THE GIRL WHO LIVED TWICE

TINA CLOUGH

THE GIRL WHO LIVED TWICE

Copyright © Tina Clough 2013 & 2021 Second edition 2021

PAPERBACK ISBN 9780473588465

A catalogue record of this 5X8" edition is available from the National Library of New Zealand

Lightpool Publishing

www.lightpoolpublishing.com

Cover and book design by Andrene Low

1

SLIPPING THROUGH A CRACK IN THE FABRIC OF TIME

Mia jerked awake, terrified, with her heart beating fast. The bedroom was completely dark and blue sparks flickered in the black void. Her body was being crushed and dragged against a hot, rough surface. Rumbling and cracking noises, vibrations and scalding heat, she laboured to pull air into her lungs. Her mind snatched for explanations and found only confusion. Her hands reached for something to grab hold of but found nothing.

Suddenly all noise and movements stopped, there was a moment of startling silence, then one last violent jerk followed by stillness.

Mia lay terrified and panting, trying to make sense of what had happened. What had happened? An explosion or an earthquake? Her heart was still racing, and her face was covered in cold sweat. The room was blurrily visible now in the usual indirect glow from the city lights. Cautiously she sat up, half expecting something to give way or fall. She turned on the bedside light, expecting cracks in the ceiling or a wall about to topple into empty space, but everything seemed normal. She got gingerly out of bed and stumbled to the window on legs that felt numb and disconnected.

The view was perfectly normal, and her fear of a big earthquake faded. She was surprised to see that the rain had stopped and the top of the Sky Tower, floodlit in icy blue, was outlined against a clear night sky. She stood there for a minute recreating

I

the sensations she had felt, shook her head and went back to bed, her legs steadier now.

I must have dreamt that I was awake and heard those noises and felt that awful pressure, she thought, I'll never go back to sleep now, not after a nightmare as realistic as that.

She left the bedside light on, closed her eyes and woke to the sound of the clock radio announcing the 7 o'clock news, bewildered and surprised that it was already morning, amazed that she had managed to sleep after all.

"Phoenix Air has confirmed that four New Zealanders were among those killed in yesterday's light plane crash just outside Manchester. No names have been released, but it is believed they were all members of one family."

Mia sat straight up in bed, instantly awake and alert, her mind full of confused questions. Were they playing a recording of an old news reading? Or had a second air crash happened, identical to the one that killed a New Zealander family shortly after Greg's death last year?

She switched to the local commercial station and caught the tail end of the same news item. Confused and frightened she got up and pulled on track pants and a T-shirt, turned on the computer and went straight to the BBC news site. The headline about the plane crash was at the top of the page. Her eyes raced down the lines, her sense of disbelief growing by the second – every single detail was as she remembered it. Did it not happened a year ago, was she experiencing a particularly detailed event of déjà-vu?

And then she saw the date under the BBC banner – 'Updated 19.23 Thursday 10 August 2006'. A cold shiver of fear ran down her spine and her mind stumbled around trying to make sense of things. Today was Friday 17 August and yesterday was Thursday 16 August 2007. With trembling fingers, she clicked on the NZ Herald website and stared at the date – Friday 11 August 2006.

Mia was sweating now and breathing fast, on the brink of panic. Had she had a stroke? Or was she in some kind of realistic-seeming, psychological state where her mind had snapped back to the past? Had she imagined a whole year? But it must be true, the websites agreed. What had happened to her?

She was on the verge of crying, but a sense of self-preservation made her battle the tears. If she let go and cried, she might not be able to stop, and what she must do was calm down and try to work out what had happened.

Should she ask for help? But no, she shied away from the idea nearly straight away. Would anyone believe her? Would they insist on doctors and psychologists? It might be dangerous to expose her delusion or whatever it was to others. It felt safer to try to achieve some sort of calm and work it out alone, at least for now, if that was possible. She checked her emails; nothing was dated later than Wednesday, 9 August 2006.

Half an hour later she was pacing around the living room, frustrated and confused. She had reached no conclusions and several times she had stood with the phone in her hand to call her sister Sarah, but each time she pulled back. The thought of telling her or anyone else was unbearable. How would Sarah react? Would she suggest it was a mental breakdown, take her to hospital? Whatever the truth was, she would rather struggle on alone.

And then, for no apparent reason, her heart was beating too fast again, and she knew she was going to be sick and ran to the bathroom. She came out gulping for breath, drank a glass of water and wiped her clammy forehead with a tissue. She must try to figure it out without asking for help and going to work was out of the question.

At half past eight, showered and dressed, and with a cup of coffee in her hand, she cleared her throat, rehearsed her words and called the office. Alice in reception listened to Mia's excuse of a tummy bug and was instantly sympathetic.

"Oh, you poor thing, you've not been looking well lately. You should have taken a decent break, not just soldiered on like this – it can't be good for you. It's only been two months and you never took more than a few days off at the time. Look after yourself - I'll tell Alan you are not coming in."

Mia mumbled a vague reply and put the phone down. If it was two months since the accident, it confirmed what she already knew in the back of her mind. She was back in August 2006. And she was not having a mental breakdown, time really had rewound a whole year. She found it hard to believe, but there was no other explanation. Whatever this was, temporary or permanent, it was real and not a delusion. That awful graunching movement in the night must have had something to do with it, though it seemed insane. That sort of thing happened in sci-fi movies, not in real life – but it had.

An hour later she felt calm enough to ring Sarah at work. She repeated the story of the tummy bug and, as usual, big sister Sarah was immediately concerned.

"That's not like you, Mia. Wonder if you ate something bad? Would you like me to pop over after work with something from the pharmacy?"

"Oh no, don't worry - I've got cans of chicken soup and crackers. I'll eat something harmless when I feel a bit better. It's probably one of those 24-hour things and I have the weekend to recover."

"I don't suppose you'll feel like coming over for dinner tonight, then? What a pity! But if you feel better later today, please come - you don't have to eat or drink anything. The others will be there about seven. Barb is coming, though she only got back yesterday morning, and Lorna is bringing her wedding album - they just got it from the photographer this week. I'm cooking something nice, and I've hired The Kid Next-door to do the dishes."

Mia struggled for a natural reaction. "OK - if I improve during the day, I'll come along tonight. It would be lovely to see Barb."

She put the phone down with a mass of tangled thoughts revolving in her mind, because now she knew that she had been taken back to a crucial moment in her life.

2
____

The previous day Mia arrived home late with her shoes drenched by the sideways rain. She kicked her wet shoes off, changed out of her office clothes and caught sight of herself in the dressing table mirror – brown hair, short and curly-wavy, pale face, little make-up, wide mouth. She ran her fingers roughly through her hair and shook her head and her curls simply returned to their places, she looked exactly the same again.

I look so boring, she thought, was I always this mousy, or have I become more mouse-like?

In the year since Greg died, her life had gone from bad to worse. She had lost interest in the outside world and the tedium of having nothing productive to do outside of work constantly weighed on her. Having distanced herself from her former friends, she had found no substitute activities or new friendships and could not muster the energy to do anything about it. She often contemplated having another glass or two of wine to make it easier to go to sleep at night and then dismissed the idea. Drinking alone raised vague fears of a slippery slope towards solitary alcohol dependence. Her doctor had prescribed sleeping pills after Greg's death, but after a fortnight she had stopped taking them for the same reason that she shied away from the second glass of wine. The idea of being dependent on anything, legal or illegal, frightened her.

. . .

Now, after more than a year, Mia slept at the most five or six interrupted hours per night. She would close her eyes and her mind would take her back to February 2006 when she and Greg decided to sell their tiny flat. Greg had got a new job as sales manager with a big brewery and was earning a lot more, and Mia had finished her degree and had a good job at Concept Marketing, working as the assistant to a section head. Full of heady optimism they took a bigger mortgage and bought a brand-new apartment in a tower block in an area advertised as "nearly in St Mary's Bay" and felt as if they had won the lottery. It was spacious and light with large windows nearly down to floor level to the north-east and a recessed balcony where they could have a table and a couple of chairs.

Straight after signing the paperwork, they made a pact not to buy anything major without discussing it first. Mia had money in a trust established by her parents, but the capital could only be accessed before she turned thirty, if the trustees agreed or if there was a risk of serious hardship. And then Greg came home one evening in May with his eyes glowing and told her that he had bought his Dream Machine, a second-hand Ducati, offered for instant cash sale at a price not to be resisted.

Mia was angry and disappointed; they had an agreement and Greg had broken it without even a phone call to discuss it. For the first time in their life together she wondered if he was complacent and counting on her trust money to save them if things went wrong. Their overdraft was now at the very limit and left no room for emergencies for a while. When she pointed this out, Greg confirmed her unspoken thought by accusing her of having no sense of fun.

"Do we have to worry about emergencies? The trust is our safety net."

For the first time they went to bed on bad terms and there was a subtle change in their relationship; Mia worried that their differing attitudes to money would always come between them. During the four weeks leading up to Greg's accident she never once suspected that there could be another reason for the sense of estrangement she felt.

· · ·

On a wet evening one month after buying the Ducati, Greg went for a 'quick spin' on his dream machine and ended his life under a truck on the Harbour Bridge. He was buried in Raglan, where he had grown up and where his parents, brothers and sister still lived, and the funeral highlighted how few people there were in her own family. She only had her sister and brother-in-law, an aunt and uncle and a couple of cousins, but the little church was filled to overflowing with Greg's extended family and their friends; he had multiple aunts and uncles and hordes of cousins.

But only a couple of months later, her fragile comfort was shattered by an unexpected blow, and even now, after all this time, the betrayal made her squirm with humiliation. Greg's possessions had been returned to her, but it had been some weeks before she felt able to look through them. On an impulse she had charged and turned on his cell phone, which was miraculously undamaged, and found messages which made it obvious that Mia's friend Barb and Greg had been having a long-term affair. She became obsessed with finding out who had known about it and not told her.

Barb, who had been in England since a week or two before Greg's accident, had only just returned when Mia found out, and she became convinced that nearly everyone in her circle of friends must have known. And then Sarah let it slip that she and James had suspected the affair. They had seen Greg and Barb using a keycard to enter a lift to the hotel room floors at the Sky City Casino one evening some weeks before Greg's accident, when they themselves were on their way home from drinks with friends.

Mia broke down in a storm of frantic emotion. "How *could* you know a thing like that and not tell me?" she cried. "You and everyone else who knew - you've all betrayed me! How could carry you on as normal and not tell me?"

"Mia, I thought it was for the best - I couldn't bear to maybe destroy your marriage if it was a one-off thing. And with Barb going off to the UK I thought I'd have time to think it over."

Sarah's voice was shaking with emotion. She knew that having known and not told Mia was an act of passive betrayal. And now that it was out in the open, she found that she could not explain it to her own satisfaction, and she felt guilty and frightened for Mia's mental state.

Mia was beside herself with tears running down her face and her fists clenched. "I don't care, that's a ridiculous reason – you've all made me feel like a fool! Everyone must have laughed behind my back when they were with Greg and me. And think of all the times I would have said something about our plans for the future, and how happy we were! I must have sounded like a total idiot, and they would all have been pitying me behind my back."

"Please, darling, calm down," Sarah was close to tears herself. "Don't torture yourself, it wasn't like that! I hated knowing, but I couldn't bear to tell you in case it had already finished."

"Well, it hadn't, had it? I can't stand this, it was going on right up until he died - he was probably getting ready to leave me. He knew I didn't like motorbikes, but Barb was always going on about how sexy they are and how she loves them. I bet he only bought it to impress her."

A year later she still relived those weeks in her mind and felt that first flush of disbelief and fury, followed by humiliation. And she couldn't talk about it. How would she know if people would just pretend that they hadn't known? The only protection for her wounded pride was to not talk to anyone at all about how badly hurt she still felt, and she gradually withdrew from her circle of friends and isolated herself.

When the actions of a colleague at work caused a humiliating setback to her career a short time later, it was the last straw; Mia withdrew from all social interactions, apart from seeing Sarah and James, and descended into unrelieved depression.

3

———

But now, in this fantastical situation of having been moved back in time, she was surprised at her own composure. She still wanted to scream and rant and demand explanations, but the conversation with Sarah had given her the kind of reality check she needed. And now she knew exactly where she was in time and space. The dinner at Sarah and James's place had been in August 2006. It fitted perfectly; about two months after Greg's funeral and very shortly before she had found out about Greg's affair with Barb.

Standing in front of the large window in the living room, looking out over the city she thought back to that time a year ago, well, it was really 'now', of course. Barb had only just come back from London and the party was the first time they had met since Greg died. And now here she was – 'rewound' to a point in time when she had not yet discovered that Greg had betrayed her. And a blinding insight cut across other concerns with stunning clarity. Maybe she could change it all and salvage her pride. If she exposed Barb in public, she could avoid being seen only as a victim. But would she stay in this time strand? Did she care if she ended up back in that other time? Her life in This Time was the actual present for now and whatever she did, even if this didn't last, was better than nothing. And how would she know if everything was going to play out the same way this time around? She needed something else to use as a test, to see if this timeslip thing was consistent. Had everything reverted to how it was?

She looked around, outwardly focused for the first time since she got up. The sofa was back in its old position, at right angles to where she had re-positioned it a few months ago in That Time, and last night's shopping list was no longer under a magnet on the fridge. A sudden rain shower swept over the city, and large drops splattered against the window. She traced the path of one drop after another while she thought of what to do next and decided that a stock-take would probably be useful. Starting in the hall, she went through the apartment opening every cupboard and drawer, looking in the pantry and the fridge, mentally noting changes. If she had been asked yesterday to list what changes she had made in the past year, she would have found it hard to think of very many. Now she could make a list as long as her arm. The two paintings that Sarah had persuaded her to buy at the giant art sale were still there, so they had obviously been bought before this date in 2006, but a framed van Gough print that she had given to Sarah was still on the wall beside the front door.

She was missing two pairs of shoes and a jacket, but on the other hand she had her favourite shoulder bag back - undamaged instead of deeply scratched after being caught in closing lift doors just before Christmas. Today, in This Time, was after she packed up Greg's clothes, but before she had turned on his cell phone and discovered about Barb. As far as she could see there was nothing out of synch, everything seemed to fit her recollection of how things had been in August 2006.

Some things in cupboards and wardrobes were arranged differently, and she noticed that she still had that favourite hand cream that she could no longer get by Christmas. She made a mental note to go out and buy every tube she could find, and then she laughed with a note of hysteria at how prosaic that thought was in her present dilemma. Every now and then she would pause briefly in her search, wondering how the time-shift worked and marvelling at her periods of relative calm.

And she must prepare herself, so she could give an impression of fitting in and not arouse suspicion. Mentioning something nobody has heard of yet would be catastrophic. She stood in the hall, considering the print that was still there, though she had given it away, and told herself that even if the rational part of her brain refused to believe it, here she was - returned to the past. Confused and intermittently terrified but determined too in an excited kind of way; living in an altered reality was beginning to seem like an opportunity.

By eleven she was sitting at her desk in the study with her 2006 diary in front of her, trying to make a plan and list key things to consider. If she tried to work through too many things at once, she would lose the plot, she must be methodical and stay calm.

She swung around on her chair and contemplated the messy room with dismay. Because she and Greg had very different habits, Mia had claimed the desk area to the left of the computer and Greg was supposed to have the other end. But somehow things crept across and took over the entire desk - piles of papers and bits and pieces he never threw away turned the desk into a storage dump. They had gone to a DIY store and bought wall tracks, supports and laminated shelving, and covered the whole wall above the desk. The mess moved up and the desk stayed relatively clear. Now Mia studied the shelves and thought how cluttered they looked compared to how they had been when she sat there last night – or whenever it was that she last sat here - but she could sort it out again.

The car! She hurried to the kitchen and checked her car keys. Yes, of course, she said out loud, these are the keys to the Honda that I sold last October, when James found me that demonstration car. I'll have to remember to look for a white Civic again instead of a silver-coloured Ford. And now I'll have to go through that awful period again of turning the windscreen wipers on every time I go around a corner.

And then without warning her stomach turned into a knot of fear again. She was bound to get things wrong, there were so many things she knew that others had never heard of. What if she came out with something that was still in the future, and they thought she was mad? Or maybe she really was insane and delusional? Wouldn't she be the last person to know? She had to exert all her willpower to pull her mind back from the brink of panic and regain her calm.

. . .

She picked up the pen and started jotting things down.

1 Damage control re Greg and Barb?

2 Check news for recent events.

3 What is going on at work?

4 Make a list of future things to convince Sarah and James. Any others?

5 Try to find out if it happened to anyone else.

It was hard to keep her focus on one thing at a time. Her mind strayed into speculation and fear, or suddenly presented some new aspect to investigate and check. First, she must decide how to use tonight's dinner to her advantage. she must confront Barb. It might be the only chance she had to get it right - to take control and to not be at the mercy of others and seen as a victim. It would be especially effective to do it where others would see her being assertive, it would give her a different starting point for the future.

She closed her mind to speculation about the meaning of 'future' or if she really had a future, went to make another cup of coffee, and ate a banana while the water boiled. Grabbing a couple of crackers and a piece of cheese she sat down again with a clean sheet of paper and talked aloud, as she rewrote the plan in brief bullet points.

- Check recent local events of significance.
- Read all last week's news - for normal conversations.
- Try to recall exactly what was happening at the office.
- Do NOT reveal truth to Sarah and James yet.
- Confront Barb for advantage/strength, take her by surprise at the party: Make it public, tell the story, include things I found out later.
- STAY CALM

Now her mind felt steadier again, and she circled "Barb" and put an exclamation mark in the margin. She resolved to be businesslike and look at the situation constructively, as if it were a job, and not even think of 'tomorrow'. It was pointless wasting energy on worrying if this would last, so she would grab the chances that presented themselves and use them.

As she trawled through news on the Internet, she found that she had forgotten a lot in the past year. She read news from the last couple of weeks in more detail and decided that she had better stay clear of the Iraqi war, anything to do with films and the whole Don Brash saga – and television programmes were out of the question.

Somehow this bizarre situation had brought out something from deep inside her. She knew now that she could control mind when she was on the verge of panic and force herself back to rational thought. She had never had to cope with change alone, there had always been someone there beside her, first her parents and then Sara and lately Greg; older and presumably wiser voices who guide her, but perhaps she was stronger than she had ever realized. She had often felt that she was different from those around her in her reactions to things, but she had thought of it as being less passionate, more passive. It was interesting to speculate that her quietness and lack of assertiveness might have concealed an inner strength even from herself. And though she was scared, she felt confident as well and strong enough to plan. It was crazy, but she hoped it would last.

Leaning back in her chair and tapping her front teeth with the pen, she considered her job. How far ahead was the merger scenario at this date in 2006? Had the merger rumours been officially confirmed, had any redundancies been made public? It was such a large takeover; it had affected the share price and made the business news, and those who knew where she worked might ask questions. A quick search on the Internet revealed that the merger was regarded as a given but no formal announcement had been made, which made it easier. Nobody would expect her to know any more than anyone else.

Mia spent an hour going through papers in the study and skimming through a few magazines, but it took self-discipline to stop herself from delving too deeply into articles and websites. All that could wait until later, if there was to be a 'later' - for now she only needed the big picture. She made yet another cup of coffee and sat down to read her 2006 diary and old emails and gradually she began to feel that things that she thought she had forgotten were familiar and current in her mind. This Time was live and real.

I'll ignore That Time for now, she thought, my future used to be the present, my new present was my past, and I will not panic.

4

———

While catching up on the news occupied one part of Mia's mind, other ideas slowly evolved in the background and became fully fledged resolutions. She would go to Sarah's dinner and try to reclaim her self-esteem by confronting Barb, even if her future was uncertain, because she had nothing to lose. It was important to do it right, and the way it was done, how she spoke and the image she wanted to project were all equally important. This was a one-off opportunity, a chance that would never be repeated. She wanted to give an impression of strength and control – very different from the person she had been when she attended that dinner a year ago. Somehow, she must signal change by how she looked and dressed, so there was an element of surprise to give her an advantage. Dressing differently would be a good start, like donning armour before a battle or dressing for a theatre performance. If she could show a façade of strength, it would probably make her feel more confident. She had no idea what she would wear, but it must make a statement and signal a departure from the timid Mia of the past. Just a glance at the clothes in her wardrobe made it clear that she owned nothing of the right kind; everything seemed designed to make her blend into the background and go unnoticed.

If I stop looking like a mouse, she thought, maybe I'll stop acting like a mouse? I need to do something radical, and I need to do it right now, today.

Mid-afternoon she caught a bus downtown and headed for an expensive shopping arcade, where she had window-shopped in the past but never bought anything. There wasn't much time now to achieve her goal, and she knew it wouldn't be easy to change a lifetime habit of buying non-assertive clothes, but she must try. And perhaps even outrageous would be an improvement on mousy and provide the surprise factor she was looking for.

In Designers Boutique, Lorraine was feeling slightly bored on an unusually quiet Friday afternoon and hoped for some action before the end of her shift. She watched Mia come in and stop just inside the door, looking around to orientate herself. Lorraine walked towards her thinking, 'I've never seen her before, looks nice, pretty hair, but a very quiet dresser. She probably won't buy anything – this isn't her type of shop.' She greeted Mia and quickly realized that this was woman on a mission and in a hurry, and someone who needed to look around on her own. She stood back and waited while Mia went from one rack to another, by-passing some without even really looking at the garments. At others she lingered to look more closely at a few things, and after a while she went back to a couple of the racks she had already looked at and started to hang clothes over her arm.

Lorraine headed for the same point. "Can I take some things to a fitting room for you?"

"Yes, thanks, great!"

Mia picked out a dozen things and gave them to Lorraine before continuing her search, and Lorraine took the garments to the back of the shop and returned to watch with renewed interest. This girl was making very surprising choices. She kept picking out things that Lorraine would never have guessed she would even look at, trendy and on the cutting edge of the current fashion. Lorraine began to feel intrigued, not only by Mia's choices but also by the nearly tangible urgency she radiated.

As she took a few more things from Mia she said, "You might be interested in the new collection just along here."

Mia looked at the tall black girl, obviously of African descent, but with an entirely local accent and went to have a look. Ten minutes later she followed Lorraine to the rear of the floor, where a small mobile rack with the selection she had made so far was waiting outside a fitting room.

After a few minutes Lorraine said, "Just let me know when you want me to take a couple of things away or find other sizes".

Mia slid the curtain slightly open, wearing a very short wrapover dress with a deep V-neck. "Could you please take those three away and see if you have this one in a smaller size?"

Lorraine returned with a smaller size and a similar dress in a black and white 70's op-art print. "Try this one too perhaps? And try it over these tights - it would look great with boots."

Forty minutes later Mia watched an astonishing number of garments being folded and put into carrier bags and marvelled at how easy this had been, and what a radical change of style she had achieved. It was amusing to think that with her pre-knowledge of next year's fashion trends, she could turn into a trendsetter. But without the assistant's help and advice she could never have achieved a coherent look, and neither would she have had the courage to make such radical choices.

"Thanks so much for all your help!" She got her credit card out and handed it to Lorraine. "I didn't know if I was going to manage a complete change of style. You've been so creative, you made it easy."

Lorraine laughed and looked at Mia with open satisfaction.

"I think we made a good team - I hope you'll be happy with what you've bought."

Mia returned the smile, genuinely pleased. "This was the easiest shopping expedition ever – and I thought it was going to be a real challenge, or even impossible. I've never been very good at this."

"Well, you seemed to want a complete change of style - and it was fun. What about make-up - are you giving yourself a total make-over?"

Mia's face took on a less confident and slightly worried look and Lorraine thought, 'something bad has happened to her, or else she's up against something and she's apprehensive. I'm sorry I suggested it - perhaps it's too much to change at once'

Aloud she said, "You have a great face for make-up."

She was beginning felt a bit worried now about how personal this was becoming, but she pushed on. "You know how they say that the best models have that 'quite pretty' look, but the main thing is that they have regular features, a great smile and really great hair. And that's exactly what you have. I'm sorry if I'm too personal - I just thought it might be a good idea."

Mia was both flattered by the interest Lorraine was taking in her transformation and slightly embarrassed. But it was a good idea and probably exactly the sort of morale booster she needed to feel self-assured and confident.

"Oh, no, don't worry - it's kind of you to help me. It's just that I have never been very good with make-up, never experimented. I would love to be completely different tonight - I need to feel more confident than I usually do."

Lorraine began to suspect that Mia probably needed a friend more than a shop assistant. "My name is Lorraine. What's yours?"

"I'm Mia."

"Well, I know for a fact that if you know you look confident, you can act confident. It's amazing what a great looking façade can do for your self-esteem."

Heavens, she thought, maybe I shouldn't have said that - it sounded nearly insulting.

But Mia nodded and looked relieved. "Yes, that's it exactly! I might have to say or do something in public tonight, something that will need a bit of extra courage, so I thought a new look would be like a disguise and make me feel braver."

Lorraine smiled. "I know exactly what you mean. That black and white dress will do the trick; you look stunning in it – it's a very decisive-looking dress."

She handed the credit card back to Mia. "So, this is what you *could* do, if you want to have a go at the makeup as well. There's a cosmetics shop called Bliss Oasis just a few doors down on this level – they have all the top brands, and trained consultants, a very smart shop but don't let that intimidate you." She smiled to take the edge out of her last comment. "Any one of the girls there will be happy to do a demo make-up for you, so you can go home and work out if you like it. And, if you don't already have a favourite brand, try the Lancôme counter and ask for Maylene. I know her a little – we have coffee together sometimes, and she would be honest and not too pushy."

"I will - I'll go there right away."

"You can leave your bags here if you like and pick them up when you've finished – there isn't much room in Bliss Oasis, and these are pretty bulky."

Mia left the bags and set out for Bliss Oasis, glancing at her watch as she walked. She had spent over an hour in Designers and now it was after four and she had no idea how long a make-up session would take, and then must try to get a taxi, because those bags would be impossible to handle on the bus in the rush hour.

5

As soon as Mia walked out the door, Lorraine called Maylene. "A short curly brunette in jeans and a grey jacket is heading your way. She's bought some fabulous clothes, radically different from how she looks now. I think she's having some sort of crisis going on and she's determined to change her style completely. She's gone for very trendy stuff – she left it all here to pick it up after you finish with her. She needs a new make-up look, but don't push it too far."

Maylene laughed her infectious Samoan laugh. "I can see her now - she's outside, just looking in the window. Yes, pretty girl – I can do things for her."

Mia made her way towards the immaculate girl with a badge saying, 'Lancôme Consultant Maylene', a creature of total perfection. This was the sort of environment where the shop assistants might easily sneer at customers whose appearance did not meet their expectations, and she was acutely aware of her casual clothes and un-made-up face.

"Hi, Maylene. Lorraine in the Designers shop suggested that I should come and see you – for a makeup demonstration. If you have the time? I want to change how I look – completely, right now. If that's possible?"

It all came out in a rush, and Maylene looked Mia over in a considering way, a bit like a man looking at a car he knows he can

20

get for song and then turn into something that others will envy. "It will be my pleasure," she said.

Perched on a tall stool Mia submitted to Maylene's expertise. When she asked how Mia usually did her make-up, and what products she used, Mia nearly laughed. "I don't really use any make-up, unless you count the odd bit of mascara and lipstick."

Maylene smiled. "That's even better - we can regard you as a blank canvas. What did you buy in Designers?"

They discussed Mia's new clothes and Maylene was impressed. "Sounds as if you've got some really cool things, really different. I think we'll give you a sophisticated natural look but very smooth and luminous, emphasize your best points."

Mia nodded, fascinated to be the object of such intense analysis, though she had no idea what her best points might be. "It would be great if my face could match my new clothes – they're very different from anything I have, but I'm going to something tonight that's very important for me, and I want to make a certain kind of impression. A bit more assertive and stylish?"

Maylene looked at Mia – an averagely pretty and not in the least glamorous girl and speculated about love rivals or ex-partners. She turned the stool around, swivelled a circular mirror to face Mia and switched on the ring-shaped light around it. Mia watched her familiar face in the mirror, slightly thinner than it used to be, and in no way remarkable, just pale and troubled looking, and suddenly her mind was full of doubts. It was hard to imagine that applying some make-up would change anything much, but she was here now, and she would wait and see how it turned out. Maybe she would just go straight home and wash it all off.

Maylene draped a cape over her shoulders and started a running commentary on her skin colour, eyes, lack of 'brow definition', her lovely mouth and finished with 'great hair, no need to change anything there'. It was as if she was evaluating a third person, the girl in the mirror, and everything was stated factually and without emotion or apology. Every product applied, every brush and sponge used, and every technique of application was explained, patiently and exactly. Slowly a transformed face appeared in the mirror, familiar but different.

And when Maylene said, "There you are!" with a touch of satisfaction and removed the cape from round her shoulders, Mia remained silent, staring mesmerized at herself. Wat a transformation! Was that really her?

Maylene directed her to full-length mirror on one side of the shop. "Look at yourself as others would see you, from a slight distance. What do you think?"

"I can't believe it - I never knew that I could look like this. It's like some kind of magic."

Mia continued to stare at herself in the mirror, fascinated. Her skin glowed with a smooth lustre as if lit from within, her eyes seemed twice their normal size and sparkled, her mouth looked – lush, was the only word.

"You are a genius! And it looks so natural, too."

She smiled at Maylene, who met her eyes in the mirror and nodded happily.

"I love what I do, and I know I'm good at it."

An amazing number of small expensive-looking objects were gently wrapped in tissue paper and placed into two small, shiny carrier bags with plaited handles. Maylene remarked in an offhand way that she had added two alternative products for day wear, and meticulously filled in a card with all the products and when to use them, morning, noon and night. "You can always come back if you want to experiment a bit more. I'll be very happy to advise you."

Having filled in a form to become a 'favoured Lancôme customer' Mia handed over her credit card and had an attack of anxiety so vivid that Maylene immediately picked up on it and looked at her with unspoken concern.

Mia knew she was blushing furiously under her wonderful façade. "I'm sorry, I don't know - that is, I'm not sure – I mean I hope I have enough credit on the card to pay for this. I've spent quite a lot today already."

Maylene said calmly, as if taking for granted that everything would be in order, "I'll do it now."

Mia punched in her PIN and they both watched the little display until it came up with Accepted. Mia let out her breath and Maylene said, "All done!" in a neutral voice.

"Heavens!" said Mia, looking at her watch, "Time to go - forget about new shoes, I must get home. Thanks so much!"

She picked up the little carry bags, and returned to Designers, but to her disappointment Lorraine was not there.

"She's finished for the day," said the middle-aged assistant, who handed over Mia's bags from behind the counter. "She won't be in again until next week."

"What a pity! Can you please say thank you to her? She was so helpful, and I really appreciate how much time she spent with me."

Outside the warm and sheltered mall, low clouds were racing across the sky and there was a threat of more rain in the air. The pavement was crowed, and the street was a solid mass of vehicles. The thought of waiting for a bus while laden down with so many bags was daunting but getting a taxi might be impossible. And then, as if by a miracle, there was an empty taxi caught in the stationary traffic in the middle lane. She waved wildly with a hand holding two large carrier bags and managed to catch the eye of the driver who nodded. Risking life and limb she launched herself out among the cars and reached the taxi before the traffic started moving. The driver reached back and opened the door behind him, she shoved her bags in ahead of her and slammed the door just as the traffic started moving.

Mia gave the driver the address and sank back to contemplate the afternoon's insane session of shopping and transformation. Never in her life had she done anything so radical and totally self-ish. And without those two wonderful helpers she could not have done it, she wouldn't have had the mental energy or the vision to get it right. Both had helped her take it further than she would have dared on her own, too. All that remained now was to try to live up to her new look and act confident.

Opening the door to her apartment she was struck by the changes from what she had become used to in that other time, and it reminded her of the need to be cautious in conversations tonight, to stay off difficult topics. And then she caught sight of herself in the hall mirror and everything was forgotten as she stood fasci-nated for a moment.

"It's just amazing!" she said aloud. "If I met myself in the street, I'd turn round and have a second look."

She had never understood that skilful makeup could literally transform someone and what an asset that skill was. She dumped the carrier bags on the bedroom floor and looked at the still unmade bed, thinking of how she had woken to chaotic terror that morning and felt a shiver of fear again. Was she insane? Would tonight be a catastrophe? Or was she in a coma and just imagining all this, like a long, coherent dream?

Trembling again, she forced her mind away from panic, pulled the duvet up to make a smooth surface and emptied the bags one by one. And then excitement conquered her fear, because just looking at what she had just acquired made her feel changed and different from the person she had been. She went through to the living room, turned the TV on and poured a glass of wine from a half-finished bottle in the fridge and smiled. *Brookfield's 2005 Chardonnay*, her favourite everyday wine in That Time. She tried to remember why she stopped buying it and failed.

Back in the bedroom she put the glass of wine on the bedside table and contemplated her purchases without taking in a single word of the TV news coming from the living room. It was like stepping into someone else's life; able to be daring and brave and take risks. With a feeling of reckless courage filling her mind, she took a sip of wine; she had never felt like this before.

The problem now was what to wear tonight. Stripped to her bra and panties, she hesitated, then she picked up the new, short dress because it was totally unlike anything she had worn before. But should she wear it with tights or over tight black pants? She opted for the 'dress over very tight pants' look, simply because it was so unlike her usual style of dressing. She looked in the long mirror and thought, yes! This was the right thing for tonight, stylish and slightly in-your-face, a bit ahead of current fashion.

She rummaged in a drawer and found a necklace she had not worn, since Sarah gave it to her, because it had never looked right with any of her clothes. Now the longish string of over-sized black and silver beads fitted perfectly in the deep V-neck of the black and white op-art dress, and it all seemed to come together into a deliberate retro look. It inspired a bold surge of confidence, definitely not a mousy feeling and she hoped this wasn't a dream; she wanted to wake up in the morning and still feel just like this.

There was still a lot of traffic at seven, and just before the top of the rise on the Harbour Bride, the car on her left swerved into her lane without indicating. Mia slammed on the brakes and the Honda skidded before she got control again. The fact that the road had dried a bit since the last shower of rain had probably saved her, and in her mind another memory popped up. In October 2006 in That Time, she had gone to get a new warrant of fitness for the Honda and been told her tyre patterns were too shallow to pass the test. She had been forced to spend a lot of money on four new tyres then, and now she made a mental note to get new tyres next week; she might not be so lucky next time she needed to brake hard in a hurry.

In a way going to Sarah and James's place was like going home. The house they lived in had been Mia's family home, and Sarah used to say that she was the only adult she knew, who had never left home and probably never would. Their parents had been sailing a yacht from Christchurch to Queen Charlotte Sound with the girls' aunt and uncle, when they capsized in a storm off the Kaikoura coast. Mia's parents had drowned, and their aunt had been bashed against rocks and badly injured. Mia felt the pain of it still - just thinking of that phone call from her uncle gave her a cold shivery feeling. Sarah had been twenty-two and in charge of her younger sister while their parents were away. The fact that their father's body had not been found for several days had added to the stress and trauma. Uncle Jim had been Mia's legal guardian and there had been long discussions about the girls moving to the South Island, but in the end, it was decided that they were better off where they were.

And it had been far better, Mia reflected now, that they had had no big changes or adjustments of place to make. Sarah took charge and did her best to make it feel like a home but inevitably they had struggled with the practical issues of how to reorganize the house, how to pack up and dispose of their parents' clothes and to move forward. Mia had gone straight from school to work as a junior clerk in a marketing company and had worked her way up to a reasonably interesting job before she went to university and got a commerce degree, and when Sarah married James the three of them stayed on in the house on the North Shore, until Mia met Greg and married him three years ago.

6

———

The bungalow at the top of Verbena Road was lit up for a party, with the lights along the front veranda and turned on, and the front door ajar. Mia walked in, out of the damp evening air, took her coat off and hung it on the hook she always used. A sudden surge of anxiety made her nearly physically dizzy: this was it, the crucial moment when she would find out if fate would give her the chance to take back control of her emotional life. She took a deep breath to steady her nerves, put a smile on her face and walked through the double doors into the brightly lit living room.

Sarah was at the far end of the long living room facing the doors to the hall, and Mia saw her sister's face register nearly shocked surprise. When Sarah called out a greeting, her voice was louder than normal, and people turned around to look at Sarah and then turned again to see what she was looking at, and in that moment, Mia became the focal point in the room. She smiled a greeting at everyone in general and forced herself to walk straight across the room towards Sarah. Beside Sarah stood Him Next-door and Her Next-door, a childhood expression that Mia and Sarah continued to use about their neighbours, and their faces were as surprised as Sarah's. As she approached the group, Mia felt the attention from the rest of the room so focused on her that it was like a physical sensation between her shoulder blades. She kept her eyes on Sarah and tried to smile, as if there was nothing unusual going on.

"Hi darling, what a gorgeous smell! I haven't eaten all day, so I'm starving," said Mia and ignored long enquiring glances from a couple of women friends of Sarah's standing nearby. She knew them of course, nodded and turned to blend into the conversation between Sarah and the neighbours, but she could feel that people were still looking at her. When James joined them to give Mia a glass of wine, he studied her intently and then his long narrow face lit up.

"Gosh you look great, Mia. You look different - have you changed your hair?"

"Good grief James! Her hair is about the *only* thing that hasn't changed," said Sarah, and those around them laughed and commented on her dress and how gorgeous she looked. Sarah was visibly moved to see Mia wearing the necklace she had given her and exclaimed, "I thought you didn't like it! I never saw you wearing it before."

"But I love it! I just had to get the right outfit to wear it with." Mia was making a continuous effort to sound casual and relaxed, but it was hard is the face of so much attention.

"God, you look so different, so glamorous. I've never seen you wear anything like that - you look like a different person."

Mia felt her resolve gradually strengthen; confidence in her ability to change her own fate returned in step with Sarah's admiration, and she tried to sound casual.

"I thought it was time for a change - no point in sitting around and letting chance direct my life."

Her Next-door smiled her approval. "Good for you, Mia, and it's great to see you looking so well, and that outfit is lovely, very stylish."

Sarah watched as Mia responded to Her Next-door and thought how great it was to see Mia looking happy and desperately hoped that Mia would never find out about Greg and Barb. For the last couple of months, she had been intensely worried about Mia's depression and listlessness and her own inability to cheer her up. Thinking back now, the change in her was incredible. She tried to imagine what could possibly have happened to cause this transformation, as stunning as if someone flicked a switch and her whole personality has been altered.

Now she smiled and said, "Well done! I love the dress, and I'm so pleased you like that necklace after all. Oh look - here's Barb."

. . .

Sarah was looking towards the door to the hall, but Mia didn't turn around until she heard Barb's voice behind her, and then she turned slowly with a smile on her face. "Hi Barb," she said coolly, just the way she had practiced in front of the mirror at home. She made no move to embrace Barb, and her stance made it perfectly clear that she was not inviting physical contact. Barb said cautiously, "Mia, you look like a million dollars - so different."

That was the moment when Mia knew that she was going to be able to do what she had come to do and without rushing it. Something in her own altered look had alerted Barb and now she was apprehensive. Mia looked at Barb's blond bob, her pretty face, the girlie style emphasized by a top in pink and grey layered chiffon. This was the person who created misery and agony for her in That Time, who had left her to struggle with no confidence, feeling humiliated and betrayed. She could handle this; now she was ready to go for the jugular, but in a calm and controlled way.

She waited while Barb and Sarah exchanged greetings and spoke casually, hoping her voice wouldn't tremble.

"Barb, I've been waiting for you to come back! I need to tell you right now, that when I got Greg's phone back after the accident, I turned it on."

Barb's face changed from a puzzled smile to apprehension. Sarah, taken aback by the chill in Mia's voice, stood silent and watchful.

"And of course, I listened to the saved messages," said Mia slightly louder.

Instinctively Sarah reached out and touched James's arm while keeping her eyes fixed on Mia and Barb. Him and Her Next-door moved slightly closer together and watched silently, a couple of people close to the fireplace picked up the tension and turned to listen.

Barb was now visibly uncomfortable, and a flush was advancing up her neck, but she said nothing.

Mia looked at her without pity. "Anything you want to tell me? Or shall I tell you – and everyone else?"

Inside her head she listened with amazement to her own voice saying the phrases she had rehearsed and practiced that night after she got dressed; every word exactly as she had written them down in her script.

Barb's voice was thin and brittle. "Mia, please! It's not what you think - nothing happened - it wasn't really serious..."

The sentence trailed off into the silence around them, and Mia thought, 'so *this* is what it's like when a fight starts. Things get to a certain point, and then it can't be stopped - you're in it to the bitter end'.

She forced herself to smile, though it was a tight little smile, and in her mind, she turned the page to the next section of the script. "Barb, I know it all - you didn't do much to cover your tracks. Booking into the Sky City hotel was *not* a smart move - I heard about it nearly right away. I took a while to decide what to do about it, but those phone messages on Greg's phone, and the way you two talked about me – well, let's say it made up my mind. But I wanted to say it to your face, so I have waited all this time for you to come back. And I'm not interested in your explanations - all I want now is for you to get out of my sight and to stay out of it."

Barb, scarlet-cheeked and completely undone, turned and walked straight across the room and through the doors to the hall and the sound of the front door slamming was like an exclamation mark. The silence was louder than an explosion, and Mia imagined shockwaves rippling out across the room.

She turned to Sarah and said reasonably, as if in private conversation, "Well, it had to be done – I have been waiting so long to tell her, and it was getting on my nerves."

She turned to James without waiting for an answer. "Can I please swap this white for a red? Somehow it feels like the time to have a glass of a good red just now."

James laughed out loud, relieved and amazed. Mia knew he was usually uncomfortable with scenes and conflict, but this was different, more like a choreographed fight, and she could see that he had enjoyed it. Behind him the room resumed its buzz with a slightly forced animation.

Her Next-door looked at Mia with open admiration. "My God Mia, that was brilliant - stunning! You have really surprised me."

The rest of the evening was like countless other large and casual dinner evenings at Sarah and James's, but for Mia there was an additional frisson of excitement. Those she knew gradually and deliberately circulated towards her. She didn't know how many of them just wanted more fodder for gossip or how many wanted to genuinely commiserate or congratulate her on having taken action. But she realized that it didn't matter what their motivation was, so long as it gave her useful opportunities to add detail to her tale. Those who had known about Greg's affair would no longer find her a pathetic object of pity, and they would tell others.

Gretchen, who had been one of Sarah's bridesmaids, was openly delighted and made no bones about saying so. "I know Barb's been a friend of yours since school - but good on you for showing her up in public. For her to have the cheek to turn up here as if nothing had happened, it's just incredible."

"Well, you know what really stuck in my throat? It was how she wrote sympathetic emails to me from the UK after Greg died, that really got to me. But I didn't feel I could tackle her before we met face to face somehow. I suppose it seemed more appropriate for some reason - I can't quite figure it out myself."

"Oh, I completely understand that. And very effective to do it in front of an audience, not to mention how brave. I fancied I heard a drum roll as she walked out," said Gretchen and raised her glass in a toast.

There were others who echoed Gretchen's sentiments as the evening wore on, and Mia began to feel that word would spread quickly and effectively along the information networks of this particular group. Her own point of view was that the more people who found out, the better it was, and gradually she relaxed into the new role she had created. The feeling of being in charge of her destiny even carried her over a sticky moment when one gossip-vulture wanted to find out just how humiliated she had been, and what had been said about her in the messages on Greg's phone.

Lovely food was piled on the dining table, people sat or stood to eat it, and some drank a bit too much. As at most parties, there was a couple who had an argument about whose turn it was to drive home while the others pretended not to notice. Sudden bursts of laughter would erupt and every now and then someone's voice would be heard, too loud, in a little interlude of silence, it all seemed amazingly normal. Mia noticed Sarah glancing at her now and then, wondering and speculating, and Mia smiled whenever she caught her eye and continued acting as if nothing unusual had happened.

When the last guests had left Mia helped Sarah and James take plates and glasses to the kitchen, where The Kid Next-door - 14 years old and constantly thirsting for money, was tidying and washing up, intent on getting done, getting paid and going home.

Mia reflected once again that the kitchen really needed a complete makeover; it was practically the same as when Sarah and Mia's parents had bought the house about 30 years ago. It had such minimal bench space that the debris from a big dinner would have been unmanageable without someone clearing the decks as the evening progressed. And it was not just the lack of bench space, but the cupboards above the bench were still too high to be practical, and the pantry door still opened the wrong way.

Mia, standing on tiptoes to reach the high shelf to put away clean plates, said, "Sarah you should tear this kitchen out and start from scratch. I don't know how you can produce these huge feasts with no mod cons and hardly any bench space."

"Oh, it doesn't really worry me." Sarah's voice floated back from the pantry, where she was putting things away, hidden by the door. "I'll think about it after the summer, can't be bothered now. But I must admit that I do grumble about it now and then. It's not as if we can't afford to do it, it's just the thought of how awful it will be to live with the mess."

James came in from the dining room with a tray full of glasses and heard the last comment. "I don't think it needs to be that bad, you know. Brian said that when they had their kitchen revamped everything was made off site and then delivered ready to install. It took about a week to have the old stuff ripped out and the floor and painting done and then the new things were brought in, and the job was finished in a couple of days."

"OK, we can start planning it during the summer."

Sarah emerged from the pantry and winked at Mia, and Mia smiled and thought: And I know exactly what will happen, provided it works out the same as in That Time.

Finally, the house was tidy enough to call a halt. The Kid Next-door had been paid and left yawning, and Sarah looked hard at Mia. "OK, tell us! When did you find out?"

For a split second, Mia considered saying that she had only just found out, but then ironic reality caught up with her; not only was there a psychological advantage in Sarah telling everyone that Mia had known since before Greg died, but it was also literally true that she had known for ages.

"Look you two," she said, in control of her voice and hopefully of her face. "I've known for quite some time. And I *would* have confronted him about it. He might have ended the affair if I had, though it's possible he was planning to go off with Barb when she returned from London - as *she* clearly thought he would." She resisted temptation to add, 'But he was also very fond of my trust fund,' but added, "And I had to do it in person – telling her in an email just wouldn't have put a full stop to the whole issue for me."

While waiting for their response, she fancied that she could read Sarah's mind, processing the pros and cons of admitting that she and James had known and then deciding that now was not the moment. And then, all at once, Mia realized that she needed a bit of distance on the evening before she had an in-depth discussion with Sarah.

"I'm really tired," she said. "I don't think I should have had two glasses of that lovely red after half a glass of white and not eating enough during the day. I'll splash out on a taxi home and leave the car here. Enough upheavals last night and tonight to last me a while."

Despite their insistence that it would be better for her to stay overnight, Mia was determined to go home.

"I'll come over on the bus and pick up the car tomorrow - or if you come into town, perhaps one of you could bring it, if I leave you the keys?"

Fifteen minutes later she was in a taxi heading for the Harbour Bridge, once again feeling apprehensive about the future and speculating about her strange situation. What would tonight bring? Would she wake up in the morning and find she was back in August 2007? And in that case, would tonight's event have changed the future for her in That Time? Or would she find herself in yet another time? Could there be others in the same situation? Had she unknowingly met people in That Time, who had been snatched from wherever they should rightly be? And if she was now in 2006, was there another Mia continuing a different existence in 2007, completely ignorant of this Mia living in the time warp world of the past?

There were no answers and maybe there never would be, a troubling culmination to this long, exhausting and surprising day, but she would go along for the ride as long as it lasted, because as she had repeatedly told herself, she had nothing to lose.

7

M ia opened her eyes and lay quite still for a long moment looking at the ceiling and wondering what year she was in. Then she turned her head and caught a glimpse of the new dress through the half-open wardrobe door; it was still 2006 and relief surged through her, she was safe, if only for another day. The thought of waking up one morning and finding herself back in 2007 filled her with dread. However uncertain her existence was in This Time it was preferable to what her life had been in That Time.

When she got home the previous evening, she stood at the kitchen bench for a few minutes scribbling note after note about the things that had occurred to her in the taxi, though she knew there was little hope of finding answers to her questions. There was no way of finding out if logic as she knew it, applied to her situation. What she most wanted to know was if there was someone else who had experienced that time shift, or perhaps at some earlier time, but even if she could find someone who had, was it likely that they would know any more than she did?

Now she got up even though it was only quarter past seven on a Saturday morning. It was vital that she crammed as much as possible into the weekend before work began again on Monday, so first a shower, then coffee. She had developed a habit of talking to herself, as if her thoughts became better defined when she heard the words spoken aloud. The feeling of power she had gained from the events last night was overtaken by a desperate urge to continue her planning. She stood in the stream of hot water with her eyes closed, and however hard she tried to stop it, the endless cycle of repetitive thoughts continued to circle in mind.

How can I find out if there is someone else like me? Will I be able to cope at work on Monday? Do I still exist elsewhere in another timeline? I wonder if what I change in this time strand will continue developing here, even if I slide sideways into yet another time – or back into That Time? Or are the strands not parallel; is it just one and I have been literally moved back within that strand? If I get snapped back to 2007, will I remember all that happened in this version of 2006 and have a changed future there? Am I in a coma and dreaming?

By the time she was dressed, her mind had settled down, and she made her coffee feeling calm. She had to accept that the jumbled thoughts and ideas would return and might never be answered. Determined now to be businesslike and tackle things one by one and not get distracted, she sat down at the desk in the study and jotted things down in no particular order, checked them against last night's scrawled notes from the kitchen, consulted her lists from yesterday, crossed things out and considered the result again. She must identify what was most important, put things in order of urgency and tackle them one by one, however tempting it was to get side-tracked, the risk of running around in mental circles again was always there. Half an hour later, and having drawn up a new and tidy list, she was deep in thought when the phone rang and made her jump.

"I hope I didn't wake you," said Sarah, not sounding in the least troubled by the thought. "I couldn't wait another second! Last night was the most amazing thing I've ever seen. James is knocked sideways with admiration for how cool you were, and I am dying of curiosity - my mind is buzzing. I have to find out what on earth is behind all this – how you changed your style so fast, and who helped you."

Mia smiled, because this was exactly what she had expected. "Sorry Sarah! I can't talk right now, I just got out of the shower."

Hopefully, the gods would forgive her this little white lie for the sake of convenience, but she must map out consistent responses to all Sarah's potential questions in advance, so she didn't get trapped in some situation that could not be explained away.

"Why don't you come over a bit later? Give me time to go out and get something we can have for lunch - unless you and James have something planned? No? Great, I'll see you two soon then!"

"OK, I'll be there about eleven. Don't know if James will come, but wild horses couldn't keep me away. I'll drive your car to town and if James doesn't drive in at the same time, he can pick me up later."

Mia made toast and another mug of coffee and went back to her plans and started re-writing her list again. The floor around the dining table was littered with screwed-up paper, and what was evolving was a short list of practical things and on another page a much longer list of questions to consider and conjectures to pursue. She knew with complete finality that asking for help had no place in her plan, for the time being she must keep things to herself. There were four priority items on her "immediate" list: think of a way to find out if this had happened to others, get prepared to cope at work on Monday, plan how to cash in on the advantages gained last night and try to think of some way to prove what had happened.

She would regard it as a marketing assignment where she must create and sell a product called The New Mia. The product must have credibility, good packaging, capture the target market and satisfy the consumers.

Unfortunately, she could only think of two ways to find other time-shift victims, either advertise or search for Internet blogs devoted to aliens and time travel, but the blog idea filled her with distaste. That kind of site will be full of weirdoes and crazy people, she thought, and how would she possibly know if they were genuine? She might end up with some lunatic she couldn't get rid of, the sort of crazy person who really believed in time travel.

And then the mad humour of it struck her, and she laughed till she nearly cried, slightly hysterical. Was time travel not what she herself had experienced? But her sensible self from That Time still insisted that time travel was nonsense, but she was trapped in an oxymoron of a situation, and it was hard to get her head around her own conflicting viewpoints. She had to admit that if she could not explain these two contradictory points of view to herself, it would be impossible to convey it to someone else. Placing an advertisement in the NZ Herald was a start, and she would write the text early and give herself plenty of time to consider it to avoid being deluged by replies from crazy people and maybe even be tracked down in person. And while she worked on everything else on her list, she would let her memory work in the background on remembering things that could be used as proof, things that might happen again in This Time.

But first she must try to work out exactly what was going on at work, and what would have been expected of her, at this precise time a year ago. It wouldn't be as easy as planning for the evening at Sarah's place last night, not by a long shot. She knew Sarah would not be able to wait until eleven; her craving for information would compel her to come sooner. Mia set out early to get supplies for lunch and returned with bits and pieces from the deli, croissants from the bakery and the weekend paper.

8

When the entry phone buzzed and she pressed the button to let Sarah in, she had a sudden attack of nerves. What if she couldn't keep up the deception and Sarah got suspicious? She knew she couldn't reveal what had happened and expect to be believed. Would Sarah decide she was crazy and insist that she sought medical help? Would she panic? With worried thoughts running through her mind, she went to open the front door and heard the lift arriving at her landing as she turned the door handle. This was not the time to change her plans, she would just have to be careful about what she said. She needed more time to find her footing and to feel secure before she could share the truth with anyone.

Sarah was talking even as the lift doors opened and by the time they closed the apartment door behind them, there was already a backlog of questions to answer.

"Hang on Sarah – too much! Let's get ourselves a cup of coffee and sit down."

Sarah hovered while Mia made the coffee, commenting on the outfit Mia had worn the night before, speculating on the impression she had made and giggling about the amazed faces when Barb walked out.

"I've had three calls this morning already. They're stunned by the way you tackled Barb – everyone says it was a star performance and they can't believe how cool you were. I'm sure Vicky already knew about the Greg and Barb thing - she let something slip and then she tried to backtrack and wouldn't tell me any details."

"I'm sure lots of people knew." Mia tried to make her voice sound calmer than she felt and hesitated for a moment about how far it was safe to go. "As I said yesterday, I've known for quite a while myself, but when I heard those messages on his phone – well, that was pretty devastating. I couldn't just leave it - I had to reclaim my moral territory, so to speak. And I felt that I must do it face to face - and now it has the added advantage that others know that I confronted her, which also makes me feel better."

They spent the next half hour talking about Barb's treachery and what people at the party had said the previous evening.

"Do you think she'll apologize, so you can have some sort of friendship again?" asked Sarah after a while, sounding hesitant. "I've been thinking about it this morning – would you be able to?"

"Oh God, no! There's no way I ever want to speak to her again. Apologies can't fix this - I'm just going to move on and write her off. People we know will stay friends with her, of course, and that's fine. I'll just stop seeing them as well."

Sarah was looking intently at her, and she could see what Sarah was thinking: 'Is this really my quiet little sister?'

Mia decided to change the topic. "Would you like to see what else I bought, when I had my big expensive revamp day? Or shall we have lunch first?"

Sarah laughed. "Clothes first, of course – who needs food?" And then a thought occurred to her, and she added contritely, "God, I'm so sorry to go on like this! It's not as if all this does away with your grief – you're still grieving."

Mia knew that if she was going to be able to be relaxed in the company of Sarah and James, she must reassure them in a credible way that she was over the worst.

"It's OK - truly, it is. Now that I've done my thing with Barb, I feel that I can move on. It was something I had needed to do for some time - now I can grieve for what Greg and I used to have, before he got involved with her - and I can handle that."

She hoped she made it sound reasonable, but there was no way she could tell Sarah that for her, it was actually fourteen months since Greg died; time would tell if she would ever be able to.

They spent a lovely hour inspecting Mia's new clothes, discussing styles and examining every single makeup product she had bought. Sarah picked over the little tubes and bottles and wanted to know what each one was for, fascinated with the special properties of each.

"It's food for thought, you know," she said seriously. "We are so alike in how we've always gone for fairly plain - pretty but plain and never bothered much about makeup. Well, I don't mean mascara and lipstick, but the rest of it."

"I know - we've never been the Glamour Sisters, have we? We just always kept it simple. But I must say that having learnt about foundations, highlighters and blushers and all that has been a real eye-opener to me. I never understood before what a fantastic boost it is to your confidence to know that you're looking really great. It's like a magic, your self-assurance ramps up to the top of the scale the moment you look in a mirror."

Sarah shook her head. "I couldn't believe it - the minute I saw you last night, I knew you had changed, even before you said a single word. That smooth and polished look, glowing – and quite apart from the new clothes. I kept looking at you all evening, wondering how you did it. I'd love to learn how to look like that – not overdone, but really great."

"It was a master class in makeup. The girl who taught me is just so good at her job, amazing, and she doesn't try to turn you into someone else. You know what she said?" Mia laughed at the memory. "She said, we'll emphasize your best features – and I didn't even know what my best features were. A girl I know recommended her and I just went in and told her I needed to look more sophisticated and self-assured. She could tell right away that I wasn't the type for bright lipstick and false eyelashes. I'll give you her name if you like."

By the time Sarah left at half past three, to be picked up by James and go to the movies with friends, Mia was exhausted. Having probed every comment from the previous evening and gone over every detail of the Greg and Barb saga made her feel as if she had been through a wringer, and at times it had been nearly impossible to keep a tight lid on what had really happened. It was all very well to decide that for the time being she was not prepared to reveal it, but neither could she bear to tell Sarah any more outright lies than strictly necessary. At times she had scrambled for ways to put things, and a couple of times she had only managed by being slightly evasive or by diverting Sarah's attention.

"Lovely to see you!" said Mia. "I think you can stop worrying about me now. I know I'll be all right - last night was the proverbial corner I've been waiting to turn."

Sarah hugged her. "You are such a star - and I'm so relieved. Bye!"

Mia smiled at the thought of all the information and speculation that Sarah would soon pour out to James and close friends. Very shortly the grapevine would spring into action, and people would think that she had kept it to herself and not talked about it until she could confront Barb face to face. She felt a warm glow of satisfaction at having managed well so far, but in the back of her mind a little voice reminded her not to be too confident – work would be far harder to deal with.

A few minutes later Sarah called from the car. "God Mia, we got so involved I forgot to ask you - are you still able to take us to the airport next Sunday? Just so I can tick that off on the Big Trip list. I am getting so excited now - I think I might start packing tonight. Bye, talk to you later."

Mia had forgotten that Sarah and James's big trip must be coming up soon. She went back to the study to check her diary but found nothing there. In the end she found a note pinned to the little notice board. 'Sun 20 August, take S & J to airport @ 6 pm. Back on 16 Sep.' It was coming back to her now, the well-planned holiday to Poland, Russia and London, Sarah's list of museums, cathedrals and art galleries and James's list of WW2 sites and military museums.

Letting her mind drift while she did some housework, resisting the urge to push her memory for more details, and just waiting to see what came up, proved productive. Now and again, she went back to her note pad and jotted down what had occurred to her, both about events that might prove that she had 'lived in the future' and things relating to work. Maybe not everything would happen as they had the in That Time, but if she could document a few with enough detail, some might work out.

At the top of a clean sheet of paper she wrote: Ruby Maria, born 23 April 2007.

9

———

On Monday morning Mia's first waking thought was to check that she was still in 2006. There was a tingle of apprehension in her stomach; today would be the biggest test, because to carry it off at work she must perform with the appearance of total confidence. She had tried her best to prepare, but she was still uneasy. The possibility that she had made a verbal promise to do something and that she would have no idea what it was, haunted her. She must be ready to improvise or make excuses and stay calm, but she was well aware that if she couldn't then she would be in serious trouble. It was a venture into the unknowable and there was no possible way to write a word-for-word script, as she had for Friday night.

Mia got off the bus in Newmarket Broadway, unfolded her umbrella and walked the two blocks to her office, mentally rehearsing the stratagem she could use to cover any mistakes. After some thought she had decided that her best bet would be to smile and say, as if she found it was amusing that she had forgotten, 'Sorry, what was that again? Remind me!'

Dressed in a careful selection of newly acquired clothes and having taken special care with her make-up, she hoped that the magic of a protective façade would once again help her feel confident. As she walked, she carried on an internal debate about how she could reveal the story of Greg's infidelity and the way she had dealt with it. She could vividly remember how mortified she had been when she discovered that there were people at work who knew about the affair. Someone who knew Greg had found out and talked, and when he died the rumour of his infidelity had spread further. The recollection of how she felt when she had become aware of this still made her cringe.

Her primary wish was to be seen as strong and self-confident, in control of her life, instead of helpless and damaged. And if she could change how people perceived her, they might pay less attention to her sudden recovery from immediate grief. And

somehow, she must make it known that she had known about Greg's affair and had held Barb to account.

When she pushed open the big glass door to the foyer, she still didn't know how she would bridge that credibility gap; she would have to wait for the right opportunity and hope for the best. Lovely Alice greeted her from the reception desk in the foyer, glamorous and cheerful as always.

"Hi, Mia! Have you recovered?"

Mia stopped by the desk, shook her umbrella, and took her jacket off.

"Thanks, I'm fine now. I was much better already by Friday evening - it was just one of those twenty-four-hour bugs. I actually went to my sister's place for dinner on Friday night and felt completely OK."

Alice was looking her up and down – the new look was getting a thorough inspection.

"New outfit!" said Alice "You look crash hot, Mia – and I *love* the make-up! Somehow I thought you never bothered with make-up."

Mia smiled her appreciation and walked down the corridor to her office, glanced into Alan's empty room and continued to her own three doors down. She was grateful that she hadn't bumped into Josh before she had a chance to check her notes, because he was as sharp as a tack and had a killer instinct for people's weak spots.

Josh was only a couple of years older than Mia, but he had gone to university straight from school and had a few more years of experience. He had been hired just before her and was Alan's deputy in the department. It was rumoured that he had some impressive achievements in innovative marketing behind him, and he was often spoken of as someone who would go far. Mia, with the hindsight of having lived an extra year in That Time, knew that he was ruthlessly ambitious and ready to use dishonesty to get ahead. He had sacrificed Mia for his own advancement, and her reputation had suffered considerable harm, which had added to her depression.

As she hung her jacket on the back of the door, she knew that first of all she must establish if the disastrous events of 2006 were already underway. The deception, which had brought Josh unmerited praise and blighted her own prospects, might not even have started its destructive course yet in This Time. Once she knew where things were at, she would make a plan for how to protect herself from harm; it would require a clever strategy and unwavering focus.

She put a plastic folder under her dripping umbrella in the corner behind the door, sat down at her desk and turned on the computer, while her thoughts returned to the Josh debacle. What would their relationship be at this point? The safest option would be to keep their first meeting neutral and pleasant and try to give nothing away until she was sure of where she stood, but she would probably be able to work it out from how Josh acted towards her.

There were no meetings in her diary for Monday 14 August 2006, so she settled down to read emails from the last couple of weeks and check the ones she had printed out and clipped together. The habit of printing important emails and keeping them to gradually make progress notes on, was a longstanding habit and right now, it was invaluable. Others might find it pedantic, but it suited her way of working and today it was the perfect tool. She spent half an hour searching for clues, hoping that she would end up with a reasonable grasp on what was in progress, though she would inevitably have forgotten some details.

Alan appeared in the doorway in a wet jacket and wiping rain from his bald head with a large handkerchief. "Hi Mia, are you OK now?"

"Yes, thanks, it was just a twenty-four-hour bug – I'm fine."

"You'll see in your emails from Friday that there's a full staff-meeting at three this afternoon. The CEO announced it on Friday. He'll brief us on progress about the merger. Heaven knows if he'll tell us the only thing everyone really wants to know – how many jobs might be lost."

Mia looked at his kind and chubby face, which had a worried look that was completely unnatural on him.

"Are you worried about our department? Do you think any management jobs will be lost?"

"Honestly, Mia, if I knew I'd tell you. I think the most likely scenario is that they'll lay off those roles where they can make immediate economies of scale - the obvious ones and then wait for natural attrition to lower staffing levels some more. And then, if that doesn't work or they discover there are further economies to be made, they might 'disestablish' some roles - which is just a trendy way of saying that people will be made redundant."

Mia knew exactly what would happen and how many would be laid off overall, but she said nothing and tried to look suitably concerned. She looked without focus at the empty doorway after Alan had left, and her memory brought up details she had forgotten about the merger and the job losses that happened over a six-month period.

Amazing how you think you've forced your mind to give up every last possible thing, she thought, and then a day or two later another layer of facts emerges, as clearly defined as if they'd been stored only yesterday. I think I could give him the final body count.

She finished her survey of emails, made some useful notes and gradually more details were emerging in her mind. Cruising through files on the server she found the official update of the merger plans, revisited some documents she had saved in her personal folder and sent a few files home to herself to study more closely. By mid-morning she sat back reasonably satisfied with her grasp of events and began planning which task on her notepad she should tackle first. Once she got started, it was no different from any other working day and gradually it began to feel normal, and her confidence increased.

Josh came in to check if she had read a file that he had emailed to her on Friday.

"How's the sick girl then? You look healthy, but I'll keep a safe distance. Did you read my email yet?"

Mia observed him carefully from behind a neutral façade. She felt reasonably certain from his tone and look that they were still friends. She knew that once he had used her as a scapegoat to save his reputation, he had changed his approach to her. Even though he had harmed her, and they both knew it, he had treated her with pity as if she had genuinely messed up and ruined her own prospects. And she had never confronted him directly about it, just let it sit in the background like some toxic substance slowly poisoning her mind. Now it felt as if the person she had been then, had no connection to her present self at all.

"No, I haven't had time to read it yet. I'm catching up with some things I left mid-stream on Thursday, but I'll have a look at it later today."

"Okay, we'll catch up later. Be good!"

He left and she reflected on the deceptiveness of good looks. Josh was one of the cliché golden boys, tall and good-looking and with enough personal charm to have fooled her completely. She had never liked his half-flirty approach, but she had never told him to lay off. He had surprisingly turned out to be ruthless and dangerous, but forewarned is forearmed, she told herself, and perhaps this time she would be able to prevent him from ruining her career.

Left to herself again she tried to assemble her puzzle pieces. The merger was just about to be announced and Josh was still pretending to be a nice guy. Alan still valued Josh and Mia equally, though Josh automatically assumed superiority on the basis of having a more glamorous position compared to Mia's more fact-based role. And lovely Alice was not yet pregnant with the baby of the abusive man that she had decided she never wanted to see again. And last but not least, in This Time, she herself was prepared for all sorts of different reactions and actions, compared to That Time. Then she had let herself be dragged along by events, shackled by her own passivity and lack of assertiveness, now she was much better equipped to deal with what fate might have in store for her.

Her stenographer's pad with notes was a habit she had developed as a student, and over time it had been refined into a personal reminder system, a blend of general notes, ideas and inspirations, and reminders. Now she read her notes and marked items, which must be completed or taken a step further before the end of the day. Since starting this job, she had built a reputation for always meeting deadlines and in a workplace with so many creatively gifted people this made her stand out. Josh, of course, mocked her and called her obsessive and 'list dependent'. He sometimes joked about "Mia, who wouldn't remember to go home at night if it wasn't on her list".

"It works for me," was all she would say in response, when Josh trotted out the same joke again in the staff canteen, and Josh would chuckle and wink at whatever female was looking in his direction. How she detested that habit of winking! That alone should have been enough to alert her to his character months earlier, a perfect example of 20/20 hindsight. But such was her newfound confidence that even that thought failed to dent her mood.

10

The staff canteen was rarely empty, but the same combinations of people tended to go there at the same time of the day, so Mia went upstairs for a cup of coffee at eleven, half an hour later than usual. Avoiding those she usually met up with seemed like a good self-protection strategy. She got herself a coffee and was looking around to find a place to sit when someone at a table over by the windows called out: "Oy, Mia! Over here!" and she wove across the room, hearing snatches of conversations about the merger more than once.

Callum, Tex and Mandy were at a table for four and she joined them, thanking her lucky star for a chance to share a table with Mandy, whom she otherwise rarely talked to. Callum and Tex were creatives with a high profile, younger than most of the other creative teams and had won a prestigious award in Australia the previous year. Mandy worked in IT and was the company gossip, and it was rumoured that she and Tex had a thing going, though Tex was married, and Mandy had an endless supply of boyfriends.

Luck was still standing guard behind Mia, because after five minutes of merger talk, Callum gave her the opening she needed, by asking if Barb was back from England yet. She knew he had met Barb a couple of times, and he knew that she and Mia were friends. Now she made a lightning-fast decision to grab the chance to launch her new persona, because the advantage of having Mandy there to hear it was a great piece of luck; she would spread the news and Mia wouldn't have to tell anyone else herself.

"Yes, she just got back," said Mia coolly, looking at Callum and ignoring the other two. "She was at my sister Sarah's place for a dinner party in the weekend, but I sent her packing before the meal."

Her choice of words was pure ad-hoc inspiration, but it could not have come out better if she had practiced it in front of the mirror. If she had ripped off her clothes and danced on the table, their surprise could not have been greater. All three stared in silent anticipation, and then Mandy said uncertainly, "You sent her packing? You mean you told her to leave?"

Mia tried to adopt a reasonable and calm tone of voice, though inside she was fizzing with nerves. "Well, I hadn't seen her, you see, not since Greg's accident, because she'd been away on some work exchange thing in England. She left just before it happened. And she didn't know that I had known since *before* the accident that she was having an affair with Greg. In fact, I had decided to talk to them about it, but I left it too late, and Barb went off for her trip - and then Greg had his accident."

She stopped. Their faces registered a range of reactions. Mandy looked guilty and surprised and greedy for more at the same time, and Callum was stunned. Tex looked mildly curious and was the first to speak.

"You were going to talk to them about it? That seems very laid back. I would have thought you'd be furious?"

Mia looked at him and thought, 'Perfect, thank you!' Now she could elaborate in a natural way.

"Well of course I was furious - I was devastated! I mean, we've been friends since primary school. At first, I thought it might have been a one-off fling and I figured that if it might save my marriage, it was worth trying to live with it and not say anything - which I tried to do." She made sure there was a frown on her face for the next part. "But then I found out that it had been going on for quite a while and I wanted to talk to them together. I felt sure that Greg would drop her, right there in front of me, if I confronted them together. I really wanted her to experience that with me there – my so-called friend."

Mandy broke in, unable to contain herself. "So, what stopped you? Was it too hard to do?"

Mia looked sad. "The right opportunity just didn't come up

before Barb went off to England. So, I decided to talk to Greg on his own, and then he was killed, and I never got to do it at all."

Her voice trailed off, and to her surprise she was close to crying, she could feel tears pooling in her eyes. It was as if the story she had told them was new and true, the effect on her fresh and immediate. How strange and disturbing!

Callum found his voice and his opinions, and he made no bones about it. "What a treacherous bitch - unbelievable! Sorry Mia, but what a bastard Greg was too. That's the worst kind of betrayal, when it's with your friend."

Mandy was hungry for more detail. "And you had it out with her at a party at Sarah's - in front of everyone?"

She wanted it all, gory details and blood on the floor, so Mia took a deep breath, and thought that this was it, the best opportunity she might ever get.

"Yes, I did. I hadn't seen her since she came back, she'd only just returned the day before, and it all got too much when she walked in, as if she'd done nothing wrong, all smiles. I could tell she was going to hug me, and it was more than I could take. So, I took my courage in both hands and confronted her. There was nothing she could say - she admitted it, so I told her I never wanted to see her again and to get out of my sight. And she left, just walked out and slammed the door."

By this time, she had drunk her coffee, and more detail might spoil the effect, so she got up with a casual remark about having to be on time for a meeting and left.

Mandy looked at Tex without even pretending to include Callum. "God, that's ghastly! Poor Mia, what a pig of a thing to have to deal with. I think she's so together and strong, it's just amazing. To have that on her mind and not talk about it, that's really something. I would never in a million years have guessed she could be like that. She always seemed like such a timid little thing."

Tex said nothing, but Callum nodded in agreement. "I met Greg once or twice, you know. He seemed like a nice guy at the time."

Tex said quietly, "I knew about it, and I wouldn't know Barb from a bar of soap, but I've got a mate whose sister works for the brewery where Greg worked. And she had seen him more than once with someone who wasn't Mia and she said it was obvious they were in a relationship. And if one person knew, then lots more would have, and I bet some of Mia's friends knew too."

Mia took the stairs the ground floor, contemplating the group she had left behind and what the impact of what she had told them might be. She had noticed the flash of astonished admiration on Callum's face, and she was prepared to bet that Mandy was weighing up the pros and cons of spreading such tasty news. Despite the fact that many already knew about her own affair with Tex, the temptation to shock and surprise would probably get the better of her.

The staff canteen filled up early for the afternoon meeting, people came in without much talking and quietly took their seats. The large room had been cleared of café tables and someone had lined up extra plastic chairs in rows, but even so many

had to stand along the walls and in groups at the back of the room. David Wilson, a man Mia had only said hello to in the lift a couple of times, sat at a table at the front of the room with the department managers lined up beside him. As the latecomers trickled in, he leaned forward, tapped the microphone and the low buzz of voices died down.

Mia listened and watched with great interest. The speech was another test of This Time compared to That Time. She remembered this meeting very clearly, because it had been a momentous occasion, and she knew what David Wilson was going to say, or rather what he had said the first time around. If some things in This Time were going to have a different spin, she was sure she would be able to pinpoint the changes. But gradually it became clear that this was the same speech. There were no surprises - the merger was going ahead, and a media release would go out at the end of the day, the stock exchange might or might not react, but any change to the share price was expected to be temporary, and business would go on as usual.

He emphasized that he wanted them all to know that, as far as anyone could tell at this point, all jobs were secure 'apart from possibly my own' – Mia knew that joke was coming and the second time around it was still as lame as the first time she heard it.

"I want to assure you that we'll keep you informed of further developments as they happen," he concluded. "This is a wonderful opportunity for us all – merged with AMCL we will be a force to be reckoned with in the global arena and I for one look forward to it with excitement and confidence."

A bland and reassuring speech, with no hard facts and no outright promises. Probably the standard merger-speech, she thought, keep it general and don't go into specifics. Some clapped in a half-hearted way, many simply got up and left, others stayed talking in small groups or headed for their department heads at the front of the room to ask questions. Mia followed a stream of people slowly heading for the doors. She wanted to avoid being drawn into conversation, because this was not the moment for her to contribute; that could come later. Her mind was, as always, these days full of things she would need to spend time researching and reconstructing. She had written the text to the advertisement yesterday, but when she had another look at it before lunch, she was undecided about her choice of words and felt it needed fine-tuning before she submitted it. Everything she did needed an extra layer of scrutiny and attention.

11

S arah called that evening just as Mia had turned on the washing machine, but she had too much on her mind to have a long conversation. She blamed her disinclination to talk on the news about the merger and said she needed to sit down and do some thinking.

"It's one of those things you hear of others going through, but you don't think you're going to have to make decisions like that yourself," she said. "Do I jump ship now and get another job, just to pre-empt being laid off later, when dozens of others could be looking for new jobs too? Or shall I stay on, hoping I won't be made redundant and take my chances? I might not get it right either way, but I want to feel I made a reasoned choice."

She moved away from the noise of the washing machine, walked through to the kitchen and started looking in the fridge.

Sarah understood her point. "I know - that's how I would think too. James and I have been through this once already, when his brother-in-law lost his job in that big meat company merger a couple of years ago."

She was more than willing to use this experience to take the discussion further, while she pottered around her own kitchen preparing dinner, and Mia let it go on for another few minutes before making an excuse to put the phone down.

"Sorry, Sarah – my dinner's nearly ready. I'll call you tomorrow."

. . .

Being back at work had raised a new crop of questions and what she really needed to do now was to sit down and do some quiet thinking, not worrying about the merger. She got a can of potato and leek soup out of the pantry and tipped it into a bowl to heat and stood watching the bowl revolve slowly in the microwave oven.

There was one question that made no sense, and she kept reverting to it. She had woken up in her 2006 body but with her 2007 memories right up to the previous evening clear in her head, and it seemed illogical, stranger than all the rest. Perhaps she was an anomaly, the only person who in the world who could remember being moved around in time; maybe it happened all the time, but nobody remembered the time strand they came from.

She put a slice of wholemeal bread in the toaster and groaned. What was the point of using logic when she didn't know if logic applied to this? There must be some logic, of course, but how would she know what the rules were? She must try to find someone else in the same situation, or she would have nothing to go by. Or if that failed, she must find sensible people to discuss it with, but that meant that first she must be able to convince them that she wasn't mad. On the whole, she felt more comfortable with the concept of innumerable parallel lives, with lightly different twists and turns and running at different speeds.

She poured a glass of wine, carried it to the table and turned on the TV news before returning for her soup and toast.

I didn't know I had it in me, she thought, to react as I have, comparatively pragmatic and balanced - and it was only first thing on Friday morning that I totally freaked out and since then I think I've coped pretty well – with short interludes of complete, heart-pounding panic.

While she ate and watched the news with half-hearted attention while her mind filtered ideas and reached a conclusion. In the absence of facts or any way of finding anything out, the only reasonable thing would be to regard the situation as a gamble, something she could not change, only try to manipulate in her own favour. And it would either turn her future into a much better place, or she would end up where she had started. And thinking of it like that turned it into a win-win situation, which was a calming thought. Because whatever happened, she would not be any worse off and might end up better off. She returned her dishes to the kitchen, tidied up and went to put her laundry in the dryer, before going back to her research and plans.

Two hours later she stretched and yawned. She had read the emails and documents that she had sent home from work, and now she had a comprehensive picture of the situation, but she was stiff from sitting in the same position and concentrating. The first consideration now was to not miss the opportunity to put a spanner in Josh's works before he destroyed her reputation again. She needed a good plan for this and must be alert for certain key things to happen. Unable to switch off and go to bed, she prowled around the apartment, conducting a running discussion with herself.

She poured another glass of wine, turned all but one of the living room lights off and sat for a while looking out through the large window across the room. She loved the night view of lights and buildings, glimpsed sections of streets with moving vehicles and the Sky Tower floodlit against the night sky looking like the top of one of those elegant Venetian glass bottles.

When she got up and did what she had done nearly every day since July 2006, which paradoxically was both thirteen months ago and one month ago. She looked at the two paintings and revelled in the thrill they gave her. Until she went to that huge art sale at Eden Park, she had not known that art could create a sensation that touched her soul. One work was an abstract painting, which made her think of a city glimpsed through thick fog, tantalizing fragments of tall buildings in a near white-out. The other was a large, dark oil painting, of a man seen through a window, partially concealed by the reflections in the glass. His stance and look of abstraction evoked something in Mia that gave her goose bumps, and as she stood there contemplating the paintings, she realized that somewhere in the depths of her brain she had reached a decision about Josh.

I will write it down now, she thought, both what happened in That Time, every single detail – and also what I must to now, step by step. Some of the things I might have to do are a bit scary and I must get the timing absolutely right, so if I am going to carry this off, I need to keep my focus and not miss a beat.

It was after midnight when she turned her bedside light off and her last conscious thought was that she hoped she would be able to sleep.

12

___

Over the next couple of days Mia repeatedly thanked her lucky star that she had been shunted back to this particular week in This Time. Many work-related things were tagged "pre-merger" or "post-merger" in her mind, which made it easier to place key events. At work everyone speculated about the merger, and Mia listened without comment and remembered the exact numbers who lost jobs in three waves up to March 2007. Could she change anything? Should she warn some to start looking for jobs elsewhere before the axe fell? Though it might actually increase their chances of getting good jobs, it would also favour some at the expense of others. There was no perfect answer.

On Tuesday afternoon she stayed an extra hour after work looking up documents and dates relating to the work that she had done for Josh's big promotion idea. He had hatched a very ambitious plan for a concept he wanted to pitch to a large company with stores all through the country selling IT products and home appliances. It involved issuing 'smart cards' to customers to encourage them to return. Purchases would register on the customers' cards, and they would get rewards proportional to their spending. But they would also have special offers loaded on their cards simply by using them at retail outlets with text alerts to tell them what the offer was. The master plan involved the possibility of other chain stores selling different goods to be offered the opportunity to 'buy into' the system and for several retailers to share the same card, to attract

customers as a group. The advertising campaign he proposed
would be extensive and across all media. It would play on the hi-
tech aspect of the card and the chance of high value opportunistic
'treat' bargains limited to certain select customer groups.

Alan had used Mia to do research on intelligent cards, website-
based databases, mass-texting, one-day special offers and many
other aspects. She had worked on the costing with some help from
outside IT specialists and created a timeline of projected uptake
and increased turn-over to support the business case.

She knew that at this stage in That Time she had just
completed her part of the brief and passed it on to Josh. It was
tagged in her mind as only a day or two before the merger
announcement. Now she made notes, copied a couple of files to
other locations and was just turning her computer off, when Alan
came in to see why she was working late.

"I hope you aren't getting nervous about your job, because
there's no need for that. I'm determined to keep you here and I'm
sure you know how pleased I am with your work. You may have
been one of the last to be hired, but you won't be laid off if I have
anything to say about it."

"Thanks, Alan, that's kind of you. I just had some bits and
pieces I wanted to tidy up, so I can start with a clean slate tomorrow, nothing major."

Mia spent the next hour plotting the most accurate timeline she
could, based on her memory of events and what she had found in
her searches among files and documents on the hard drive. The
facts of the Josh saga were clear in her mind now, and she tried to
identify the danger points and decide on strategies to stop disaster
repeating itself.

In that other life she had spent a lot of time and used all the
resources she could muster to work out the projections and costs
for Josh's concept. Because so much of it was highly technical, she
had had to rely on 'best advice' from outside experts. The crucial
work-up along with extensive notes were in an Excel file where the
background data and the final costing were displayed in a dozen
connected spreadsheets. She had saved the file in a project folder
on the server's shared document drive, where Josh or Alan could
access it.

Just before the merger announcement, she had told Josh that

she had finished, but that the project carried a high risk of not being viable. She had gone to talk directly to him about it, instead of emailing, but he was on his way out and they had stood talking in the doorway. Now she sat at her desk, her unfocused gaze on the computer screen, and replayed the scene in her mind.

"Sorry Josh, it's a great idea but I don't think it will work – the viability is so marginal that it would be insane to try it. Particularly with something where so much up-front development work must be done at a cost that can't be accurately predicted."

Josh was instantly furious, his face seemed to swell and redden as he took a step closer, and she took an involuntary step back, nearly frightened of him.

"You can't be serious! It just can't be that bad, you must have got some of the costs wrong. Or you'll have to eliminate some of the expenses and make it viable."

Mia steeled herself not to be intimidated and stood her ground. "No Josh, I can't. Just have a look at the spreadsheet yourself – it's obvious that there's nothing to play around with – and it can't be made to look better. I'm even worried that I've under-estimated some of the costs – there is no way I can scale any of it down."

Josh had recovered some of his composure now and was coldly furious; his eyes were drilling into hers.

"But it's got to work! It's a brilliant idea and if I don't get them to try it now, someone else will come up with the same idea very shortly. You've got to fix it!"

She was glad she had not given him a chance to bargain with her; now she would just continue to refuse to budge. "No, it really is that marginal. A tiny percentage of increase on the cost side or low increase in turnover would make it a financial disaster for the client, because all he cost is upfront. You have to read the comments in the spreadsheet – it's all there and there is nothing to be done about it."

The argument was going nowhere, and she had gone back to her room with a final uncompromising comment. "Well, it's your project, but I don't think Alan will let it proceed to a proposal to the client. If anyone asked for my opinion, I'd tell them it should be canned."

From there things had developed into a complete disaster for Mia, but Josh had come out of it with his prospects untarnished. The project was accepted for presentation to the client, who liked it and work started on the design and creative input right away, closely followed by a brief to an IT company to develop the software and the interface for the smartcard.

Mia had been astounded when she heard that the client had accepted it, but she didn't make an issue of it, didn't ask Alan to explain why it had gone ahead. It was not her problem, and she knew that the risks would have been thoroughly debated by more experienced people than herself. It was even possible that Alan and Josh had asked for outside advice and made some changes to the cost structure, but she never asked.

As Mia found out later, a lot of money had been invested in the development phase, advertising space was being negotiated, location finders and photographers contracted, and many hours of agency and contractor time was invested in working on developing the interactive website and the technical side of the promotion.

By late October, when someone from the client's side raised the alarm and called for a crisis meeting, a large amount of money had either been spent or was committed for contract work. Mia first heard about a problem when a stressed and worried Alan came to ask if she could come to the meeting room.

"Sorry to spring this on you, Mia, but things are getting a bit sticky, and I hope you'll be able to shed some light on what's gone wrong with the costings in the proposal."

It had been a harrowing session. Even now she felt her shoulders tense and she cringed at the memory of that humiliating day. She had entered a room where the atmosphere was thick with unanswered questions and suppressed anger. She was handed a copy of the proposal Josh had prepared, and Alan pointed out the page with the cost projections, and she saw straight away that some figures and totals were different, and the bottom line looked a lot more optimistic than it should. She flicked to the text; there was no mention of the warnings she had attached to the spreadsheet. A chilly shiver raced down her spine – something was very, very wrong.

Questions were coming thick and fast, directed primarily at Josh, but also at Mia. The focus was on the projections. Why had nobody crosschecked them, why had nobody realized that some of the costs were not included in the totals? Josh had appeared genuinely puzzled. He said that he had been given the completed spreadsheet by Mia, who had prepared it and the figures looked good, so he went ahead and wrote the proposal paper. He stated with apparent honesty that it was not until that very morning, after speaking to the client's financial manager on the phone that he had realized that the totals did not include all the expenses. He looked concerned and confused, and he apologized for not checking, but to all appearances he was the innocent victim of someone else's sloppy work.

Apprehension had flooded Mia's mind and she felt sick. If Josh was prepared to lie, she had no way of proving she had warned him. The figures were different from her original calculation and only Josh could have changed them; those new totals at the bottom of the columns; they must have come from somewhere and they were not typing errors. There had been a formula to total each column and at a quick glance it looked as if someone had changed it to exclude the top row of expenses after she handed the spreadsheet file over to Josh. Alan asked her to explain what might have happened. Mia could tell from his voice and face that he had not been informed of the faulty additions before the meeting but had only known that the client was concerned about the accuracy of some of the data.

She had felt her throat close up, and she knew that her voice had sounded uncertain and without conviction, when she replied. "These aren't the figures from the spreadsheet I prepared. The viability is much better than it should be. And my notes aren't referred to in the text of the proposal."

Everyone looked at her and mistrust filled the room like a grey fog.

"I can go and print off the relevant part of the spreadsheet and show you."

Alan nodded and she ran back to her office, her mind in turmoil, and her fingers trembled on the keyboard as she located and opened the Excel file. She stared in disbelief – the actual spreadsheet had been changed. Cold sweat was forming on her forehead; she flicked to one of the totals cells and yes, the formula now excluded the expense row at the top of the columns. Quickly she went to the View menu and clicked on View Comments, but no comments appeared. Feeling sick to her stomach she got up from her desk, cast a despairing glance at the computer screen and walked slowly back to the meeting room.

Entering the room again was one of the hardest things she had ever done, but she braced herself and walked into a room where every face turned to stare at her. She stood behind the chair she had occupied earlier, and her voice was tight with tension. "The spreadsheet shows the same totals as the proposal paper. But that is not what I prepared. It did not look like that when I finished with it."

Before any of the client's people could comment, Alan took pity on her and told her that there was no need for her to stay, she could leave now. Dismissed and mentally demolished Mia went back to her room and sat at her desk, desperately trying to think of something that would prove that the file had been tampered with after she finished with it. She checked to see if she had ever emailed the intact file to Josh, but all she found was an email where she told him when it would be completed. She checked her own personal folder, but she had never saved a copy of it, and she knew she had never printed it out. She was stuck with looking like an incompetent or careless fool and there seemed to be no way to change it.

Alan had come to see her after the meeting and after speaking to Josh, but he had no reason to doubt that Mia had seriously messed up. The project was cancelled; the firm would have to bear the write-off of the costs incurred so far. He himself was puzzled and sad that she had made such an error; he felt it was all to do with her recent trauma and her distracted mental state, but he also blamed Josh for not checking everything before proceeding with the proposal. Mia didn't comment or cry, she just sat as if turned to stone and listened, said yes and no, but offered no explanation or excuse.

Since then, her working life in That Time had been a struggle and her confidence seriously eroded. But in This Time, she had a chance to avert the nightmare and she must get it right, both the facts and the timing. She debated the tactical options with herself: how far to go and how best to stage-manage her actions, how to credibly 'discover' certain things. She was confident that she would be able to monitor what was going on and not interfere with fate in any way that was unfair to Josh, taking into account that he might not be about to destroy her this time around.

. . . .

This afternoon she had found the spreadsheet on the shared drive, still in its original state, showing very marginal viability and complete with her cautionary comments. She had saved a copy of it on her C:/drive, where it would be safe and "date stamped". She would email it "by mistake" to someone in the company, as further proof of time and date; all she need to do was decide who the recipient should be, and what the excuse would be for sending them something that did not concern them.

And once that piece of proof was in place, she would wait to see if the story unfolded as it had in That Time. Of course, there was no guarantee that things would play out in the same way and in her heart, she hoped they would not. It would be far better if Josh didn't decide to use and abuse her, but at least now she was forewarned and ready to defend herself. She tilted her chair back and stared unseeing into the middle distance, thinking through what she needed to do; check the spreadsheet on the shared document drive every now and then, and get hold of the proposal once it was printed and then start the countdown. She must be sure that Joss had not only tampered with the data, but that he was going to present the false data to the client, and then she could unmask him before any harm had been done.

13

T he evening was clear, and it nearly felt like spring. Mia came out of the office just after seven and noticed a definite change; the air was softer and warmer. Her spirits rose as she walked down Broadway towards the supermarket, stopping to look in the odd shop window and in no hurry to be on her way home. Spring, she thought, it feels like spring, how lovely!

At the checkout she hesitated about which queue to choose and an amused voice behind her said, "Hi there, how are you?"

Mia turned to find the girl from Designer's standing behind her with a basket.

"I can never decide if it's better to queue behind six little baskets or two full trolleys."

Lorraine smiled "Let's go for this one – we can pass the time together."

When Mia had paid, she turned to Lorraine and said impulsively: "Which way are you going?"

"I live in Ponsonby. I'll catch a bus just a bit further down the block. Today was my day to finish early, so I came over this way to have a look at the shops and visit a friend who lives in this part of town. How about you?"

Mia felt an unusual connection to the tall, black girl; that strange feeling of knowing someone well though you have only just met them. They had shared a mission that had been very personal to Mia, and Lorraine had helped her further by encouraging her to have the make-over with Maylene.

"Would you like to go for a drink somewhere with bar snacks, or a cup of coffee? My treat. I am really grateful for all your help the other day and it's so nice to see you again."

"I'd love to - I'm in no hurry. There's a nice place just across the street, where I've been once or twice."

A short silence fell when they had seated themselves at a table with glasses of white wine and tapas, then they both of them started talking at once, stopped and laughed, and then conversation was easy. They exchanged basic information, and in response to a question, Mia told Lorraine that she was widowed, and Lorraine said she was single and shared a flat with her brother. The session in the shop had intrigued her and she had often thought of it and wondered how the occasion, that Mia had worried about, had turned out.

"How long is it since your husband died?"

Mia hesitated, then said quietly, "Two months."

Lorraine's eyes widened slightly, and Mia continued quickly, knowing how strange it must seem.

"I know I seem very composed about it, but somehow I've managed to get past the early stage of shock and anger, learnt to accept it."

She hesitated about how much to reveal and made a fast decision. She looked out at the now dark street while she searched for the right words.

"And that might have something to do with the fact that I knew he was having an affair with a friend of mine - it obviously influenced my reactions. And since I saw you last, I've faced her about it, publicly – just last Friday at a dinner party at my sister's. Both the dress I bought that afternoon and my lovely new makeup made feel very assertive."

Lorraine burst out laughing, and then, horrified clamped her hand over her mouth.

"Oh God, I'm so sorry! I know it isn't funny, but I did wonder what it was you were preparing for that day. Now that I know, I can just picture the scene. No wonder you were tense! I felt sure you were on a mission of some kind, personal and scary."

She chuckled again and Mia smiled in response and thought how good it felt to have told yet another person and to have established herself as someone in control of her fate.

"Tell me about your name though - were does Mia come from? I never met a Mia before. Is it Italian?"

"My name is really Maria, but my mother had Swedish

ancestry and she called me Mia, which is a Scandinavian short form of Maria. And it's an abbreviation of a Maori name too, so very suitable in New Zealand."

"I think it's lovely! I have such a prosaic name myself. My mother chose it because she felt it sounded so English – and then I found its origin is French."

Three quarters of an hour later they exchanged phone numbers and went their separate ways. Mia was cheered - it felt as if something new and fresh had entered her life. The possibility of a new friendship with someone, who had no links to the past, was an unexpected treat. Lorraine would have no reason to see her as anything but how she chose to present herself in This Time. It was like having been given a blank page and a chance to write a new script.

The following morning, she got an email from Callum asking her to join the creative department that afternoon for their usual Thursday 4.30 workroom drinks. It was tempting; she had only been asked once before, and she knew that it wasn't an open session for all and sundry. But she also wanted to get home, check emails and continue sorting out the study. Maybe they would let her take a rain check; she would reply and say that she had something already arranged, but that she would like to come along next week, if that was OK.

She sat at her desk with her mind far away, imagining what she would do if someone actually replied to her advertisement. Would she suggest meeting them in a neutral place or should she just talk to them on the phone? What if she got drawn into something she wasn't prepared for? But the reality was that getting a response from a genuine time-slip victim was so unlikely that making plans was probably a waste of time.

At the end of the day, when she was racing through a brand recognition survey full of figures and statistics, which Alan wanted to discuss in the morning, Josh came in and perched on the corner of her desk. How she detested it when people did that, it was impolite and a real turn-off. He often did this, even going so far as to casually move some of her papers to clear a space, and she had never said anything about it. Now, looking up at his handsome, friendly face, she said firmly, "Josh, would you please *not* sit on the desk - it's rude. Sit on the chair, so I don't have to look up at you."

Josh obediently moved to sit on her visitor's chair and looked quizzically at her. "Mia, my girl, you're changing just a tad - what's happening out there? Anything you'd like to share with a mate?"

Mia laughed. "Nothing is happening, at least not anything worth telling. I've just decided that I need to take a grip and be a bit more assertive. Can't be a nice doormat for the rest of my life."

"Quite right, take charge of your fate, eh? And I hear from usually unreliable sources that you've dealt to someone who needed a bit of discipline?"

Good heavens, thought Mia, how genuine and friendly he sounds. I'm glad I know he's a devious bastard, or I might be taken in.

"Ah, you must have heard of me confronting Greg's mistress - I didn't think Mandy would be able to keep such a tasty bit of gossip to herself. Yes, Greg was having an affair with a girl who used to be a friend of mine, that's quite true. It had to be done - I feel a lot better now."

Josh's face expressed genuine admiration. "You really surprise me, Mia! I would never have thought you had it in you to do a thing like that, and then to be so cool about it, too. Well done - must have been an awesome performance!"

Mia folded the papers she was still holding and glanced at her watch. "Well, perhaps not quite as exciting as that, but still a good feeling to have it out in the open. It makes up for some of the grief it caused me. Sorry, Josh, I have something I must get finished for Alan before I go. Did you want me for anything in particular?"

Josh wavered ever so slightly, his eyes swerved to one side, he hesitated and then he got up.

"No, not really, just checking on how you are and so on."

He ambled out into the corridor and Mia sat for moment looking at the doorway with narrowed eyes, thinking about the conversation they had just had. In That Time, they had already had their argument about his project, and she had to take for granted that it had already taken place in This Time too. Perhaps his friendly façade was intended to make her think he had taken her advice about how unviable it was.

And this exact chat had never happened in That Time, but

something very similar had. Joss used to drift in now and then and ask how she was getting on in a friendly way. The change now, was that she had asked him not to sit on the desk, and he had commented on the gossip about Greg, which could only happen because of what she had changed in This Time. So, nothing essential had changed in their relationship, only things that she herself had said or done, and she must wait until the proposal was out to find out if everything was on track to happen as it had in That Time.

14
____

As soon as she got home that night, she turned her computer on and opened her email account; nothing yet. She changed her clothes and checked the fridge, for the first time in a long time she felt like cooking, even though it would only be an omelette with ham, diced potatoes and onions.

There's something to be said for domesticity, Mia thought. Cooking is satisfying but undemanding, and the end result is a nice meal. And you can do some good thinking while your hands are busy.

She was just finishing her dinner when the little ping of an incoming email rang out from the study. She raced to the computer, her heart beating excitedly, read the email and groaned.

'I was thrilled to see your notice in the paper - I too came from another planet. I have waited for someone to contact me. I am so happy that you are here. I know that I came here for a purpose, and I am waiting for instructions. Please let's meet as soon as possible to make plans. Alexander.'

Oh, no! she thought, I knew this would happen. That ad was bound to attract the crystal ball gazers and the rest of the fringe-dwellers. I'll reply politely this once and if he ever writes again, I won't answer. I am living a paradox and trying to be rational about

71

it makes no more sense today than it did yesterday. What happened to me is a fact - I know I'm not mad, but this Alexander guy is surely crazy.

She took her mind off it by writing a long and gossipy email to her cousin Brett in London. He had a highly developed sense for absurdity and had always been her favourite cousin out of the three she and Sarah had. He and his two sisters had grown up in the South Island, but they had spent many summer holidays together and were nearly as close as siblings, particularly since his parents and hers had been together on that fateful yacht trip when her parents drowned.

She told him about Greg and Barb, and how she had confronted Barb at Sarah's place, and how much better it made her feel. She shared the bizarre story about a woman in Hawke's Bay who breastfed an orphaned puppy, and how an Auckland parking warden had been sacked for making suggestive little drawings on people's parking tickets. Writing nonsense to Brett was a lovely anti-dote to her worries, and she felt relaxed and cheerful when she finished.

Another couple of emails arrived in response to her advertisement, both as crazy as the first. She replied politely to all of them with the same non-committal message and dug through her brief-case for the note with the text for the advertisement.

Did you slide through a crack in time? Are you stuck in a different time or place from where you started out? I want to hear from anyone who has experienced what I have.'

Very simple, and just the email address to reply to. People could make of it what they wanted, but the chance of it being read by someone who really understood it, was probably miniscule. She would know if a genuine time-slip victim turned up; there would be some description of the sensation of moving between timelines or some other aspect that she would recognize as genuine. During the month that Sarah and James were away she would have plenty of time to start a quest for events that she could use as proof of her story, to make it safe for her to tell them at some unspecified time after they got back.

. . .

The morning bus was packed, the driver took the corner into Newmarket Broadway too fast, and people were flung against each other, but Mia barely noticed. She was on autopilot thinking ahead to the next few days and what she needed to get done. Walking towards work she carried on an internal conversation with herself. She could call Lorraine and ask her over for dinner the following week, maybe to watch a film or just sit and talk. Would she think that was too boring? Maybe she would prefer to go out some-where? Should she give her the choice or just suggest something?

There was an inherent dilemma in feeling so close to someone whose tastes and interests she did not know, but the idea was growing on her and by the time she arrived at the office she had made up her mind to call her. She couldn't quite put her finger on what had created the bond she felt for the other girl. Though she knew that Lorraine had come to New Zeeland as a young child and felt one hundred percent a New Zealander, she was still exotic in a particularly appealing way. Maybe it was something as simple as the way her eyes were so alive and interested, or perhaps it was the experience they had shared when Mia bought her new clothes, but she fancied that there was more to it than that. It was that indefinable thing she had read about, when you meet someone new, and you feel as if you already know them, you feel very comfortable and safe with them straight away. Mia imagined that this happened to certain people more than others and she had never experienced it before, but she knew that she and Lorraine had formed an instant connection.

The day got busy with Alan working towards a tight deadline and demanding more and more information, and finally deciding he wanted the summary of a statistics in a brand awareness report for a client to look different.

"Because we are attaching an unasked-for plan with this report, I want to support our pitch with something, not just rely on the concept being great and the figures good," he said. "Sorry I can't be more specific, but you know the sort of thing I need – that final little presentation twist that will make all the rest of it fall into place and become irresistible. I know our proposal is really good, but it needs that extra something."

Mia nodded. "OK, give me till mid-afternoon and I'll have

something for you. Maybe we could simply make it more visually appealing? I could turn it into something cute – perhaps colour-code the bar graph to match the client's logo colours or something."

He was instantly contrite. "Don't go to too much trouble! I know how busy you are and it's not your job to design pretty presentations, but you do it so well."

"That's OK Alan, it won't take long, and I quite enjoy fiddling around being creative. It's a nice break from dealing with facts and figures."

Alan had no sooner gone than the IT department called and said they wanted to load some new software, which meant no computer access for twenty minutes. She managed to put them off to a bit later in the morning, so she could take an early lunch break while they did their thing, and then have an uninterrupted run to the end of the day.

Mia was quietly reading a report on the internet and making notes of things that might come in useful in the future, when a man she recognized as Callum's section manager knocked and came into the room.

"I'm Grant, from the mad creative side – we met at that Christmas drinks thing upstairs. I wonder if you would you mind if I ask Alan to lend you to us for a project?"

She smiled. "Can't imagine what on earth I could do for you – a very different universe from mine. And Alan keeps me pretty busy."

"It won't take up too much of your time, probably a two-hour meeting next week and then a couple of hours per week - it's not long-term. But I'll only ask Alan if you think you would like to do it."

Mia knew that this had happened in That Time, too – but would it work out differently this time? "Why are you asking me? You've got people who have been here much longer than I have."

"We want someone with strong analytical skills, but it's got to be someone who can communicate well with those on the team - let's face it, most of the team can't tell a percentage from a ratio. Two of our people suggested you, so I came along to ask."

Mia felt the pleasant glow of being appreciated and kept her fingers crossed that nothing would scupper it this time around. "By all means, go ahead and ask Alan. I'd love to do it."

She remembered the project that Grant was talking about; it would have been her first big step up, if the Josh drama hadn't intervened and ruined her prospects. If she could reshape the course of events this time, the project could give her a push up the ladder. And if Grant was already talking about borrowing her, then the Josh disaster was not far away. She must make sure she kept herself informed, because things were beginning to fall into place in a way that made sense timewise.

And then she suddenly remembered that she had not emailed that spreadsheet in its original form to anyone as evidence. Quickly she checked the file on the shared drive, holding her breath, but it was still as she had left it. She scanned the list of staff names in the email address book and decided to send it to the person directly above Josh on the address list for internal staff. She had no idea if she had ever set eyes on 'Joe Christie', he might be the tall guy on the top floor, something to do with corporate finance.

'Josh – please don't forget what I told you about the embedded comments! They are as important as the figures in this case. I know you don't agree, but I still maintain that this is not a viable idea. The clients need to understand that the impact of even a 5% lower increase in turnover than what is projected, would turn it into a loss situation, and so would higher than anticipated up-front development costs for the IT. Mia.'

She attached the spreadsheet and pressed 'Send'. Now she had the evidence in her Sent folder and a copy of the original file saved and date stamped on her personal folder; the insurance she had so wished for in That Time, the life-raft that would have saved her. And right on the button, a minute or two before the IT guy came and she would have to turn her computer off, a reply from Joe: *'Think you sent this to the wrong person?'*

She replied right away. *'Sorry, I was in a hurry to get it away to Josh Welsh before the IT man turns up to fix my computer, and here he is right now.'*

This made it even better than she had first thought, unasked-for perfection. Whatever happened later, she had evidence to prove the original state of the spreadsheet, and she could even be excused for not having remembered to send the extra little warning to Josh after all, what with having to leave her computer just then. She smiled to herself at how well this was working out, as if fate was on her side in this timeline and went off to have an early lunch.

15

The big room was nearly empty with only a scattering of people having a cup of coffee or a quick lunch before rushing off to something more important. She made a cup of coffee and sat down at the same table by the windows that she had shared with Callum, Tex and Mandy the other day. That day and her impulse to tell them about Greg had been inspired, there was no way she would have done it better even if she had been able to plan it ahead of time. It had come out just right and created a gossip item which had done her reputation a world of good, and just thinking about it made her smile.

Behind her a voice said, "Well, fancy that! Here we are again."

And there was Callum with a mug in his hand. He sat down across the table from Mia and looked at her sandwich. "That's a very early lunch! I'm having a late morning tea break."

She smiled. "Yes, but the IT guy came to load something on my computer, and it might take a while, so I thought I'd get a head start on the afternoon. Hey, thanks for the recommendation to be part of that project. I presume it was you? Grant came to see me - I'm very flattered."

"Oh, good! We hoped you wouldn't mind that we didn't ask you first if you were up for it. But when Grant asked for suggestions, we gave him your name thinking you might be able to relate to our crazy creative minds, somehow?"

"It should be fun – and I'll learn something new."

"Would you like to join Tex and me for a meal sometime before we get going with the project? We go out after work about once a week - we just ramble on and catch up on bits and pieces. Some of our best stuff comes into our heads while we're bashing ideas around over a meal and bottle of wine. I'll call you or message you next week." He looked at his watch. "Sorry, I must be off."

Running down the stairs Mia mentally ticked off her list of problems she wanted to solve and thought about Alice. Maybe she should try to intervene and change things in Alice's life. In That Time, Alice started dating someone new, became accidentally pregnant and then discovered the new man was a total bastard and had convictions for violence against women and fraud, which Mia had heard about when Alice's low spirits became obvious. How and when could she warn Alice? She counted backward in her head: in August 2007 Alice had probably been about eight months pregnant, so she might have conceived in December. Which meant that sometime between now and December she would meet the bad guy, but how would Mia know just when, and how could she prevent history repeating itself?

Back at her desk she picked up her phone, called Lorraine and left a message asking her to come for dinner one night the following week, her choice. The afternoon flew past; she had come to grips with where things were at now and felt confident. She revamped the statistics sheet for Alan's report and created a new version with customized colours. Taking out the bar graph and replacing it into an exploded pie chart with 3D effects and colours to match the client's logo gave it enough zing, she thought. She emailed the new version to Alan and thought that she had rarely felt so energetic and confident. Just before five Sarah called and asked if Mia was going to be at home early afternoon the next day. She and James were coming across to the city to do some last-minute shopping and might call in.

"Come for lunch," said Mia. "I'll do something simple, so we can eat whenever you arrive."

She was tidying her desk when Lorraine returned her call, and they settled on dinner at Mia's place on Tuesday night. Mia put the phone down feeling a surge of happiness, turned her light off and called out 'good-bye' to the other rooms as she walked out to the foyer.

Alan hailed her as she went past his room. "Great design, thanks Mia! And have a good weekend!"

Alice was just leaving, and they walked away together talking about what they were going to do that weekend. Alice was frank about her quest to find a man. "I just look out wherever I go. I go out with the gang and wherever we are, I check out the talent. If I see someone, who looks likely and not with a girl, I try to create a conversation somehow - it's the only way I'll ever meet anyone new. I've had several dates that way, but nothing lasting. I don't want to be the eternal bridesmaid at everyone else's wedding - I am going to be thirty-two before Christmas and I need to get a move on."

Mia was amused and tried not to show it. "Perhaps you should just wait and let fate take a hand?"

But Alice shook her bouncy curls. "No, no, no - it might take forever! It's time I was in a relationship again - I haven't had a long-term one for years and I'm really ready for it now. And I don't want to date someone I've known for ages, just for the sake of it. There are a couple of guys in the gang who are kind of interested, but it's so dull. I mean, I know everything about them already, where would the romance be?"

Mia laughed. "Well, I'm not much help, Alice. I don't go out much and I've no idea where to go to meet new men. But if I come across some guy who seems OK, I'll let you know."

They parted at the bus stop, and Mia thought how fortunate this conversation with Alice was, because now she could ask every now and then how the great man hunt was going, and when that nasty Romeo turned up and lit Alice's fire - well, plenty of time to decide at the time what she would do about it.

And then a chilly shiver ran down her spine, when she thought that she might not be here then, she might be back in That Time. She had achieved so much in This Time, taken charge of her fate and started to build a new and different life; she couldn't bear to think she would lose it.

16

Sarah and James turned up laden with parcels and both started talking at once.

"We have had such fun..."

"Bought lots of things, some are for the trip."

"Found an adaptor that works with just about all foreign wall sockets, and those funny socks you wear on long flights, so you don't get blood clots."

"And a present for you!"

Mia laughed. "Why did you buy something for me? It's your birthday soon, not mine."

Sarah handed over a purple bag. "Here it is – we're going to ask you to do something for us, so it's more like a bribe than a present."

Mia pulled out a lime green merino wool top, so fine and thin it was like knitted silk, with a deep scoop neckline.

"This is gorgeous! It will be perfect with my new look – how clever of you. You'd better have a big task for me if I'm going to deserve this. And I haven't bought your present, Sarah, not yet. You'll get it when you get back."

"I'm the one asking the favour," said James. "Somewhere in one of these bags is a wedding present for George – you remember George? Best man at our wedding, lives in Western Australia?"

"Of course, red hair and freckles, and very entertaining."

"That's the one – well, he's getting married next Saturday, very quietly at his parents' house, because his father hasn't got long to live. I just realized last night that I hadn't organized a present, and now it's too late to get it mailed today. So, could please you go to the post office and buy a box and send it off? We have the card, and we'll sit down and write it now, but the present needs gift wrapping."

She gave them a pen and took her new jumper to the bedroom, held it up in front of herself to see what it looked like and had a sudden and nearly irresistible impulse to confide in them, to tell them the truth and not hold it inside her like a bubble of suspense and excitement and fear. To be able to share what had happened, answer their questions, and to be believed. But no, it would cause disbelief and worry, and time was too short now, it would take hours of explanations and discussion to convey her story. I must wait until they come back, she thought, and then I'll tell them everything and by then I might know a lot more. She put the jumper on the bed and went to get lunch organized.

When Sarah and James picked up their parcels and left, Mia's thoughts reverted to the question of what it was that was making her feel dissatisfied with the flat. For a couple of days, she had looked around now and again and tried to pinpoint why nothing seemed right. In that other time, she had moved a few things and got rid of a few things she didn't like, a bit here and a bit there over a period of a few months after Greg's death, but nothing major. But now everything seemed dull and badly put together with nothing to recommend it apart from functionality.

The urge to change every aspect of her life was like pent-up energy needing release. She wanted to be surrounded by a style that resonated with her newly discovered self-assurance, a bit like what she had done with her appearance. She stood there looking at the living room and tried to pinpoint what she really wanted the place to look like.

After a few minutes she came to the conclusion that part of the problem was that there were too many things, the room was cluttered. And she didn't like the sofa which was squashy and shapeless, the coffee table and the little side tables were different heights and made of different coloured woods; a random collection of things that said nothing about the person who lived there. And she knew how this had happened: Greg had some furniture when they met, and she had taken a few pieces of furniture from the house at Verbena Road, and the result was boring. She stared at the bowl that her parents' friends the Gordons had given them for a wedding present and wondered why it was sitting there on the table, when she actually disliked it. Perverse was the only word for it.

She turned slowly, studying the space and what was there, and decided that the only way to tackle it was to get rid of every single thing that she did not positively love, to be quite ruthless even if the object was a gift. And then, once she had cleared the decks, she would be able to reassess what was left and decide what she needed to buy to make it work.

In her mind the idea that the colours and shapes must work together as a whole grew stronger, and she imagined looking through the big opening in the wall from the kitchen to the living area and seeing a balanced composition, something that made her feel pleasure, a little like those painting did.

She shook her head and smiled at herself. This was such an unexpected thing to suddenly come into her head, like a change of personality and she wondered why she had never before realized how important this was, a bit like how she was only now beginning to know what she herself was really like. It must be the shock of what had happened, it made her understand that she was not just as others had made her believe she was, she was a different person inside.

Maybe that was due to how there had always been someone older and wiser to guide her: her parents, Sarah and then Greg, and she had never stopped to consider if she really needed so much advice and why she did not just make her own decisions. I was passed like a parcel, she thought, from one to the next, even if I didn't need to be, I allowed it to happen. It was as if invisible threads anchored me to the perception that others had of me, but all it takes is just a little jerk to break those threads. They didn't mean any harm, but they were over-protective, and I might even have encouraged it.

She started in her bedroom and hours later she realized that at some stage she must have turned the lights on, it was dark outside, and she was starving. She headed to the kitchen for soup and bread and decided to make a list of things while she ate before she forgot all the ideas that had popped into her head while she worked. She laughed at herself; never in her life had she made so many lists as she had in the last few days: things to do, things to research, what to buy, how to defeat Josh. One list after another. She studied the chaos she had created in just one evening, left the list on the bench and continued her ruthless pursuit of a new environment.

It didn't take long before the flat was a jumble of things that she was getting rid of. There were piles of linen and towels from Verbena Road, and clothes she hadn't worn for years sliding into shapeless piles. Ornaments, crockery and excess cooking utensils in a jumble on the bench tops in the kitchen, and some framed posters and prints leaned against the hall table. She would need boxes, extra-large rubbish sacks to take things to the second-hand shop and to the clothing bins in the liquor store parking lot. It would take most of Sunday to get it sorted out, before and after the airport trip.

At quarter to ten it felt like time for a change, and she went to check her emails and maybe play a game or two of computer solitaire before going to bed. There was a reply from Brett with some family news and a couple of links to clips on You Tube, but they could wait until tomorrow. A spam email offered her a mysterious chance of immense riches if she registered on a website, and then, there it was - a message from someone, whose name she didn't recognize:

"My neighbour is an elderly man, and he has no computer. He wants to reply to your advertisement in the NZ Herald. He has asked me to send you the following message: My name is Carl Morgan. I think I can help you. My phone number is 09-320 1826. Via Thomas Livingston."

Mia had a funny feeling in the pit of her stomach. This sounded different, calmer and more normal. What harm could there be in calling him? She glanced at the time and decided to do it right away. After half a dozen rings, just when she had decided that there was nobody home, he replied. "Carl speaking."

"Hi Carl – I'm the person, who put that ad in the paper. I hope I'm not calling too late, but I just got the message from Thomas."

"No, it's not late for me - I'm an old night owl. I must say I'm impressed with that computer mail, very fast. I'm not used to these things. And I didn't expect you to be a woman."

"I would really like to talk to you," said Mia, ignoring the problem of being, surprisingly, a woman. "Can you tell me briefly what happened to you – just so I know we're talking about the same thing?"

"Well, I had a very strange experience a long time ago. It felt as if I was being forced though a narrow pipe of some kind. I remember it got very hot, and it was pitch dark. I thought I had died, but it took quite a long time. When it started happening, I was just walking down the road on my way to work and suddenly everything went black. I thought it was an earthquake, and that I had been swallowed up by a crack in the ground. And then when it stopped, I was in a different age."

He sounded gruff and factual, as if he didn't expect to be believed.

"That's right," said Mia, and her voice was trembling. "That's just how it was for me, only it happened in the middle of the night, just recently. How long ago did it happen to you?"

"I've been here for 20 years now, and I think I'm here for good."

Mia thought for a moment, trying to gather together all the theories and questions she had stored up. "How far back in time did you get shifted?"

"Back? I didn't go back, I went forward. I was twenty-four years old in 1946 and walking to the tram stop at half past six in the morning on my way to work. I was moved forward to 1985 and found that I was a 63-year-old man. And I can tell you, it wasn't funny, it was bloody awful!"

Mia was stunned; for some reason the possibility of moving forward in time hadn't occurred to her. She had assumed that things went backwards. She thought for only a second.

"I would really like to meet you and tell you what happened to me. We might be able to help each other somehow. Would you mind?"

"That's why I asked Thomas about the funny address, and he told me it was this sort of computer mail. Thomas is my neighbour and he's very helpful. Well, he's really my landlord. I said I thought it was someone looking for a person I used to work with a long time ago, and I didn't show him the ad, I just gave him the address thing, just in case he got worried I would get into something tricky."

"I can't tell you how pleased I am that you did that! I would love to sit down and talk as soon as you have time. Where do you live, Carl?"

"I live in Eden Terrace, in a flat at the back of a house, granny-flat I think they call it now. It's not very big, but I'm comfortable here. Thomas is the man who owns the place; he lives in the big house at the front."

Mia wrote down the address and thought that she knew where that was, in a funny little pocket of small industries down the slope beside the top of Mt Eden Road, light industry with a few houses still left. She had gone there once with Greg to see someone at a panel-beating place.

Quickly she considered the mess in the apartment, when she would have to set out for the North Shore to pick up Sarah and James, and how she could time it to work.

"Would it be all right if I come and see you mid-morning, perhaps about ten? I'll bring some biscuits and we can have a chat."

She put the phone down feeling stunned. It was nearly surreal to find that there really was someone else it had happened to. She jotted down a few of her thoughts, things she wanted to bring up with Carl and took the pad with her to the bedroom. As she sat in bed reading, something else would occur to her and she jotted it down to make sure she would remember all she wanted to ask Carl. She read until her eyes shut, blinked them open for just long enough to turn the light out and went to sleep.

17

Sunday morning was a blur of activity from dawn. Mia went up and down in the lift with bags of cast-offs and then she was off to the charity clothing bins at the liquor store, a quick visit to the supermarket to beg some cartons and to buy biscuits and a fat roll of large plastic rubbish bags. Back at the flat she filled boxes with crockery, ornaments, and anything else a charity or second-hand shop might want. Clothes and linen went into large black rubbish bags, and soon boxes lined the passage, and piled-up bags made an untidy mountain in the corner by the front door. She stood back to consider and realized that it would take several carloads to get rid of this, and then she would need a trailer to shift the rejected furniture. A problem to ponder, but she would ask Sarah and James if the Salvation Army shop in Birkdale was still open or if they had any suggestion.

A quick wash and change and then Mia picked up the pad and the biscuits and ran down the stairs to the parking lot behind her block of flats. Ponsonby Road was busy as usual, the cafes tables on the pavements were full of locals, talking and reading the paper, their dogs tied to their chairs. It's like a village in a city, she thought, and I bet half these people know each other at least by sight, and all their dogs know both them and each other by smell.

A few minutes later she found the turning she wanted, Nikau Street - short and steep with the back of the TV3 building on the right, then around a couple of corners and she was there.

86

The main house was a large old-fashioned villa with a deep veranda across the front and down one side, and a tall picket fence lined with neglected-looking roses. There were two letterboxes on the gatepost, one with the number Carl had given her, so she parked on the street and walked down the drive past the side of the big house. The garden went a long way back and Carl's flat was a small cottage at the far end. As she approached a short, stout old man with a shock of white hair came to the open door.

"You must be Mia. Come on in, I've got the kettle on." He shook her hand and ushered her in. The front door opened straight into a living room with an open kitchen at one end, 1940's oak furniture, some nice rugs and a couple of landscapes in heavy frames. It looked comfortable and homely, and through a door to another room, she saw a cat sleeping on a bed.

"Coffee or tea?" Carl busied himself with the kettle and cups, while Mia put her bag and keys on the arm of an armchair and came to stand next to the kitchen bench.

"Coffee thanks – milk and one sugar. I brought some chocolate biscuits."

She opened the packet of Tim Tams and Carl handed her a plate to put them on, which made her smile. It was obvious which armchair was his, the table beside it was laden with books, his reading glasses, a metal ashtray full of bits and pieces and a small radio. Over one arm of the chair hung a folded tartan rug, ready for a chilly evening. The domestic permanence of the room and the old-fashioned style made Mia feel comfortable, as if she had been here many times before. She sat down in the second armchair and realized that now they both faced the blank screen of the TV, so she got up and moved her chair a bit, so she and Carl could look at each other.

"That's better," said Carl approvingly. "The chair was that way because the last person who visited was Thomas – we watched the rugby together the other night. He's my only visitor these days, apart from you now."

He stirred his coffee and looked searchingly at her. "Now then, young lady - you start your story, and I can ask you questions as you go, and then I can tell you how my life has been, and you can ask me things. If that sounds like a good idea to you?"

. . .

An hour later they were back in the kitchen end of the room, making another cup of coffee, and Mia was surprised at how open she had been. She had told Carl absolutely everything, including her plans to change several aspects of her life this time around. Carl had asked many questions and shown a keen grasp of the possibilities she had to make changes. There was no doubt whatsoever that Carl and she had both been wrenched from their lives to another 'strand of time' as Carl called it. He had laughed at her expressions That Time and This Time when she used them.

"That's a good one. This Time and That Time - I like that. I haven't bothered to find words for it, but it's good to have a proper phrase when you talk to someone."

"Carl, it's so strange to sit here with you and talk about it - as if it's a normal thing. I haven't been able to tell anyone in case they would think I'm mad or something. I know it's real and that I'm not mad, but I can't figure out how to put it to someone else, so they'll believe me."

Carl nodded. "I know what you men. I have the same problem, and apart from the very first year, I haven't told anyone but Thomas, and that was only after knowing him for a couple of years. He bought this place when I'd already been in residence for about twelve years, and he let me stay. That was four years ago."

"Did he believe you? Or was he too polite to say?"

"Oh well, who knows? He says he believes me. I don't know that he does, but it was the first time I had told anyone since things went really wrong in my first year in this time strand, and I might not have made a very good job of explaining it to him."

Mia pricked up her ears. "How did things go wrong back then?"

"Oh well, I haven't told you my whole story yet, have I? You see, you've gone backwards in time, so you know exactly what's happening, you know who everyone is and how things work. I went forward by about thirty-nine years I think it was, and it was like landing on another planet."

"You poor man," said Mia. "I never thought! I suppose you found you had friends and family, and you didn't even know who they were."

"Yes, I had friends and a job that I didn't know how to do, and I'd been married and was widowed. It was probably lucky that my wife had died - think of the complications otherwise. I didn't know who my in-laws were or what my wife had been like, or if we had children – nothing at all! Turned out I had a car that I couldn't drive, though I had a legal licence. I didn't know how to get from A to B, had never seen a TV – I was completely lost."

He made a wry face at the memory. "The only good thing was that I woke up in what was my house then, which was a bit of luck, because if I had materialized back on the street, where I was when it happened, it would have been much worse. How would I have known where I lived? As it was, I didn't know where I worked or where the shops were or anything. And the money had changed, too – there were no more shillings and pounds, so it was like being in a foreign country."

Mia was shocked. "God, it sounds like living in a nightmare. I never thought of how difficult that would be. How did you cope?"

Carl cleared his throat and said: "I ended up in the loony bin for nearly two years. They decided that I must have had some sort of catastrophic breakdown and somehow lost my memory. You see, when I found out what year it was, and that I'd lost near on forty years of my life, probably forever, I really thought I would go mad. In fact, I didn't know if had perhaps lost my mind and my memory. My mind thought I was a young single man just starting out on the main part of life, and then suddenly I was near retirement in a body ready to slow down and take it easy."

Mia was horrified "And I suppose nobody believed you?"

"No, of course they didn't – not that I blame them. I stayed at the mental unit and let them treat me and then I resumed my life with some support. By selling the house – that's the house my wife and I had lived in for thirty-odd years, I made quite a lot of money which is invested. I sold the car too and just kept enough furniture for a couple of rooms as you can see. Now I rent this and live on the pension and the interest from that money. I do very well, but I have no friends."

"What about your family or your wife's family?"

"Good lord, no, my wife's family thought I was mad! They didn't want anything to do with me, when I came out. Turned out I didn't have any family of my own by that stage, apart from a couple of nieces and nephews, and they were the same. Couldn't be bothered with a mad old uncle. My wife and I had no children, so there was nobody really. And friends were no use - I didn't even recognize them when they came to visit – which they did at the start. I never went back to work, of course, came out a pensioner."

Mia felt her eyes fill with tears. "Oh, Carl! I can't bear to think of how ghastly it was for you - how you managed to cope is beyond me. Compared to you I'm having an easy time."

"But you know, it's not been bad at all for the last 15 years or so, after I got used to all the things that had changed. And I'm very comfortable here and I have money enough to do what I like. I read a lot and I watch documentaries and films on TV. I grow tomatoes and bits and pieces in summer. Every now and then I write some little things and put them in a drawer - it entertains me and keeps my mind busy. And I've learned to cook too. I'm a pretty good Italian cook these days, you know! And Thomas – he's a good friend now and we get on really well."

Mia's mind was racing ahead, thinking of the questions she wanted to ask and things to discuss; this was more intriguing than having been moved a year backwards in time.

"But wait a minute - that means that though your body is eighty-four or eighty-five, you feel mentally only forty-five or so - or am I getting confused? I hope it's OK that we talk about it?"

Carl reached across to pat her arm. "Of course, it is - I'm glad to have you to talk to. Well, that thing about what age my mind is, that's been a bit of a poser for me. I *feel* that I have only experienced forty-five years, yes, that's right – first the twenty-odd years before it happened and then the time since I came into This Time. But my mind isn't the mind of your average forty-five-year-old, because the old brain inside my head has actually lived through the full eight and a half decades, as has the body – as you can see!"

He paused while Mia thought this over before he continued. "You know the funniest thing is that in That Time, as you call it, I was a heavy smoker, but I'd never drunk anything alcoholic in my life. When I sorted myself out in This Time, I found I had no desire to smoke at all, but when I was released from the loony bin, I discovered I like wine. Which again proves that the body had lived through changes that I can't remember. Interesting thing, this time shift thing."

Suddenly Mia realized that it must be well past lunchtime. "I have to go now, but you must come and visit me, Carl. We can't leave it here – I feel as if you're family now, in a different way from ordinary family."

Carl took her hand in both of his. "You are such a good girl, Mia, and so well balanced. I never thought I'd find anyone else who'd been moved to another strand of time – I think we're very lucky to have found each other. You must come and have dinner here one night and I'll cook you something special."

Mia kissed his cheek. "Thank you, I'd really like to do that."

Driving home Mia thought of all she had learnt, and the many questions it raised. How did different time strands interlock? Were there rules for which actions in one strand affected other strands? Or did they not affect each other; were the strands separate and moving at different paces - somehow split off from the original strand for some peculiar reason, like branches with little twigs growing out from them?

Lunching on the balcony in the warmth of the late winter sun, Mia read her book and tried to keep her mind off the jumble of thoughts churning round in the back of her head; a twenty-minute break and then it was back into action. In the bedroom, she paused - a lot of clothes and minor objects had already been removed, but now she must decide about the furniture. The dressing table must go even though it had been her great-aunt Mary's, it was ugly, and she knew Sarah didn't want it. And the bed, did she like it? She studied it with a frown; she and Greg had bought it when they moved into the first flat, but the heavy bed ends were a nuisance, it was hard to make the bed without bruising your knuckles. Something lighter, more minimal but still queen sized would be better and much easier to make.

The bed joined the dressing table on the list of things to go, and she turned yet another page on the pad and started a list of things to buy, starting with a bed and bedside tables to match, and maybe some new linen.

By the time she finished in the living room and sat down to complete her shopping list, it was clear that more things were going than staying, and the list of replacements was long and detailed. She must decide on a style and colours, visit websites, make notes and go shopping. Great therapy and something that would signal to herself every day, and to anyone who came to visit, that the slightly timid and non-descript Mia was gone, and someone more decisive and clearly defined had taken her place.

She stretched her arms above her head, pushed her shoulders back and considered the implications. She knew she would end up spending a serious amount of money on top what she had already spent on a new wardrobe - and that was a work in progress too. But with the mortgage paid off by Greg's life insurance, her income was a bit more than her needed, and if she didn't use her savings to buy a new car, as she had done in That Time, she could well afford a major change of style. She might go into overdraft, when the credit card fell due, but that would soon be covered by income again and then in November she would get the quarterly interest from her trust.

The rest of the afternoon until she had to leave to pick up Sarah and James, was spent in front of the computer, trawling through interior design sites and furniture retailers, avid for ideas and inspiration. She made a mental note to check the bookstore in the airport terminal and buy all the design magazines she could find.

18

At six that evening Mia drove away from the house in Verbena Road with Sarah and James. The house was locked, and everything was switched off, the fridge was cleaned and the rubbish out, and Sarah had checked and double checked that Mia had her key to the house and remembered the alarm system code.

"Don't fuss, Sarah!" said James from the backseat. "Mia knows the house as well as you do, she used to live here for goodness' sake. Just forget it all and relax - this is the start of our special holiday."

Sarah laughed. "I know, it's just me. Forever trying to make sure nothing ever goes wrong - once cast in the role of Big Sister, forever a Big Sister."

Mia smiled to herself, remembering her thoughts earlier that day. By the time Sarah and James got back she might have moved even further away from the little sister who needed help and protection.

As they cruised along the motorway towards the airport Mia told them of her plans to get new furniture and how much she was getting rid of, and their positive response amused her. If she had told them a month ago that she was changing practically everything they would have worried about her and offered to help – already their relationship was changing.

"What fun," said Sarah, happy on many accounts and relaxed now that they were truly on the way. "It's like an adventure, isn't it? I'm so pleased for you. You seem to have turned the page somehow and started a new chapter."

93

Mia smiled and said casually, "I don't know how to explain it. Somehow I seem to have processed a whole lot of grief and sadness very fast in the last little while."

This was literally true, of course – her words fitted based on Sarah and James's reality and they were also true for herself, who had had a whole extra year to adjust; this convenient double meaning that fitted two truths always made her smile.

"I think having it out with Barb was important and it closed a whole chapter that you didn't know about," she said with her now usual disregard for the truth. "It had been on my mind for such a long time and being able to face her like that made the most enormous difference."

And then as an afterthought she added, "I am sorry I caused a bit of an upheaval at your party, though! It got a bit more dramatic than I had planned."

James laughed. "It was awesome, Mia - I loved every moment. I never liked Barb that much to tell you the truth, though she was your friend - a bit too fond of very flirting with all and sundry, even plain old James."

Sarah turned in the front seat to stare at him. "You never told me that! When was this? Lucky, I didn't know, or she would never have got inside our door again."

"Ages ago, poppet, and not worth mentioning. I made it clear I wasn't interested, and I must have done it properly, because she never tried again. But I must say I kept a bit of an eye on her just in case she set out to make trouble for anyone else we know."

From the way James's voice changed on those last words Mia understood that he had only too late realized what he had said, and now he probably hoped that Mia wouldn't ask any uncomfortable questions.

Sarah had noticed and tried to avert attention and save him. "I suppose you must have scared her off then, must have been your irresistible charm that got her tempted."

"Well, I don't want to contradict you about James's irresistible charm," said Mia lightly. "But the fact is that she tempted Greg too and was successful – surely that's the proof of the pudding?"

"You know what, Mia?" said James, suddenly changing the subject. "I know what you should do about all that stuff you want to get rid of. Instead of trying to find a second-hand shop to take it to, you could look in the Yellow Pages and find an auction place. When my grandmother died my parents got an auction firm to come and give them a price for the whole lot, and they just took it all away. Probably gave half of it to charity or took it to the dump, but they literally emptied the house. Perfect solution for you and no hassle at all. You might not get the top price, but it would surely beat making lots of trips and hiring a van or a trailer. You don't even have a tow bar on the car, do you?"

"Perfect!" said Mia. "That's one problem solved then - I'll call someone tomorrow. Much easier than any other way."

Three hours later Mia was back at her desk making a note of the phone numbers to three auction firms to call the next day. With the five design magazines she had bought at the airport spread out on the dining table, she turned pages backwards and forwards, comparing minimalistic and uncluttered interiors, and slowly a mental image of what she would do emerged. She would only keep a couple of antiques and the faded old Persian rug from her parents' home, the desk in the study and her favourite bucket-shaped armchair. The rest could go, and from then on, her freedom of choice was endless; she could be as radical as she liked. She went to bed with her head full of happy plans.

19

Mia cursed campervans in the Monday morning rush hour and red lights conspiring to delay her progress. It was a long time since she had driven the car in the weekday rush hour, and she had forgotten how easy it was to get stressed and irritated. She heaved a sigh of relief when she finally arrived at the garage, and after a short consultation about the choice of new tyres, she set out on foot for the short walk to work.

She started her day by calling the auction firms to find a helpful company that could come as soon as possible and remove what she had decided to discard, and her third call produced results.

"If you can't be home for us to do a pickup during the day I can come in the evening. We do it all the time now that everyone's always at work, eh? Give me the address and I'll come tonight, but not till about eight. I've got another job to do at six and yours could fit on the back of that, if your stuff isn't too big and bulky?"

"It's not that much, enough to fit on a big domestic trailer maybe? Perhaps a bit more."

"Good-oh. I'll be there at eight or maybe a bit earlier, depends on the job before. I'll bring the paperwork."

She gave him the address and told him where to park, and he was brief and businesslike. "OK, see you tonight then."

The rest of the day passed in a blur of activity. Her energy seemed nearly inexhaustible these days, and Alan made a face of mock amazement when she returned to his room for their third ad-hoc meeting that day.

"You are turbo-charged today, Mia – I can hardly keep up."

Half an hour later they agreed that this was the final version of the report for the presentation she had shown him; it all stacked up, there was just enough detail and they agreed they would be surprised if the client found it anything but completely convincing.

"Well, that's good," said Mia, making an opportunistic grab for a favour. "Because I'd like to have Thursday off. I need to get some things done – but if I'm done early, I'll come in for the rest of the afternoon, if that's OK?"

"Fine with me – you've done so many extra hours lately that we'll just write it off as a treat to compensate – take the whole day."

Mia left a few minutes before five and declined Alice's invitation to stop for a chat as she walked through the foyer.

"Sorry Alice, I'm on a mission tonight. Let's take a coffee break together tomorrow - come and get me on your way upstairs. I must run now."

Outside it was still light and quite warm. Full spring was only a flutter away; you could feel it coming like a tinge of increased colour gently seeping into the cityscape.

Picking up the car from the garage and stopping at the supermarket took longer than she had expected, but she made it home by quarter to seven and was putting away her shopping and eating a banana, when the man from the auction firm buzzed her from the entrance.

"So, what have you got here then?" He parked his large flat-deck trolley in the hall and looked around at the sliding tower of bags and boxes. He was a massive man, nearly as wide as he was tall and dressed in shorts and work-boots, and he had the biggest calf muscles Mia had ever seen.

"Let's write it down and we can decide as we go what's going to be sold in the shop as we go along. I'll write you a cheque for the shop stuff before I leave, and then I'll list what's going in the auction."

"Do you have a second-hand shop as well?"

"A very good second-hand shop, missy – we like to call it an antique shop, it's very popular, not as messy as those places usually are, so it looks upmarket."

He laughed. "We know how to do it. We usually advise people to put the less valuable - I won't say rubbishy - stuff in the shop. It turns over fast there and doesn't clutter up the auctions. And then we keep all the good bits for the next auction. We have an auction every four weeks – very popular they are too. Here's the first form."

This was clearly a man, who wanted to get home and have his dinner. Mia filled in her personal details, signed a contract and was handed a pad with forms in triplicate. Listing things was a slower process and her new friend was very honest.

"Oh no, not that one!" he said decisively when she suggested putting a box of mixed ornaments and small kitchen gadgets on the list for the shop. "That stuff might not be valuable, no. But in an auction people love a box of mixed bits and bobs. They imagine they're going to find something really special in amongst it. It's really competitive at times and people get as silly as chooks outbidding each other for stuff that they don't even know what it is. And sometimes we get it back, the whole box, for another auction later on. We sort through the boxes first, to see if anything is worth separating out to auction on its own."

He laughed again and his large belly wobbled alarmingly. Mia obediently put the box aside to go on the auction list instead, and they set to work. In the end it took five trips in the lift and then the job was done, and somehow, they had managed to dismantle the bed and get everything down to the truck.

Now the only thing left in the bedroom was her great-grandmother's Scotch oak chest, dark with age and with a satin sheen from generations of hands rubbing it with beeswax polish. She looked around and tried to imagine a new bed and bedside tables, but all she saw was an empty room with dents in the carpet. It made her smile to think that based on her new ideology that she would not give houseroom to anything that she did not positively like, she had even got rid of some wedding presents.

There were another two crazy email replies to her advertisement, and one from Thomas Livingston, passing on an invitation from Carl to come for dinner on Sunday. Mia replied saying she would be delighted to and that she would bring something for dessert.

20

When the entry phone buzzed on Tuesday evening, the salad and the four-cheese sauce were prepared, the smoked chicken breasts neatly cut into slivers and Mia was setting the table, with only the pasta to boil. Lorraine came to a halt in the doorway to the living area, looking across the room to the large windows.

"Is that a million-dollar view or what? I bet you never get sick of it!" She held out a bottle in a shiny gift bag and shrugged her jacket off. 'The wine is possibly not up to the standard of the view."

Mia laughed. "Well, let's not exaggerate – maybe a quarter of a million-dollar view, but I love it - and no, I never get tired of it." She noticed the way Lorraine glanced around the nearly empty room and grinned at the way she tried to not look curious. "I had a man from an auction firm here last night, and he took masses of stuff - not just furniture but all sorts of things. I went through every cupboard and drawer and made ruthless decisions. I've only really kept things I positively like and want – come and see!"

She led the way around the rooms, enjoying having someone to tell her plans. "See, an empty bedroom, apart from the chest of drawers, because I love it and it was my great-grandmother's. Study still intact, reasonably furnished spare bedroom, at least I left the bed here so I have somewhere to sleep. Living area, as you saw: one armchair and two large cushions, the TV on the floor, dining table and chairs. Most ornaments gone. Isn't it lovely?"

Lorraine laughed that wonderful laugh again. "God, I think it's amazing – the energy! Did you win Lotto?"

"No, no – nothing too exciting, but Greg was insured, so I'm mortgage free. I'm using my savings for this instead of buying a new car, which I had been planning to do - much better for my morale - to love where I live."

"You are so lucky! My brother and I flat together, which means that we cope really well, and we only have one vehicle between us. Paul's a policeman, so he's quite well paid, but I'm going back to university next year, and I'm saving all I can. Mind you, you have lost big chunks of your family and that's not really lucky, is it?"

"I know - it's like some cosmic ledger that ends up balancing one part of your life against another. But I didn't know you're a student. Did you have a break to earn some money?"

"Yeah, I'm doing a law degree. I get the student allowance of course, but that's not enough these days, and I didn't want to graduate with a loan debt, so I'm doing it in instalments. First, I worked for two years after school and saved money and then I did two years study. This is another year of earning and saving hard. Next year will be my final year and then I'll have my degree, and I'll rush out and earn some real money."

"Good for you! I did a marketing degree after I had worked for a few years. I only finished it last year, but we lived on Greg's income and some money I had from my parents. But how come you don't work for a law firm in your in-between years? Wouldn't the pay be better?"

"I actually get very well paid at Designers. I look after the whole business when the owner goes overseas with her husband – which they do for weeks on end. I do the staff roster, pay the wages and the bills and do the bookkeeping. She pays me manager's wages for every hour I work, because it gives her heaps of freedom to do whatever she likes."

"What a great job – and she must trust you completely. Perfect!"

"Yes, it is, but the best thing is that I can put myself on the roster, so it fits my second part-time job with a law firm; just casual hours that change from week to week. It doesn't pay as well as the shop job, but it's a chance to learn and earn."

They ate their dinner and laughed together at the fact that Lorraine had brought a bottle of the same chardonnay that Mia had a half-finished bottle of in the fridge. After the meal they stayed at the table, finished a round of Brie and talked about everything under the sun. Mia talked about Sarah and James, and Lorraine told her about Paul, her own ambitious plans for the future, and about her mother.

"Dad died a few years ago and Mum lives in a little house in Meadowbank and works at the local TAB - she's been there for years and it's not that interesting, but as she says, 'not a job that's going to disappear in a redundancy'. I could have stayed on at home with her, but she has quite a busy social life and I need to be closer to the university. Flatting with Paul is great – he's between girlfriends and I don't have boyfriends." She grinned. "And flatting with your brother is way easier than with anyone else, believe it or not. I'm not going to get into a relationship until my career is going strong - I'm definitely a member of the Me Generation. And anyway, I've never found a guy who was interesting enough to go out with more than a couple of times."

"Well, why not?' Mia smiled back, 'There's no reason why you shouldn't look around as much as you like without making a commitment. I didn't, but perhaps I should have."

"True! And by the way, I waved to you from the bus the other day, but you didn't see me – you were with a curly blond girl."

Mia told the amusing tale of Alice's burning desire to settle down and the Great Man Hunt. "I do hope that I'll catch on early, when she first meets that bad guy, before she gets ...."

Then she stopped, confused and embarrassed; this was the first slip she had made, and she knew it was due to the wine and feeling so relaxed with Lorraine, who was now looking searchingly at her, head tilted to one side.

"Before she meets the bad guy? How do you know she'll meet a bad guy? And who is he?"

Mia made an instant decision; this was it, and if Lorraine thought she was a lunatic and left, then so be it. She got up and picked up their plates.

"Let's make coffee and take the other bottle of wine out of the fridge. I want to tell you something very strange if you have the time to listen."

Lorraine glanced at Mia now and then as she helped clear the table but kept the conversation to questions about where to put things. When they were sitting on the cushions with their wine glasses topped up and mugs of coffee, Mia cleared her throat and started her story with a feeling of apprehension like a hard lump in her chest.

"This is going to sound quite mad, and I understand completely if you don't believe what I'm going to tell you. I'll start at the very beginning, with Greg's accident and go from there. Ask as many questions as you like."

She recounted the whole fourteen months in broad strokes, including the demoralizing effect of the Barb affair, Josh's deceit and what happened on the night of the time shift. She explained the use she had already made of her knowledge of what could or would happen over again, and how she had found Carl.

When she got to the present she stopped, feeling light-headed and empty, and oddly relieved. Lorraine had drunk her coffee and poured herself another glass of wine, but she had listened without asking one single question.

Mia smiled weakly. "You'll make a fantastic lawyer one day - I've never met anyone who can listen like you."

Lorraine looked back steadily. "That's the most amazing thing I've ever heard - like something out of a science fiction novel. And I can't understand *why* I do, but I do believe you."

Mia felt tears pool in her eyes. "Oh my god, I think I'm going to cry. I thought you might just leave politely and hope never to bump into me again. Thank you!"

"Ah, but we can't leave it there. I must know more - tell me again about what happened that night, and the things you did the next day. Was that really the same day that you came into the shop and bought all those clothes? The very night of Sarah's party?"

"Yes, it was, and it seems quite bizarre to me too, now. I can't understand how calm I was after those first few hours of being totally freaked out - it's like it happened to someone else."

"Perhaps that's exactly what made you able to do it." Lorraine was intrigued and thoughtful. "Perhaps because it was so unreal, and it felt like a 'borrowed life' you felt free to be really radical. Whatever the reason, I'm *very* impressed."

Lorraine had many questions and Mia answered and explained as well as she could, until in the end there was nothing more to tell. It was half past eleven now and Lorraine yawned.

. . .

"I would really like to sit here all night, talking about it, but tomorrow's a working day. One thing though - I do think you need to do something quite clever and formal to prove beyond a doubt that this is what we say it is. Not that the whole world needs to know, but it would be great insurance to have some proof. And I think I know how we can do it."

Mia was touched and grateful by the way Lorraine said 'we'. Apart from Carl, who already knew that the phenomenon was real, she had not told anyone, and she had not expected to be believed without concrete proof.

"I've thought of how I might do it," said Mia, twirling her glass between her fingers and looking absently into the middle distance. "I've started a list of things I can use as proof when I tell Sarah and James. Some are personal and relate to them. But perhaps I should tell someone else about an event that might happen again, something so big and remote that nobody could have foreseen it - and then if it *did* happen again, that person would be my proof."

"Not enough!" said Lorraine decisively. "I have an idea of what we could do, which would be more formal and properly documented, if you like. You'll have to put up with the future lawyer in me coming out. Say that you think of a couple of world events of the type that people can't just say, 'Oh that happens at regular intervals, anyone could have thought of one of those.' No, it would have to be very specific, time, place, outcome – definitive facts of the kind you couldn't predict or guess, unexpected things that took the world by surprise. When you've written down as much detail about each event as you can possibly remember, we take what you've written to a Justice of the Peace or a Notary Public and ask them to seal the paper in some tamper-proof way - perhaps we bring sealing wax or do something to make it absolutely impossible for fraud to take place. We leave the envelope there and after the events we invite certain people to be present - and open it."

Mia looked at Lorraine, who was clearly enjoying herself, and nodded.

"OK, let's do that, but let's have a couple of complete outsiders witness the envelope sealed and deposited. Perhaps we could ask a lawyer or someone to come with us to a police station, and we could seal the envelope there in front of them and leave it with them to be kept as evidence."

"We might be able to take it to Paul's station and ask his boss to be a witness - or bring a solicitor, and then leave the envelope with one of them."

Mia tried to recall things that had happened in the last year that she could use; preferably something not too close to the time just before she slipped back to 2006, or they would have to wait nearly a year for the proof. A war or a disaster, but what? And suddenly like a flash it struck her and with eyes sparkling with excitement, she exclaimed, "I know - that cathedral fire in St Petersburg. Perfect!"

She sat up straighter on her large cushion and smiled triumphantly. "It's brilliant, because it's one thing where I know the exact date. When Sarah and James were away, I knew that they would be in St Petersburg on the twenty-fifth of August, because it's Sarah's birthday and she particularly wanted to celebrate the day there. She's had a thing about Russian history and art all her life. The cathedral's main dome collapsed - it made the news because of the artworks. I think the dome was wooden, though that might not be right. I saw it on the BBC website and panicked of course, but later that day they reported that no tourists were injured - I don't think anybody was killed."

"Great timing - we can use that and whatever else you think of, and get it documented. But heavens - let's see, the twenty-fifth is Friday this week. We must get on to this in the next couple of days. Awesome luck!"

"Trinity, that's the name - Trinity Cathedral. And I've just this second thought how I could use that fire to convince Sara and James too. I'll find out the phone number of their St Petersburg hotel and leave a message for them not to visit Trinity Cathedral on Friday. And then I'll need at least one other event, just in case the fire doesn't happen this time around."

And then she took that thought a bit further and shook her head. "No, I can't leave them that sort of message – imagine the hotel receptionist calling the Russian intelligence agency and saying I'm in league with arsonists! I only thought of a message to avoid having to explain the whole thing over the phone."

"Easy," said Lorraine. "You call them first thing in the morning on that day – first thing at their end I mean – and say don't go to that cathedral, it's going to burn. Refuse to say how you know, just say 'don't do it' and then explain afterwards."

"OK," said Mia. "I know they record phone conversations there, a lot – you know, just keeping tabs on people, but surely they can't record *every* single tourist's calls?"

Lorraine smiled. "I'm sure they don't! And I'll ask my friend Miles to come along - he's at that law firm I told you about, so he would be the respectable witness. And I can bring Paul's video camera and film the paper being sealed in the envelope. Wouldn't that add a bit of wonderful credibility?"

"Very clever – would you like to be my lawyer when you have qualified? I'll make sure I write down every single detail I can remember and have the paper ready."

21

Early the next morning, Mia woke up with her mind already in gear and racing. She felt energetic and excited and got up even though it was only quarter to six.

The cathedral fire was one thing, but what else could she come up with? It was no good thinking of something that happened months later, she wanted things that would prove her story sooner rather than later. It was important to have at least two events documented, and she wanted them to be close together. If the first one didn't happen there was still a chance with the second, and she didn't want to wait for months to find out.

She sat in her solitary armchair with a cup of tea and enjoyed the sunrise and tried to remember what had happened just after Sarah and James got back, and what they had discussed. Had she told them something that they hadn't heard of - some event in New Zealand? And then it struck her that they had talked a lot about how Steve Irwin had been killed by a stingray and it had happened while they were away. She remembered James saying, that until they arrived in London, he had never realized how truly world-famous Steve Irwin had been; it had been all over the UK the papers and on TV. And even as she thought about it, more details popped up in her mind.

Gripped by a frantic sense of urgency, she wanted to write it up straight away and then she could fine tune it after work, if necessary. She sat at her desk and put her mind to work trying to tease out more detail about the Crocodile Hunter's death. The cathedral fire was fine, she knew the date and the place, even if the minor details were lost, but she wanted as much detail as possible in her description of Irwin's death.

Twenty minutes later she had finished a statement, tidily divided into two parts, with bullet points of everything she could recall. She had managed to dredge up quite a lot about both events and more might surface during the day. Eating a banana and yoghurt for breakfast, she read her printed-out document and wondered what her witnesses would think about it when they read it.

Statement made by Maria Margaret Dawson on 23 August 2006.
I believe that the following two events will take place as described.

St Petersburg – Fire destroys the main dome of The Trinity Cathedral on 25 August 2006

- *Wooden main dome.*
- *Repairs going on, fire started by accident.*
- *Photos on internet of main dome ablaze and people carrying icons and paintings to safety.*
- *All art works rescued as fire progressed.*
- *Nobody killed.*
- *One turret/tower also damaged.*

Steve Irwin killed by stingray while filming TV series.

- *Film crew captured it live on camera, but film will never be shown.*
- *His wife was not there.*
- *Sting pierced his chest and punctured his heart.*
- *In Australian waters, Great Barrier Reef?*
- *Daughter (6 or 7) interviewed - says she will appear as planned at conservation event.*
- *Between 25 August and 18 September 2006*

Signed:
  In the presence of:
  Date:

There was no need to add more, there was more than enough detail to avoid being accused of generalistic predictions. Provided that things happened as they had in That Time, there could be no doubt that she had made genuine predictions. She saved it on a USB stick and put it in her bag. Once signed, the paper could be sealed and left in the safekeeping of someone trustworthy and then the waiting would begin.

On the bus she had another flashback: There had been speculation that Steve Irwin would be given a state funeral. She remembered thinking that the Australians were getting a bit hysterical, but it might be a great detail to include, not the sort of thing you would have expected. At work she found the number to Hotel Astoria in St Petersburg on the internet, made a note of it, and went to the stationery room to get a robust brown envelope, so now all she needed was something to seal it with. Did lawyers still use sealing wax? Lorraine would know and she would ask her right away; the feeling of urgency was still strong in her mind.

"Have you spoken to your lawyer friend yet? OK, when you do could you ask him if they still have sealing wax in lawyers' offices, and could he bring some? Are we making it tonight or tomorrow? No, tonight's fine with me, I'm all ready and I can get some string somewhere. I have the document on a USB stick in my bag, so I can print it here, and I've nicked a good envelope to put it in."

"Did you manage to come up with a second event? It's so frustrating that I can't help you remember."

"Oh yes, I forgot to say, I have the perfect thing. I won't tell you now – I'll keep it as a surprise for when you witness the document. I can't wait - if these things happen, or even one, it will prove my story is true."

She added that extra detail to the document, saved the change back to the USB and printed it; now she was ready.

. . .

Time flew and never had so many boring little jobs got done so fast. Callum called and asked her to join him and Tex for dinner the next night.

"We're going to that little Chinese place down the road straight after work. We're usually finished and on our way home by nine thirty."

Having said yes, she put the phone down and thought how busy her life was getting, a far cry from the lonely and isolated existence she had withdrawn into in That Time.

Alice and Mia went up for an afternoon cup of coffee together, a bit later than usual and the staff canteen was nearly empty. "Mia," said Alice and looked seriously at her over the rim of her mug. "I've been thinking about the merger. Do you think we can do something?"

Mia shook her head. "I don't think anything could stop it now. It's like a natural disaster – we can only watch and hope."

"I know - I'm not talking about the actual merger, but all the damage it could cause for staff. I know they say they can't predict if there will be redundancies, but I'm sure they know more or less exactly how many salaries they want to slash to make it all work financially."

Mia nodded; she knew that Alice was right. "But what could we do? It might be that we get laid off ourselves."

"Yes, but I think we could both cope. We probably wouldn't find it as hard to get new jobs as some of those really specialized people in Creative. And you and I don't have families to support. I was thinking of some sort of support group, like finding out where to go for help and advice when the time comes and being prepared to help each other."

Back at her desk Mia felt guilty about how little she had known about Alice in That Time, and how she had never got to know her, but grateful now that she had another friend in the workplace.

22

Lorraine called late in the day to say that everything was set up for straight after work.

"My solicitor friend Miles and my brother Paul will meet us at the Gillies Avenue police station at half past five. Paul said he thought it would be better not to go to his station, and Miles knows one of the higher-ups at Gillies Avenue from court work, so he's organized for us to go there. Miles didn't want to involve anyone at his firm for some reason – being a bit cagey, I think. And Paul was concerned that there could be talk of collusion, if staff at his station were involved."

"That's fine," said Mia after thinking it through. "So long as we get it witnessed by respectable people and then kept somewhere safe. It'll be nice to meet Paul, too."

"Wild horses couldn't keep him away." Lorraine laughed. "He's as cute as he is clever, but he is also the world's worst nosey-parker. He says he's coming to be cameraman because he doesn't trust me to do it right, but he's really just coming to try to find out what it's all about. I haven't told him anything about your story, just that we want witnesses and safekeeping for some notes you have made."

At half past five Mia joined Paul and Lorraine, who were waiting outside the police station. Mia could quite see why Lorraine had said he was cute; he was adorable, hugely tall and broad with a small boy's round face and innocent smile. Paul in turn studied

Mia with a keen and speculative glance – he was clearly curious, but he asked no questions.

Miles arrived and proved the absolute opposite of Paul, short and tidy in a dark suit, with an already receding hairline at thirty-something. His bright eyes took everything in, and he too studied Mia carefully. I bet he never misses anything, thought Mia, he looks as sharp as the proverbial tack.

"Well, how about we do whatever it is we came to do?" Paul was suddenly businesslike. "Not that I have the least idea what this is about. Lorraine's refused to tell me anything, but I'm willing to be her slave as usual."

"Oh, do shut up, Paul. It's not my secret to tell and you invited yourself, as you well know!"

The officer behind the counter escorted them to an interview room, sparsely furnished with a table and some chairs. They stood in silence, not looking at each other and waited until a tall dark man in his early forties came into the room. His eyes ran over them one by one, and Mia thought, that's the police look.

Miles stepped forward. "This is Superintendent John MacFarlane. John, this is Mia, her friend Lorraine and Paul, who is Lorraine's brother and a police constable. I'm going to let Mia explain what she wants to do – as I told you, I still don't know what this is about."

John MacFarlane looked calmly at her and waited for her to speak, and suddenly she felt flustered, even though she had carefully rehearsed how she would put it.

Without speaking she put her bag on the table, took out the A4 sheet, the envelope and the string, and turned to face John, who was standing across the table from her.

"I have a sheet of paper with certain, ah ... guesses or predictions on it. These refer to things that might happen in the near future. I want everyone in this room to read the paper, sign their name and write the date in their own handwriting, next to their name and to say their full name out loud so it's recorded on the video. Before anyone reads the document, I would like everyone here to give me their word that *nothing* relating to this will be revealed to anyone without my permission."

She looked around and saw that Paul was filming, capturing

her speech. The others nodded their agreement, and Mia cleared her throat and continued.

"When everyone has signed the paper, I want Paul to take a close-up shot of it. Then we will fold it in full view of the camera and seal it in this envelope, put the string round the envelope and..."

She suddenly realized that Lorraine had not told her if Miles had been able to bring sealing wax, but Miles saw her hesitation and held up a square stick of red sealing wax. "Here it is - sealing wax and I brought our firm's seal to impress in it."

Mia smiled at him. "Thank you! Here is the document."

She turned the sheet of paper around to face John. Lorraine and Miles came closer to the table to read it, and Paul continued to film. John MacFarlane looked at Mia after signing his name and considered her carefully, expressionless and neutral, and unblinking she met his gaze and said nothing.

The other two signed one by one and Paul approached the table, focused on the paper and then stepped back while keeping it in view. Lorraine took the camera from him so he could sign, and Mia folded the paper, put it into the thick brown envelope and tied the string around it as one would around a parcel. She tried to be careful to keep her hands from obstructing the camera's view of the envelope.

Miles said, "Put the envelope on the table please."

He got out a cigarette lighter, heated the end of the stick of sealing wax and dropped globules of red wax on the string in four places on the front, pressing the stamp into each spot of hot wax to make it adhere to the envelope. Then he turned the envelope over and did the same on the back and Mia picked it up and handed it to John MacFarland.

"Will you please keep this safe here until after the first of the predicted events? If that event happens, I would like to ask that you all help me to try to prevent the second event."

John took the envelope. "Would you all like to follow me - and Paul, continue to film this, please."

He led the way upstairs to a room that was obviously his own office. He hesitated for a moment, walked around the desk and opened the drawers, one after the other until he found what he was looking for.

"I'll give you a receipt, Mia. As you can see the pages are dupli-cates and numbered, so it's an official receipt, but I must admit that we don't normally do this sort of thing. The only reason I agreed was out of curiosity."

He smiled and put the envelope in the bottom drawer of a filing cabinet and locked it. "I'm the only person who has a key to this cabinet, so the envelope is perfectly safe here."

Paul lowered the camera. Mia felt exhausted, as if she had run a marathon or held her breath for minutes on end, and Lorraine said excitedly, "My God, that's the most amazing thing ever – you could save Steve Irwin's life!"

John looked searchingly at Mia again. "Are you a clairvoyant? Or a medium of some kind?"

"Oh God, no, not at all," said Mia truthfully. "I don't believe in that stuff."

He looked increasingly puzzled. "But you think you can foretell the future?"

Mia had to reveal a little more than she had planned to, but she had to answer his question. "Well yes, I think I know that some things will happen. I might not be right about both those things, because I'm not sure how this works yet. I'll tell you more if this works out, even if only one or the other thing happens. The whole point of this exercise is to validate that I can predict *some* things that will happen in the future."

Miles and Paul looked intrigued and glanced at each other, but they made no comment and John broke the meeting up.

"I think we all remember both events, so we'll wait and see. Let's meet here after the cathedral fire – provided it does happen."

Lorraine interrupted. "If the fire happens, we won't know until Saturday. St Petersburg is eight hours behind New Zealand. Mia isn't sure what time of the day the fire happened – I checked the time difference. So why don't we meet here on Saturday afternoon? That will have given the media time to post it on websites, so we can check. Let's say four o'clock, if that suits everyone?"

Mia gazed at her in silent appreciation, impressed with her attention to detail; she herself had not even thought of the time difference.

Once outside there was a distinct sense of anticlimax and nobody knew quite what to say. Miles went off to his car, and Mia, Lorraine and Paul walked slowly along the street without speaking.

Suddenly Mia couldn't wait to be alone, to stop thinking about how this would turn out. "Thank you both for coming along," she said politely. "I'll just catch the bus home and go to bed early, I think. Lorraine and I were up so late last night, and I woke up quite early this morning."

They seemed to understand her mood, Lorraine gave her a hug and Paul patted her shoulder. "We'll drive you home, Mia. It's no trouble."

They were quiet and thoughtful during the trip across town. Mia was torn between wanting her predictions to turn out to be right, so her story could be verified, and feeling apprehensive about Saturday and possibly having to tell three new people her story. How would they react if the fire did happen? It was such a strange tale, and anyone could be excused for not believing it. If she herself had been in the position of the others, she would never believe it without proof either, Lorraine was the exception. When Paul stopped to let her out, she said a brief goodbye and got out of the car without further conversation.

Mia closed her front door and turned the lights on, relieved to be alone at last. A rummage through the pantry produced a tin of pumpkin soup and she sat at the table, surrounded by design magazines and sheets of paper, eating her dinner and trying to make notes about colours and styles of furniture, but concentration was beyond her, and she soon gave up. She jotted down some things to remember: Thursday, morning off, look at furniture, work afternoon? Dinner with Callum & Tex. Saturday, more furniture? 4 pm at police stn, Sunday, dinner at Carl's.

After a long hot bath, she went straight to bed and slept like a log until the clock radio woke her in time for the morning news. She opened her eyes, slightly tense as she was every morning, and quickly took stock. The deep relief she experienced each time she had reassured herself that she had not been moved back to That Time had not diminished with time. It felt luxurious to wake at seven on a weekday morning and not need to get ready for work, and she had plenty of time before the shops opened. She sat over a cup of coffee getting her shopping list sorted and stapled magazine cuttings to it for reference. Before going out she rang St Petersburg to leave the message for Sarah and James and got through to Hotel

Astoria straight away. The receptionist spoke nearly perfect English and was politely professional.

"If you can wait one moment, I will try the line to their room."

Mia was quick to stop her calling the room; the last thing she wanted at this stage was a long conversation with Sarah.

"No, please don't put me through, just take a message if you don't mind and tell them I will call them before they go out tomorrow morning and to wait for my call. My name is Mia. I know it's the middle of the night at your end and I don't want to wake them up, just give them the message first thing in the morning, please."

"We will deliver a note to call you with their breakfast - I see they have ordered breakfast for seven am."

23

Before leaving the next morning, she walked slowly through the rooms with a second mug of coffee in her hand, contemplating the look and feel of the nearly empty rooms and vaguely thinking of all the ideas her design research had given her, and it set a mood that remained fresh in her mind when she set out on her shopping expedition.

She felt happy and buoyant again, even slightly philosophical about her attempt to prove her story. So, what if those particular things didn't happen? All that would prove, was that things change - it didn't mean that she was mad or lying. She would just have to start over and find some event that really did happen again in This Time.

The bus was not nearly as full as it usually was at the time she normally went to work, and she got a seat with nobody beside her. She got the list out of her bag and mentally added up approximate values and decided it might come to ten thousand dollars, or very nearly. She would pay by with money from her car savings account and just about clean it out, but she didn't mind. This was far more important than a new car, it was to do with self-esteem and a dose of aesthetic pleasure every single day.

The sky was blue, and the pavements were filling up with shoppers; she was fizzing with pleasurable anticipation. To take time off work and go out to selfishly spend thousands was a heady adventure.

Inside the Freedom shop she was swamped by the urge to try to find everything at once, but common sense prevailed. She stood in the middle of the store checking her cuttings and getting her bearings, working out where on the floor things were displayed. A young man approached her, but she declined his offer of help and explained that she wanted to wander around on her own first.

The key pieces were the bed and the sofa, and half an hour later she had looked at many sofas and sat on a few. She did the round again before dismissing all but two styles, both exactly right and available in neutral colours that would fit her look. One was available as a two-seater, and that clinched it. The two-seater and a matching chair would be perfect, not too large for the room.

Selecting the bed was more difficult, because what if it wasn't comfortable after all when you got it home? How do you properly test a mattress in a shop? A young assistant came to the rescue.

"Pick a mattress that feels a bit firmer than you think you want," she said. "Most people regret picking something too soft - once they get the bed home and spend a few nights on it they wish they had picked a harder one. And if it's really too firm when you sleep on it, then you get a soft topper pad."

"Thank you," said Mia. "Good idea – I think I'd better test a few to get a feel for it." She lay down on the first of the beds she had been contemplating.

"Don't lie on your back, unless that's your normal sleeping position," said the assistant, who was clearly an expert. "Curl up on your side or however you normally sleep."

Mia turned on her side and knew within seconds that the mattress was too soft, though it had felt quite firm when she lay on her back. Ten minutes later she made her choice.

"I'll have this one, please, and also two of the matching glass-topped bedside tables. And then I want the TV cupboard unit, the one in aluminium and opaque glass over there, and the two-seater sofa called Imara in the colour called Pale Chocolate and..."

"Stop, stop!" said the girl, holding up both hands and laughing. "Not so fast - let me get an order pad and we can start making out a proper list."

She returned with a pad and grinned. "Now, if you don't mind, would you please take me to each item and show me, so we are quite sure I'm getting it right? A bit slow, but much safer."

They did the circuit again; everything was written down and the colours confirmed, and Mia spotted a few minor things to add to the list. Back at the counter the order was entered into the computer system, and the girl handed and Mia an invoice. "That comes to $6180 and then the freight if you want it delivered."

"That doesn't sound right," said Mia, studying the invoice. "It should be a couple of thousand more – look, the price of the sofa is wrong for a start."

"Yes, but what comes up on the invoice is the discounted price - the regular price less 25% up to the end of the month," said the girl cheerfully. "It's our end-of-winter sale - didn't you notice the banners at the entrance?"

"No, I had no idea – what luck!"

Mia arranged for delivery first thing on Saturday morning, paid and left smiling. She was doing very well timewise; it was only two and a half hours since she left home. And having spotted those nice cushions and a couple of lamps was a bonus she had not planned for.

With time on her hands, she sat in a café for an hour enjoying an early lunch and reading the courtesy newspaper, occasionally looking up and letting her thoughts drift. Her goal now was to keep busy until Saturday afternoon and to try to keep her impatience in check. If New Zealand was eight hours ahead of St Petersburg, then she would be able to check if the fire had happened well before four o'clock on Saturday, because she was reasonably sure that the video shots she remembered had been taken in broad daylight. With new furniture coming on Saturday morning, she would have no problem filling in the time until the afternoon. Her mood varied between determination not to worry if the prediction was wrong and feeling sure the fire would happen. It felt a bit ghoulish to rely on the misfortune of others for her own satisfaction, but there was no way she could prevent this from happening anyway.

On an impulse she went into a glamorous-looking 'home shop' and bought some stylish new linen for her new-look bedroom and half a dozen luxurious bath towels. The result was three super-sized and surprisingly heavy carrier bags, and by the time she reached the office her arms felt as long as a gorilla's.

She stopped at the reception desk and dropped her bags on the floor with a dull thump.

"Have you been spending money, Mia?" Alice's eyes twinkled wickedly.

"Damn, I was hoping nobody would notice. But it's not more clothes - I promise. It's just a lot of new linen. And hello to you too!"

Alice grinned. "Well, I hope it was fun! To change the subject though – remember that I told you about my cousin Linda's wedding in a couple of weeks, on the ninth? I just heard last night that the dinner is going to be in a big marquee, not inside, so it could be as cold as sin. I mean, at this time of year you can't bank on warm evenings, can you? And I want to look sexy and gorgeous, you never know when there's going to be some talent around."

She paused, and Mia said, "And?"

"And - my very nicest dress that I'm hoping to wear is slinky and bare-shouldered. Not the sort of thing you can wear a jacket with."

"Get yourself one of those really thin shawls, you know what I mean, one of those silk pashmina things – or maybe they're wool. You could wear it so it kind of slips off one shoulder, that would look sexy and keep you warm at the same time. And think how you could use it as a prop – trail it seductively behind you like 1930's diva."

They smiled at each other, delighted with the prospect of Alice being warm and sexy at the same time.

"Great idea - my mum has one of those, but it's not a colour I like. Oh dear, how sad! I'll have to go shopping."

Mia was laughing at herself now." It's so funny that I am standing here being a fashion guru. I've never handed out dress advice before in my life – a new experience."

"But you are so trendy these days, and you changed your look completely, very cool - everyone says how clever you are."

Mia carried her bags to her office contemplating the strange new world she was living in, and how crazy it was that she was getting a completely opposite reputation after being Miss Mousy for so long.

. . .

The first thing she did was to check the original spreadsheet file on the shared document drive, but nothing had changed; she must wait and be patient. Or it might be that Josh was more honest in This Time. She knew that Josh's betrayal had contributed hugely to the pathetic wretch she had turned into in that other life. It had robbed her of her self-esteem, and she had lost the will to communicate with people and simply drifted through life. Now she was acutely aware of the need to take steps to protect herself, but she must still give him the benefit of doubt.

"Amazing how short the day seems, when your working day starts after lunch," she said cheerfully when Alan came to talk about a changed deadline for a project.

He looked at the large shopping bags in the corner behind her desk. "Looks like you got a lot done in one morning. My wife used to love that shop. I think most of our linen came from there."

"I hadn't been inside the place before, but it's a wonderful shop. I just walked in on an impulse after I finished the big-item shopping. If you think these bags represent a lot of shopping, you would be amazed at what I did in the first two or three hours this morning." She smiled. "Come to think of it, I'm amazed myself."

Alan smiled, delighted with her mood. "My God, Mia, it's as if you've had a personality transplant. I would never have thought that serious shopping was your thing."

"You are right - it didn't use to be, but somehow I needed a change of scene. I sent nearly everything I own to the auctioneers."

She saw the look on Alan's face and added, "Greg's life insurance paid off the mortgage."

"Well, you are both unlucky and lucky then." Alan generously looked pleased for her. "There couldn't be anything worse than losing someone you love, and then having to worry about money as well."

"That's so right. And because I've got over the worst shock now, I decided to get rid of lots of old stuff and start again in a new style – kind of more cohesive, if that makes sense. I'm thinking of it as a kind of therapeutic interior decorating event."

Because he seemed genuinely interested, she told him of that sudden idea, ripping everything apart and ruthlessly sorting and discarding. She described the man with the wobbly belly who came and took everything away, and how she had looked at pictures in glossy magazines and found the style she liked and then continued from there.

Alan was fascinated. "What a fantastic thing to do! You know, I really admire the way you cope with how your life has changed, and not only that – then you generate even more change. Perhaps that's what I should do."

He looked thoughtful for a moment, and then he said decisively. "Yes, that is *definitely* what I should do. I feel as if I'm always expecting Pam to come in the door from some errand, even now after all this time. I feel kind of surprised sometimes that her towel isn't there in the bathroom. I just recently threw out her cosmetics and things – it seemed so cold-hearted that I just couldn't get around to it."

He hesitated. "You know, I would really love to come and see your place, when you've finished the make-over. I might get some ideas about how to revamp my place. I think that's what I need – a complete change. I might be able to move on, if things don't look the same as they used to."

"That's more or less what I felt. I needed to change things, so I could look forward instead of backwards all the time. I'll invite you for a meal one night, after I get it sorted - perhaps a couple of weeks from now. And then you can start planning how to change things for yourself - it's not actually that hard once you figure out where to start."

24

After checking with the admin department that they would be able to identify the call she was about to make and tell her the cost, she closed her door and called St Petersburg. Once again, she spoke to a receptionist with perfect English.

"Can you please put me through to the room of Sarah and James Collins?"

"Yes? Mia!" James's voice had an urgent quality, as if he was bracing himself for bad news. "Is everything all right? Has something happened? Yes, yes Sarah, I *will* let you speak to her, just hang on! Sorry, Mia, your sister is very concerned - I'll hand the phone over to her."

"Mia - what's going on, are you OK?" Mia only now realized that her message had rung alarm bells, and that both Sarah and James were seriously worried.

"Sarah, listen, what I am going to tell you is *very* important." Mia chose her words carefully. "Can you hold the phone so you can both hear me? OK? I know this is going to sound completely bonkers. Just let me tell you one part of it, and then you can ask me questions, but I might not answer all of them. And Happy Birthday - I nearly forgot!"

She started on her carefully scripted tale, taking it step by step and trying to not overwhelm them. "There is a cathedral called The Trinity Cathedral and I don't know if it's on your list of things

123

to visit, but I want you to stay away from it today, or at least not go inside."

"Have you heard something about this church? Is it dangerous to go there, terrorists or something?"

Sarah was full of questions and Mia knew she had to stem the flow and go about her explanations in her own way.

"I'm not going to tell you the full story right now, but I'll tell you enough for you to take it seriously - the rest has to wait."

Trying to speak as if this was a perfectly ordinary and reasonable story, she continued, "I feel fairly sure that there's going to be a catastrophic fire in the Trinity Cathedral today, 25th of August. I don't think anybody will be injured, and a lot of valuable artworks will be saved. I don't know why the fire is going to break out, but I think it is possibly to do with some repairs they are doing. And I can't tell you how I know - and I could be wrong, it might not happen."

"God, Mia! This isn't a bit like you. Did you have some sort of dream? What do you want us to do?"

Keep it calm, thought Mia, I must sound reasonable and not too crazy. "I don't want you to do anything apart from *not* go into that church. I think I have advance knowledge about a couple of things, but I can't tell you any more now, but I will when you get back. I have created a double-check here which involves reliable witnesses. If it turns out that I'm right, you will hear the rest of the story later, but not over the phone - when you get back. I know it sounds mad, but please trust me – this is as strange to me as it is to you."

She finished the call despite Sarah's voluble frustration at not being able to tease anything more out of her, but Mia knew that if she gave any more hints or details, she might not find another point where she could cut the story off.

James had the last word. "We're damned well going to find out where this cathedral is and at least go there to look at it – I promise we won't go inside."

Mia put the phone down, and it rang while she still had her hand on it. Callum had remembered his casual invitation.

"Tex and I usually have the traditional Thursday beer with the team first and then we're going out for a meal. Why don't you come up and join the team at five and we'll leave together when we're ready?"

As Mia came up the stairs, she heard voices talking and laughing and thought that the creative floor was like a different planet from the rest of the building. Somehow the space was a blend of louder voices, more movement and an atmosphere of free spirits and creative anarchy. When she entered, she saw Tex perched on a chair, holding up a large sketch pad with both hands, and a cluster of people standing around looking up at him.

Callum spotted her and beckoned her over. "Come and look at this."

As she approached, she saw that it was a rough felt-tip sketch of a landscape with some trees and a road in the foreground. Then Tex turned the pad upside down and one or two people said, "I still can't see it." Others laughed, and suddenly Mia saw it too. By turning the sketch upside-down it had become a picture of a naked couple standing half concealed behind shrubs, and the road had become a horizon of hills.

"That's so clever," said Mia and Callum nodded.

"I know - he's something else, our Tex. He did that while he and I were chatting in one of our break-out rooms this afternoon. He never sits down without a sketch pad and a pen."

They left the noisy crowd in the workroom just after six and walked to a restaurant only a couple of blocks away where Mia had never been. While they waited for their food, they discussed the new project over a glass of wine. Two or three creative teams were competing for the brief, but before the creative work could start, they would all be involved in brainstorming the basic concept.

"This is not how we usually do things, it's a completely different approach, like an experiment," said Tex.

"And you need someone to provide some financial and practical input while you develop your thinking?"

"God yes, it's a huge and ambitious basic idea, and Grant doesn't want us to get too far down the track without some checks along the way – that's checks with a 'ck' by the way. And it's going to need a huge cheque with a 'q' from the client too."

Mia looked at ginger-haired and lanky Tex and smiled. "That trick sketch you did was clever!"

Tex grinned. "I didn't tell anyone, but I had practiced that one before – just so I can do it fast and get it right without turning the pad up the other way to check it every two seconds. But I'm pleased it worked. I might try to make up another one of the same kind - it was fun."

Callum interrupted, delighted to boast on behalf of Tex.

"He paints too, you know. He's as much an artist as any regular artist, if you know what I mean?"

"There are lots of people, who work in advertising or as sign writers, who paint. Last year I met a fellow from South Africa at an ad agency downtown – he's quite well known, I think."

Mia was immediately interested; this sounded familiar. "It wasn't David Thompson, was it? He's from South Africa and works for an Auckland agency."

Tex looked surprised, so she had to explained how she knew.

"I actually have one of his paintings. I went with my sister to that huge art sale at Eden Park a while ago, and I bought one of his paintings – just fell in love with it the moment I saw it. And then I googled his name to see what I could find out about him, and the only thing that came up was stuff about the firm he works for and a short bio."

"I'd like to see it some time, I've only seen a couple of photos in a magazine."

When Mia finally said she must go home, Callum offered to drive her.

"My car is parked behind the office, so we'll just walk back and get it. Tex, did you come in by car today or do you want a ride?"

But Tex wasn't going home; he had a mysterious errand elsewhere.

25

As the two of them walked back towards the office, Callum vented his frustration with Tex. 'I bet he's off to meet Mandy again and he'll tell Debbie that our dinner went on longer than it did. That affair is bound to blow up with a loud bang one day – no way can he keep on with this double life without someone telling on him. I keep saying that he must either break it off or leave home, but he's such a damned idiot about it – he won't listen. The longer it goes on before Debbie discovers the worse it's going to be for her - I'm very fond of Debbie and she doesn't deserve this. Sorry, I forgot about what happened to you. Of course, you know all this better than anyone."

The evening was warm, and Mia carried her coat over her arm, enjoying the feeling of being outside at night wearing only a jumper. Callum's car was the only vehicle left in the parking lot behind the office and as they walked towards it, Mia had an idea.

"Would you mind if I nip inside through the back door and pick up my shopping? That way I won't have to drag it home on the bus tomorrow night? No, no - I'm fine, you stay here, and I will be back in a minute – I've got my card. Could you hold my bag perhaps?"

She swiped her security card, pulled the door nearly closed behind her and walked down the long dark passage towards her office with the muted light from the foyer at the far end. As she walked, she pulled on her coat to have two hands free for the bags,

127

and she was nearly at her own room before she noticed a thin strip of light in the crack of the door. Had the cleaner left her light on? And she could see a narrow band of light at the bottom of Josh's door, though it was shut. She stopped and held her breath, waited and listened, a sound from her room. Mia advanced slowly until she was level with the open door to Alan's secretary's room. Very carefully she stepped sideways into the doorway and as she did so, she heard the unmistakable sound of a filing cabinet drawer shutting, and then immediately another drawer being pulled open. She bent down, removed one shoe at a time and put one in each pocket of her coat, before she tiptoed out into the passage and closer to the door to her room. Without crossing to that side of the passage, she could just see a slice of the room through the narrow crack in the door. Josh was standing with his back to her with a folder laid flat on top of the open file drawer. He was flicking rapidly through the contents looking for something.

What was he up to now? The last thing she wanted was for Josh to catch her watching him, so she moved slowly away and crept back down the corridor in her stockinged feet, around the corner and out. She closed the outer door with gentle hands, slowly and silently. Callum was waiting just outside.

"I was just starting to feel that I shouldn't have let you go in alone if you had heavy bags - thought you would have been out in half the time. Where are the bags?"

Mia grabbed his arm. "Shush - can we please get into your car right away and then park on the street out front? I'll tell you why in a minute, just let's go right away - please, let's go!"

The urgency of her half whisper was enough to tell him something was seriously wrong. They got into the car and Mia watched the back door as Callum drove quietly out along the side of the building without turning his lights on. He turned into the street and parked twenty metres down from the main entrance, turned the engine off and swivelled in his seat to look at Mia.

"What the hell was that all about? What did you see in there?"

Mia never took her eyes off the side mirror. "I want to stay here with the lights off until someone comes out the backyard driveway. Would you know what Josh's car looks like?"

"Which one is Josh, is he the chubby guy in admin?"

"No, that's William. Josh is that handsome shit on my floor," said Mia with great feeling.

"Oh him, he drives a Mazda MX5, dark green with a black soft top. Are you going to tell me what's going on?"

Mia kept her eyes on the side mirror.

"Do you think you could do a U-turn and park facing the exit? Then I'd be able to see better, and I could talk at the same time?"

He started the car and waited for a gap in the traffic, did a swift U-turn between passing cars and parked on the other side of the street.

They both kept their eyes on the driveway. Traffic swept past in both directions, headlights and taillights weaving a bright pattern, and pedestrians broke up the faster movements of the cars. Mia tried to concentrate and not divert her gaze; it would be easy to miss someone coming out with the street so busy.

"I went down the corridor and I saw the light on in my office - the door was open just a crack. So, I took my shoes off and crept up to have a look. Josh was in there going through my filing cabinet, but I didn't feel up to confronting him there and then. Most likely the entire building was empty apart from him and me, and I wasn't sure what he was doing - it didn't feel very safe. But I want you to see him actually leave, to confirm he was here. There wasn't another car in the car park, so he'll be on foot. His car must be parked on the street."

"Well, if that doesn't beat all! What the hell was he up to? And why did you call him a handsome shit? Is there something going on?"

Mia was just about to reply when she saw a man emerging from the driveway across the street.

"Hey, look - there's someone coming out now!"

A row of cars passed and when the line of sight was restored the man had disappeared. Callum swore and was ready to jump out and run across the street to chase him, but as he reached for the door handle a car indicted that it was pulling out from the curb further down, on the other side of the street.

"That's it – that car pulling out, it's him!" Callum sounded triumphant as if he had engineered a perfect revelation. "An MX5, a pre-97 model with the flip-up lights, you couldn't miss it, it's a classic - that's him all right."

They watched Josh drive past them, but his face was obscured by traffic passing between them and Callum's identification of the car had to be sufficient.

Mia let out her breath. "God, was that weird. And I've just realized I still have my shoes in the pockets of my jacket. OK, we can leave now."

She directed Callum to her address and forestalled him before he got started on what she knew must be a long list of questions.

"Why don't you come up to my place and have a coffee or something. I'm sure you have questions you want to ask, and I owe you an explanation, I think."

She briefly explained the lack of furniture, put the kettle on and retreated to the bedroom. Her tights were ruined from the rough asphalt in the car park, so she swapped her skirt for jeans and pulled socks over her dirty feet. By the time they sat down on the cushions in front of the view, she had had time to consider how much she could safely tell Callum.

"This is going to sound a bit crazy, but it's really good that you were there and saw Josh drive away. But let me start at the beginning – I've had a feeling lately that Josh is up to something, and I think it might be to do with his latest project. I did the costing and some of the research for it and made some notes for him. It doesn't look very good at all, actually it looks very risky, but he doesn't want to take that on board. I have a feeling he's going to ignore my advice, and maybe even pretend I didn't give him the detailed notes I made - or worse still, change the figures I gave him, so it can go ahead to the client proposal stage."

She took a sip of her coffee and paused to give Callum a chance to say something, but he just looked at her expectantly.

"So, to be on the safe side, I made a copy of a crucial Excel file and saved it in my personal folder a day or two ago. Just in case he decided to change something and then blame the resulting disaster on me. I can't tell you the details or why I'm so edgy about it, but I am very suspicious. When I saw him in the office tonight, I wondered if he *is* going to doctor the file and he was making sure I haven't got a printout of the original version somewhere in my room."

She stopped talking. It sounded completely mad, more like the ravings of a paranoid than anything else.

But Callum said quite calmly, "OK, so let's say that's what he was doing. If you are right, you'll be able to check the shared file first thing in the morning and then you'll know. But tell me one thing, wouldn't Josh expect you to notice that the original had been changed long before the proposal goes to the client? I would have thought that you would know as soon as you saw it and start a real ruckus?"

"Oh yes, I would. But I'm not involved in the next step of this particular project, I only did the research and the costings, and I've kind of handed it over. So, Josh might think he is safe and can do whatever he wants - take a chance in case he can pull it off. I think he feels his concept is brilliant and new, and he wants to give it an airing and kind of have the intellectual property rights to it for the future, even if it fails financially. I think he really believes his own golden boy reputation."

She found it hard not to sound bitter when she spoke about Josh, and she wondered if Callum would wonder why.

"But wouldn't he get blamed for the disaster, I mean if they did use it and then the whole thing went wrong? What good would it do him to have "given his idea an airing"? He'd still look like an incompetent twat, wouldn't he?"

"I don't think so," said Mia seriously. "I don't believe he thinks like that - I've thought about it a lot this last week. He was absolutely furious when I told him that it wasn't going to work - he tried to bully me into taking out some of the costs. He was ready to choke me when I refused. I think he might let it go on for a while, as long as he can, and then when someone clicks that it's doomed, he'll say that I did the work-up and there was nothing in my costing to alert him. And then we'll probably find that he's changed something, and it will look as if I messed up."

She stopped and looked out into the night, considering how to make this credible. "It sounds like a paranoid melodrama, I know. But I really believe that he will change that spreadsheet, and he hopes that I won't be able to prove that it was ever different. Which means that his brilliant idea will have been talked about and it would only be circumstances that prevented it being tried. I will be made to look like a fool and it could ruin my career with the company."

Callum was frowning and trying to think of options to help her. "How about you check the file in the morning and if he's changed it you go to Alan and say, this costing was a disaster and now it's been changed, and I didn't do it. And that would be the end of it."

"No, that won't work - it's not enough. I need to know for sure what's going to happen. How can I not let it go on? All I need to do is keep an eye on how the situation develops. If it goes the way I suspect, then I will stop it before any damage is done. And now I know that he's been in my office, and I have you as a witness, so that's a bit of circumstantial evidence to back me up. And I have a copy of the original file safely tucked away, just to prove what it looked like when I finished with it."

She paused and thought for a moment while Callum's eyes never left her face.

"I *do* need for him to be caught doing real mischief and be seen to be a cheat, Callum. Not because of nastiness on my part, but because I know of something he did a while back, something very bad - and it caused terrible trouble for someone else."

"Did you know Josh before you started with us, then?"

Mia shook her head and thought she had to be careful how she phrased the next part.

"No, I didn't know about this previous thing until after the event, but it's a fact and I know everything about it. I know the person he did it to, you see. He must be shown that he can't do this again or he'll just continue to trample on others as he climbs the ladder to the top. He has proved that he is a liar and a cheat, and I have to make sure it doesn't happen again."

Well aware of the irony of talking about a misdeed committed a year ago, but still to happen, so to speak, Mia decided not to answer any questions Callum might ask, but he took her word for it.

"I can see that you're not going to tell me what it was, and I guess that it would be pointless to try and persuade you. But promise me one thing - if this turns out the way you think it will, then you'll tell me the whole story."

Mia got up and stretched and felt really tired all of a sudden. "I'll fill you in over a bottle of wine, but not until it's all sorted, so please don't talk to anyone about it. And thanks for waiting with me and driving me home, I appreciate it."

At the front door he turned, put his hands on her upper arms and gave her a little shake. "You are so amazingly focused. God knows why I'm going along with this crazy thing. I'll see you tomorrow."

His hands felt warm and comforting. He pulled her closer and kissed her gently at first, then with greater urgency. Before she could either respond or withdraw, he stepped back, smiled and closed the front door between them. His voice came through the door; she could hear the smile.

"Don't forget to lock the door."

She returned to the living room and stood by the window looking out at the glittering lights and considered what she felt. The answer was 'nothing' - she felt absolutely nothing. It was the first time in years a man other than Greg had kissed her, and though she liked Callum and he was good-looking and fun, the kiss had meant no more than a handshake. She admitted to herself that she had enjoyed the solid comfort of the male touch, but aside from that there was no response of the kind he might have hoped for.

She shook her head at herself and thought that she hoped it was just an impulse. Right now, she didn't need any complications, she had enough on my plate already. Then she turned off the lights and went to have a shower and scrub her dirty feet before going to bed.

26

When Mia arrived in the office the next morning, Alan was in his room reading something and by the state of his desk it looked as if he had been there for hours already. She thought about him telling her that he needed a change and wondered if he sometimes woke too early and came straight to work because it was preferable to being alone at home. She made a mental note to remember to ask him for a drink or dinner once the rush of new furniture and everything else was over.

When she turned from hanging her jacket behind the door, she noticed a manila folder on the corner of the desk. In it were some spreadsheets she had done for one of the first projects she had worked on with Alan. She was surprised only for a moment before realization dawned, and just then Alan walked in, holding a lever arch file and a pen.

"Mia, do you remember a little while back I mentioned I wanted to change the way the internal reports are presented? It was when we talked about changing the layout of the graphs in a proposal. And you came up with an idea of using those spread-out pie charts?"

"Yes, exploded pie charts - we could easily do something similar with your monthly report, if you don't like the way it looks."

"I was reading up on business psychology and they said that we take things in differently, better actually, if the format changes now and then. If there's an element of the new and unexpected, it kind of forces us to really consider what something actually says, and we process the information differently. I get a bit pissed off sometimes, when I sit in management meetings, and you can pick up straight off that half the people there haven't read the material beforehand."

"Right! So, you figure that if you change the format, they won't be able to just skim over it while they are in the meeting, and then they won't know how to discuss the result, so next time they'll read their stuff before the meeting?" Mia laughed at the prospect, both amused and impressed.

"Yeah, hopefully something will change. How about you show me how to do it, so I can do it myself in future? I really do need to learn a bit more about Excel. Can we sit down together now so you can at least show me how to do that chart format?"

"Of course, but let's do it in your room, where we have a bit more space in front of the computer."

As they moved toward the door Mia pretended to be struck by a thought and picked up the folder from her desk.

"Were you looking for something before I came in? Did you find it?"

Alan looked puzzled "No, why? What's that?"

Mia feigned innocence. "It's a folder with some data printouts from last year, one of the first briefs I helped you with. I haven't had it out of the filing cabinet since. It was lying on the corner of the desk when I came in just now."

"Who would have taken that out – and why? Are you sure you didn't leave it there last night?"

"No, you know me by now - I have a double copy of the tidiness gene and I always tidy my desk before I go home. There was nothing at all on this side of the desk when I left, only that little stack of papers on the far side. And anyway, I haven't looked at this stuff since we finished working on it."

She tried to look suitably concerned. "I can't imagine why anyone apart from you would want to go through my files,"

The episode must have stuck in Alan's mind, because later that day he sent an email memo to everyone in his section, saying that although people didn't lock their filing cabinets, it would be a good idea to either check with others before searching for things or leave a note that a file had been needed.

· · ·

Alice came past on her way to get a cup of coffee and stopped in Mia's door. "Coming for a cuppa, Mia? I'm on my way now if you're ready."

They went up the back stairs together and Alice said, "Tomorrow morning I'm going out to buy a shawl to wear to the wedding. What are you up to this weekend?"

"I'm having a huge clear out in the flat, really radical. I've got rid of lots of things and I have some new furniture coming in the morning, so I'll be busy getting organized."

"What fun, you lucky thing! Oh God, I'm sorry, Mia – I didn't mean that you are lucky - I just meant it's fun with some new furniture. God, I am such a klutz at times, my mum says every second time I open my mouth, I put my foot in it."

Mia smiled. "Don't worry about it, I know what you mean, it's not a problem."

When they parted after coffee Alice apologized again and impulsively Mia invited her to come for a visit the next day. "Provided you come before lunch because I've got something organized for the afternoon."

It was late in the afternoon when Mia saw Josh for the first time that day. He sauntered into her room with one hand in his pocket, the very picture of cheerful innocence.

"Hi Mia, how's it going? I heard from Alan that someone's been in your drawers – sorry, no pun intended."

Mia tried to keep her expression casual and friendly. "Yes, someone must have been going through my filing cabinet after I left yesterday. There was a folder on the corner of the desk when I got in this morning. Nothing important, just some printouts I hadn't looked at for months - but it seemed a bit odd. I thought it might have been Alan, but he didn't know anything about it."

She stopped and said nothing more, deliberately waiting to see what he would say next. In her mind she pictured Josh last night, standing in front of the filing cabinet, no more than a meter from where he was standing now.

Josh shrugged. "Well, you never know, do you? Perhaps it was the cleaner? Or someone else looking for something they needed, though it does sound a bit weird."

"Not to worry," said Mia casually. "There is nothing in those drawers that would be useful to anyone. And everything I work on is on the public drive on the server anyway."

"Ah, well, I suppose you're right. Nearly time to go home, must go and tidy up my mess. Have a good weekend!"

He strolled out and Mia sat looking at the empty doorway, considering the difference between That Time and This Time. Now she was on high alert for a repeat of Josh throwing her under the bus, and she would monitor him closely. It was intriguing to try to predict what would happen next, because her own actions in This Time had changed a raft of minor details, so some things might play out differently. She turned off her computer and got up; time to leave and she still had those heavy carry bags to bring home on the bus.

27

Saturday morning the entry phone buzzed five minutes after she got out of the shower; the furniture delivery was downstairs, at least an hour earlier than she had expected.

'When they say, first thing" they really mean it,' she grumbled to herself as she hurriedly pulled on a pair of jeans and dragged a brush through her damp hair, while the men loaded the lift downstairs. Six trips later the flat looked like a badly organized furniture storeroom, and the men surprised her by assembling the bed before leaving.

"Can you please sign that you've got everything, and we'll be off."

Quickly she ticked off the items, but halfway down the list she realized that the bedside tables had not been delivered. The men went back down to check the truck and returned in five minutes with the tables.

"Are you OK moving all this stuff around? Do you have someone to help you?"

It was a kind offer, but she was impatient to be alone, so she could start on her project without anyone else suggesting things.

"I have a friend calling in this morning to help. But thank you!"

They gathered up the cardboard and plastic wrappings, took their trolleys and left. Alone again, she stood for a moment relishing the feeling of excitement and thinking that she did not want to share the excitement of doing this with anyone and breakfast could wait.

. . .

It was half past eleven before she was done. In the living room everything had been moved around several times before she got it just right, and then there were the minor tweaks – the sofa half a meter to the left, so it didn't cut in on the view from her armchair, the other armchair a bit to the left, so someone sitting there could see the TV.

Once the big pieces were in place, she spent a lovely half hour deciding where her few remaining ornamental pieces would go. She was being very particular about how she placed them, trying to make each one show to best advantage. The Trudy Kroepf cast glass bowl must be where it was lit properly both in daylight and at night, and the modern crystal piece that had wedding present from Sarah and James needed a dark surface to sit on to look its best.

When she had finished, she looked around, satisfied and excited. Now there were only five ornamental objects in the whole big room, and it looked amazing. She was just thinking of breakfast when the entry phone buzzed.

"Hi Mia, it's Alice. Is it all right if I come for a coffee?"

"Of course, come on up." She pressed the button, turned the kettle on and went to open the front door, Alice got out of the lift glowing with excitement and fun. "I can't wait to show you the shawl I bought, it's gorgeous."

They walked into the living room and for Mia it was as if she saw it for the first time, the way it would appear to a visitor.

"Wow!" she said out loud, and then she turned apologetically to Alice. "Sorry, but I think I'm a bit over-excited. I've just this minute finished making my new bed and I've spent the last three and a half hours getting things right. The new furniture was delivered before eight this morning and I hadn't really seen it as a whole until now. It's like being in someone else's house - weird."

Alice looked around, taking it all in. "Mia, it's stunning – just perfect! I love the colours and that TV unit made of – what? Metal and white glass? My God, it looks like an ad for the perfect interior."

They did the full tour and then went to the kitchen to make coffee, and the door buzzer went again while Alice was getting out the Danish pastries she had brought.

"I don't know who that would be," said Mia in response to Alice's look. "I'm not expecting anyone."

It was Callum who, as he put it, "was just going past and thought he would call in". And Mia laughed at his face when he walked into the living room, utter surprise.

"The fairies came in during the night and got it sorted," she said and was pleased that no mention was made of his previous visit or any of the events that had led to it.

Mia made another cup of coffee and Alice showed off the shawl she had bought for the wedding.

"Ta-da!" she said and flicked it out of the bag and held it up. It was deep turquoise-blue silk with dragons embroidered in red, gold and lime green - vivid and luxurious. Mia and Callum exclaimed at how beautiful it was, and Alice was as delighted as a little girl with a new party dress.

"Mia said a shawl would be perfect with my black slinky dress, because it's so bare-shouldered," she told Callum. "She said I'd be able to drape it over my shoulders like this and let it slip or trail it behind me like a seductive diva!"

She strolled across the floor to demonstrate the diva look, let the shawl slip first off one shoulder and then let it drop, trailing it behind her in one hand, and Mia laughed. "I knew you would be a natural at that!"

It was a surprise to find that Callum and Alice had never really had a conversation before.

"Well, let's face it," said Callum when Mia expressed disbelief. "I might have worked there for three years, but I never come in the front - I use the back door, so we hardly ever see each other."

Alice was her usual sparkling and vivacious self and to Mia's amusement Callum was forced to have opinions on things he had never considered before.

"Really, Callum!" Alice was incredulous. "I can't *believe* you never stayed up all night and had pizza for breakfast! You must have led a very sheltered life."

At quarter to one Mia broke it up. "Sorry guys, but I must get ready to go out. I've arranged to meet a group of friends and can't keep them waiting, but it was super tto see you both."

Alice and Callum went off together, making arrangements for Callum to drive Alice home, and Mia thought how amazing it was that since getting up this morning she had only given a fleeting thought now and then to the cathedral fire.

She took the coffee mugs and the plates to the kitchen and noticed that the phone cord in the kitchen was disconnected and stood for a moment trying to work out what had happened. But the penny dropped when she pictured herself moving the big shopping bags from the hall to the kitchen bench when the furniture was delivered; she must have pulled out the phone cord when she shoved the last bag along the bench.

The bliss of modern technology - Mozilla swung into instant action when she turned the computer on. She went straight to the BBC site and scanned the foreign news items. And found it! Her heart skipped a beat; it had happened on Friday afternoon just as she had remembered. Avidly she read the short notice and clicked on the link to a more detailed article, and it was very much as she had described it in her document. The main dome was made of wood and had collapsed during the fire, a minor turret had been destroyed and the entire interior was damaged by water and smoke. There were photos of people watching the blaze from across the street and helpers carrying artworks to safety.

Her spirits soared on the knowledge that now she could prove her story, or at least prove that she could predict that certain things would happen. Which, she thought, unless you believe in magic, proves I must have 'been here before' so that's something, at least.

Now she must prepare for meeting the others and plan how much to reveal: the whole truth or just that she can predict things?

The Danish pastry had not been enough after all the hard work and there was plenty of time until she had to leave. The phone rang while she was making a toasted sandwich.

"We're absolutely baffled - how *did* you know? We were there – we saw it, we video-taped it!" Sarah was nearly shouting with excitement. "It happened, the dome collapsed in a huge shower of sparks, we spent a couple of hours watching - and there was an enormous fireball type thing, a huge explosion from inside – spectacular."

James must have snatched the phone from Sarah. "Mia, we can't wait until we get home, we're both dying of curiosity. You must tell us how you knew."

Mia thought fast; they would have to know sometime and at

least there was some proof now. She decided to give them a short version.

"OK, can you try and arrange yourselves again so you can both hear me? I'll tell you the basics, but the details will have to wait. I can't do the full-blown version over the phone - I need to see you face to face when I tell you the whole story."

"OK, we're sharing the receiver now," said James. "It's five in the morning here, we've hardly had any sleep, but we couldn't get through before, must be the Russian phone system."

"No, it was my phone - accidentally unplugged. I pushed things around on the bench this morning and I didn't notice that the plug thing got pulled out of its socket - don't blame the poor Russians. So, here's the brief version."

She gave them a summary of the event in the night, of waking up to find that time had been wound back by a year and taking that fateful Friday off to research where she was in relation to certain key events. She finished with her decision to take hold of her life and change her future, and the whole time she spoke there was not a sound from the other end of the line.

"Are you still there?" she asked, hoping they hadn't been cut off and she would be forced to repeat the whole saga.

"God yes, we are still here," said James. "I suppose we're just literally struck dumb. Do continue!"

Mia turned the oven off and went on to relate her reasons for confronting Barb, but she thought it was better not to reveal that she remembered that Sarah and James had known of Greg's affair. She told them of other things she had figured out and about the strange little ceremony at the police station the other night, but she deliberately did not mention Josh or finding Carl, or her prediction about Irwin's death. It was too complicated and would mean a lot more explaining; too much for now.

"So, now you know it all, or very nearly. Maybe now you can understand how I seemed to progress so suddenly - I know you wondered at how I got over my initial grief and had the nerve to change just about everything. You see, to me I was well over a year since Greg died, not just two months. And along the way I had found out a lot of things that I was powerless to change in what I call That Time, but in This Time, with more forewarning and more determination, I can change my future, so it'll play out differently."

"Mia," said Sarah in a voice tinged with awe. "Will you be able to prevent disasters and people getting murdered, that sort of thing?"

With one hand Mia took the toasted sandwiches out of the oven and put them on a plate and got a mug of coffee organized.

"I don't know yet. I don't even know for a fact that *everything* that happened in That Time will happen again in This Time. My memory's no better than yours or anyone else's, so I can't recall every detail of events – to me they are memories from a year ago. I tried to think of a second thing to document along with the cathedral fire, something reasonably close in time, and it's much harder than you think to pinpoint exactly when things happened. And then there's the possibility, like I just said, that some things won't happen this time around. The most important thing now is that you two do *not* mention this to anyone at all. Not to anyone, not even Brett when you get to London. It is crucial that this isn't talked about until I know more about the whole thing. I don't want to risk becoming a celebrity freak."

Sarah understood immediately. "Of course, we'll keep it to ourselves. We can talk to each other, which is great - or I might burst my boiler before we get back, but we promise not to tell anyone else."

Mia put the phone down relishing the relief of having been able to tell them and not be met by disbelief. The details could wait until they were back and could sit down face to face. She carried her lunch through to the dining table thinking of Sarah and James and how they would now have time to digest what they had heard and then be ready for other aspects. Perhaps she would be able to do something to prevent a few bad things from happening, though it would have to wait for now. Trying to persuade Steve Irwin not to go diving with stingrays would remain her top priority.

28

Mia arrived at the police station at five to four, and there was nobody outside, so after a couple of minutes she went inside and the constable behind the desk looked up.

"Are you one of John MacFarlane's visitors? OK, come through here and I'll show you the way."

He opened the door behind the counter and Mia followed him to a corridor, where he stopped and pointed.

"I can't escort you up, but I think you've been here before - turn right at the end of the passage and take the stairs to the first floor, second door on your left."

She heard excited voices through the half open door to John's office and paused briefly before going in, feeling unaccountably nervous. When they noticed her there was a moment of complete silence and then a cacophony of questions and exclamations broke out.

Mia held out a hand as if to ward off a physical assault. "Please, I can't hear you if you all talk at once."

John spoke over the others. "Let's give the girl some space, please. How about we all sit down and talk calmly instead of this onslaught?"

He gestured towards the round conference table by the window and pulled his desk chair over to provide a fifth place. They sat down, quiet now and all eyes were on Mia. John took the lead.

"We read the document before it was sealed, so we all know that Mia's first prediction was exactly right. I'm in a quandary myself about what to think of this and I would appreciate some kind of explanation. There are also a few things we need to talk about, provided that Mia wants us to and given that nobody objects to me chairing this meeting?"

Nobody replied - all comments seemed suspended, and John looked expectantly at Mia, who thought for a moment before replying.

"Yes, you're right. I do owe you an explanation, and I would appreciate a bit of support and input from you. I have a lot of questions running in circles in my head and talking things through might help me work things out. Do you all have time to listen?"

Paul laughed. "Mia, do you honestly think that anything in this world could get us out of this room until we've heard your story – even if it takes all night?"

There were murmurs of agreement from the others. Mia looked at Lorraine as if waiting for a signal to start, and Lorraine said calmly, as if nothing could surprise her.

"Well, starting at the beginning and continuing to the end is always a good idea. And by the way, I think it would be good to give them the whole picture including Greg's accident, and the Barb debacle - just so what has happened in This Time makes more sense."

When she saw the look on Mia's face she added quickly, "You can leave the personal bits out if you want, it's just that it would put everything into context."

John got up. "Let's go down the hall to the canteen and bring back a couple of pots of coffee and some mugs, and then we can sit back and listen without interruptions."

They returned from the canteen with coffee and biscuits and John closed the door before they settled down around the table again. Mia sat for a moment collecting her thoughts and then she started her story and taking Lorraine's advice, she began with Greg's accident and continued chronologically forward. Few storytellers have had a more spellbound audience, there was not a single word spoken by anyone else. The only sound in the room, apart from her own voice, was the occasional sharp intake of breath at certain points of the story. When she described the switch from

That Time to This Time there were gasps of surprise from the others.

It took nearly an hour and when she stopped, her throat felt gritty. She had been taut with concentration from the first word to the last, and she had hardly touched her cup of coffee. All the details had been included; how she had found Carl and how surprised she had been to find that for him time had been 'fast forwarded' instead of 'rewound', the message left at Sarah and James's hotel and that they had gone to the cathedral and actually witnessed the fire.

John got to his feet and stretched his long, lean body. "Good God," he said quietly. "I think this is the moment to break out the wine - I bought some stuff on the way here to celebrate with. Back in a moment."

He returned with a laden tray and put two bottles of wine and five glasses on the table and went back for a plate of cheese and crackers before he resumed the role of chairman. There had been no conversation while he was away. It was as if a spell had been cast on the group and they were in a strange state of waiting without comment or thought. Mia felt empty and tired and was happy not to have to talk.

John picked up the thread again. "When I knew the fire had happened and before you arrived - and before I had heard the whole story - I thought of some issues we might want to discuss. Firstly, how can we prevent Steve Irwin from going for that fateful dive? Secondly, is there something else we need to do, something which Mia remembers, which we can try to prevent? And third, what kind of help do you need from us, Mia? Even before I heard the whole story, I knew that whatever it whatever this ability of yours is, you might need support."

Mia felt her eyes pool with tears, and Paul reached for the box of tissues on the table and handed her one. In a slightly muffled voice, Mia said, "You can't imagine what a relief it is that you believe me." She blew her nose and started again. "I think all John's points are good, and I think we should start with the Steve Irwin thing. I can't put an exact date on it, but I know we don't have a lot of time, so it's urgent that I find a way to approach him and make him believe me."

Lorraine reached over to unwrap a triangle of blue vein cheese and a disk of Brie, put them tidily on their wrappers, opened a packet of water crackers and poured wine into everyone's glasses. John watched her absent-mindedly and was just about to say something when Miles spoke up.

"We could make a DVD copy of the video Paul made the other night, courier it to Steve Irwin and then call and talk to him when he's got it. You can direct him to the news stories about the fire to prove you are telling the truth and ask him to reconsider his plans."

Lorraine looked around, got up and walked over to John's desk, returned with a paper knife and started cutting the cheeses into slices. John looked at her and smiled. "Good idea! And do you know - I was going to record Mia telling her story, but I don't think I turned the recorder on."

Lorraine continued to cut the cheeses and spoke without looking up. "I saw you turn it on just before Mia walked in, and the little light is still on. Let's leave it on for now."

Mia was taken aback and hesitated to say anything, but Paul had been watching her face and spoke for her.

"I think we need to hear it from Mia, it's her story – and her life. Do you want any of this recorded? It's obviously your call."

While he spoke, Mia made a quick decision that having the recording might be a good thing. "No, that's fine. It's a very good idea actually, now that I think of it. It continues the documentation, and I think we should mention that today is Saturday 26 August 2006."

John nodded. "It's a little old-fashioned tape recorder, and the machine time stamps the tape, so that's double verification. I should have asked you before I turned it on, sorry. What do we all think of Miles's suggestion about the DVD?"

It took some time to refine the idea of sending a copy of the video, but as Paul reasonably said, "It's so clear and simple, what else could we do that would be that effective? He's can't possibly dismiss the warning about him when he's watched the video."

Lorraine agreed and suggested that they should leave the original document where it was, sealed up and untouched. "We all know that things happened just as the document predicts, so we don't need to check it. You can see the actual text on the video, Paul and I checked it last night."

"John, you looked as if you wanted to protest just then?" Miles looked at John, who hesitated before he turned to Mia.

"Mia, I think Miles's plan is perfect. But I want to say right now that I feel quite concerned about you. I think the audio tape should remain private to us five and only ever be played to those you decide should hear the whole story if you don't want to retell it 'live' again - there is such a lot of private stuff on it. I can keep it here under lock and key. But my main concern is that your privacy must be maintained, for as long as you yourself want it to be."

Lorraine glanced at John, put a slice of Brie on a cracker and handed it to him. "I agree with John, Mia - you must be protected," she said decisively. "Imagine what would happen if this story broke in the press - it would turn your life into a nightmare. You would be hounded by reporters, and it would end with half the world believing you and the other half calling you a fraud. And some would want you to make them rich, some would want you to help them commit all kinds of fraud - someone might even want to harm you to prevent you revealing something they imagined you knew. It's too awful to contemplate what it might do to your life." She popped a cracker into her mouth and looked at Mia.

While Lorraine was speaking Mia had considered the scenario she painted.

"You're right, both of you," she said and held her wine glass out for a refill. "I knew from that first day that it could be dangerous to let on what had happened - that the consequences might be more far-reaching than I could foresee. And once the story is in circulation there is no way of calling it back. But I must work out how to reach Irwin and get a DVD to him, with a short letter, and then maybe call him as well. I hope you will all stand behind me in this and not talk to anyone outside this room about it?"

She looked at the faces around the table and everybody nodded their agreement.

"Well, that was easy," said John cheerfully, looking around at their serious faces and nodding heads. "That's unanimous. The last item is if there's anything else you remember that we could prevent. And I don't mean crimes only."

He smiled at Mia's disbelieving face. "No, anything at all, but crimes included of course, seeing they are close to my policeman's heart."

Lorraine was still thinking of Mia. "If anything leaked out and people started pestering you, then you could just deny it - say you have no idea what they're talking about. All the evidence, including the audiotape could remain here where only John has access to it. But if we send a DVD to Steve Irwin, then we have added a factor we can't control. So maybe we shouldn't send it - maybe you should just try to persuade him to believe you first of all."

Paul and Miles spoke at the same time and Paul let Miles go first.

"I don't think that would work. If you're as famous as Steve Irwin, you probably get lots of crank emails and calls. Why would he believe this any more than anything else people fire at him? And you have to admit the story sounds totally insane until you see the evidence."

"Too right!" Paul agreed. "We must convince him first, and then talk to him. If he goes to the media with the DVD then it's out there and we can't do anything about it. But if he *does* believe it, then we could ask him to destroy or return the DVD and he might do it. It's that old chicken and egg thing - which comes first. Cause and effect and all that."

He got up and went across to the window, leant against the window frame and frowned down into his wine glass, and Mia thought how unexpected it was that he had such strong opinions. I mustn't let that little boy face fool me, she thought, he is very much an adult.

Paul continued, "If we are all available, I think we should go somewhere to continue this discussion over a meal, or else order something in. I think it's important that we don't leave this discussion unfinished." He flashed a smile in John's direction. "I don't want to be insulting, but these chairs are torture after a couple of hours."

"There are several things I'd like to put up for debate," John said. "Not just practical things, but more ideas - like how does this time switch work and can we try to guess how cause and effect connect across timelines. And that's just for a start."

29

M ia studied their faces carefully. They all seemed to genuinely care about the consequences of whatever decision was made, and she wanted to acknowledge their concern.

"I would really appreciate it - but I think the next part of the discussion should include all of us who are here now, so if tonight isn't OK for everyone, then we'll make a date for another day."

They looked at each other and nodded, and she wondered if they had deliberately kept the evening clear, prepared for whatever might eventuate.

Mia took the lead. "I don't really want to go out to eat. Sitting in a restaurant and talking about this doesn't feel right - and I'm really sick of this hard chair too. We can go back to my place and pick up some take-away food on the way. I've got wine and even some ice cream, I think, and we can be comfortable while we talk - and nobody can overhear us."

John volunteered to get their food orders from his favourite Asian take-away place, and Lorraine offered to go with him. "Just to make sure we don't end up with everything full of chili and extra hot."

"OK, Miles and Paul can follow me or come with me," said Mia, "and we'll go straight back to my place. Lorraine knows the way on her own."

Mia turned lights on and showed Paul and Miles the bathroom, put some wine in the fridge and started getting plates and cutlery out. Paul turned up beside her and helped carry things through and asked for a corkscrew and glasses. Miles reappeared and strolled over to the window to admire the view and Paul joined him. They opened the door and went out on the balcony and Mia looked and smiled at how completely different they were. One tall and dark-skinned with wide shoulders; the other a head shorter, skinny, pale, and freckled. She could hear their voices in animated discussion, but not their words, and glancing out from the kitchen, she noticed Paul shaking his head at things Miles said and wondered if they were arguing about her story or discussing sport.

When Lorraine and John arrived laden with bags of Thai food, Lorraine made a surprised and appreciative face at Mia when she walked into the living room. "What a difference – gorgeous – you've been quick!"

The containers of Thai food went straight to the dinner table, and as they passed food around and filled wine glasses, the conversation was casual and general, but after a while they returned to the point where they had left off in John's office.

"After dinner we should Google Steve Irwin and some Australian news sites and see if we can find out where to contact him – and try international directory service," said Lorraine. "We might have to send it to his Zoo – I bet his home address isn't available online."

Paul raised his glass in Mia's direction. "A toast to the most amazing time-traveller ever – totally cool and level-headed."

Lorraine and the others joined in the toast, but Mia shook her head. "Don't you believe it - that's not how it was. You should have seen me that Friday morning – complete panic doesn't even start describing it. My mind was a mess, and at one stage I was so scared and confused I was physically sick - not level-headed at all. And I still have flashes of absolute terror now and then, mostly in case I get flipped back into 2007 – well, I did until recently." Talking about it made her realize that this had not happened in the last few days. "I think talking to Carl has calmed that worry a bit."

John disagreed. "You don't rate yourself highly enough, Mia. What you describe is only the immediate shock reaction – I'm sure we all agree that what you've done since then is very brave, very cool."

Lorraine said, with a wicked smile in Mia's direction. "And

apart from that, she has managed to tidy all her cupboards, invent a new personal style, sell most of her furniture, refurnish the whole flat, wreak revenge on a false friend and start planning to teach a cheat a lesson. *And* organize to have new tyres put on her car. And my God - all I've done is go to work, eat dinner and moan about what's on TV."

They all laughed and went back to the topic of most interest. "Paul and I were discussing things earlier today, after we knew that the cathedral fire had really happened," said Miles. "Lorraine was at work, so Paul and I sat in a café and came up with theories about how you could have known that the fire would happen: clairvoyance, time warps, time travel, and even reincarnation. We didn't get very far."

He looked at Mia with raised eyebrows, but she was not ready for a theory debate. "Before we start on this - who wants dessert, and or coffee? Let's make ourselves comfortable before we continue."

They cleared the table, Mia made coffee and they abandoned the dining table for the new seating. John looked around as if searching for something and without apparently having noticed his roving gaze Lorraine said, "You left it on the hall table, when we came in."

He left the room and returned with a large box of chocolates. Mia noted with amusement that Lorraine seemed to have developed a way of communicating with John as if they knew each other well, some form of non-verbal communication. And she wondered what it signified, so soon after their first meeting. Were they just accidentally and naturally attuned to each other, or was something else developing under her very eyes?

She re-ignited the discussion. "I think my problem is trying to understand the logic of it – that has nearly driven me crazy. I can theorize to a certain point, but then it all becomes blurred by the fact that I don't know if B comes after A, or if it comes after Z - or if A possibly equals 4, if you see what I mean."

She thought for a moment and frowned. "I want to work out how it hangs together, but it seems there is no way to do that. I get confused and frustrated, and sometimes I think that maybe we're just tiny cogs in something so huge and complex that we'll never understand it and there's no point in even trying to work it out."

She looked around at the four faces, all serious now. "But, as I said before, what really terrifies me is that I might suddenly find myself back in 2007. And if that happens, what is the logic that governs what happens then? Would I remember this, or would my memory remain here in This Time? Would you still know me? Would I remember you?"

John took a different tack. "What I would like to know is how it was when you woke up that Friday morning. You said before that everything in the flat had reverted to what it had been like in the August 2006 – that any changes you had made after that date no longer existed?"

Mia nodded. "Yes, that's right. I once again had my old car for example, new clothes were no longer in my wardrobe. I was worried that some things – like Greg's affair with Barb – might not have happened in This Time, because I had to know that before I did something about it. But it had, and so far, I've not come across anything significantly different from what I expected."

"OK, in that case tell me this – and I know it's only a couple of weeks – but have you come across anything new - anything at all in This Time - not related to your own life, which has been added?"

Mia thought for a couple of minutes. Had she noticed any references to news or events that seemed completely unexpected or new?

She shook her head. "No, I don't think I have. But I haven't really thought of it from that angle, more along the lines of whether things I expect to happen as This Time moves forward will happen as they did before. You see, I did begin to think of what would happen if someone else had also come back from a different time strand into this one, and once here in This Time they changed something and how would that affect things further down the track? Like me planning to unmask Josh at work."

Paul nodded. "Like if you changed how something played out here and now, and then went back and checked in 2007 – would the effects be noticeable there? Or will the changes only affect how the future shapes up in this time strand as it moves forward? In other words, have you actually been moved back in time within one time-line, so to speak, or are we in a time-line, which got split off from your first time strand, are they no longer connected? Is this strand a separate line, will everything here only affect the future in this strand? God, it sounds muddled, but I kind of know what I mean."

"Yes! What you said just now fits my ideas exactly. I was thinking that perhaps there are untold branches in the timelines, and the one that I was sort of flicked out of will continue as if nothing happened. In which case, I am still there in 2007 and I will continue to live out my life in there, but from here I'll never know how that life develops. And here in This Time I'll have another life along different lines perhaps. And nothing I do here, now that I am here, changes anything apart from the future in this particular strand."

John spoke slowly, thinking as he talked. "Yes, that's fine, but I have a problem with that - if that's the case, then how come you didn't just flick back into your body and mind as they were in 2006 in this time strand? How did you take your mind and memories and experiences from a whole extra year in That Time with you to This Time? Obviously, you came back into your body as it was a year earlier– or I presume you did?"

Mia smiled at him. "I went to bed in 2007 with nail varnish on and woke up in 2006 without I – just as it was a year earlier."

Miles grinned. "It's hilarious. Here we are discussing the laws of the universe and theorizing about time shifts in a way that could confuse Einstein, and Mia proves a crucial point by noticing if she has nail varnish on. Girls!"

Lorraine snorted derisively. "You're totally missing the point, Miles. There's no doubt that women will end up running the world because they can mix practical trivia and life-changing philosophy. We can change the baby's nappies, think of what to have for dinner and sort out a better way to distribute the country's health budget – at the same time."

Mia laughed and reverted to the idea that John had raised. "You *are* right, John - if I didn't have my memories from 2007, I wouldn't even be aware that I'm in a different year, would I? Somehow some rule was broken, and my 2007 mind flicked over to This Time where it's 2006. And the same goes for Carl."

Lorraine narrowed her eyes in thought. "So - if several or maybe dozens of strands exist, then they might be like little blood vessels coming off a main artery - and maybe they even sub-divide further? And in all of them various changes occur after the point of break-off, and that leads to different futures. Or perhaps they move at different speeds? What happened to you could be that you were moved from one strand to another in a straight sideways move, but the strand you surfaced in had moved a bit slower, so it was a year behind?"

Paul stared in delighted amazement at his sister. "That's pretty good, bet you are right - it sounds completely convincing."

"Well, we'll never know, but I quite like the idea myself," said Lorraine modestly. "And if remembering your life in your original timeline is an anomaly, then there might be lots of people who have got shifted – they just don't know it."

They sat in silence for a moment considering the possibility that they might all have started out somewhere else, but they would never know, and then Mia pulled them back to the original discussion.

"I must say that speaking to Carl was the most wonderful thing for me, because he's gone forwards, and it gave a new angle on the whole problem. He was fast forwarded about forty years, poor man. And his memory of being a young man was in an old body - a 60-something-year old body, but the interesting thing is that his mind is still only middle-aged when it comes to experience and memories. His mind thinks he has only lived about forty-five years in total or something like it, first what he remembers from his original life, and then the twenty years since he 'woke up' in This Time. But from a physical point of view his physical bran is actually 85 - and that brain acts its age. I'm sure he has exactly the same problems with short-term memory and learning new things as any other octogenarian."

It was late when they finished the discussion. They agreed that the only way to get Steve Irwin to take the warning seriously, was to send him the video, and Lorraine searched the Internet and found the mail address to the Zoo. They discussed the letter Mia would write to accompany the DVD, and Paul promised to bring two copies of the video on DVDs the next day, so Mia could courier one from work on Monday.

It was late when they exchanged email addresses and phone numbers and agreed to meet the following Saturday at John's house in Parnell. Paul felt sorry for John being faced with a horde for dinner and said he and Lorraine would bring dinner, but John surprised them.

"No, don't do that, I like cooking, and I don't often cook for visitors - it's all good."

After they left, Mia pottered about tidying up and thinking of the evening's discussions. She wished she had found something other than Irwin's death for the second predicted event, something that felt less like being responsible for somebody else's life and death. But overall, the relief of having the support of people who believed her story made her feel more relaxed than she had since her world shifted on its axis. She had Carl, who was a fellow victim of the same cosmic joke, and his neighbour Thomas, who possibly already believed Carl's story or at least was used to the idea. She had got over the first hurdle of getting Sarah and James to believe her by having concrete evidence for them to see for themselves. She yawned at herself in the bathroom mirror, dried her hands and turned the light off, knowing she would sleep like a log.

30

Putting the warning to Steve Irwin into words was unexpectedly hard. Mia tried to imagine how the letter would look to the person who opened the mail. How would she capture their attention and get them to take the message seriously and pass it on? In the end she kept it simple and said that the DVD contained video evidence of two predictions she had made, and that one of them had already happened exactly as she had described it.

She continued: '*My second prediction is of a diving accident involving you. You were being filmed while diving with stingrays and as you swam directly over one of them, it raised its tail, and the barb went into your chest. You were then taken to the surface, to a boat.*'

For some reason she was reluctant to say that the barb through his heart and killed him and left it to his imagination. And neither did she mention her own bizarre story in the hope that he would be more likely to pay attention to a straight-forward premonition, than believe an outlandish idea of what amounted to time travel. She put her name, email address and phone number at the bottom of the letter before she printed it. She sat looking at it for a long time, but decided there was really nothing else she could say. Short of going to Australia to convince Irwin face to face, she had done all she could.

She was in the bathroom transferring a load of washing to the dryer when the entry phone buzzed, and Paul arrived at the door dressed in his uniform, looking particularly dark-skinned and handsome in his light blue shirt.

"Lorraine has discovered that if you go to the airport, even though it's Sunday, there's a way of getting the parcel on a plane to Sydney today."

He followed Mia into the living area. "And then it gets picked up and delivered by regular courier anywhere in Australia. It's expensive, but it's far quicker than giving it to a courier company at this end. I made two DVDs, one for you and one to send."

"Thank you - I'll go out to the airport and get the disk sent off this afternoon. Have you got time for a cup of coffee?"

But Paul had to leave. "Thanks, but I must go, I'm on duty and my partner's waiting downstairs in the car. I'll see you on Saturday, if not before."

The airport was messy and there was yet another building project going on, which complicated things, and she got lost the first time she drove around looking for the name of the air freight company. In the end she made a full circuit before finding a place to stop to call them and ask how to find their depot.

Driving back towards town she tried to picture the reaction of whoever would open the parcel. If Irwin himself got it, he might sit down and watch the recording straight away. But say someone else opened it and put it to one side? Could she have done something more to make it more credible? The thought that so much hinged on how she expressed the warning in the letter plagued her, and it was hard to stop thinking about it.

Worried thoughts continued to revolve in her head as she headed for the Mt Eden shops, one of her favourite parts of the city. It was like a self-sufficient little town, not the slightest bit concerned about what went on outside its boundaries; she would have liked to live there, but the area was expensive and out of her reach. After circling a couple of blocks, she managed to park the car and walked along to the bakery that made little chocolate gateaux. She chose an undecorated one to take to Carl's place and continued to the wine shop for a bottle of merlot, thinking that if it didn't go with what he was cooking, he would enjoy it another time. Dawdling outside a gift shop, admiring desirable but unnec-essary objects in the window, she thought contentedly that with

her new minimalist lifestyle, temptation played a correspondingly
minimal part.

31

Carl met her at the door with a big smile. "Let me take that bag. You shouldn't have brought so much, what's all this? Wine, oh good, I love a merlot. And a box – aha, gorgeous cake. I have ice cream we can have with that. And what's this – a CD? Did you mean for this to be in the bag?"

Mia smiled. "Yes, it's a DVD that I thought we could watch on your computer, but then I remembered on the way here that you probably don't have one."

A voice from the doorway said, "Evening, Carl." He was a tall and muscular man with a tremendous scar across one cheek, which pulled his face and twisted the corner of his mouth on one side.

"And you must be Mia – I'm Thomas."

He shook her hand and looked carefully at her, and she thought he probably wanted to make sure that she was not about to trick Carl into anything.

Mia smiled at his serious face and turned to Carl. "If you had told me someone else was coming, I would have bought a bigger cake."

"There is plenty of cake for three, and with ice cream it'll do us very well. Well, you've met now. How about a glass of wine before I start cooking?"

Carl poured three glasses of wine and raised his in a salute. "Here's to us! Mia, I have a confession to make, and I hope you won't get up and leave when you hear it. I've told Thomas a little about you, just enough so he knows that you're like me, but you've moved from the future backwards - opposite to me."

"You don't need to worry," said Thomas. "I know how to keep a secret, and I haven't mentioned Carl's story to a living soul. He told me about you, because it backed up his own story – seems he thought I didn't really believe him."

Mia noticed that he did not say if he really did believe Carl, and thought how clever and diplomatic that was, and now Carl and she could take it any way they liked. Two slightly anxious faces looked at Mia, which made her laugh.

"It's OK Carl, I don't mind – if you trust Thomas, then so do I. And perhaps Thomas can show you the DVD on his computer seeing you don't have one. It's the proof of the pudding so to speak about both of our stories."

Thomas looked intrigued. "You have proof? That sounds inter-esting - why don't we take our glasses and go across to my place and watch it now? I must admit that I'm very curious. How about it, Carl, is there time?"

They pulled up chairs around the computer in Thomas's living room and Mia hesitated about whether she should explain who these witnesses were, but it felt too complicated just then. The main thing now was the proof, and the back story could wait.

"We could have played this on the DVD player and watched it on the TV," said Thomas but stayed where he was. It was the first time Mia had seen the video and watching it, she was impressed with how comprehensive and conclusive the whole thing seemed. It was crisp and clear, and the document was clearly visible and easy to read. The way everyone introduced themselves, the setting, the signing and sealing of the envelope – it all came together as a structured and credible scene.

There was a short break in the filming after they moved to John's office when he gave Mia a receipt for the document. When the recording resumed it was with Lorraine in a different setting, a bedroom, where she sat at a desk in front of a laptop. Paul's voice set the scene: "Today is Saturday 26 August 2006. It is 8.45 in the morning and my sister Lorraine and I, Paul, have checked the BBC website and found the story of the Trinity Cathedral fire in St Petersburg, just as described by Mia in the previous section filmed on Wednesday 23

August. The envelope remains in John MacFarlane's locked cabinet at the police station. Lorraine and I are both completely convinced that there's no way anyone could have faked a prediction of the fire two days in advance in such extraordinary detail. I'll try to film the computer screen, hoping to show the date on the website."

The camera was brought closer to the computer monitor and zoomed in on the screen, and Lorraine's voice could be heard in the background.

"I'll pull the curtains so there's less reflection."

Then came the swishing sound of curtains being pulled, and the computer image became more clearly defined. There was a slight flicker across the screen, but the story headline and the BBC banner were clear to see and then the recording ended.

Carl and Thomas continued to stare at the blank computer monitor when the video had stopped playing until Carl found his voice. "By golly, that's the most amazing thing I've ever seen, incredible. Nobody could doubt it, Mia, nobody!"

She needed to break the mood, she felt overwhelmed by what she had seen. It was so intense and there was a sense of unreality watching it as a spectator. When it had taken place at the police station, it had seemed quite natural, though a bit nervous, but watching it made her realize the dramatic impact. And the additional part with Lorraine and Paul reading the BBC website was stunningly convincing.

"Let's go back to Carl's place and we can talk while he cooks," Mia said and got up. "I think I'm as gob-smacked as you are – seeing it like this is unnerving even for me. You can keep the DVD for a little while, if you want to watch it again, but you must keep it somewhere safe."

Thomas took the DVD from the computer and put it back in its case. "I'll put it in the snuffbox safe. It'll be completely safe there, and we can get it out and watch it on the TV before we give it back."

Mia was intrigued. "Snuffbox safe? Do you collect snuff boxes? I don't think I've ever seen one."

"You have to show her, Thomas," said Carl. "They are the most wonderful little things you ever saw, Mia, and each one has a story.

He has a safe to put them in when he goes away. I'll go back to the cottage and start dinner."

"OK - come and have a look and we'll follow Carl across in a minute. They're in the dining room."

He led the way to a rather bare and formal dining room with a huge fireplace. Against one wall stood a waist high table whose top was a shallow display box with a glass lid and inside, arranged on dark green felt, were eighteen or twenty tiny boxes.

Thomas lifted the lid, took one out and put it in Mia's hand. She had never held anything so exquisite: a tiny oval gold box, no more than four centimetres across, with a hinged lid and on the lid an enamelled scene of a landscape with a chateau and a lake in perfect miniature detail.

Thomas took it out of her hand and opened it. "This one was made in France about 1760. Snuff was very fashionable among the upper classes. The aristocracy and wealthy people had boxes for all occasions - like fashion accessories. They made popular gifts, and people commissioned them with a particular colour scheme or a scene that had some significance to the person who was going to use it."

Mia lifted another tiny box out of the case. "Look at this miniature portrait of a young girl and a spaniel – it's lovely, such perfect detail."

She opened it and read the engraved text on the inside of the lid.

"Sir William Knowles from his daughter Caroline 18th December 1808".

Thomas smiled. "You've picked one of my favourites. It's special because there's documented provenance – which means that I know who made it, where it was made and what the inscription relates to. And I know who has owned it after the original owner and so on - it's a very interesting one."

He took it and closed the lid, and then flicked it open using only the fingers of the hand holding it.

"That's a little piece of snob-value dexterity from the era. In London the elegant Regency dandies had little mannerisms, and that's one of them – I suppose it singled out the ones who were in the know from those who just aspired to be fashionable. When I read about it, I practiced with this particular box till I'd learnt the trick."

Mia had never met anyone with a hobby like this, and the

historical connection and the tiny perfection of the boxes enchanted her.

She smiled her thanks. "Thank you for showing me – they are lovely! Some other time I would really love to look at them all properly and in daylight and hear their stories. But we'd better not keep Carl waiting."

As they walked across the dark garden, Thomas told her that he had bought his first antique snuffbox in an English antique shop about fifteen years earlier and had collected them ever since.

"Some I have bought in auctions in Europe by being an absentee bidder. Technology has made that much easier, but I still like it best when I can wander around galleries and antique shops and actually see and touch them before I buy one."

Carl was busy at the stove and Thomas set the table, obviously a familiar routine, and Mia leaned against the dividing counter between the kitchen and the room itself and studied the two men while she listened to them talking. Thomas was probably late thirties or maybe early forties, and Carl was in his eighties, and it was easy to see that they were genuinely close friends, not just landlord and tenant. She felt pleased for Carl, who would otherwise be very lonely; he deserved the support of a good friend after all he had been through.

They ate pasta with pieces of bacon, red peppers and capers in a cream sauce, and what Carl called a winter salad from his garden.

"I've got this perfect corner you see, where the sun blasts down more than half the day even in winter and it's up against the dark wall, so it stays warm. In the summer I grow tomatoes there, but during the winter I raise a crop of leafy salad things, just bits and pieces and some winter veges."

It was not until they had finished dinner and were sitting down with a cup of coffee in front of the fire that Mia brought the conversation back to her story. At some stage during the evening Thomas had become another trusted person and she was completely frank.

"What I'd like to do is to get a copy of the audiotape that was made during the second meeting at the police station yesterday. John MacFarlane – he's the older of the two police officers who were present - he said he would duplicate it as an audio file, so you can listen to it on your computer. And then you'll have the full chronological story, complete in every detail as I told it to those who were at the meeting. And we taped the discussion that followed too - when we debated where to take things from here."

She gave them a brief outline of what they had done to warn Steve Irwin about the possible accident and mentioned the uncertainty of whether it could be assumed that what had happened in That Time would occur again in This Time. Thomas and Carl both had plenty of theories and it was obvious that they had discussed this many times before. After a few minutes Mia simply sat and listened until Carl interrupted himself.

"Sorry Mia! Thomas and I are old hands at theorizing about this. Over time we've developed a range of ideas, but we have always been working from the only thing we knew – that I was moved forward in time. Your case has added another dimension, and then there is your interesting prediction experiment - more grist for the mill."

Thomas walked across the room and picked up a bottle of wine to top up their glasses. Mia studied him and thought how strange it was that when he moved across the room towards the kitchen, she saw his face from one side and saw an intelligent and good-natured face with a ready smile. When he walked back, she saw his other side, and the scar combined with his height and muscular build gave a completely different impression; he looked brutish from this side. She could imagine that many people found his face off-putting, and how hard it would be to live with negative reactions.

Suddenly it was quarter to midnight and Mia jumped to her feet. "How did it get so late? I'll turn into a pumpkin any minute! I must go, it's a working day tomorrow. Thank you so much for having me." She started looking around for her things. "It's been great - I hope you'll both come and have a meal at my place soon – how about Sunday? You can't imagine how wonderful it is to be with people who understand things, it nearly makes me feel normal."

She picked up her bag and her car keys and kissed Carl's cheek, and Thomas walked her to her car.

· · ·

He returned to help Carl tidy up after dinner, and while they were doing the dishes, Carl said casually, "If I was forty years younger, I'd ask her out. She's just lovely, that Mia! I think she liked you."

Thomas made no comment, just continued drying cutlery and putting it in the drawer with his back turned. Carl looked at his reflection in the window over the sink and wondered if he dared take the comment a step further but thought better of it.

Half an hour later Thomas walked across to his own house, let himself in and locked the back door. While he cleaned his teeth, he studied his face in the mirror. He turned his head, first one way and then the other. He was a scary sight from one side and OK from the other, but he had deliberately sat down at the table, so Mia would see the scarred side while they ate. He knew that his need to show women his bad side was perverse, challenging them to like him. He pushed the thought to one side and went to bed.

32

———————

The office felt claustrophobic and everything Mia did seemed irritatingly trivial and uninviting. She longed for this endless Monday to be over and tried to understand the reason for her listless mood, and why it made everything she tried to work on seem so boring. Maybe it was like the post-baby blues you hear about; the build-up is intense and full of anticipation and excitement, and then suddenly it is over. And nobody would dare to admit that after the first week, they think, "Is that it? Where are the tickertape parades and the brass bands?"

The previous weeks had been full of activity and new ventures, new people and discoveries, and time had flown. She had been full of energy and had felt capable of anything. Now she sat at her desk holding a pen and looking blankly at the pages of a report she was editing and wondered how she would last to the end of the day. The thought of Irwin's reaction to her letter and the DVD had been uppermost in her mind since she first opened her eyes that morning.

Grant Clarkson came by to discuss her involvement in his project, keen to progress her involvement.

"Alan seems pretty relaxed about it - he said he was happy for us to map it out between us. I don't think we are likely to use up too much of your time."

"How long will it go on for? I can be flexible with my time most weeks, but sometimes I might have to negotiate with others to be available."

"Oh, it will definitely need to be flexible. I'm giving the teams two weeks for the preliminary brainstorming sessions and a bit of detailed work-up in amongst it. And you'll be up to date with their suggestions and plans and able to critique them from a business angle. And perhaps we'll want to involve you for a bit longer with whichever creative team gets the go-ahead."

Mia entered the first project meeting on Wednesday in her computer diary and felt marginally more upbeat when Grant left. This was something new and different and it would give her an insight into the whole development process. Until now she had only contributed to projects on an ad-hoc basis when her skills were needed; the opportunity to see the entire process was excit-ing, provided nothing ruined the pleasure of it in This Time.

Just after three, Alice called from reception and asked if Mia was ready to go for a cup of coffee. They went up the stairs discussing their respective weekends, and Mia sensed a restraint in Alice, as if she was holding something back. Perhaps a casual remark would relax the situation.

"I loved that shawl you bought on Saturday – you looked gorgeous prancing around showing it off."

"Did you really think so? I was a bit worried afterwards that I'd got carried away and behaved like a real twit."

"Goodness no - not at all!"

Mia was genuinely surprised; surely this wasn't what Alice was worried about.

"You looked so sweet and funny, like a little girl with a new dress."

"Mia, tell me honestly," said Alice in an up-tight voice when they had found a quiet corner to sit. "Are you keen on Callum?"

Mia understood instantly that she must make a very clear statement now, but she was also acutely aware of the fact that Callum might be more interested in her than she was in him.

"Not in the slightest, if you mean in a romantic way. I don't know him that well - he only called in casually on Saturday. He dropped me home on Thursday after I went out with some of the guys from the creative side, but that's the only other time he's been to my place before Saturday."

Alice relaxed visibly, relieved and pleased.

"I didn't know him at all, really, and I never thought he'd be my type – from just observing him, I mean. I never had a proper conversation with him before, but I really like him. We had such fun talking on the way home from your place – he's good company and we seem to have the same sense of humour. But then I got worried in case you were already interested in him – I wouldn't want to get in the way or anything."

"You go for it, Alice! I'm bound to get to know him better, because I'm going to work on a project with the creative teams but forget the romantic bit - he's not my type."

She knew with absolute certainty that she would never fall in love or even have a casual affair with him, but the idea of Alice and Callum getting together was an intriguing idea. She must nurture this developing connection because it fitted so well with her plans to prevent disaster for Alice.

Aloud she said, "He seemed very taken with your performance with the shawl, and he took it really well when you teased him. Actually, now that I think about it, he seemed to like being teased."

Alice brightened up and finished her coffee in one gulp. "Duty calls, Wendy wants me to be back bang on time today, because she's got loads of mail-outs to put in envelopes. And if I don't let her go, she'll come out at the end of the day and ask me to help her - she's just looking for an excuse."

When they parted, Mia reached out and touched Alice's arm.

"I really mean it – go for it. I have a good feeling about you and Callum."

And Alice giggled and walked down the corridor with a new spring in her step.

Back behind her desk, Mia reflected on the many little things that made this time strand different from That Time. So far, everything that was different had been instigated by her and she felt a prickle of excitement when she considered it in detail. She had made a decision to change her style for Sarah's dinner evening, to publicly denounce Barb, to change the apartment, and she had told Josh not to sit on her desk. None of those things happened in That Time and all of them would have consequences downstream. She hadn't come across anything yet that was different due to the actions of anyone else, though it might happen later on. And if she was right, then Alice and Callum getting together could mean that Alice would not get into a relationship with the abusive guy.

She found herself planning to mention it to Carl and Thomas on Sunday. In fact, she wished she could talk to them right now; Thomas had such a thorough way of thinking things through, he considered his answers; he would probably never reply just for the sake of having something to say. She forced herself to abandon speculation and returned to the boring report and the rest of the day's tasks.

When she got home that evening, she gave in to the urgency she had managed to keep at bay all day, dropped her bag and jacket on the floor in the chair in the hall and went straight to the study to turn the computer on, only to find that there was nothing from Steve Irwin.

It felt as if someone had slammed a door in her face. Even a completely dismissive response would have been better, because then she would have been able to start an email dialogue or get John or Lorraine to email him in the hope of convincing him. This way, she would never know if Steve himself had seen the DVD, and she had no way of communicating with him to reinforcing her warning; it was a dead end. But maybe there would be something tomorrow, she comforted herself, maybe the little parcel had not been delivered as soon as promised.

Seething with frustration she kicked off her shoes and changed out of her office clothes. She could try again to find a private phone number for the Irwin's, because if she could only speak to him, she might be able to convince him that the warning wasn't a hoax. Mia searched and read everything she could find on the Internet and the only number she could find was the one to the Zoo. She dialled it with trembling fingers, rehearsing in her mind what she would say, but the reply was that he was away "for a few days" and no, they could not give out his cell phone number.

* * *

At nine on Wednesday morning Mia went to the first meeting with the creative teams, and sat quietly while Grant set the scene, outlined the process he wanted them to follow, gave them a deadline and then left the room. As soon as he had gone, mild mayhem broke out, and Mia sat back with her pad and pen untouched on the table in front of her and said nothing for the rest of the meeting. At times she found it hard not to laugh out loud, she could feel the corners of her mouth twitching, but she gradually began to see that there was a mad kind of structure developing. They all seemed to find it natural to constantly interrupt and contradict each other, but they were actually developing ideas and going forward. She wondered if they borrowed each other's ideas sometimes, and if it led to trouble, or if the things they tossed around in sessions like these were without ownership. By the time Grant returned two hours later, they had made progress of sorts, and she felt that the meeting had been productive. Grant set a time for another meeting the following Wednesday, and everyone drifted off in different directions.

"So, what did you learn?" Grant laughed at Mia's expression, and she had to admit she was amazed. "Well, at least now I know how creative people hold meetings – that's a start, I suppose. I'll have to get used to the chaos aspect and maybe practice how to make myself heard in case I need to contribute or ask questions."

"We are a noisy lot sometimes, I must admit, but you'll see some results emerging soon. They will continue to work on it in their own individual ways between now and then, and we'll discuss what they come up with and let them critique each other's concepts. Normally I wouldn't continue to involve both teams after that, and if I did, I would meet with them separately, but this time we're trying a new model."

Mia admitted that she could see some advantages. "Maybe this mass approach means they'll reach a critical mass of creativity, and the result will be brilliant?"

"Yes, or they might kill each other – I wouldn't like to bet on it. In any case it's a good thing that you see it from the start and understand how they develop things. Your input will be needed sooner rather than later. If either team asks you to talk to them between meetings, I would like you to do that, if you can fit it in. You are their rational fact and cost resource."

. . .

Mia had only been back at her desk for five minutes when Callum turned up. "So - how did you like it?" He hovered in the doorway, and Mia gestured towards her visitor's chair.

"Come in and sit down.' She smiled and shook her head. 'I must admit it was a bit of an eye-opener for me, not the kind of meeting I'm used to – but I'm glad I'm getting the chance to see how you work and to be in on it from the start. I'm sure I'll learn a lot, but I felt a bit like the fifth wheel today."

"You're right – I think you will learn a lot. But we'll involve you more as things go on, so you will be part of it."

He made no move to leave, so Mia decided to try and find out what else was on his mind.

"I didn't realize until Alice told me that you two didn't know each other properly,' she said innocently. 'I thought everyone knew Alice more than just in passing. She's such a great girl - and she knows how to be a good friend, too."

She watched as a little spark appeared in Callum's eyes and thought that he really was interested in Alice. Maybe he was concerned because he kissed her the other day, and then he turned round and got intrigued with Alice five minutes later.

Aloud she said, "If you play it right, I think you could get invited to be her partner at that wedding. I know she hates the idea of going on her own, and she hasn't anyone she wants to ask."

"Really? I would have thought there would be guys lining up to be asked. She said she doesn't have a boyfriend, but she must be in demand, surely?"

"Oh yes, she has plenty of guys wanting to date her, but she's a bit choosy."

The rest of the week was no better than the start, and by Thursday evening there had still been no response from Australia. Mia rang Lorraine to vent her frustration, but Lorraine was more philosophical.

"Don't fret! Just wait and see what happens - if Irwin isn't injured or killed before your sister reaches London, then we can ask him if he changed his plans or took precautions or whatever. Or maybe his fate is different this time around."

"I know - that's what is driving me crazy. Sarah and James get to London on Tuesday next week, so it's not long now."

33

Mia mooched around the apartment most of Saturday, unable to settle down to anything constructive. Miles called and offered to pick her up on his way to John's place for dinner, saying he was picking up Paul too and would be outside about quarter to seven. Mia wondered vaguely where Lorraine was, but she was probably out somewhere else and would go straight to John's.

She diverted her impatience by making a real production of getting dressed. Not that she had to dress up, but with new and interesting clothes it was fun to experiment, and she managed to kill an hour, doing her face, and trying on different things.

John's place was hard to find, though it was in a short street just off Parnell Road, and they drove past it once without realizing and had to make a second circuit around the block and then finding a place to park necessitated another detour. As they walked towards the two-story townhouse, Mia listened to the men talking without taking anything in, deep in thought about Alice and Callum. Paul pressed the doorbell and to Mia's surprise Lorraine opened the door.

"I got here early, so I'm helping with the preparations," she said casually and led the way up the stairs with no signs of having anything to hide. John was in the kitchen and turned around to say hello but stayed where he was.

Lorraine said, "I'm not allowed near the cooking end, so I am being the maid," and John said, "Nonsense – it's just that I like cooking without anyone giving me advice. Why don't you all have a drink and give me one too? I put some bubbly in the fridge, so we could start with that."

Mia watched fascinated as Lorraine went straight to the right cupboard and got out champagne flutes. She had clearly had champagne here before, and if she had, it must have been in the last week; Mia watched and wondered.

"It smells fantastic!" exclaimed Paul when they sat down to eat. "And it looks great too – what exactly is it?"

"Smoked salmon baked in a crust of breadcrumbs, herbs and orange zest, with steamed baby leeks as a side and mashed parsnip," said John and reached for the wine bottle. "But I forgot to check if everyone likes fish – if you don't, you can have a double helping of dessert to compensate.'

"Very impressive," said Miles later and accepted another helping of salmon. "Where did you learn to cook like this? It's as good as a five-star restaurant."

John smiled. "It's not that special. I was married for a few years, and my wife taught at a restaurant school, so it was inevitable that I picked up a lot from her. Whenever we ate out, she would figure out what the ingredients were and how it was put together and sort of rate the meal, so I learnt both theory and practice."

He topped up his glass and added without any sign of grievance, "We divorced a few years ago – she left me to marry an Australian, a vegetarian of all things, and I bought this townhouse - and here I live my quiet and orderly life and amuse myself by cooking nice food."

He raised his glass, and they toasted the idea of a quiet and orderly life before Lorraine changed the subject.

"Well, we managed to avoid fretting about the Irwin thing for an hour and a half - which is a great relief, because I know Mia's twitching to find out what's going on."

Mia sighed. "This week's been torture. I just can't stop thinking of it. I alternate between hoping I'm completely wrong and wanting it to happen – I think I'm losing my mind. At least we know that if it *is* going to happen it will be before Tuesday, because that's the day Sarah and James get to London, and I know they'd heard about it before they got there."

As the evening progressed speculations about Lorraine and John had continued to pop up in Mia's mind, and now that she was alert to it, she saw little signals of mutual attraction. She wondered if Miles or Paul had noticed, but there was no sign that they had; maybe men paid less attention to these things.

It was nearly midnight when the party broke up, and there had been no further discussion about time strand theories. It was as if they had put the topic on hold by unspoken consent until the next stage was reached, which was calming and a nice change from the last two times they had met.

Miles drove Paul and Mia home, despite his several glasses of wine and made light of Paul's offer to drive.

"If we get stopped, I'll have to lie down on the floor, so they don't see me," said Paul. "I would be in real trouble for being in a car with a DIC driver."

"But worse for me," said Miles carelessly. "I'd look great in court, wouldn't I - first defending a client and then being in the dock myself."

Mia was only half listening; she was thinking of Lorraine saying that she would help John tidy up and then drive herself home and admitted to herself that she was envious. She could recreate in her mind that intense feeling of wanting to be with someone all the time, of hardly being able to resist reaching out to touch the other person, of being held and making love and going to sleep with someone. Would she ever feel like that again?

When they dropped her off, she went inside and got ready to go to bed with a stream of thoughts running through her head. After Greg died, she had shut herself away and she hadn't thought of sex at all until just recently.

Is it because I've taken charge and got some confidence back that I'm thinking of it now? I looked at Paul and noticed how attractive he is, and I was tempted to reach out and touch his arm, but I think that was more to do with that wonderful colour and silky look of his skin than anything else. I feel the same way about Lorraine's skin – I often want to reach over and touch her. Perhaps I am coming to life again generally, not just in action, but inside.

. . .

She turned her bedside light out, pushed her pillow into shape and closed her eyes, and just before sleep claimed her, the image of Thomas's hand holding that exquisite little snuff box surfaced in her mind.

The morning was wet and the big windows in the living room were streaming with rain carried on a strong wind from the north-east. Despite the temperature inside being the same as always, Mia felt chilled. She put on a thick sweatshirt and socks and sat down to breakfast, thinking of her day. She had invited Carl and Thomas for dinner, so she must decide what to cook and then go to the supermarket, and there was some washing and ironing to do. To think that only a few weeks ago she had been looking around for things to do to pass the time, and now she hardly had time to keep up with it all. She thought of Sarah and James, who were due to arrive in London soon and the knot of anxiety reappeared in her chest. If anything was going to happen to Irwin, it would happen soon.

Shaking herself to dispel the mixture of guilt and anticipation that gripped her, she got up from the table and went to put the washing in the machine and fetched her recipe folder. She wanted to cook something special, not just a simple dish that could be thrown together in a few minutes, however delicious it might be.

Leafing through the folder she scanned the mix of cuttings and the occasional recipe in someone's handwriting. It was like going through an album of memories: here was the Floating Island pudding her aunt used to make, and on the next page a cutting from a magazine with pictures showing how to stuff chicken legs with feta, pine nuts and grated zucchini, which she mentally marked as a possibility. Her mother's recipe for Beef Stroganoff was tempting on a rainy day and so was the Cuisine recipe for beef sautéed with picked walnuts.

This was the first time she had looked at her recipe folder since before Greg died, and it was not until the washing machine beeped, that she finally made up her mind: Beef Stroganoff, Hasselback potatoes and her favourite mixture of peas and thinly sliced leeks. By the time she had transferred the washing to the dryer she had decided on a dessert, so she wrote her shopping list and went out into the uninviting rain, grateful that the wind had died down.

It was a surprise to realize that it was still only nine o'clock. She had woken early and got on with the day without considering the time. The supermarket was unearthly quiet and nearly empty, the aisles seemed twice as wide as usual. She read the labels on ice cream packets to find one made with real vanilla seeds and had a serious conversation with the butcher behind the meat counter about whether it was a waste to buy top quality steak for the Stroganoff. She rambled through the aisles in a dreamy way quite unlike the rush and crush of weekday shopping and emerged to find that the parking lot was still nearly empty, and the city felt hushed in the cloak of grey drizzle.

34

———

It was the perfect dull Sunday to stay inside and prepare for guests, and with a Dolly Parton CD playing in the background, Mia started preparing the Stroganoff. She looked at the lined-up ingredients from her mother's recipe and knew that the mix of tomato paste, sour cream, mushrooms, onion and wine would be delicious - impossible to go wrong with this one. She had always enjoyed cooking for special occasions and having the time to do it without rushing added to the pleasure. The casserole went into the oven to cook slowly for an hour and a half; after that it could sit and cool, ready to be reheated at dinner time. She peeled potatoes and searched for the big wooden spoon that she had bought especially for Hasselback potatoes. Her mother had always served potatoes done this way with Stroganoff, and she could see no reason to break with tradition.

"There are two tricks you have to know about Hasselback potatoes," her Mum used to say. "The first trick is to put the peeled potato in the wooden spoon and holding the potato and the spoon firmly together while slicing very thin slices through the potato until the knife meets the rim of the wooden spoon. That way you avoid slicing right through the potato by mistake, which is easy to do when you slice deep and thin. The second trick is to baste the potatoes several times with butter while they roast, not just once or twice like most people do."

. . .

Mia thought of how much her mother would have liked to see what she was doing, while she sliced her potatoes very thinly and put them in a bowl of cold water. It was not lunch time yet, but it was already hours since she had breakfast. She sat at the table with a sandwich and a cup of coffee looking out through the rain-washed windows without really seeing the view. Her final year in That Time had taken her into new and frightening mental territories, and she treasured the present. The opportunity to take control had changed her life, but in the back of her mind a cautionary little voice whispered that things might not last; what she had unexpectedly been given, might be taken away. A shiver ran briefly down her spine, she shook herself to dispel the feeling and went to tidy up the kitchen.

The study was still a work in progress. To get it back to where it had been in August 2007, she had been forced to repeat the sorting and discarding, piling things into stacks on the floor and gradually emptying shelves and drawers. She paused in the doorway and tried to estimate how much she had left to do and sighed. Most of the clutter was sorted out, though some was left in a pile in the corner to be gone through at a later date, and the shelves were tidy again. Now she must tackle the file cabinet and a couple of document boxes that had always lived under Greg's end of the desk. The first things she saw when she opened the bottom drawer were the registration papers for Greg's Ducati, and she realized she had never claimed the insurance for it; a reminder of how dysfunctional she had been in That Time. Now she would claim the insurance and the money could go towards the new furniture. There was an ironical justice in the thought that Greg's motorbike extravagance would subsidize the revamp of the apartment. She smiled without malice and put the papers to one side.

Early that evening, on her way to open the front door, she glanced around the living area, checked her face in the hall mirror and realized that right now she felt happy, truly happy and pleased with life.

Thomas carried a bag with two bottles of wine, and Carl handed her a bouquet of very tall dark blue irises wrapped in clear cellophane.

"I hope you have a tall vase, but these were so splendid we couldn't go past them."

She kissed his cheek. "Thank you! And as luck has it, that's one of the things I bought in that furniture shop during my mad shopping spree– a very tall vase. Come on in and I'll put them in water straight away."

Carl went to the windows to look out at the view and Thomas followed her to the kitchen.

"We can put this one in the fridge to keep it cool or you can keep it for another time." He held up a bottle of chardonnay. "And I bought a bottle of late harvest Riesling in case we're having dessert, and that definitely needs chilling."

The domestic activity of opening wine, handing out glasses and nibbles and putting the flowers in water made the occasion casual and friendly and broke the ice. Carl admired the view and the new furniture and said he hoped the rain would stop, so they could see further. He was interested in everything, so Mia showed him the rest of the apartment.

"I've never been in an apartment up high before," he said. "I never thought it would be like this. I thought it would be very cramped. When you see the balconies so close together you think each flat is tiny - but your place kind of goes around the corner – and it had a balcony in the bedroom as well. I never thought of that!"

Mia showed him that he could see the Sky tower if he looked in the right direction. As she was pointing it out, she sensed that Thomas had come over and was standing immediately behind her, she could feel the heat coming from his solid body. She glanced over her shoulder and saw him looking not at the view but down at her; there was a brief moment of stillness, then Thomas stepped back and looked round the room.

"You've done a tremendous job with the décor, Mia. Very stylish, but it still looks like a home. I went to see a client at home recently, and the place was like a display in a shop - not the slightest sign that anyone lived there, elegant and sterile – probably done by a stylist or whatever decorators are called these days."

Carl turned from the window to study the room. "I only see other people's homes on TV, but I can see that this very smart and lot better put together than my place. Or Thomas's for that matter."

He grinned at Thomas, who was obviously not put out by the

comparison. "Quite right - my place is a boring mess. I inherited some furniture from my mother, and I've never got around to sorting the place out, so a lot of stuff is there by default, so to speak. And not having any creative ability, I haven't done anything about it. Perhaps I could hire you as a consultant, Mia?"

Mia was quick to disclaim any merit. "It was easy, because I had sorted out the look I wanted in design magazines - and all I did was get rid of absolutely everything I didn't positively like, which left very little - in fact, hardly anything at all."

Not wanting to make Thomas feel that his house needed the sort of look she had created here, she added, "And your house is a lovely old villa with high ceilings – you might like to furnish it in a style that suits it."

Carl's sense of 1940's economy got the better of him. "I hope you didn't just give all your stuff away to some second-hand shop, Mia. You need to be careful when you're living on your own and there's nobody else to tide you over, if you get ill and can't go to work."

"Oh no, I gave the lot to an auction firm, and they have what they call an antique shop as well, so they have paid me up front for the stuff they put into the shop. The rest will be auctioned – actually, any day now. Not that there was anything worth a lot of money – just some things from family, the bed we bought when we got married and lots of crockery and ornaments, old linen and stuff. I got so ruthless that I even got rid of a few wedding presents I didn't like."

Thomas chuckled and raised his wine glass. "Here's to you - just the sort of person I need to come and be ruthless at my place. Name your fee and the job's yours."

His words and tone were joking, but his eyes were hard to read; was he serious? She avoided replying directly by picking up the wine bottle and turning to Carl. "Can I top up your glass, Carl?"

The half hour before they sat down to eat was punctuated by Mia's visits to the kitchen to baste the potatoes, and when she announced that dinner would be ready in a couple of minutes, Carl went off the bathroom, and Thomas followed her to the kitchen to ask if he could carry something.

"You could help me decide which wine to have." She pointed. "We are having Beef Stroganoff, so we must have a red. There are three different ones over there by the phone, so please open the one you think would be best and put it on the table."

Thomas looked at each bottle carefully. "I think we'll have this Te Mata cabernet-merlot – it's a wonderful wine, lots of personality to go with the beef. Did you buy it especially for tonight?"

Mia felt herself blush. "No, I've had it tucked away for a couple of years. Greg wasn't a wine drinker, so I've been waiting to share it with someone who'll appreciate it."

She bent down and took the potatoes out of the oven to avoid looking at him, felt his searching glance like a touch, but all he said was, "I look forward to it."

The meal was a great success. Carl had never had Stroganoff and decided it had completely changed his mind about casseroles. "Next time you ask us for dinner you'll have to make it again, it's just lovely."

Thomas confessed he was a terrible cook, who could only produce grilled sausages and mashed potatoes and often bought frozen meals for convenience.

"It's a bit like the inside of my house. I don't know how to be creative, but I know how to appreciate the creativity of other people. I know that what you've achieved is great and I know that this food is top class, but I couldn't do any of it myself."

The conversation ranged from politics to TV programmes and Mia was interested to find that Carl had a complete grasp of everything on TV and liked the most surprising things. And he in turn was stunned at the gaps in Mia's TV education.

"You mean you haven't watched Outrageous Fortune?! I can't believe it - it's hilarious, I never miss it. I hope they do another series after this one."

Thomas was more a film and book man than a TV watcher. He and Mia discovered that they both liked John Irving and agreed that they got impatient waiting for his next book, because he took such ages to write them. Mia mentioned Ken Follett's *Pillars of the Earth* and then had to explain to Thomas what the title referred to, as he had not read it.

"I'd love to see the medieval cathedrals," said Mia, her eyes alight with enthusiasm. "They have everything, not just the stupendous architecture, but centuries of embedded history and art. One day I'll go to Europe and do a tour of cathedrals."

"Yeah, they are wonderful. You stand there and imagine you can feel all the grief and joy and drama that have seeped into the stones over centuries. It's like being part of a historical continuum. Well, you're obviously supposed to feel religious, but I'm afraid that's beyond me. I have to be content with appreciating how beautiful they are."

Carl, who was still slowly eating, looked up at Thomas. "Remember when you were there last and you sent me a postcard from that wonderful church in Paris, what was it called – the one that has two levels? I've still got the card - I use it as a bookmark."

"That's Sainte-Chapelle - a gem of a place, I go back to it nearly every time I'm in Paris."

The conversation reverted to books; Mia and Sarah had been brought up in a household where reading was part of daily life and she loved discussing books. Thomas had not, but he had acquired the habit because he was curious and liked to find things out.

"I read more non-fiction than fiction - a lot of history and biographies from the historical eras that interest me – mainly the period from the Restoration to the end of the Peninsular Wars. And, of course, I read everything I can find about snuff boxes."

"I guessed that when you showed them to me." Mia and laughed. "Being smart and putting two and two together. And some time I would really love to see them properly and hear the stories. I wasn't just being polite when I said that."

"Of course, he'll show you," said Carl. "He loves showing them off – the trouble is that he never has anyone to show them to. I'm always telling him how lucky it is for me that he never brings any friends home, or has a girlfriend, because I'm the one who benefits. He has time to spend with me, which is really nice."

When Mia brought the dessert, Carl was fascinated. "Fancy pouring alcohol over ice cream, never had anything like it before. It smells delicious, what is it?"

Mia got the bottle of Bailey's out to show him what it looked like. "Oh yes, I recognize this - they used to have ads for it on TV a few years ago when they still allowed alcohol advertisements. I'm going to get some of that next time I go shopping."

Thomas laughed. "I agree, Carl. This is a dessert that even I could make, it's just that I never thought of it before."

They moved to the comfortable chairs to have coffee and Thomas looked at the painting of the man in the window and the irises in the vase on the table below it.

"The colour of those flowers is perfect next to that marvellous painting, very effective."

"Yes, it works, doesn't it?" She said no more, but a thrill of excitement ran through her; he recognized the effect.

And then they inevitably reverted to the Irwin situation, it was like a conversational magnet. However hard she to avoid the subject, it crouched in the back of her mind, like a beast waiting to leap. This time Thomas started it and asked if there had been any response from Irwin, and Mia shook her head, reluctant to talk about it, but she must reply.

"No, nothing. It's driving me mad with frustration, but there's nothing I can do now - apart from wait."

"They're probably very careful not to make it easy for people to reach them at home," said Carl. "You read about celebrities getting hounded - I can't imagine what it must be like to have people always watching you and commenting on what you do. And imagine how much mail they probably get."

"Yes, I'm sure you're right, Carl, but there is a risk that they will overlook my little packet among all the other stuff."

"When's the 'deadline' for the Irwin accident? Sorry, no pun intended. You said last Sunday that you knew it must have happened before a certain date." Thomas echoed Mia's own thoughts.

"If it *is* going to happen, it must be today or tomorrow, I think. All I can remember for a fact is that Sarah and James had heard the news before they got to London. And they get there on Tuesday evening – that's UK time, so it's Wednesday morning for us. I remember James saying that he had never realized that Irwin was truly world famous until they got to London just after it happened, and it was all over the media for days."

Thomas studied Mia's face and said slowly, "You're really worried about this, aren't you? Do you feel that if he's killed, you will be partly responsible? And if he doesn't get killed, you might never know if they aborted the dive, or if your prediction was wrong?"

Mia was slightly unnerved by how accurately he had summed up her conflicting emotions, but it was a nice that someone understood that mingled sensation of hope and fear.

"Exactly! There is constantly a feeling of apprehension in the back of my mind – fear and hope sort of mixed up, if that makes sense? On the one hand I want to save his life, of course I do - but on the other it would prove a point if he were killed. God, how I wish I had never thought of that accident, when I drew up that proof document! It's made it too personal - it makes me feel like an executioner."

"I can see that, but if it happens you must remember that you didn't cause the accident - and you did your best to prevent it happening again. You are a marginal player in this drama - you can't change things unless others choose to listen to you." He gave her a wry smile. "You don't really hold the power of life and death even if it feels like that right now."

Mia eyes filled with tears; she got up and walked over to the table to get the bottle of Bailey's and replied while she had her back to the others, trying to sound casual.

"You are right - I *was* beginning to feel that I'm personally responsible for saving his life."

She returned and handed the bottle to Thomas. "I'll get us some clean glasses for this." As he took the bottle, his fingers brushed against her hand, and a surge of intense physical attraction flashed through her like an electric shock. She walked back to the kitchen and imagined she could feel her hand tingle and nearly stumbled.

My God – I want him to touch me again, she thought, and if Carl wasn't here, I might throw myself at him. This is mad, can you fall in love so fast - or is it just lust? I must pull myself together or he will notice.

When they left just after eleven, Carl hugged her, but Thomas only said goodnight. She closed the door and stood for a moment leaning against it, trying to decide if he was uninterested, just kind and perceptive, or if he was attuned to her feelings because he was attracted to her. He had said or done nothing that he might not have said to any good friend, not even shaken her hand on arriving or leaving. Perhaps he did not feel that electrifying touch when she handed him the bottle.

She continued to wonder about her reaction to Thomas, while she stacked the dishwasher and tidied up leftover food, pleased that she had managed to conceal how she felt and hoping it had not been obvious. There was something about him, a reserve or a barrier of some kind. Every now and then she had felt that his attention was strongly focused on her, but then the connection was severed as if it had never been, for no apparent reason. She decided that however much she was attracted to him, she could not let him see how she felt, or it might skew her friendship with Carl.

She stared blankly at the casserole soaking in the sink and her thoughts reverted to Steve Irwin; within the next 24 hours the suspense would be over. She knew sleep would be slow to come with so much going on in her mind and tried to close her mind to worry.

35

———

Mia was leaning towards the computer screen scanning lists of document titles, frustrated at the time she had spent searching for the file she wanted. She knew she had seen it recently and it had the words 'as projected' in the title. The search function had unfortunately brought up two hundred and fifty-two files with names that included the word 'projected', and she had only eliminated a dozen so far. She plugged on for another few minutes before the penny dropped, and she leaned back in her chair and laughed helplessly. Of course! The file she was trying to find didn't exist yet; she had remembered sitting there admiring the formatting and thinking it might be useful to copy one day, but that wasn't in This Time, it happened in That Time. The thought of plagiarising something that did not yet exist was irresistibly funny.

"Well, you *are* having fun! Care to share the joke?" Josh was standing in the doorway looking amused and suddenly she felt flustered.

"No joke - just early onset of memory loss, I'm afraid. I managed to completely confuse myself just then."

Something flickered behind Josh's eyes, but all he said was, "Oh, well, that sort of thing sometimes happens on a Monday morning," and continued on his way.

Mia looked at the empty doorway, puzzled and trying to interpret his reaction. What was that strange expression that flitted

187

across his face; something like satisfaction or even elation - but gone in a split second? All she had said was ... and then she got it. She had said that she had confused herself, and maybe Josh had thought what a great quote that could be, when the so-called errors in that spreadsheet were discovered way down the track.

She turned back to the computer, located the crucial Excel file on the shared drive, and Snap! there it was: he had done it. The totals were different; she flicked her cursor over the cells in the 'Totals' row and saw instantly that Josh had indeed done exactly what she remembered from That Time.

He had taken the top row of expenses out of the formula, and that reduced the total expenses, so the viability looked good. And the embedded comments had been removed, just like in That Time. She wished she could go to Alan straight away and tell him, but she must be patient and make sure the proposal was final before she spoke up. Josh might say he hadn't done a final check yet and brush it off. But she could not let it be presented to the clients with false data like last time, it would damage both her and the company, so she would continue to monitor progress.

She went out for lunch in a café, eager to be away from the office and give herself some space to think without interruptions. There were two key things to keep in mind: she must find out when the presentation meeting was to take place, and where. Sometimes it was at the clients' place and sometimes at the office, but the date would be in the diaries of Josh and Alan. She thought it might fit Josh's personality to have a flashy leather diary with brassbound corners like a mogul of the past, and she would try to get a look in his office. Alan used his computer diary but there was no chance that she could access that. She would have to pretend to come across the printed version of the presentation before it was sent out and then press the alarm button.

She was prepared for it to take a few days before a good opportunity presented itself, but serendipity decided to play a part that afternoon when Alan came to see her.

"I've told them to put the call through to you, if the marketing chap from Jobling & Brown calls – hope you don't mind? You know all the details of that costing as well as I do, you did the brand research. Josh and I have a meeting at Hillman's, and we'll be lucky if we make it back by five."

. . .

She made sure they had left before she picked up a couple of pages of work notes and headed for the copier, made a set of copies and walked back to Josh's door. There was nobody in sight in the corridor and no sound of anyone approaching; feeling furtive and devious, she went in holding her papers like a shield. If anyone came in and found her there, she would pretend that she was dropping off some papers for Josh. The computer was on, and his satchel was on the cabinet beside the desk. By walking along the desk towards the wall, she kept out of sight from the door and could just reach the satchel by leaning across the desk. There was no diary there or on the desk; he might have it with him and she would try again later.

She stood thinking for a moment, weighing up the risk of going to the other side of the desk and having a look at the pile of papers on his filing cabinet and then maybe even checking the computer diary. Being caught snooping was not part of her plan. She picked up a pen from the desk, so she could claim to be writing a note on the papers she had brought, and carefully lifted the untidy pile of papers on the filing cabinet, no diary there either. She double-checked the desk and the top of the cupboard and found nothing. Finally, and watching the doorway as much as the screen, she flicked a fingertip on the mouse. The screensaver folded back to reveal an open Word file and, at the bottom of the screen, the Outlook icon, open and minimized.

It was the work of a second to click on it. With her heart pounding in her chest, she switched from the email folder to the diary and scanned the entries. Her eyes flew down the columns, her mind busy trying to interpret abbreviations and initials. She changed the display to Month rather than Week and found what she was looking for – on September 12, a three-hour block of time had been marked off from 2 pm for the presentation meeting. The word 'here' must mean that the meeting would be held in the third-floor meeting room, just as it had in That Time. Just thinking of the humiliation that she had faced in that room made her skin crawl, and her resolve strengthened. Josh deserved what was coming.

Feeling increasingly nervous, she quickly restored everything to its original state and minimized Outlook, leaving the computer exactly as it had been. The screensaver would pop up again before

Josh returned, and there would be nothing to show that she had been in his room.

Quickly she picked up her papers, checked that there was nobody in the corridor to see her coming out, and returned to her own room. Today was Monday September 4, so the report might not be finished, printed and bound until next Monday, or maybe even Tuesday morning, if things were busy. Reports and proposals were often given to Lisa to copy and bind at a very late stage, and she had heard Lisa complaining about how everyone seemed to leave things to the last minute. She would leave it until Monday, then get hold of a copy and take it straight to Alan. And when Josh tried to use her as a scapegoat, she would 'remember' that she had saved a duplicate of the original in her own folder. And if need be, she could eventually remember that she had emailed it to someone by mistake – ample proof of its original state at that date.

Mia sighed and thought of how complicated it must be to be always involved in this kind of game, to juggle half-truths and strategies. It was hard to believe that people could be bothered making whole careers out of lies and deceit. How did they ever remember all the twists and turns of what they were involved in?

The excitement and stress made Mia forgot to fret about Steve Irwin's fate for the remainder of the afternoon. When she got home, she turned the radio on and the first item on the 6 o'clock news was Irwin's death. She stood as if frozen and listened to the scant details – exactly as it had happened before. Tears ran down her cheeks and she wanted to howl with frustration and sadness. When the phone rang, she tried to stem her tears, and heard Lorraine's awestruck voice: "I just heard it on the news - he died!"

"I know," sobbed Mia. "I can't believe it – he did that bloody dive again and he wasn't even careful!"

"Now, hang on, darling. He might not have got your warning, you know. Whatever the reason, you have definitely proved that your story is true. Not that I ever doubted you, however mad it seemed."

Mia managed to stop sobbing and struggled to control her voice.

"I know - you've been marvellous. Can you do me a favour, I

feel a bit funny – it feels as if I've lost someone I know. Can you just text the others and tell them that I'm in a funny mood and I'd rather not talk to anyone tonight? To just send a message if they want to communicate?"

"Of course, I will, don't worry – they'll understand. Would you like me to come over to keep you company?"

"No thanks, not that I don't want to see you, but I just need to have some time to process this. I'll be back to normal again soon. We'll talk tomorrow."

The minute she put the phone down it rang again, and this time it was Thomas. Her heart skipped a beat at the sound of his voice, and she made an effort to sound normal.

"Mia, are you OK? I just heard the news."

"I am OK, thanks. I don't know quite how I feel – conflicting emotions you could say."

"Have you been crying? Your voice sounds strange."

And at that she started crying again and it was a moment before she could talk. His concern had completely undone her composure and she felt as upset as she had when she first spoke to Lorraine.

"Sorry - I've just been talking to Lorraine, and she calmed me down with her wonderful logic, but now I'm all in pieces again."

"I'm not surprised. I imagine you feel pleased that he proved your story and devastated that he didn't listen to your warning - all at the same time?"

He was only saying the same thing as he had said before but hearing him say it and knowing he perfectly understood her feelings touched her heart.

"Yes, that's it - in a way I feel as if I killed him. I don't know how you do it – you seem to understand."

There was a pause and when he replied he sounded slightly distant. "Well, I'm glad if it helps you feel better in some way."

It was awkward to know where to go from here, but Mia wanted to restore normality before putting the phone down. She could sense that he was guarded, that he might regret having been so personal. Perhaps he felt threatened by her frankness, or worried that she would want to be more than friends, so she thanked him for calling and said goodbye. But she remained standing by the kitchen bench for several minutes, trying to recapture the surge of comfort she had felt when they spoke, while at the same time she warned herself not to wish for anything more.

The evening stretched out before her like a tedious challenge, it felt as if someone had pulled a grey veil of gloom over her. To create a diversion, she walked to the kebab shop three blocks away and bought her favourite vegetarian kebab with plum sauce and sour cream. She carried it home in the insulated bag and ate it while watching a silly film of the kind she would normally never bother with. This is sadness therapy, she thought and refilled her wineglass, tomorrow will be better.

36

Sitting at a corner table in the staff canteen the next morning. Mia noticed that Alice kept glancing towards the door and wondered if she was keeping an eye out for Callum. She was amused and pleased, it would be nice to have something positive to balance out the negative impact of Irwin's death. If Alice and Callum made a go of it, at least she would be able to stop worrying about one thing. She knew Thomas was right and there was no way she could prevent every bad thing she remembered from happening again. She must learn to let some things go.

Aloud she said, "Are you all set for the wedding this weekend? I'm keeping my fingers crossed for fine weather."

Alice radiated excitement. "Guess what! I was going to tell you anyway, but now that you've brought it up - Callum's going to come to the wedding as my partner."

She watched for Mia's reaction and was clearly relieved when Mia was genuinely pleased. "That's great – you'll have much more fun if you bring a partner."

Alice looked as if she had personally invented Callum and all his good qualities and was just opening her mouth to say something, when her eyes lit up. Callum was crossing the room towards them, and Mia thought they must have synchronized their watches, because Callum didn't normally appear this early. Alice smiled happily while she listened to Callum telling Mia about the film they had seen at the weekend. It was a long time since Mia had watched a developing romance and it cheered her up to see the way they looked at each other.

She returned to her office in much better spirits, determined to avoid feeling responsible for everyone and everything, and when John rang after lunch, she was pleased that she could discuss the Irwin event calmly.

"I think we should meet and discuss where to from here," he said firmly. "We need to be on the same page, as they say. I am slightly concerned about you, and we must make sure we all know what you want and fit in with that."

Mia was puzzled by the way he sounded as if he suspected or knew something, but she thought it might just be the natural cautiousness of an experienced police officer.

"OK, let's do that. Why don't we meet for a drink at my place tomorrow night after work – I'll call the others and let them know."

"I'd like to call them myself, if you don't mind. I want to signal that we need to meet and make a commitment as a team, that whatever you want to happen will happen, nothing more and nothing less."

"What are you thinking? I can tell there's something on your mind – what's wrong?"

"I just worry that someone on the team might try to take advantage of you and your story – try to exploit you for fame or financial gain. Don't worry, I might be wrong, but an open discussion and an agreement by everyone on the team would make me feel happier."

Mia's mind was racing through ideas and speculation. It couldn't be Lorraine or John, which only left Miles and Paul. Something must have been said at some stage and alerted him, but what? Nothing either of them had said or done had triggered any alarms in her mind, but she was happy for John to take the lead and do what he thought was necessary.

"OK, that's fine with me, makes very good sense in fact. We discussed earlier that my life might become impossible if the media got hold of this, so let's do it. And I agree - it's better that you call the others and set the scene."

"I will – what if I tell them six tomorrow at your place, or as early as they can make it? I've checked Paul's roster and he is available, but he's got to leave at twenty to seven or so. Can I bring some beer and crisps or something?"

"Some beer would be good. I have wine and nibbles - we'll keep it simple."

For the rest of the afternoon John's words echoed through her mind. She had suspected from the start that Paul was interested in her, but perhaps he was more interested in using her for gain or fame than the usual male/female reason? Or was it Miles? And if it was, what was he after? She would let John lead the discussion, but she must state her wishes strongly and not hesitate to tell them what she wanted or didn't want.

On and off during the evening she tried to imagine how someone could exploit her, and how it would affect her. Some people might want her to recall crimes and accidents and warn those who could be injured or killed, but that thought was in the back of her mind anyway. But being able to prevent injury or death for a limited number of people could surely not present enough financial opportunity for the sort of exploitation John was warning her about. And the use-by date of her potential value was less than a year away. She only had a limited window of opportunity to offer, and then her usefulness would be over. She retired to the study and turned the computer on, hoping for something to divert her attention.

37

The next evening, they all made it by quarter to six and John got the discussion underway as soon as they had seated themselves.

"I'll start this off and try and keep it brief, because Paul has to be away early, so we don't have a lot of time. If we can't reach a conclusion that meets Mia's needs, then we'll have to continue another day. We are here to discuss how Mia's information can be useful and who can use it - and Mia will have the final say. Irwin either ignored or did not get the warning. At the moment, Mia can't recall anything else that we might be able to prevent. But that's not to say that things won't occur to her as time goes on – we all know what a funny thing memory is, and how things spring to mind for no particular reason."

Lorraine raised a finger to interrupt. "Perhaps we should go around the group and hear everyone's ideas? I've been thinking about it a lot since Irwin died. I think that anything, however nebulous, that Mia remembers - even the slightest chance that her knowledge could save someone's life, should be explored."

Paul was coming at it from a policeman's angle. "I think she should concentrate on big crimes, robberies and murders – that sort of thing. And hypnosis might help. If we could get the context of where and what, then we might be able to prevent some major incidents and save a lot of tragedy and suffering."

Mia smiled at him, relieved that so far, this nice man didn't seem to want to profit personally, though it might not do his career any harm if he was instrumental in preventing a major crime.

John was nodding in agreement. "That's a thing that occurred to me too. The big dramas would have been in the news and in the papers, sometimes for days on end, so we're more likely to tease out enough information from those rather than isolated accidents, say."

Lorraine stuck to her point. "There's no reason why Mia wouldn't remember other things as well – we should try for as much as possible, even if it doesn't contribute to a reduction of police time."

"Of course - but what sticks in your mind is the big stuff, you must agree?"

"Yes, but isolated things too, like an accident where the victim reminded you of someone or was the same age and had the same name as someone you know. Those details make events memorable - I just want Mia to keep an open mind."

Mia spoke for the first time, feeling as if they were talking about someone else. "I've been thinking of all those things since yesterday. I think waiting for the outcome of the Irwin drama - sort of put my mind on hold, but now I'm trawling through memories again. And if I remember anything, big or small, I'll work on it."

Now Miles spoke up and he sounded vaguely irritated. "It's all very well working from a humanitarian angle, so to speak but there are other things that Mia could achieve. The Melbourne Cup is coming up in a few weeks and the Trophy race in Hawke's Bay – both of them with major gains to be made. If Mia can retrieve the names of the winners we could make a nice sum of money on a simple bet. Or if there was an interesting development on the share market say, or the sale of a major company – think if we could have bought 100 shares each in Trade Me two weeks before the sale – we'd be rich!"

John spoke mildly, as if this was a new, but not particularly interesting thought.

"Well, those things could happen, of course, but they aren't important in the way preventing a disaster is. I think we need to keep our priorities focused."

Miles looked aggrieved. "I don't mean that we should do one at the expense of the other, it's just that all aspects are worth the effort. And apart from anything else, Mia might well want to sell her story. Imagine what the interest would be, if a teaser or two appeared in the media, and then hey presto there was a TV programme about the proof she set up, the events which followed and so on. It would be huge! There could be a TV series, speaking engagements, a book, a film even - the possibilities are endless. All it needs is for someone to mastermind it and manage it to best effect. Mia, you'd never have to work again."

Mia was stunned and looked at Miles as if he had turned into a monster. Lorraine spoke up in her place. "Miles, you sound as if you already have an idea about who could manage this?"

Miles mistook her meaning; he was too fired up to hear the slight sarcasm in her voice. "Yes, I do. I've thought about it a lot and I think we could manage the whole thing as a group. Or I would be happy to take it on. All it takes is a strategic plan and a tough negotiator to maximize the profit."

Mia could see that both Paul and John were about to respond and found her voice just in time to get in first.

"*No!* When I first told you my story, I made it *absolutely* clear that I was telling you something in confidence." She looked around and stopped when she got to Miles. "There is absolutely no way I want to become famous for this - it would drive me mad. I remember John saying that it could change my life forever and not for the better and he is right."

"But think of the money, think of never having to work again!" Mile's voice was one notch louder now, he was carried on a wave of combined enthusiasm and frustration. "Don't listen only to the cautious voices, Mia. Listen to practical common sense. You'll be set for life if it's done right, and I would be happy to manage all the legal aspects for you. It's a chance you will never have again. It needs to be started while Irwin's death is still news."

John had been watching Mia closely and now he intervened smoothly. "Mia, it's your call – and you have told us what the boundaries are and reminded us of what we promised at the outset. We will keep your story private unless you tell us that we can talk about it. Hopefully, we have all kept this confidential until now?"

It was clear from the way he looked around at the group that this was not a rhetorical question, he wanted an answer.

Lorraine looked straight at Mia. "I haven't mentioned it to a soul, and I won't unless you say I can."

"I have kept it completely to myself and will continue to do so," said John and looked around again, checking off each face in turn.

Paul sounded sincere. "Absolutely – same as John. Nobody will hear it from me."

Each person had ticked the box and now they all looked at Miles, who was beginning to look flustered and angry. "There's no need to look at me like that. I haven't let the cat out of the bag."

Mia felt she needed to put a stop to the debate before Paul had to leave. "I can only repeat what I already said - I'm quite certain that I only want to use the information for good." She smiled and tried to inject a bit of levity. "And in 'good' I include putting a bet on a winning horse in the Melbourne Cup, if I remember the winner's name, which isn't likely – but if I do, I'll make sure I tell you all, so we can all share the opportunity. And that goes for anything similar, I wouldn't keep anything advantageous to myself."

She took a deep breath and continued with more serious emphasis. "But I do *not* want publicity of any kind. No media interest or fame, I can think of nothing worse. I'd rather do the nine-to-five routine to earn a living and have an ordinary life than become part of the media freak show and have everyone think I can work magic for them."

John nodded. "And don't forget that if the general public got the idea that you know things in advance, there might be someone out there who'd be prepared to try something nasty to prevent you spiking their guns. It's not a risk worth taking."

Paul got up to leave and Mia followed him to the door. He hugged her and said quietly, "Don't worry, Mia. Your story's safe with us, and we won't let you down. But if you remember that horse I look forward to some unearned money for Christmas."

They were silent until the door closed behind him. Mia asked if anyone wanted another drink, but nobody did, and Lorraine picked a few things from the coffee table and took them to the kitchen, the discussion was over. John followed Lorraine with a couple of beer bottles, and Mia and Miles were left in a slightly tense silence. She could imagine that Miles was struggling to accept that his ideas had been vetoed, and to save him having to make the first effort towards normality she took the lead.

"Are you sure you don't want another glass of wine, Miles?"

He got to his feet. "No, thanks, I must go. I have a date to play squash tonight."

Mia closed the door behind him and went back into the sitting room to find John and Lorraine back on the sofa, pouring more wine and opening the round of camembert, which had sat untouched for the duration of the meeting.

"Ouch!" Mia sank down into her chair. "Can you pour me another one too? God, that was a bit of a revelation. You obviously suspected?"

John nodded grimly. "I've had a feeling all along that Miles had his eye on the main chance. He struck me from the start as someone on the make, an opportunist and as we know, happy to drive when he's had too much to drink, so lacking in common sense. Don't know why I felt like that, really - I only knew him very superficially from a court case or two when he called me about this at the start. But I didn't take to him when I got to know him a bit better."

Lorraine was thoughtful and a little embarrassed. "I'm sorry I got him involved. I've worked with him on and off in one of my part-time jobs, but I've never had any reason not to trust him."

"Don't worry – it's not your fault. You couldn't have known he'd be like this and in any case, he's not been untrustworthy yet, just on a different tack." Mia smiled at her and then returned to John's comment. "Provided we can trust Miles to keep his word there seems to be no need to worry. Do you agree John?"

"I hope you are right. I noticed that he was the only one who spoke in the past tense, no mention of the future. He said he "hadn't let the cat out of the bag" but he didn't say he wouldn't do so in the future. And everyone else was very specific about that, but perhaps it means nothing - I'll reserve my opinion of Miles until he's proved himself."

Lorraine shook her head. "I completely missed that = I must start paying more attention to how people word things, because that one went right over my head. Did you notice it, Mia?"

"No, it didn't register at all, I'm afraid. How about we have something simple to eat seeing it's getting close to everyone's normal dinner time?"

After an exploration the fridge and the pantry, they put together an omelette with fried onions and tinned mushrooms, a token gesture of a salad, and bread and cheese. They took their plates to the table and settled down to their impromptu meal. Lorraine passed the pepper grinder to Mia and studied her thoughtful face.

"What's on your mind? You look as if you're deep in thought."

"I am - but I've been pondering things for a while now. I've known from the start that the only way to contain this story is to make sure only very few people know - and that those who know are trustworthy. Apart from us – I mean the original group -Carl and Thomas know, but I would trust them both with my life. Actually, I wish Thomas had been here today. He has a kind of presence, very quiet and calm, but I think he could put a sort of mental barrier up around Miles to contain him, if you see what I mean?"

John was counting on his fingers. "Including you that makes seven. And your sister and her husband know, so that's nine. I think that's quite enough!"

"That's all very well," said Lorraine. "But even if we're fairly certain that eight of us aren't going to tell anyone else, we have to be prepared for the possibility that Miles might. And if he does, then we are going to need to plan in advance how we manage the situation. It's exactly the same as having plans for risk management in a business – if you don't think through every potential disaster in advance, you're bound to miss something when there's an emergency going on."

"But it's worse than that," said Mia. "I sent that DVD to Steve Irwin and there might be untold people in Australia gossiping about it right now - it might be in the papers over there and we just haven't found out yet. Anything could happen at any time from now on."

John finished the wine in his glass and poured himself another. "Lorraine, we'll have to take a taxi again, we're over the limit, both of us - this is getting expensive. But back to the subject on hand - I don't think we can do anything about the DVD apart from wait and see what happens. Hopefully, it's either been thrown out or buried in a pile of stuff in the office at the Zoo."

"That's what I've been hoping too. I think they didn't respond for one of two possible reasons: either the DVD never reached them before he died or they got it and dismissed it as a hoax, in which case they probably threw it out. But let's say that something appears in the New Zealand press tomorrow. What will I do?"

Lorraine reached over and cut another wedge of cheese. "I think you should just deny it. Isn't that the simplest thing? If you're evasive they'll scent blood and hound you. If you tell self-protective lies, you'll get tangled up or they'll find out somehow. I think the best protection would be to deny any knowledge, along the lines of: 'I've no idea what you're talking about.' Who could prove otherwise? There's the video, the audiotape and copies of the DVD, but we know where they are and that they're all safe."

Mia made a face. "I suppose that might work - apart from the DVD I sent there isn't much anyone could lay their hands on to disprove it."

"I think that the evidence should be in a safe or a bank security box." John sounded very certain. "Everything should be in one safe place. Apart from the DVD you sent to Irwin of course – and who knows, you might even get that back one day unless it's been thrown in the rubbish."

"At the moment my DVD is in Thomas's house," said Mia and reached for the wine bottle. "Let me have some of that before Lorraine drinks it all! I took it over to show Carl and Thomas when I went there for dinner, and they are keeping it for the time being, because it turns out that Thomas has a proper built-in safe."

"OK, that's good. Eventually you'll have to collect the rest from me at work and put it in that safe or in a bank box. I'll put that recording on a couple of CDs for you, so you have everything in a slightly more modern format. But even if the plan is for you to simply deny all knowledge, I still think we should discuss it. It could be that you'll need legal advice or some mention of the law to get people off your back, if they start putting pressure on you."

By the time Mia locked the front door behind them it was just before ten. It had been an interesting evening, but once again she wished Thomas had been there. It would have added another viewpoint and something else she found hard to define; not protection, more a rock-like quality of integrity and dependability, which she imagined he brought to every occasion. She smiled ruefully at the thought that she might be falling in love with him, turned the hall light off and went through to the study.

There was an email from Sarah, James and Brett - Sarah made no reference to Mia's secret and it was obvious from Brett's paragraph at the end that they had kept their word and told him nothing. And then she realized that there was no reason for Sarah to comment on Irwin's death. She had never told them what the second prediction was, so at least they would not be tempted to let it slip to Brett, while everyone was talking about it.

38

———————

Mia was late coming home from work and the phone was ringing as she unlocked the door, she sprinted through to the kitchen and grabbed the receiver. An unknown woman's voice asked for Mia Dawson and Mia instantly felt slightly uneasy.

"I am Mia Dawson. How can I help you?"

"My name is Grace Wright, I write a syndicated newspaper column called "And what have we here?" – you've probably seen it - and I wonder if I could interview you about that amazing prediction you made about Steve Irwin's death and also - let me see, where is it? Ah yes, a church fire in Russia."

Mia's blood ran cold, and she was instantly on the alert, mentally preparing herself to put on a convincing performance. She made an effort to sound natural, and hoped she managed an incredulous and slightly amused tone.

"My what? Prediction? I think you've got the wrong person."

"Oh no, I don't think so."

"Whoever gave you that information is trying to hoax you. I've no idea what you're talking about."

The woman's voice was firm and insistent.

"No, I have it from a reliable source. I was told that your sister was in St Petersburg and saw the fire and that you had told her in advance that it would happen. As I say, we have a lot of detail and I've checked the event on the Internet."

"Well, whatever you've been told, I can assure you that you have been misled – someone's trying to hoax you. I have no magic powers - you can't possibly believe such a silly story."

Now the woman was irritated, and Mia heard the slight threat underlying what she said. "No wait – don't put the phone down. He said you would deny it, but I know there is absolute proof that you made these predictions - and it has been documented with witnesses and everything. Do you deny that?"

"This is just nonsense - goodbye."

She put the phone down and took a deep breath to steady her nerves; she was trembling. She felt as if she had been through a long and arduous ordeal and needed to recover before doing so much as taking one single step. After a moment she returned to the hall and shut the front door, which she had left open in the rush for the phone. She took her jacket off and looked at herself in the mirror above the hall table, surprised that her face looked calm and ordinary and showed nothing of the turmoil inside her mind.

She was about call Lorraine and John to tell them, but after a moment's consideration she changed her mind; she wanted to talk to Thomas first. She went to the study where she had his and Carl's numbers on post-it notes on the wall and stood in front of the desk dialling; not calm enough to sit down, fingers not quite steady.

"Thomas speaking."

His voice at the other end was so normal and so composed that she felt stronger and more capable the moment she heard it.

"Thomas, it's Mia. I am sorry to bother you, but I think I need some help."

"Of course. Tell me what I can do."

His brief reply was so like him, so competent and calm that she felt her shoulders drop in relief.

"A journalist is on to me, someone called Grace Wright, she writes a weekly column in the paper. She called just now and I'm about to call that policeman friend I told you about and Lorraine. They were here yesterday because John was worried this would happen. Sorry, I'm getting ahead of myself. John thought one of the original group - you know the ones who witnessed my document - might try to use me for his own ends, commercial fame and gain. John and Lorraine will probably come over and I would really like you to be here. Would you mind?"

"Of course, I don't mind. I'll come over right away. Is there anything you need?"

Mia nearly told him that the only thing she needed was him, but common sense prevailed, and she said, "A bottle or two of wine would be useful, thanks. I seem to spend a lot of time discussing my fate over bottles of wine these days and I'm not sure what I've got left. I only just got home."

"OK, I'll be there shortly. Have you thought of dinner? No? Well, how about I bring something we can share if need be? See you soon."

Lorraine replied to a background babble of laughter and many voices. She was appalled at how soon their risk plan was needed. "My God, that's incredible - and it was just last night we discussed it. I'm in South Auckland at my mum's place. She is having a baby shower for someone I went to school with, and John is in a meeting till about eight or eight thirty. I'll text him and tell him to meet me at your place. I can't get away much sooner than he can anyway."

"Thanks Lorraine, that's great. Don't rush - Thomas is coming over, so we'll just wait for you."

She tidied up a bit and got out a packet of grissini which was the only wine-accompaniment left in the pantry. These days she seemed to forever be buying cheese and crackers and crisps, not just one packet at a time but by twos and threes, which was a routine she was still not quite used to. She changed into jeans and one of her new tight T-shirts and brushed her hair - very aware of how she looked, wanting to look pretty. In front of the mirror, she studied her 'new' face for a moment and decided that the new style of make-up made a difference, but the greatest change came from feeling confident.

Too much on edge to settle down, she paced from the sitting room to the kitchen and the bedroom in a meaningless circuit until the buzzer went. She pressed the release button and went to open the front door straight away, standing with her hand on the door handle listening to the lift coming up.

Thomas came out of the lift carrying two shopping bags. She looked at him and all she could say was, "Oh, thank you!"

She felt as if safety was at last within reach. Thomas put both bags on the floor in the open doorway and pulled her towards him.

Her head fitted neatly under his chin, and she could feel the warmth of his body through his jersey. They stood like that for a moment, his arms holding her against him and then he said in a perfectly normal voice, "It's all right, we'll sort it out."

He let her go, but neither of them stepped back and they stood for another moment with their bodies touching but their hands at their sides, then Mia took a step back and looked up at his face.

"Thank you – again. Somehow it was quite threatening to find how much information she had about me - and she was so pushy."

"Let's get rid of this and sit down and then you can tell me all about it". He closed the door, followed her to the kitchen and started unpacking the bags.

"Sushi!" said Mia. "Lovely, it's one of my favourite foods. Do you want some now? John and Lorraine probably won't be here until nine or so."

"Well, if they haven't had anything by then, they can have some too - there's more in the other bag."

Mia desperately wanted to tell him all that had happened. "Let's have a drink first – I just want to tell you a couple of things right away, so I can settle down and enjoy the food."

They sat down with glasses of wine and Mia started telling him about the meeting the previous day and how it was all due to John's suspicions about Miles.

"I didn't know who it was he suspected, but it had to be either Paul, that's Lorraine's brother, or Miles."

"Why couldn't it have been Lorraine, even if she's a friend? You haven't known her very long, have you?"

"Because John and Lorraine are having some kind of relationship and if he thought she was the problem he'd be able to deal with it without involving the whole group."

"OK, that makes sense."

Mia took a sip of wine and continued, serious and still tense. "John said we needed to synchronize our thinking and make sure that everyone was honour bound not to do anything I didn't want. He spelt out very clearly what he was worried about, media exposure and possible exploitation. Lorraine and Paul were both very strong and direct in agreeing. But Miles put up an argument, saying I must consider that this was the chance in a lifetime, He raved on about how I could earn enough money never to have to go to work again and more, much more. I think he had spent a lot of time thinking about how to gain most media traction - he offered to manage the whole media campaign."

Thomas had a cynical smile on his face, which in combination with the scar made him look decidedly dangerous. "I bet he did. He wouldn't have suggested it without some idea of personal gain, the rat!"

Mia smiled at this, her fist smile since she got home. "You don't know how right you are - you haven't met him. When I first saw him, he made me think of those white rats that people keep as pets - he's pale and has nearly invisible eyelashes. But I must say I was taken aback when I heard him describe a marketing strategy culminating in a book and film rights. And he got more and more irritated and frustrated as the meeting went on."

"How did the others react? Were they surprised?"

"Paul was – he got angry and Lorraine too – she clearly knew about John's suspicions but hadn't wanted to believe him. You see, she's the one who got Miles involved. She has done holiday and part time jobs for the law firm he where he works, so she felt responsible. But John wasn't surprised. He had worked through the whole scenario – and he was the one who warned the others right at the outset that I could be at risk if my story becomes public knowledge."

She was going to explain why, but Thomas's face told her that he understood the implications.

"When we played the DVD at my house, and you told me the tale it was one of the first things that occurred to me. There's no way we can allow this to become widely known. We'll discuss ways and means when the others get here, and in the meantime maybe we should have something to eat?"

Mia was full of contrition. "Oh God, I'm sorry - not only do I drag you out at short notice, but you probably had a busy day or got no lunch."

He laughed. "No, it's not that bad. I got taken out for lunch by clients and had a lovely meal."

"I didn't know clients took their accountants out for lunch – you must be good!"

He grinned. "I'm not actually a standard account now. These days I specialize in international tax matters and the tax laws in different countries, so I mostly deal with clients who have investments or business dealings overseas. Many of them are wealthy and a few are influential, and every now and then someone gives me a tip for a good investment. It's a very interesting job."

They ate sushi with their fingers and drank more wine and discovered that neither of them enjoyed Indian food and they both loved Japanese and Italian cuisine. Mia was surprised to find that Thomas had never been to the Italian film festival, and Thomas educated Mia about the various roles of accountants and about his own role as a consultant.

"I never do any of the stuff you think of as normal accounting at all, haven't for years. I'm in a partnership with two other specialists, both lawyers, and we hire ourselves out at an outrageous hourly rate. We research and give advice and come up with strategies. I spend hours just sitting in my office reading and researching tax laws in other countries - some weeks I don't talk to a single client. Just recently one of my clients offered me a job in Hong Kong, but I can barely cope with the humidity of the Auckland summers, so I said no. But I do go there quite often because it's a lovely place to visit."

They were discussing getting more sushi out of the fridge when the buzzer went again. Lorraine and John looked like a long-term couple, thought Mia when she let them in, and wondered how on earth they had progressed to this stage so fast and acquired the mannerisms of two people who have spent a long time together? John lifted Lorraine's jacket off her arm and put it on the hall chair along with his briefcase and she handed him a deli bag without looking to see that he was there to receive it, while she turned to tidy her hair in the mirror.

"There's some gorgeous cholesterol-laden crisis stuff in that bag, Mia. We haven't had dinner, so I bought some goodies on the run. We seem to be here more often than we're home these days. We should keep spare pyjamas here and save ourselves the expense of taking taxis home."

39

Introductions were made and Thomas pointed out that there was sushi in the fridge. This is a nice kind of chaos, thought Mia as she watched everyone organize their own plates, food, dessert, glasses and all they needed. They milled around for a few minutes, and then suddenly it was done – they were sitting round the table eating dinner, out of step with each other, chaos resolved.

Mia grinned and John caught her eye. "Now, what's up, young lady? You look amused."

"Oh, nothing really. Just wondering how it is that Lorraine and you have only been here a couple of times, and Thomas only once before, but everyone seems to know where everything is in the kitchen. I must be far too fond of letting my guests do all the work."

Lorraine spoke around a mouthful of sushi. "You must get out of the habit of calling everyone under thirty-five a young lady, John. You're not that old!"

The perfect opportunity thought Mia and said innocently: "How old are you really John? Forty-one, forty-two?"

Lorraine was delighted. "Well, that's what I always tell him. He thinks he's ancient and you think he's only forty-one."

John frowned a mock warning at Lorraine. "You're out of order, young lady - it's rude to discuss my age in front of others." He turned to Mia. "I am a bit older than that – I've just had my 47th birthday. When you get that close to the half-century you start reflecting on life – Lorraine prefers to call it pontificating."

They continued a casual conversation until they had finished eating and were ready to sit down with a cup of coffee, and then Thomas set the ball rolling.

"Mia's filled me in on what happened yesterday when you met. But I haven't heard the details of the call she had tonight from that journalist - perhaps you could tell us now, Mia?"

Mia put her coffee cup down and thought for a moment. It was important to tell them exactly what the journalist had said, and she related the phone conversation slowly, pausing now and then to make sure she got it right.

"I think that's it and with the exact words we used. I wouldn't like to put a spin on it, because it's important we can somehow work out how much she knows, from what she said. I know who told her – of course, we all do. That comment about documentation and witnesses could only have come from one of the team and there's only one person, who wants the story to get into the news."

Lorraine had sat quietly studying her fingernails, while Mia spoke, but now she looked up.

"I think you did well to keep your cool and not give her anything that she could get her teeth into - and that tone of disbelief and ridicule was good. She might be left wondering if the story really is true, or if her informant has set her up. I think you should continue to say that you have no idea what people are talking about, if it ever comes up again."

Thomas was thinking along other lines. "Mia told me that all the documentation is to be kept together and I'm happy to let her keep it in my safe, but there's that DVD that was sent to Irwin – that worries me. *And* I'd like to be sure that Miles didn't manage to take any photos with his phone when the document was signed."

It was obvious that nobody had thought of this. They looked at each other and tried to cast their minds back to the evening at the police station.

Mia found she could visualize the scene amazingly clearly. "The others were focusing on me and on the document, but I have a very clear picture of where everyone stood and how people moved in relation to each other and to the table. At the start I told them what I wanted them to witness, and everyone was looking at me, but I was looking around at their faces and nobody had a cell phone or a camera in their hands - well apart from Paul, of course. Then they moved around the table in turn, to read the document and to sign it, and I continued to watch them from the sidelines - because I wanted to make sure everyone signed and dated their signatures. I feel absolutely confident that Miles never had anything in his hands apart from when he put his hand in his pocket and produced the sealing wax I had asked for."

John and Lorraine both stared into space, with the look of people mentally running through a scene from the past, but in the end, they agreed that Miles had not taken any pictures.

"That's a relief," said Thomas. "I was worried that Miles might have some independent evidence. Let's hope there's nothing we've missed."

They looked at each other in silent agreement and nodded.

"And Mia, maybe you should put a password on your Word file, so nobody else can open it, just to be on the safe side? Yes, I know, I know – it seems way over the top. Must be the careful and cautious accountant in me coming out, but it can't do any harm."

Lorraine smiled at Thomas. "I can see that between you and John we are going to be kept on the straight and narrow – no chance of just taking a punt and hoping everything will turn out OK."

"God, I should hope not," said John. "You won't last long as a lawyer if you take that line."

"But how *are* we going to deal with Miles? Or are we going to ignore him from now on?" Mia was thinking out loud. "It's not that I want to punish him - well perhaps I do, actually. At least I want to tell him what I think of him. Shouldn't he be sort of warned off?"

The others all spoke at the same time, but the message was overwhelmingly clear. Miles must be told what they thought of him, and Lorraine had an additional idea of how to contain him.

"I think maybe Thomas could go and see him? It would be completely unexpected, because Miles doesn't know Thomas, he's probably never heard of him, so it would add a bit of impact. And he could introduce himself as a consultant, no need to mention accounting or tax law. What I think Miles needs to be told, is that Mia and the rest of us will deny anything he comes up with."

"That's a good idea, if you agree, Thomas," said John. "Which I hope you will. Mia said you had a sort of presence, and I can see what she meant. A warning from you would come across in a way that I couldn't achieve. And you being a stranger adds weight too."

Mia knew that Thomas had flicked a glance in her direction when John quoted her. She hoped her face would not betray her feelings and tried to sound calm.

"I think that's a very good idea. The only other thing I've

thought of since that phone call, is that Miles might try to get hold of the DVD – the one we sent to Australia. Do you think we should try and get it back before he tries?"

After a lengthy discussion they agreed that for many reasons no attempt should be made to retrieve the CD, mainly because it was unlikely that anyone would want to admit they had been warned and ignored it.

"If you give me the name of the firm Miles works for, I'll call him first thing in the morning and ask for an appointment to see him," said Thomas. "I'll make sure he understands it's urgent. And I'll report back to you all when it's done."

There was a flurry of activity as they rose, cleared the table and tidied the kitchen. Then John and Lorraine left, and all was quiet again.

"I'll write down John and Lorraine's numbers for you - and the name of Miles's law firm," said Mia, but as she turned aside, she caught Thomas' eye.

His face was closed and set, quite unlike his usual expression. She stopped and looked directly at him, but his expression didn't change, his voice was steady and even. "You were going to get me those numbers?"

Mia nearly let the moment pass, but then she thought of how they had stood earlier in the evening with his arms around her, and now he seemed like different person altogether. She took a couple of steps closer and looked directly into his face.

"What's wrong? Are we taking too much for granted? If you don't want to tackle Miles, someone else can do it."

"I'm perfectly happy to deal with Miles – in fact, it will be a pleasure. There's nothing wrong."

His voice was calmly dismissive, and she felt as if he had slapped her. Why was he so remote? How could he change like this right in front of her eyes? She must have said or done something he found unacceptable, and her mind raced through the evening's conversations trying to find a clue. She remained in front of him looking up at his face and then it struck her like a blow on the head. It was his scar! He thought she had told John and Lorraine that he looked scary or like a thug. My God – how could he sit there after that and be so cool, when all the time he must have been feeling hurt and disappointed in her.

Pity and affection overwhelmed her, and she once again felt like crying, but this time for him. She took a step closer, reached up and put the palm of her hand over the scarred side of his face. He flinched and nearly pulled away, but his expression did not change.

"Thomas, this is *not* the 'presence' I told John and Lorraine about! I was talking about your personal impact – serious, competent and not a person to cross."

She lowered her hand and now she didn't know what to do with it, it felt as if it didn't really belong to her.

Thomas spoke evenly. "I'm aware that my face makes me look dangerous - there's no need to apologize."

Mia nearly left it there. She was sad and upset, and maybe anything she said or did now would turn out wrong. She turned to go and write that note, but her emotions overruled her, and she swung back and looked straight at Thomas with tears starting in her eyes.

"That was *not* what it was! You have to take my word for it. I can't bear to see you feeling like this."

He made no reply, just looked aside as if unable to meet her gaze. Overwhelmed by guilt and sadness, Mia said in a voice that came out croaky, "I think I love you, Thomas Livingston."

There was total silence for a few seconds. He looked down into her face with a look of complete surprise, and then he slowly reached out and took her face between his hands and bent his head and kissed her, slowly and gently at first and then with increasing passion. His arms moved down to close round her back and Mia lifted her arms and crossed her wrists behind his neck, holding him close, while tears trickled down her cheeks. He lifted his head and wiped the tears with his fingers, and his face was still serious, but his eyes were alight - she knew they needed no words.

They stood like that for a moment and then he smiled, "Well, I wasn't expecting that!"

She reached for one of his hands and kissed his knuckles. "Neither was I."

He moved back a bit and leaned against the kitchen counter with his feet planted wide and pulled her with him, so she stood between his legs, very close to his chest and their faces were not so far apart.

"You are such a shortie - we'll have to grow you a bit taller."

She ignored the comment about height but stored away the

feeling it gave her, to treasure later, that implication of a shared future.

She felt nearly dizzy at her own emotional risk-taking and the fast-evolving situation.

"I meant it you know. I've never felt like this with anyone before – as if I've known you forever. I don't have to know you, to trust you."

He pulled her against his chest and spoke into her hair. "Ah, cara Mia - I fell in love with you when we watched that DVD of you doing your thing with the document at the police station – it was instant. I never thought I would get to say it - it never entered my head that you would be interested. Most people can't cope with my face."

She could feel the steady beat of his heart, his whole body felt solid and warm and safe. How could this gorgeous man imagine that he was unlovable – it was tragic. The thought of how many years he must have lived like this made her heart ache.

"Well, I love you now, and I think I'll probably love you forever."

She raised her face and kissed his chin, and he tilted his head forward so their foreheads met. "Let's go to bed."

Much later, as she lay with her head on his arm, her cheek sweat-glued to his skin, he asked casually, "Are you on the pill?"

And Mia laughed. "No, I'm not. But never mind, if I have an instant baby, it'll be company for Ruby. It's another thing I know might happen."

"And whose baby might Ruby be?"

Mia smiled in the dark. "Ruby is Sarah and James's little girl, whose birthday is the 23rd of April – that's 23rd of April 2007."

She felt his body vibrate with laughter, and then he turned on his side and pulled her close again. "My God - this is so weird - I'll need time to get used to it. But I'm glad your memory is only one year ahead of mine, or we'd never have a normal life."

"You'll have to remember not to mention Ruby, when you first meet her parents," said Mia, "Because I think that Sarah only discovered she was pregnant a couple of weeks after they came back from their trip, and we wouldn't want to spoil the surprise for them. Heaven knows why she didn't notice earlier - she'll tell us she's baffled, and we must remember to be thrilled and surprised."

"Anything else I should know? Imminent bridge collapses, trains and flights not to catch, shares to buy?"

"Mm, yes, I do have a list somewhere of things I remember. But some of them I can't place in time, and some I know *when* they happened, but I can't remember enough detail. You can help me work on it – talking might bring more out. The others suggested a hypnotist, but I am reluctant to mess with my mind – I think more or less constantly of the possibility that I might find myself back in That Time again and hypnosis sounds a bit dicey. But if I can manage to save some lives and some grief it would kind of make up for Steve Irwin dying." She added, as an afterthought, "And if I do get shifted back to 2007 again, and if I remember this, I'll come and find you!"

They feel asleep like that, close together with Thomas's arm around her. At some stage in the night, they must have moved apart, Mia was drowsily aware of a hand reaching out to locate her, moved closer and slept on.

40

Mia opened her eyes and looked straight into Thomas's eyes. He kissed her nose and said, "You look very peaceful when you sleep - like a cat."

"How long have you been lying there looking at me?"

"Oh, not long, perhaps ten minutes."

Mia traced his scar with her forefinger and smiled. "Do you still love me?"

"Let me show you."

At half past eight Thomas dropped Mia at her office on his way home to change his clothes. He leant across and kissed her before she got out.

"I'll call later. Remember I love you. And I'll pick you up about half past five."

She stood on the pavement and watched the car blend into the traffic and disappear. She already missed him, but there was a warm glow in her chest. Alice was at her desk, lit up with curiosity.

"Mia! Who was that? Did I see a fond farewell before you got out of that car?"

Mia felt her face grow pink and thought how ridiculous that was for a single, adult woman but somehow, she felt no older than sixteen this morning.

"Well, yes - it was a fond farewell. But keep it to yourself for now, it's very, very new and I don't want everyone talking about it."

217

Alice's eyes were shining. "Oh Mia, I'm so pleased for you. Will you tell me all about it?"

Mia looked at Alice and thought, I'm so lucky to have a friend like this, how did I miss getting to know her in That Time?

Aloud she said, "I'll tell you some of it, very soon. Let's go out and have a gossipy lunch one day next week."

"That's a date - I can tell you all about the wedding and you can tell me about your new man."

With a mental apology to Alice for how she would never tell her the full story, Mia made her way to her office. The morning was a string of short bursts of work interspaced with dreamy pauses, when she gazed into the far distance and her mind dwelt on the previous evening and night. Some of the images she conjured up make her feel quite hot and bothered. She would catch herself deep in a daydream and snap out of it, only to drift into another reverie half an hour later.

At lunchtime Thomas called to say that he had arranged an appointment with Miles at half past two and all he had told the secretary was that he was a partner at Bond, Livingston & Thompson.

"I did that on purpose, because most people think we're all lawyers and it's really only clients and other accountants who understand that I'm an accountant. I thought it might create a bit of useful apprehension, when he finds out why I've come to see him."

"Very smart! What did you say your firm was called, let me write it down – it feels funny not to know where your office is or anything."

He repeated the name, and she scribbled it on her pad and then burst into laughter. "You do realize how funny that is?"

"Oh, yes and it's quite deliberate. People never forgot the name once they have seen our letterhead with the initials. One client suggested we should re-locate to Rye in the UK for maximum effect."

She texted John and Lorraine and told them that Thomas had an appointment to see Miles and within minutes Lorraine called. "Have you seen the paper? There's a mention of you in that woman's column, but not your name."

"My God, she's not giving up then - what does it say?"

"It's only a paragraph. Here it is: *We hear that a young Auckland woman not only predicted Steve Irwin's death but did so in exact detail and had her prediction videotaped and witnessed by police officers some time before the event. It seems Irwin was notified but chose to ignore the warning. When we contacted the lady in question she denied any knowledge, but we were informed by someone who witnessed the original prediction, and we will continue to investigate.* Thank God, there's no mention of anything that could identify you."

Mia had to agree – the paragraph was surprisingly low-key.

"I really thought she would name me despite my denial. Once Thomas has seen Miles, I doubt she'll get any more details out of him. But she knows my name already of course and can easily ramp it up a bit. I hope Miles warns her off, but he might not have any influence over her."

"Well, whatever she's going to do, it's just gossip if you continue to deny it all - so long as she never gets to see the evidence document or the DVD."

Mia put the phone down and swung around to face her computer and saw Josh standing in the doorway.

"God, Josh, you gave me a fright!"

She made a mental note to either close her door or sit facing it during any future conversations with Lorraine. Not that anything she had said this time was very revealing, but she still felt exposed.

"Mia, my girl, you seem to lead the most intriguing life these days. I hope to goodness you're not getting tangled up in anything illegal?"

Mia bristled at hearing him call her his girl but decided to keep the upper hand by not getting involved in petty sparring.

"Illegal - what on earth makes you think that?"

"Well, I heard you talking about someone called Miles warning some unknown female off and it sounded so exotic I stopped to see what else you were going to come out with."

He grinned but made no move to leave, and Mia decided she would risk a little dig. "Josh, I'm beginning to think that your good-looking exterior hides a seriously dubious inner person. I'm sure your mother would be ashamed of you eavesdropping."

He was relaxed and amused, immune to the insult. "My mum thinks the sun shines out of every one of my orifices – she would never believe you."

He left with a smirk and Mia texted Thomas telling him to read the column in the paper before seeing Miles. The rest of the day was uneventful and slightly boring. Most of the jobs on her desk were routine and undemanding, but in the back of her mind other concerns revolved slowly. That list of events that she might be able to prevent should be worked on soon – the little team could become a think tank. Not that any of them could remember the future, but there would be avenues to explore and people to try and to contact when she had come up with sufficient detail about something.

As she had told Thomas yesterday, she would not consider hypnosis. At first, she had thought it might be useful, but now she was shying away from the idea. Her mind and memory had been violently sideswiped into a time strand where they did not belong, and the thought of tampering further scared her. Then her mind jumped ahead; would Thomas stay the night again? Should they tell Carl? Would she manage to get hold of a copy of Josh's proposal on Monday? She shook her head and told herself to stop wasting time and carried on with the work in front of her.

The afternoon dragged. At quarter past three, she had still not heard anything from Thomas, she began to worry and found it hard to concentrate. Finally at quarter to four he called.

"Sorry it took so long, but when I got to Miles's office, he was in a client meeting that was running over time, and I had to wait for twenty minutes. They were very apologetic, but I wasn't going to go away and waste the opportunity. All I can say is that I put on my best performance of authority and veiled legal threat, and I don't think he's going to try anything again."

Mia was delighted. "Thank you so much - I knew you'd be effective. Did he argue or try to deny it?"

"Oh no, not at all. I said that you had consulted us as experts in international law and business, and we will represent your interests from now on. And if anything turned up in the media or involving commercial interests, here or in other countries, we would take action on your behalf."

"Boy, I wish I'd been the proverbial fly on the wall. I bet you were magnificent – was he really scared?"

Thomas laughed against a backdrop of traffic.

"I could stand here all day, breathing diesel fumes and listen to flattery. It's a new and heady experience. But yes, he was scared – I think he suddenly started considering what being sued would do to career. Now it all depends on how much he has already revealed to that journalist, because she might know more than she has let on so far."

Just as they were saying goodbye he exclaimed, "Got it - chronoclasm, that's it! Chronoclasm – I've been trying to remember the word for days."

"What does it mean?"

"I read it somewhere years ago - it's in some book I've read more than once. I have a hunch it might be out of a story by John Wyndham, you know, the guy who wrote The Triffids. He wrote about someone who got shifted to a different time and the result was called a chronoclasm."

"Well, it's nice to know there's a word for it – makes me feel nearly normal. See you at half past five."

She looked at the scribbled word on her pad – chronoclasm and looked it up on the internet but all she found was Chronoclast, which was a heavy-metal rock album. Well, she knew that chrono was to do with time, so she tried clast, which turned out to a word describing fragmented rock. What a strange coincidence that an author had invented a word meaning fractured time decades ago for a sci-fi novel and built into it was a reference to rock fragmenting. And the sensation she had experienced, when she was moved between time strands was very much like being dragged through a cleft in a rock, uneven and gritty. She pondered the strangeness of time and space for a moment, then turned her attention back to work.

Alan came for a brief visit, aware that he had not seen her to speak to all day and asked how she was getting on. "I'm fine thanks, Alan. How are you? Did your exploded pie chart make an impact?"

He looked morose and shook his head. "The meeting is next week - we send the papers out in plenty of time. I have a feeling they're going to say something like *Please do it the way it used to be, it was easier to read that way*. And I can't say that I deliberately did it this way to force them to think. It can be very frustrating to deal with boards and management teams – people think they know everything and don't need to look at the details."

Mia smiled at his grumpy face.

"You'll have to come up with some reason to make them believe they aren't keeping up with modern business practice if they can't accept the change. Maybe you could add a footnote with some trendy management phrases to justify the change?"

"My goodness, I don't know what I did with my little problems before you came along. Of course, that's what I must do, but it can't be a footnote, the thing's already in the mail. Baffle them into submission, ha? Now if I could quote something - I'm sure you can come up with something that sounds authoritative."

They smiled delightedly at each other, conspirators in the struggle against demands from above. Mia promised to think about it over the weekend and come up with something before Wednesday.

She texted sketchy details to John and Lorraine about Thomas's meeting with Miles, cleared her desk and wrote a cryptic "check report" on her pad as a reminder to herself to find a way to lay her hands on a copy of Josh's proposal. Calling out a cheerful goodbye to Alan she went outside to find Thomas already waiting. He leant over to kiss her before he pulled out into the traffic, and she looked at his profile, and for some reason a memory of their lovemaking the previous night flashed into her mind. She felt her face go hot and Thomas looked across at her as if he could read her mind.

"Anything wrong?"

"No, I was just thinking of something."

He flashed another quick glance at her, before changing lanes and turning a busy corner. "Something from last night?"

How did he guess? Surely, he couldn't read her mind.

"Well, yes actually. How did you know?"

He smiled but kept his eyes on the street ahead. "Just a lucky guess - I've had a day of delightful erotic flash-backs myself."

Mia laughed. All of this was lovely and funny and not in the slightest bit like anything she had experienced before.

"I feel as if you can see into my head – a bit disconcerting I must say. I'll have to keep my thoughts in order."

"Don't worry, I'm sure it was just a fluke. But last night was spectacular."

She smiled at his profile. "It was - marvellous. I think we're particularly good at it."

His hand reached out and covered both hers and gave them a little squeeze. "Good." And that was all he said, but she knew by now that with him a single word could speak volumes.

Without discussion they drove towards Mia's place. "I've

nothing but what's left of the sushi from last night in the fridge. But there's dried pasta and a few bits and pieces in the pantry. We should go shopping on the way."

"No shopping - I'm not sharing your company with a lot of strangers unless we are threatened with starvation and absolutely have to buy food. Let's eat pasta and bits and have some time on our own."

"Should we call Carl? Won't he wonder where you are?"

"You're right, he will, I was thinking about it this afternoon. When I go away, I always tell him when I'm coming back. He keeps an eye on my place and takes my mail in, so he'll wonder what's become of me – I'll call him as soon as we get to your place."

41

Mia checked the pantry while Thomas was on the phone to Carl. She heard him say that something unexpected had come up, but that he would be home tomorrow morning and would come over for a coffee. Carl must have said something funny, because Thomas laughed and said, "You'll have to wait - I'll tell you tomorrow."

He turned towards her. "Carl asked if I'd found a woman and stayed at her place for the night. He has said similar things before and of course I've never had anything to tell him, so it's going to be fun to see his face when we walk in and tell him tomorrow morning. If that's OK with you, of course?"

"Goodness, yes, of course we must tell him."

He opened his briefcase, took out a bottle of champagne and put in the freezer.

"We can't have that for half an hour at least - it's got to be really cold. What shall we do while we wait? Go to bed?"

"Yes, please!"

An hour and a half later they opened the champagne and sat down with chips and dip, also from Thomas's briefcase.

Mia laughed at him. "I'm beginning to think you carry a briefcase just to have something respectable looking to carry food in."

"I nicked some extra supplies from the fridge in the boardroom to save time. Don't tell anyone – it's not something I normally do."

The evening sky was clear, and they sat in front of the big window looking out over the lights of the city.

"Would you ever be able to tear yourself away from this, do you think?"

He sounded casual, and if there was serious intent behind the question, he kept it well hidden. "Not that I object to living in an apartment, if you should ever feel that you wanted us to live together."

Mia's mind raced through the layers of implications behind this innocent-seeming statement and decided to continue laying her soul bare. Telling him she loved him yesterday in the kitchen seemed to have unlocked a talent for emotional risk-taking.

"Do I want to live with you at some stage? Well, let's say that you would have to build razor-wire barricades to keep me away. And we would obviously have to live in your house - we can't leave Carl on his own, he might need looking after as he gets older – and he would be lonely."

"In that case we must do some serious things to the house. I've never got around to getting it done, but it needs the kitchen and both bathrooms ripped out and rebuilt. And maybe a few walls could be taken out too, to make it more open. I'm sure we could get an architect to suggest something clever."

Mia tried to remember the layout and failed.

"Heavens, I've only been inside the place once and it was dark – I've no idea what it really looks like, but I'm sure we can do something with it. I remember thinking how lovely the outside was when I came to have coffee with Carl the first time. Isn't it strange that we really only just met and here we are discussing living arrangements? Other people would think we're mad."

"I know – but I can't help it. I feel we belong together, and time has nothing to do with it. But I'm warning you now – the inside of that house could be used as a set for a horror movie. Let's get someone really good to help us and then you can work it out. You've got great sense of style and you can do what you like – I know I'll enjoy it."

They left it at that and sat in relaxed silence for a few minutes before Mia said, "You know, I don't know a thing about your family, you have to fill me in. You know already that my parents are dead, and I only have one sister – and I don't have a lot of close relations, not compared to most people."

"My father left the family when I was about nine or ten. He wasn't a good father, and he should never have settled down to have children. He was laid back and funny and he drank too much." Thomas looked into the middle distance without focus, reliving his childhood. "Since I grew up, I've found out bits and pieces from my mother about how he used to stay out all night, presumably at some woman's place and then come home full of cheer as if nothing had happened. He was never mean, and he never hit anyone - he just didn't care very much about us."

He made a wry face. "And then he drifted off and came back now and then for a visit, and then that petered out too. When my mother was dying, we tried to trace him and found that he had died a few years earlier in a road accident. Apparently, my mother knew, but for some reason she hadn't mentioned it to us."

"How long is it since your mother died? Do you miss her?"

"She died of breast cancer about five years ago. No, wait a minute; it was just before my thirty-second birthday, so it must be seven years ago. We all loved her. Both my brothers are married and have children, but I would think most of the kids are too young to remember her. Yes, I do miss her – she had a wacky sense of humour, and she was curious about everything. She was the kind of person you could have the most marvellous and varied conversations with, and she was a mean Scrabble player."

Over dinner they talked about Mia's list of future events, and she fetched her notepad from the study to remind herself.

"After I thought up the two original proof events, I've jotted down a few things now and again as they've occurred to me - the sort of things that could possibly be averted. I haven't checked them on the Internet, so some of them might already have happened – it's hard to recall exact dates. You can tell me which ones you've already herd of and we'll cross them off the list."

She searched through the pages of notes, frowning.

"When this weird thing first happened, I started an orgy of list-making. There were so many things to try and keep track of and plan for, and I became obsessed with being prepared and not forgetting anything. I was terrified that I would get things wrong and confuse people or expose my pre-knowledge. Here it is, let's see. The first thing is a terrible tourist bus crash in Waikato, where quite a few people lost their lives, and two or three survivors lost an arm for some strange reason – mini-bus I think."

Thomas shook his head. "There have been many accidents involving tourists, but that's bigger than anything I can recall. I think I'd remember it if more than one person lost an arm."

"Mm, yes – I might be able to dredge up some more detail. I've got a feeling there was something wrong with the bus or the driver, no warrant of fitness, bald tyres, no licence or something like that. In any case there was a call for stricter rules for tour operators after it happened. The tour was Korean, I think, or maybe Taiwanese, and the driver ran his own travel company as well, a sort of one-stop shop."

"We should be able to do something with that, as you say. What's next on the list?"

"The next thing is big, and it went global - it made the head-lines for days and weeks. A massacre at a school called Virginia Tech somewhere in the US, probably about six months from now, but maybe even further ahead – lots of kids killed. The killer was a student, he'd been banished from one course because of his strange behaviour. I remember reading that a teacher sent him to the school psychologist, but they didn't do anything. I'm not sure, but I think he might have been of Asian descent – I must think a bit more about that." She frowned at the memory. "I read every-thing about it because Greg had a nephew who was at school in the US, and we were appalled at what came out about how people can buy guns over there. That one should be easy."

She turned the page and groaned. "What a scribble – I can only read parts of it - I probably woke up and wrote it down in the middle of the night. But it's about a robbery of a security van in Christchurch, which ended with one guard and at least two bystanders being injured by gunshots - just before Christmas and I think it happened outside a suburban bank. As I said, once I start thinking and talking about it, I might remember more details. And the last one is the derailment of a goods train in the Manawatu Gorge after a rock fall, autumn or early winter next year, perhaps May or June 2007? I think two goods wagons and the engine fell into the river - huge mess and disruption."

For a moment Thomas just sat there looking stunned and then he started to laugh. "Good grief - it's amazing to think those are just the big things you can think of off the top of your head. If we work this right, we could change so much for lots of people. We really must set up a meeting and get going with all this. John and Lorraine would want to help."

"Oh yes, we've already discussed it and they want to be involved, and Paul will be keen to help too. But there is another thing we discussed at the meeting the other night. When I said I didn't want to make a fortune out of my story, I also said that if I remembered something that we could make a reasonable gain from, without hurting anyone else, then I'd share the information with the group."

Thomas looked searchingly at her. "And you've changed your mind?"

"Oh no, not at all! Well, obviously I'm not sharing anything with Miles. But I've remembered some clues about the winner of the 2006 Melbourne Cup and if I'm right the winner wasn't expected to even be placed and the odds were very - whatever-it-is that odds are – big? good? long?"

"Great - we're well matched, I have no interest in horse racing and don't know one end of a horse from the other. But I'm sure Lorraine and Paul and maybe John might need some extra cash. I have enough, but a bit more is always good."

"Yes, that's what I thought too. I can't remember the names, but the first two horses both had names that had something to do with music, which I remember thinking was funny. I think there was something else linking them too, but I haven't put my finger on it yet. We had a sweepstake at work, and I didn't win a thing. I drew the second favourite and got nothing. I'll park it in the back of my mind, and I might remember some more."

"You have until the first Tuesday in November or whatever it is, so it's no panic. Perhaps you will pick them out as soon as they publish the list of entrants the week before the race. How about we go back to bed now?"

42

___

The next morning Mia and Thomas went straight from bed to coffee and toast on the balcony. The morning was a reminder of what summer would be like. They had woken up early, made love, gone back to sleep, and finally made it out of bed just after nine.

"I can't believe it's only September. It seems like summer."

She pushed up the sleeves of her kimono, stretched out a leg and put her foot on Thomas's lap.

"Hey, stop that, I can't eat my toast with that sort of disturbance going on."

Mia smiled. "Disturbance? It's just a friendly foot, it's not even moving."

"No, the foot isn't moving, but something else is. I'm finding it hard enough to concentrate on eating anyway, what with you sitting there covered in nothing but a silky robe with no buttons and parts of it sliding this way and that. But the foot's just too much."

She laughed, moved her foot to the floor and held up one hand, ticking things off on her fingers.

"What do we need to do today? First get showered and dressed. Then we go to your place. We must remember to take something nice for morning tea and visit Carl. And we must do some shopping, at least for this place – we're running out of everything apart from Weetbix and jam, and we might want to talk to John and Lorraine. And Paul, of course."

Before Thomas could reply, the phone rang, and Mia went

229

inside to answer. She instantly recognized the journalist's voice and braced herself to come up with a response that would end the conversation.

"Not you again - I don't understand why keep calling. I already told you I've no idea what you're talking about!" The tone of her voice caught Thomas's attention and he turned his head to listen.

Today Miss Wright was trying a cajoling approach. "I totally understand that you don't want any damaging publicity, of course you don't - but we could do a really interesting piece about what happened to you without revealing your identity. With my sort of column, I know how to keep a confidence."

"But I've got nothing to tell you. Nothing exciting has happened to me for a long time. Someone's been tricking you."

"I *don't* think so, because the person who told us has now been warned off by your legal advisors." Now her voice turned mocking and arrogant. "That must mean there's truth in the story, don't you agree? It's entirely up to you, but I can write a piece about it, whether you help me with facts or not. It's too good not to write up and it would be far better for you to cooperate and have input into how we present it."

Thomas was beside her now, saying quietly, "Do you want me to deal with it?"

Mia shook her head and mouthed, 'No, thanks'.

"I know that you can write whatever you like, but you've got to remember that if you identify me, I will deny it. It's such a ridiculous story - most likely your readers will think you've lost your marbles. And if anyone asks me, I'll say that I agree – you must be mad."

She pressed the off button and looked at Thomas. "Miles has told her that you came to see him and warned him off, and as she rightly said, that means there's something in it. But if we continue to deny everything there isn't much she can do, is there?"

She was slightly unnerved by the woman's persistence and wanted a solution to finish the whole thing once and for all, but she knew this was not the end of it.

"No, probably not, but she could be a nuisance and make your life miserable. Maybe we should discuss it with the others if they're available this weekend? Miles could have told her a lot of detail before I warned him off and we can't discount the possibility that she knows all the names. We must have the same answers if we get approached."

Mia's phone rang in the car on the way to Eden Terrace, and John asked if they could meet for a drink sometime soon to discuss what the next step was after Thomas's visit to Miles.

"We were going to call you anyway," said Mia. "That journalist called again this morning. When are you and Lorraine available, and Paul too, of course?"

"Why don't you come to my place tonight, if that suits you. I'll cook something simple, and we can have a relaxed evening. I have to go in to work tomorrow for a few hours, so I don't want to be too late. I'll check if Paul's off-duty. Come about seven."

Thomas parked on the drive. "I don't use the garage - it's pretty close to Carl's cottage and his garden, and I'd rather let him have his peace and privacy, so normally I just park here beside the house."

He put his hand on Mia's shoulder and turned her around. "Let's walk back and go in the front door, so you can see it as it's meant to be seen. We'll go and see Carl a bit later."

The front garden was just a strip of lawn between the front of the house and the picket fence. Wide steps led up to the front door and a deep verandah ran the full width of the house and continued down one side. The posts and rails were elaborately turned and there was a clear-leaded fanlight over the front door.

"It was built in 1909 and it's never been altered much," said Thomas and unlocked the door. "Not structurally, anyway, but someone did something fairly awful in the kitchen and bathrooms, probably in the 1970's. I've had the veranda floor re-piled and replaced right along the front and halfway down the side stretch, where things were a bit suspect. And the ceilings are insulated – the height of the rooms makes it hard to keep the place warm."

The central hallway was generously wide and ran right through the house from the front door to the back door, with a corridor off the left halfway along.

"That's lovely - classic Edwardian villa, I didn't remember that." Mia was impressed.

"That's exactly what I said, when the real estate agent first showed it to me. I love this type of house. But what happened was that just after I bought it, the business, which was new then, got busy and I never set aside the time to fix even the worst parts. And then I kind of got used to it, I suppose. Remember - I have warned you." He laughed. "I'll show you the worst things first and if you try to run for it, I bet I'm faster than you and I'll catch you."

The kitchen was dreadful, he had not exaggerated. The woodwork and cupboard fronts were painted in dreary brown and dull yellow, with tile patterned vinyl on the floor and a hideous 'feature wall' on the wall opposite the door.

"Right!" said Mia decisively, looking around the gloomy space. "This does need fixing. I think you're right – the only rational thing would be to rip the lot out and start again."

"But wait – there's more! You haven't seen the bathrooms – truly dreadful."

Mia stopped in the doorway and exclaimed in a tone of horror. "Good lord! How on earth have you lived here and used this bathroom every single day? It's atrocious."

"I know," he said meekly. "I told you it was bad. I just had so much to do for a couple of years and then I stopped noticing. Let's rip this out too and have a splendid bathroom – at least it's plenty big enough to do things with. And the second bathroom that someone added decades ago is just as bad. But the rest is rather gorgeous, and I've always thought that taking a couple of walls out would improve it – admittedly I can't imagine which walls should go, but I'm sure you'll work it out."

"One idea could be to make a big open space of the kitchen and the dining room – a sort of kitchen cum family room cum dining room? It would make a lovely big space and it would make it a lot lighter."

Before they knew it, they had been there an hour and it was half past eleven. Thomas looked at his watch.

"Good lord, we've forgotten Carl again. Let's go over right away and have that cup of coffee. He always has his lunch at 12.30 and then he has a siesta, so you can't visit him until about three o'clock."

43

When they were sitting down with coffee and pastries in Carl's living room, he looked from Mia to Thomas and back again, and said calmly. "So, what have you two got to tell me?"

Mia suspected that he had phrased it so they could either tell him something relating to the two of them or just say whatever came into their heads. But Thomas was ready for him. "You could say that last time we three were in this room, we were three friends and now we're one couple and a shared friend."

Carl was delighted. "Very good, Thomas - I've just won a one-hundred-dollar bet, because that's where I thought you must have been the last two nights. Bet you rang me from Mia's place last night?"

"How on earth did you suspect we were together?" Mia was amazed. "And more importantly, who did you have a bet with?"

"I had a bet with myself because the only person I ever have a bet with is Thomas, and I couldn't do that this time, could I? I sort of felt when we were at your place for dinner that Thomas was so keen, he hardly dared look at you. Am I right, Thomas?"

Thomas glanced at Mia and grinned. "You know me far too well, my friend. The only surprising thing is that Mia feels the same way. It's like beauty and the beast, a real fairy tale."

Mia knew that the opportunity to put a stop to this once and for all in a natural way might never return, and for her it was important that it was out in the open. She got up from her chair and stood behind Thomas with her hands on his shoulders and shook him gently.

"I never, ever want to hear you say that again! We're not like beauty and the beast at all. Your scar makes no difference to anyone who knows you. You are a wonderful, gorgeous man and I've been attracted to you from the very start."

How lucky, she thought, that an opportunity to say this had come up with Carl present. Thomas' assumption that he was repulsive and not fit for anyone to love had seriously worried her, and here was Carl to back her up.

"I always thought it must be that he wouldn't let the girls get close to him," said Carl without hesitation, speaking directly to Mia. "Not that they weren't interested – I'm sure they were."

Let's continue, now we are on this subject, she thought and returned to her chair. "So how did you get that scar anyway?"

Thomas hesitated, cleared his throat. "I was sixteen at the time and tried to help a friend, who was attacked by a gate-crashing drunk wielding a broken bottle outside a school dance - that's why it's so jagged. And because I heal with those bumpy scars it's created real tension across my cheek."

"What happened to your friend?"

"Oh, he was fine, nothing happened to him. I tried to grab the bottle, and the guy turned on me, so I was sort of between them. After I was slashed, I got him down on the ground – that's the crazy guy, not my friend – and the others managed to get the bottle off him."

"My God, real hero stuff - you could have been killed."

"Yes, I know. I had nightmares for weeks afterwards. I used to wake up in the night terrified, thinking I was on the ground with this maniac, and he was going to cut me again and finish me off for good. Horrible experience."

Carl said gently: "You are a handsome man, Thomas, scar or no scar. And for those who know the story, that scar is more like a medal."

Mia changed the subject, satisfied that she had achieved her objective, and told Carl about the pushy journalist.

"I can't believe the things that are happening to you, Mia. I don't like that journalist saying she'll write about you whether you want it or not. I suppose she could name you too."

"I don't want any publicity at all - I want my life to be private, not debated by strangers. So, we're meeting with the others tonight to discuss what the consequences could be if Miles really did tell that woman everybody's names. She could start hounding them too, so it's important that we all say the same thing."

Carl was thoughtful and silent while Thomas and Mia continued talking, but suddenly he said, "You should really think about where you would go, if your name gets into the paper – I mean if you feel you're at risk from someone. Once your name is in the paper they can find out where you live and work. And the others can be found too if they are named, so you couldn't stay with them. Where would you go to be safe then?"

Why had she not thought of this before? "I don't know, Carl - I hadn't thought of it like that, but I hope it won't come to that – it's a bit farfetched, I think. And I couldn't stop going to work anyway, I have to be able to live a normal life and I don't want to go into hiding."

"I'm not saying it's likely to happen, but it might. And I'm not talking about staying in hiding for a year or anything like that." Carl frowned and thought for a moment. "But say you found out that someone was following you or watching you, where would your safe place be? You can't stay at Thomas's house, because that Miles bloke might have told people Thomas's name. You can't stay with me, because I live on Thomas's property, so that's just as bad."

Thomas and Mia looked at each other and had no answer.

"We can discuss it with the others tonight and make sure we have a plan in case it's needed, but I think the risk is remote." Thomas was trying to keep the discussion from becoming too scary because Carl was getting agitated. "The others are sure to have some good ideas."

Mia smiled to reassure Carl and hastened to reinforce Thomas's words "I promise I'll let you know what arrangements we make, so you know that I'll be safe."

"Yes, make sure you do that, please - you're important to me, even though we haven't known each other long. We share a very weird experience and as far as we know we might never meet anyone else like us, so we have to look out for each other."

At Parnell that evening they spotted Paul just getting out of his car and they walked along together, and when John opened the door for them Paul was just saying: "Lorraine's here more than she's at the flat these days - I have to cook for myself all the time – it's like living alone."

John just smiled and ignored Paul's grumble. "She's making dessert, which is something I never do, so that's a bonus. I must say it's strange to share the kitchen – not that I'm complaining, mind you."

"You'd better not," said Thomas. "I've cooked for myself for years and I think the bliss of having sole possession of the kitchen is over-rated."

The discussion over dinner was intense; everyone had ideas of what would be the best solution to Mia's problems. By the time Lorraine served the dessert they had worked through the options and Lorraine volunteered her mother's place.

"Mum would be happy to have you any time you need a place to hide. She loves company and she's got a spare room that never gets used."

"But won't her place be as dangerous as your place? Your surname is so unusual and there can't be many people with that name in the phone book?"

"Ah, but she has a different surname. Paul and I have our father's name, but mum uses her unmarried name, so there is no obvious connection. You could stash some gear at her place, just a few spares, so you could get away fast, straight from work or something."

Paul agreed. "It's perfect, Mia - you would be safer there than most places. We can take you there once, so you can find it easily if you need to. And if you had to go there, Lorraine and I would stay away until it was OK again."

He looked at Thomas and then at John. "Maybe it sounds a bit over the top, but the only way to make sure Mia is safe is to physically isolate her from everyone who's linked to her. I don't suppose you have a police safe house sitting ready and waiting, John?"

John shook his head. "No, that's not an option – not unless there is a threat, but your mother's place sounds like a good idea. Let's hope we never need to worry about it."

Thomas reverted to the subject of media attention. "We should decide what we'll say if the media get on to us. Mia and I think that complete denial is still the best recipe. If we all deny any knowledge, then Miles is the odd one out - and he has no real evidence to prove his story."

They decided that whoever was contacted would respond as

agreed and let the others know, but the end result was an anticli-max; there was little they could do, apart from talk about it.

When Lorraine went to the kitchen to make more coffee and Mia joined her, Lorraine took hold of both her hands and spoke in a low voice. "You and Thomas? What's going on?"

"I wanted to tell you in person, but since we discovered how we both feel, I haven't seen you to talk to. The most instant romance in history – we're moving in together."

"I don't believe it – have you lost your mind? A few days into an affair and you're moving in together? You've hardly known him five minutes!"

She was both excited and concerned. "It's either true love with capital letters or you're both quite mad. I don't suppose you've thought of a prenuptial agreement to cover the risk of losing your invested funds? Just in case it doesn't work out?" She tried to make it sound like a joke, but her eyes were serious.

Mia laughed. "Thomas has *far* more money than I have - he's the one who should worry. For all he knows, I might just be after his money."

"I am so pleased for you – he's a lovely, lovely man and exactly what you deserve."

The evening wound up early, on a note of frustration and disappointment.

"I think I need an early night," said Thomas, and Lorraine sent a sly smile in Mia's direction.

They took a taxi and left the car to be picked up in the morn-ing. Mia sat leaning against Thomas, holding his hand and relishing the solid comfort of him. While he paid for the taxi she looked up at the clear sky where the stars were hardly visible, concealed by the city's light pollution.

And later, in bed, she remembered the stars and said, "Did you know, that if you go down into a deep hole, a well for example, and look up at the sky you can see the stars even in bright daylight? I'd like to do that one day – I don't know how it works, but it seems like a miracle."

"I think I've heard that too – probably something to do with the fact that light beams don't bend. Let's try it if we come across a suitable well."

And Mia lay in the dark thinking of un-bending light beams

and tried to picture how it worked, but it was late and scientific analysis after three glasses of wine and athletic sex didn't work. "It sounds reasonable, but I'm too sleepy to be clever – let's park it until tomorrow."

Mia woke to the sound of the landline phone and went to the kitchen to pick it up. The weather had done a U-turn again and a steady westerly wind was pushing showers of slanting rain across the city and as she picked up the phone, a seagull blew nearly sideways past the kitchen window on a strong gust of wind.

When she returned to the bedroom Thomas looked at her with a silent question and she said bleakly, "That was the courier company. They're tracing everyone who sent anything via their firm on a certain flight – the one the DVD parcel went on. A bag was stolen from their depot at the other end – including my parcel. The bag's been found burned in a suburban park – they apologized and told me to make a claim."

Thomas lifted the duvet. "Hop back in, darling."

She got in beside him and lay on her back looking at the ceiling, feeling empty and sad, and Thomas pulled her to him and kissed her forehead. "At least you did your best – that's all you can do."

44

When the automatic doors opened for Mia, Alice called out from her desk, her voice excited and happy. "Hi Mia, are you on for a coffee this morning?"

"OK - come and pick me up when you're ready to go. Do I take it you had a great weekend?"

"Oh, the wedding was perfect – really great! And guess who was there?"

Alice's eyes were sparkling with mischief. Mia realized she would never get it right and admitted instant defeat. "I have no idea. Who was it?"

"Josh!"

"Really? How did he get to be there?" She was alert and intrigued now.

Alice turned to make sure there was nobody around and lowered her voice. "He wasn't invited as such - he came as partner to one of my cousin's friends - she had never met him before."

Mia sensed that this was not all Alice had to tell. "And?"

"After dinner he came over and sat down at our table for a while. I think he just wanted to find out why we were there – Callum and me, I mean. And then he started talking about you."

This was intriguing, but Mia tried to sound only moderately interested. "Really? What did he say about me?"

"Well, not much, but he asked if you and I were friends, and I said Callum and I both know you outside work. I wondered if he might be keen on you, but I don't think that was it - sorry, I don't mean that the way it sounded! But it was odd the way he brought up your name out of nowhere, he didn't mention anyone else from work."

Alice's instinct for drama had been whetted and Mia decided this might be a good time to plant a few seeds, so she lowered her voice. "Mm, yes – that *is* odd. He has been a bit funny lately and the other day I found him eavesdropping when I was on the phone talking to a friend. He even commented on what he had heard me say – weird!"

"Yeah, we both thought it was strange the way he kept bringing the conversation back to you, but we never worked out what he was after. Mind you, he'd had quite a lot to drink from the look of him – the conversation wasn't going in a straight line at any time, and Callum got quite impatient with him."

"Don't worry, I'm a bit wary of Josh at the moment. I don't know what he's up to but if I find out, I'll tell you."

It was only a question of time now before people would be talking about Josh's deception and she was relieved that Callum hadn't told Alice of their evening vigil outside the office. Later, when it was out in the open, it wouldn't matter, but for now she appreciated his discretion.

At ten she made a quick trip upstairs to the administration office on the excuse that she wanted to bind some copies of a report. She printed a copy of an old report and went upstairs. The large office on the second floor was in its normal state of concentrated activity. Lisa was busy in the workroom off to one side, where the copiers and the binding machines were, and looked up when Mia entered and noticed the papers in Mia's hand.

"Oh, *please* don't tell me you need something in a hurry, I'm completely booked out this morning."

Mia waved her bundle of papers vaguely in the air. "I need four copies of this bound, but I can do it myself. I know how the binding machine works. So long as I am not in your way?"

"No, go ahead. If it's only black and white you can use the small copier right now. I'm doing 20 copies of a 48-page job at the moment on the colour copier, and I won't need the binder till later."

"Why are you so busy on a Monday morning?" Mia put her originals on the smaller copier and turned around to speak to Lisa. "Is it because of the merger?"

"No, it's just your typical rotten coincidence that Lawrence and Josh both have more than one thing on the go at the moment - they have one deadline each first thing this week. More to come in a couple of days too! So, I'm the one who has to cope with the last-minute panic."

Mia smiled at her cross little face. "You are too obliging Lisa, that's what it is. Everyone relies on you getting things done even if you've had no warning. I didn't realize Josh had two deadlines coming up – I did some of the work for his proposal for Nicholson's. Is that the one you're doing today?"

"Have a look, it's over there on the table. I haven't even looked at it yet. I'm finishing Lawrence's one first, and then I'll tackle Josh's stuff."

Mia opened the two manila folders on the table; one was the Nicholson brief. She flicked through it casually and said to Lisa.

"I'll just make a quick copy of this, just in black and white. If they're going out today, I won't get a chance to see a bound copy. It's always nice to see the final product, when you've spent a lot of time working on it in the early stages."

Ten minutes later Mia left with a copy of Josh's proposal at the bottom of her little pile of useless reports.

The visit to the admin room had taken a bit longer than planned. Alice came to pick her up for coffee before she had time to read the proposal, so she tucked it into her top drawer and went upstairs for a coffee.

Alice started telling Mia about the wedding as they walked down the corridor to the stairs. "It was so lovely – everything was so pretty, and they had those big gas heaters that look like jet engines, so it wasn't cold at all, even though we didn't get the warm weather they had promised. Callum met lots of my family – there are dozens of them, so that was good, and my mum thinks he's lovely. My dad never comments much on people, but he seemed to think he was OK too."

"Did he realize he was in for the full family inspection? Hope he wasn't stricken with complete panic."

Alice giggled and replied with pretend nonchalance: "Well, we have progressed you know. We spend most of our time together now."

As soon as they found a table, Alice switched topics.

"Now it's your turn - tell me who the new man is? Is it serious? What does he do? And how long have you known him?"

"Heavens Alice, how many questions is that all in one go? His name is Thomas, and he lives next-door to a friend of mine, so that's how I know him. We've been spending a lot of time together and it's beginning to look serious."

She felt her face break into a spontaneous smile and wondered if she was blushing.

"How wonderful - I'm so pleased for you. It's only a few weeks ago that you seemed really depressed and we were all so worried about you. You must have fallen in love all of a sudden." She smiled at the thought "Isn't it funny how that happens? A friend of mine had known a chap for ages and never once thought of him in a romantic way, and next thing there's this great romance going on. She said it was just as if they looked at each other one day and something went click."

"I know, isn't it marvellous? I feel as if we're made for each other, and he's not been married before - no ex-wives and no children, so everything's nice and simple."

Mia thought how lucky it was that she could avoid saying that she had only just met Thomas; the more ordinary it seemed, the better.

"And where does he live and all the rest? I hope I'll get to meet him some time?"

"He lives in Eden Terrace, and he works for a firm of international legal advisors, but he's really an accountant."

"Awesome! He's a good catch then, not that it matters when you love someone. I'd be happy to go and live in a shack with Callum, so long as we were happy together."

Mia made a pretend sarcastic face. "Yeah, right! And you wouldn't complain about hand-washing nappies in a bucket of cold water I suppose?"

She was joking, but Alice went bright pink and Mia had to backtrack. "Sorry, Alice, I didn't mean to be so personal. It was just a silly joke."

"I know – it's just that we were talking about babies yesterday and it seemed so weird that you should bring it up just today. Not that we're planning to have a baby or anything, but we were saying we both like kids and we both feel a big family is a great thing, at least three or four. Which counts as big these days."

"I think so too. I only have one sister, and when our parents died, it seemed as if there was nothing left. The two of us somehow didn't feel like a family. We were very close, and we still are, but if there had been three or more of us it would have added a bit of emotional bulk and felt a bit more solid."

Going downstairs again, Alice said she was looking forward to a closer view of Thomas soon and Mia didn't know if it was wise move, but she made a snap decision to warn Alice.

"The first thing you'll notice is that he has a great scar down one side of his face, so he looks quite different depending on which side you see – either quite dangerous or just kind and lovely – but inside he's one hundred percent kind and lovely."

45

As soon as she was alone in her room, she closed the door, got the proposal out of the drawer and flicked through it to find the paragraphs with the financial calculations, and her heart skipped a beat. It was exactly as it had been in That Time; the expenses were low enough to make the viability look good instead of marginal. Quickly she found the actual spreadsheet table in the appendix, and there it was, the expenses were all there, but the totals didn't include the top row of expenses. By now she knew the spreadsheet by heart and there was no need to check the details. Grimly she shut the report, which now looked like a proposal that any client would be delighted to accept. At least until someone sat down and added up the expenses by hand, she thought, and that would not happen until it was too late.

But what now? Since she had started planning how to protect herself in This Time, she had processed many scenarios in her mind, but now when the time had actually come, she felt apprehensive. She re-read the relevant parts of the proposal, checked her copy of the spreadsheet and then the email with the spreadsheet attached, which she had sent as evidence to that chap on the top floor.

All the pieces she had so carefully prepared were in place and she hoped nothing could go wrong this time. But now it was urgent that she left her room quickly because the last thing she wanted was for Josh to come in for a chat before she had taken the matter to Alan. She took her copy and nearly ran to Alan's room.

He was busy reading something and didn't notice her until she closed the door behind her.

"Have you got a moment?"

He looked up, startled, and glanced at the closed door. "OK, provided it's not going to take too long. I have to write an addendum for report for the board - they want more statistics. And we have two client presentations due - today and tomorrow."

Mia put the copy of the proposal on his desk. "Sorry Alan, I think this might take some time, but it *is* serious. Before I start - did you see the final version of the Nicholson proposal?"

"Yes, of course I've seen it – that's one of the client meetings I mentioned. Looks good, doesn't it? Josh might just make his name with this one."

"Who proofed it?"

"Josh proofed it himself. I picked up a couple of minor errors and told him, and he fixed those. Why are you asking?"

"The costings spreadsheet has serious errors in it - and because of that the proposal looks good. If those errors weren't there you would *never* give this proposal to the client – it's extremely marginal. I would call it high risk, more likely to go wrong than to scrape through."

Alan looked alarmed. "Mia, sit down. We need to talk about this - you did that viability study yourself. When did you discover the errors?"

"When I read the document just now – I picked up a copy in the binding room just out of curiosity, and straight away I saw the figures were wrong. I checked against the Excel file on the shared drive, but that's the same as what's in the proposal, the column totals miss out the top row of expenses."

She took a deep breath and tried to sound as calm as possible, but her heart was beating very fast, and she felt breathless.

"The spreadsheet I handed over to Josh did *not* look like that – and the comments I had added to the spreadsheet are no longer there. I put them into the original version of the spreadsheet to warn Josh that the project was unviable, and which expenses were high-risk, hard to estimate accurately and therefore potentially under-estimated."

She was talking without taking proper breaths, overcome by tension; she paused, took another deep breath and tried to calm herself.

Alan looked out the window for a long moment, thoughtful and worried, then he turned back to Mia.

"Are you saying that someone deliberately tampered with the spreadsheet to make the proposal look as if it's worth presenting?"

"It's the only thing I can think of. It's not the kind of error that happens just by chance. It is quite deliberate – all those cells where the totals formula has been changed to omit the top row – that *can't* be an accident. It could happen if someone changed one by mistake and then copied the formula to the other total cells, but the fact that the embedded comments have disappeared too? It's too much to be a coincidence, Alan. I'm sorry, but however it happened, the proposal simply can't be presented to the clients."

"Do you have a printout of the original spreadsheet? Just to compare with?"

Mia understood what he was trying to establish and had no issue with it. It would be her word against Josh's and Alan needed to be sure of his facts.

"I think I still have a copy of the original file on my personal drive, I usually keep things there until they are finished. I remember saving it on the shared drive when it was done, and then I told Josh it was finished. Come through to my office, where I'm logged on and I'll show you."

They walked to Mia's room in silence, and just like Mia had done, Alan shut the door behind them. She sat down at her desk, opened her personal folder and found the subfolder called 'Projects' while Alan watched over her shoulder. "Yes, there it is – Nicholson.xls."

As she spoke, she clicked the file open and scrolled down the spreadsheet.

"See, the totals at the bottom of the columns are completely different - and look at the end result. And you can see my comments."

Mia swung around in her chair and looked up at Alan's worried face. "After I told Josh it was nearly finished, I went to see him, and I told him straight out that the project looked very marginal and could easily slide into a loss situation. He was angry, furious actually, and we argued about it. He wanted me to change things, so it looked better, take things out – he was very ... forceful, but I told him to read the notes and look properly at the whole thing – far too risky. I said it wasn't debatable, and I could not change anything and left him to it. I thought he would calm down and accept it. Then I picked up the proposal in the copier room this morning, really surprised to find it had got to that stage - and found this."

Now Alan was getting angry. "This is unbelievable! Think of the damage to the company – he must be mad to try a stunt like this. What sort of proof can you give me that this copy of the spreadsheet is exactly as it was when you gave to Josh?"

Mia felt like a bad actress, but she had to go through the steps to establish proof of her assertions.

"I know this is what it looked like – we can check this file to see when it was last modified and then do the same with the file on the shared document drive. The shared one must have been changed later."

With Alan watching closely, she checked and proved her point; the shared file had been modified later than the one on her own drive.

Alan straightened up and reached across the desk for Mia's phone. "I'm calling the CEO." He walked around the desk and stood facing Mia while he talked. "Hi David, I have a serious issue here, which I need to discuss right away. If you're free I would like to come up now. Thanks, I will. And I'm bringing Mia Dawson with me."

He turned to Mia. "Let's go, he can see us now if we come straight away. I want you to log on as yourself on a computer in his office and show him the original on your personal drive. And bring that copy of the proposal, please."

46

They took the lift in silence. Mia had only been on the top floor a few times and she had never set foot in the CEO's office, but his PA was expecting them and motioned for them to go straight in.

Alan dived straight in. "David, this is Mia, presume you've met? Good – we won't waste any time. Mia came to me just now with a very worrying story and she has just shown me proof that she has her facts right. If you don't mind moving aside, I would like Mia to log on to your computer under her own name, so she can access her personal folder and show you what she just showed me. And meanwhile I'll tell you the story."

David Wilson looked hard at Alan and then at Mia but made no comment before he logged off and got up from his desk. He motioned to Mia to take his place, and he and Alan sat down at the round conference table by the window, while Mia sat at his desk with a feeling of unreality.

Alan gave David a brief version of Mia's story and described how they had checked the "last modified" dates on the two computer files, and how Josh had asked her to change the costings to look better. Mia listened and realized that the facts were brutally damning when told as a coherent story. Alan pointed out the discrepancies in the proposal document and opened the page in the appendix to show David the table of expenses. David reached over and took a calculator from his desk, checked the figures and got up.

"OK, let's have a look at those two files."

Mia first showed him the file on the shared drive, and the date when it had last been changed, and then her own copy of the file with a much earlier 'last modified' date. She opened the spreadsheet and demonstrated the differences to David, showed him the changed totals formula and the disappearance of the embedded comments.

"Well, there's no doubting that, is there? But as extra insurance I'll ask IT to check who it was who last modified the file on the shared drive."

"Can they actually tell who did it?" said Alan in surprise.

"Yes, they can tell whose log-on was used. That would prove it beyond any doubt," said David and Mia said, "I can assure you it wasn't me."

David was obviously keen to discuss the next step with Alan in private. "Thank you, Mia – great work. This would have been a disaster for our reputation. Heaven knows when it would have been discovered and how much money would have been already spent.' He shook his head in disbelief. "And what did Josh think he would get out of it, eh? It's a mad scheme. You can go now. Alan and I will ask Josh to come up and explain a few things, and then I'll take it from there – no need for you to worry about that. And please keep it all to yourself for now."

Alan nodded. "I'll come and see you later."

Mia left in a state of disbelief at how fast things had moved. In her imagination she had anticipated a drawn-out process, maybe over days, but everything was happening with bewildering speed. To avoid having to meet Josh on his way upstairs, she went down to the second floor and dawdled away twenty minutes in the staff canteen until it seemed safe to assume that the risk was over. She took a mug of coffee with her back to her room and shut the door behind her.

She couldn't imagine settling down to work now, and neither could she go for lunch until Alan came back downstairs; it was like being in limbo. Her focus was completely on the Josh drama, and she knew she wouldn't be able to concentrate on anything else. She was staring absently at her screensaver, sipping her coffee and wondering how to pass the time, when Thomas called.

"How's your day going?"

"Very interesting, to say the least - I can't wait to tell you all about it. You know that treachery drama I told you about, how I got shafted at work last year - right about this time? It exploded today."

"Is it going to plan?"

"I don't want to talk too much about it right now, but yes – it's going to plan so far. It's actually moving with amazing speed. I'll tell you all about it tonight."

"That reminds me of what I was calling about. I'm taking clients out for dinner tomorrow night, and I hope you will come. They're a married couple, and we never talk business over dinner. I take them out once or twice a year when they are in the country - they are what we call key clients, and I like to look after them. And they're an entertaining couple to spend an evening with."

"I'd love to - I haven't been to a good restaurant in ages. I'll see you after work."

She put the phone down and gazed unseeingly into the middle distance, deep in thought. I have this new life where I go out for dinner and meet new people, a real life with plans and a future. I am so lucky! And all the things I'm finding out about myself – that I can be proactive and assertive, and stronger than I thought I was. It makes me sad to think of another Mia perhaps still existing in That Time, depressed and lonely.

The phone rang again. "Mia, can you please come back upstairs? Josh has been here - he has been suspended and he has left for the time being. We'd like to talk to you again if you've got time."

Mia made her way to the top floor by going out to the foyer and up in the front lift to avoid any possibility of bumping into Josh. I'm not averse to facing him, she thought, but there might be a real risk of having my nose bloodied if I meet him just now – heaven knows how he would react.

Alice's desk was manned by her reliever, who paid no attention to her, and she wondered how soon the rumours would start flying round the building. It was a bit nerve-wracking being an inside player at this level, and she had no idea of what David and Alan might expect of her.

. . .

Half an hour later she went back downstairs, better informed and with specific instructions and knew what to expect. Josh was formally under suspension for an act that would result in instant dismissal. There would be no further investigation – the facts and proof on hand were enough, and Josh had been given two days to get legal advice and consider if he wanted to contest their evidence. The only thing they wanted from Mia was an assurance that she would not talk to anyone about it until he had been definitively dismissed. She must also write a summary of the spreadsheet incident from start to finish for the personnel files.

"I'll make a statement to staff once Josh has been dismissed." David looked as if doing this sort of thing was all in a day's work for him, not particularly stressed or even worried. "After that you're free to talk to people about the things you discovered, but only your own direct experiences, you can't quote anything Alan and I have said."

Mia wrote her statement as soon as she was back at her desk; the sooner she did it the better, she wanted to put this behind her and look forward. What with her new level of involvement in a creative project and having made a good impression on the CEO, her prospects looked good, and it was pleasant to speculate on a different future and feel that a major hurdle had been overcome, and Josh could no longer damage her.

Writing the statement turned out to be far harder than she had anticipated, and in the end she did it with bullet points in chronological order to avoid using any phrases or expressions that might sound like value judgements on her part. She printed the statement, dated and signed it and went to put it on Alan's desk.

He beamed at her when she walked in. "Well done! You've saved the company from a potential disaster, and you made a good impression upstairs – David commented on your judgement and your focus. He wants me to bring your salary review forward - how about we do it tomorrow instead of in December?"

Mia was reluctant to talk about it so soon; it felt mercenary. "Thank you, but there's no need to do it right now – it feels like I'm benefiting from someone else's misfortune."

"God no, not at all. Josh was acting out of self-interest, to gain something for himself, reputation or admiration for his clever promotion scheme. And I'm sure he would have put the blame on you when the errors in that costing were discovered – as they would have been sooner or later, he must have had a plan to save himself. So don't feel sorry for him! He's the author of his own fate and I think he would have sacrificed you without a second thought."

"I know you're right – I already figured that he could have used me as a scapegoat. But let's leave it until he has accepted his dismissed - it will feel more pleasant when he's really gone."

They set a date for Mia's review for the following week, and she returned to her room. On an impulse she rang Lorraine, who was at work in the Designers boutique. She was definitely not going to start telling her about today's drama over the phone, but it was nice to have a chat. They talked about this and that and decided that having dinner out next week might be nice. Just as Mia was about to put the phone down, she had an idea.

"And another thing, Lorraine. I'm going out for dinner tomorrow night with Thomas and clients of his, to a smart restaurant. I want to wear that short black and white dress I bought from you for Sarah's dinner, but not with trousers. I tried it with tights and shoes, but it didn't look right – perhaps it's me, not the right proportions? Any ideas?"

Lorraine didn't even need to think. "No, I don't think you should wear it as a conventional dress - it ruins the idea, and definitely not with stockings and high heel shoes. Try it with black leggings and high-heeled boots. That will work and it's dressier than the trousers. Have you got nice boots?"

"Oh yes, I've got a lovely pair, very indoors kind of boots. I'll get myself the right kind of tights and do that, it sounds good. Thank you. But I must come in and get another couple of dressy things - I'm obviously going to need them in this new life. Perhaps you could find some things for me to try on? If you don't mind being both legal advisor and stylist?"

She put the phone down on Lorraine's catchy chuckle, looked at the mess on her desk and decided that what she needed was lunch. She picked up her bag and jacket and headed for the foyer, telling Alice that she would be back at two.

47

With a copy of the paper and a helping of pumpkin soup with toast in front of her, Mia took her time and enjoyed being out of the office. Turning a page, she came across the dreaded column *And what have we here?*

Her eyes flew down the lines and her heart nearly stopped when she saw her name halfway down the column. She backtracked and read the paragraph from the top.

"We have further news about modest Mia, who made the accurate but unheeded prophesy of Steve Irwin's accident. Despite Mia shunning publicity and refusing to be interviewed, we now know that she also predicted a cathedral fire in St Petersburg and was again accurate in every detail. Our witness tells us that the fire took place on the stated date, and everything happened exactly according to the prophecy. We can't help speculating about what other uses this extraordinary talent could be put to. We believe Mia is communicating with the police regarding undisclosed incidents – which no doubt bodes ill for some! Our investigation continues, and we hope to bring you more news soon."

A sound of outrage escaped before she could control herself, and the couple at the next table turned to stare at her. Embarrassed she turned the page and started reading something she was not in the least bit interested in, while she calmed down. She finished her soup with worried thoughts swirling through her head. What if

Grace Wright printed her full name next time? Had Miles given her more information, despite being warned not to? She knew that the St Catherine's fire had been mentioned when Grace first called her, so Miles must have told her that at the start. Bringing it out now, as if it had just been discovered, was just a journalistic ploy. Maybe he hadn't told her anything more and Grace was just spinning it out for effect. She texted the others and told them to check the paper, but her nerves were jangling and her peace of mind ruined.

That evening Thomas was going back to his place after a late Zoom meeting he and his partner were having with a prospective new client in a different time zone. The apartment seemed empty and quiet without him, and Mia was thinking of what needed doing, when she the woman from the garage called and apologized for disturbing her evening.

"I'm sorry to call you at this hour, but I am trying to contact quite a few people. There is a possibility that the tyres we fitted on your Civic are faulty. We've had a recall notice from the manufacturer, and we need to take the tyres off the wheels to check them, so we would like to have the car for a few hours tomorrow if possible."

"That's OK – what time do you want me to drop it in?"

"The workshop is going to be flat out and we are short on parking space here. If it's OK, we'll send someone around to your work about midday tomorrow to pick the car up and then we'll deliver it back as soon as we have done the checking. Would that suit you?"

"Yes, that's fine. I'll give you my cell phone number, so you can let me know when someone's on the way."

"Great! We want to get these checks done, so people don't set out on long trips with tyres that could start delaminating."

With nothing more enticing to do, Mia got her pad and read through her list of future events, trying to tease some more detail from her memory, but after quarter of an hour, she admitted that trying to force her memory was not going to work.

She flicked through CDs looking for something she hadn't played for a while and found one her cousin had given her a couple of years ago – blues music from the American South. She turned the CD over and read the song titles, but the only familiar one was "Midnight Special", and then the words Delta Blues a bit further down caught her eye and she sat up straight and said, "Yes!".

Delta Blues was the name of the Melbourne Cup winner and that brought back the memory of what linked the first and second placegetters: both horses had Japanese owners. She pictured sitting down and telling Thomas about her big day with so much going on and the culminating luck of remembering the Cup winner's name. She sat there for a moment holding the CD, quietly relishing her luck, before she got up and put the CD on to play, got her book from the bedroom and spent the evening reading.

Thomas called the next morning just as Mia got out of the shower, and she ran naked and dripping to the kitchen where she had left her phone, and then back to the bathroom to get a towel.

"I missed you last night, cara Mia. The meeting went on forever - it was just as well you didn't wait up for me. I didn't get home until after two this morning. What did you do?"

"I found something that reminded me of the name of the Melbourne Cup winner, so that problem is solved – feel free to be as greedy as you like."

She laughed and told him what she had remembered. "You'd better make a note of it! And the Josh saga is just about over – it happened so fast, the perfect storm. I never expected it to be like that, over in a day. Now there's only the formal dismissal still to come, but it's a given. It was such a big day - and I feel so relieved now that the worst is over. I can't tell you how good it was to get home last night and just blob out – aimless and worry-free."

She moved the phone to her other hand and tried to anchor the towel under her armpit to stop it falling to the floor. "You will hear all about it, blow by blow, when I see you."

She shook her head at the memory of the events and the speed things had moved at. "Isn't it funny how you feel sorry for people, even when they deserve what happens to them? I know he's a villain and he brought it on himself, but I still pity him in a way."

"For heaven's sake - don't waste any pity on him. He was going to sacrifice you on the altar of his own ambition, and you know from last time that he wouldn't spare a thought for your fate."

"That's exactly what Alan said, too – well, he didn't mention last time, of course. I know you're right, but when I think of how he must feel…"

"Mia, what he is feeling is most likely shame and embarrassment – and probably not for what he did, only because he was found out. But I love you for being soft-hearted, it's a very endearing trait."

"I'm not that soft! Not like the marshmallow I was in that other life – then I couldn't bear to confront anyone, and I let people walk all over me. I think I'm getting quite assertive this time around."

Thomas laughed, affectionately disbelieving. "Yeah, right! But I must brag a bit too – it was such a brilliant meeting last night. We secured a new key client - very key in fact, he may well turn out to be our biggest so far. That's why we ended up being so late. The meeting was over by midnight, and we stayed on at the office and had a couple of drinks and discussed future developments. One of the great things is that this new guy has contacts and networks that could be very useful to us – heaven knows that even one or two more clients of his calibre would add enormously to the business."

"That's good, so long as you don't end up working twelve-hour days to cope with it."

"If we got one or two more like him, we would add another lawyer or accountant to the team to do some of the groundwork. At the moment we three do all the front-end work ourselves and we have one admin person, so the idea of hiring another professional is a big step forward. Do you want me to pick you up and take you to work?"

"No, thanks, I have to take the car. I haven't had time to tell you yet - the garage called and said they need to check the new tyres – something's wrong with a certain batch and they need to the car for half a day. So, I'm driving to work, and they'll pick it up at lunchtime or whatever. I'll have it back by the end of the day."

"OK - I'll call you later about the arrangements for tonight. You haven't forgotten about the dinner?"

"Heavens no, I'm really looking forward to it. I must go – if I don't get a move on, I'll be late for work."

Parking behind the building proved impossible because she was late, and the parking lot was full. She drove back out to the street and parked in a metered space about a block away and hurried back to the office, making a mental note to remember to feed the meter or move the car mid-morning.

Alice had been on the lookout for her. "Do you know what happened to Josh? I've been told that he's not going to be here for 'a while' and to pass everything on to Alan. And more information to come later - a real mystery. But I hear he left after you and Alan were in Mr Wilson's office yesterday."

The unspoken expectation was clear, and Mia knew that she had to tread a careful path between telling outright lies and revealing too much, too soon.

She stalled by asking, "How on earth did you find that out?"

"Mandy was on the top floor about something, and she saw you and Alan looking serious, and in a hurry - she told me when she came in this morning. And Lisa told me that Alan took all the reports she had just bound and said they were no longer needed."

"I'm sorry Alice, but the full story isn't mine to tell, and I don't want to speculate about it – not just yet anyway."

She moved closer and lowered her voice. "I think there will be an announcement from the CEO either tomorrow or the next day, and I've promised him not to talk about it until then. I really think the best thing would be if you talk as little as possible about this until it's official."

"OK, I'll do that - but only because you look so serious. But you'll have to promise to tell me what you know as soon as you can – I'm at the helm of this ship and I need to know what goes on."

Mia gave a mock salute and continued to her room considering what she would tell Callum and Alice. The sooner she was able to be open about it, the better – if Mandy was spreading rumours already the place would be fizzing with half-baked theories and mad stories before lunchtime. She got to her desk and remembered she never mentioned the car and called Alice.

"I forgot to say that a mechanic will turn up at lunchtime to collect my car. I couldn't park in the back yard, so it's on a meter down the road. Can you call me on my mobile – just in case I'm not in my room when he arrives? I have to show him where the car is and give him the key."

"Of course. And I'm sorry if I tried to gossip about Josh earlier – it's obviously serious. I won't say anything until the CEO tells us whatever he's going to tell us."

Alan came in, dropped a small pile of folders on her desk and sat down to discuss what of Josh's work he wanted Mia to take over.

"I've passed on a couple of things he was working on to Rob's section, but these are the ones I want to keep a close eye on. I've made some notes, but nothing in-depth yet. We need to sit down and put our heads together to make sure we don't miss anything. This *would* happen just when we're so busy on all fronts – Sod's Law. And it's always hard to pick up something that's been taken to the halfway stage by someone else. I hope you can fit it in along with that project you're involved with."

"I'm sure we can sort it out between us. Did you hear anything new about Josh?"

"No, but the day is young, and things might happen sooner rather than later." He shook his head. "If he has any sense, he won't contest it. There's so much evidence now and David told me they have they can prove that it was Josh who made the last changes to that spreadsheet of yours, so it's cut and dried."

An hour later an email from the CEO arrived, obviously sent to everyone in the company saying that Josh Greene had been discovered in serious misconduct, that he had been given time to take legal advice and had done so, but that he had decided to not dispute the allegation and he was no longer an employee. It was a very carefully worded statement. scripted by someone who knew employment law and there was no mention of either resignation or dismissal. And literally seconds after she had read it Mia got a call from David Wilson.

"Morning Mia! I just sent out an email memo. I'm aware that there's a lot of speculation is going on in some departments – I believe our internal Gossip Central has done a great job already this morning and managed to make a lot of people very curious."

She knew he could only be talking about Mandy and laughed. "I know she's been busy - I've been asked about it already."

"Feel free to tell people the facts of what you discovered but remember that anything we discussed in my office or any comments of mine or Alan's must remain confidential. It's lucky you found so much before you talked to Alan. It's very hard for the employer to let other staff know the facts without breaching the employment laws, but we can't stop you telling your side, what you know firsthand."

"If it's OK, I'll tell a few and they'll no doubt tell others. From a personal point of view, I *would* like people to know the facts – just so they know how serious it was and how deliberate."

"Exactly! It's important to me that you share what you know. These things often end up with a mishmash of gossip and assumptions based on whatever people tell each other. And before you know it, you've got all sorts of rumours about unfairness and people having been set up by management and goodness knows what. The law protects the employee but not the employer. Josh can tell any kind of story he likes, but management can't put the record straight without breaking confidentiality."

Mia was surprised at the passion in his voice and hesitantly ventured a personal comment, hoping he wouldn't object, but she really wanted to know. "You sound as if you've experienced this - to feel so strongly?"

He laughed without amusement. "Yeah, I certainly have - and it became a nightmare for me personally. But that was some years ago and now I'm very grateful for your role in this. Someday I might tell you about that other drama – you'll be amazed. But this time you found out just about every damning aspect on your own and had the proof of it – and the IT people are no doubt already talking about how I asked them to confirm who changed that spreadsheet, so more or less the whole truth will become public knowledge."

Mia put the phone down and sat for a moment thinking of how being moved around in time had given her unexpected opportunities that had never come her way in That Time. She sent a compassionate thought to Carl, who had been moved forwards in time and how he had suffered through no fault of own. It was chance that had put her here in This Time and given her a better life, not personal merit. She shook herself into action, and started on one of Josh's briefs, trying to get a grip on what she could contribute before handing them back to Alan.

48

Though she was reluctant to take a break and disrupt her train of thought, she felt obliged to play her role as truth spreader on behalf of David Wilson, so she called Alice.

"Come past and pick me up when you go upstairs for coffee – if we can find a quiet corner, I'll tell you what happened with Josh."

"You bet! Wild rhinos couldn't keep me away," said Alice. "My relief is coming out at quarter past ten today – see you then!"

Half a minute later she called back. "Is it OK if I tell Callum so he can hear it too?"

"Goodness, yes, invite anyone you like. I can only tell you what I know first-hand and once I've told one person it's on public record –my side of it is not a secret."

True to her word, Alice arrived at quarter past ten on the dot. Mia looked at her expectant face, laughed and shook her head. "Nope - I'm not going to tell you one single thing until we're upstairs. I need to sit down and concentrate, so I get everything in the right order."

"Oh, all right – I asked Callum to meet us up there and he said he might bring Tex, if you don't mind. Better that we all hear it at the same time, anyway. My goodness, what a lovely drama!"

Not for the first time Mia reflected on the seeming naiveté of Alice's comment. But she knew that Alice was not naïve, she simply made remarks that sometimes seemed childish, because she was straight-out honest and said what most people only thought in the privacy of their own minds. And if they were to say them, they would dress them up to disguise the fact that all they want is a good piece of gossip, whereas Alice didn't bother with the window-dressing to make it more acceptable.

Mia smiled affectionately at Alice and said, "Drama is right! The most amazing thing I've ever been involved in."

Once ensconced in the chairs around their favourite table, Mia told the whole story from the beginning: Josh's fury over the project costing and their argument when she refused to doctor the figures, the evening she returned to pick up the shopping bags from her office and found him going through her filing cabinet, and her suspicion that he was up to something. How she then came across the proposal in the copy room and noticed that her costing calculations had been altered.

Alice, Callum and Tex sat spellbound as she told them how she had remembered that she had saved a copy of the spreadsheet on her personal drive, which had provided dated proof, and that she had an additional piece of evidence that she had not needed to use - the email she had mistakenly sent to Joe on the top floor with the file in its original state attached.

Callum felt that he had a stake in the drama, having been there the evening Josh searched Mia's files and told the others how they had sat waiting in the car so he would see Josh emerge, and how they had seen him drive past.

"That night, you said you knew of something else he had done in a previous job. Was that a similar thing?"

Mia had to be careful now - she was reluctant to tell direct lies, but she must explain her early suspicion of Josh and what she had told Callum that night.

"I found out about it from someone who worked in the same place as Josh," she said. "It's few years ago and they kept it very quiet - the staff there never found out exactly what had been going on. It seems to have been very nasty, but Josh sailed on without a backward glance and an innocent person ended up covered in mud instead, as if it was their fault. And there wasn't the slightest doubt that he'd done it – there was nobody else who could have."

Alice looked thoughtful. "Wonder what he actually did? It's funny he got hired here - wouldn't they have found out what he had done."

"I think sometimes employers don't want to admit that someone took them for a ride, so they pretend it never happened, they want to avoid looking as if have they sloppy procedures."

Tex, who had been sitting quietly listening, spoke for the first time since Mia started her story. "I heard of someone who did something really bad recently. She struck a deal with the employer – she agreed to resign quietly, and they paid her a sum of money, and they both signed some sort of document saying that neither side would tell how much they paid her to quit or why. So officially she was not dismissed – she resigned. My sister who told me the story, said that it was because the company didn't want anyone to know that an employee had been able to diddle their systems."

"So, they were prepared to let a dishonest person go on to an unsuspecting employer, and they pay her off as well, just to keep their reputation? What a joke!" Callum was outraged. "It makes a mockery of references, doesn't it?"

"Yeah, I know," said Tex. "But I think some bosses ring the previous employer and have a quiet chat when they're thinking of employing someone. Not about a reference, more as if they are checking the person really worked there or something, which means the last boss can give them a hint without putting it on paper."

When Alice and Mia went downstairs again, Mia thought of something. "Why didn't Mandy come with Tex? I thought she usually joined him and Callum for coffee? I always think of them as a group."

"Tex and Mandy are finished. Not that it was ever official in any way, but lots of people knew they were having an affair. I knew because Mandy told me a long time ago, when I had seen them together in her car one night. She told me at the end of last week that she's not going to waste her time on something that'll never lead to a real relationship. But if you ask me, I think *he* finished it and now she's just trying to make it look as if she hasn't been dumped. Tex isn't going to make any comment, so she can say whatever she likes."

Mia wondered if her revelations a couple of weeks ago had hit a nerve with Tex. She remembered the look on his face when she told him and Callum about how she found out that Greg had been having an affair with Barb, and the effect it had had on her.

She plugged her phone in to charge and went back to the pile of Josh's folders. An hour later Alice called to say that the mechanic was in reception already. Mia picked up her keys went out to the foyer, listening to Alice telling her the guy was apologizing for being early, which seemed comical to her.

"Hi, I'm Sam," said the guy in blue overalls and smiled. "I'm a bit early - I'll take the car now and bring it back about five, if that's all right?"

"Yes, that's fine. I'll show you where it is."

They went out on the street and Mia steered him to the left, tucked her phone into her trouser pocket and started removing the car key from her key ring as they walked.

She went to the outside of the car and said over her shoulder, "I'll just get my notebook that I left in car this morning" and unlocked the driver's door.

As she turned to give Sam the key, a large white van pulled up close alongside her car and Sam took hold of her arm. For a split second she thought he was worried that the van would knock into her, but the side door of the van slid open, and she was pushed and pulled into the back of the van by Sam and the man inside. She landed on her knees on the metal floor and was shoved further in by Sam who jumped in after her. They were moving away even as the door was closing. Mia struggled to her feet. "What *are* you doing? Let me go - you can't do this!"

The other man grabbed her hair at the back and slapped her hard across the side of her face. "Shut up!"

The windows in the back were painted over and the light was dim. Beside her was a large metal cage pushed against the back doors. They went around a corner at speed, and Mia nearly fell sideways, and the men barely managed to keep their balance. The older one swore viciously and a voice from the front seat said, "Sorry, Fish!"

Mia's mind was a whirl of confusion and fear. The man called Fish pushed her towards the cage, Sam opened the door in the front, and Fish put his hands on her shoulders and made her crouch, pushed her in and closed the door. The van swerved and her ankle twisted as she lost her balance and fell helplessly further into the cage, landing hard on her left hip. Grunting in pain she rolled onto her back and as she did, she remembered the phone her right trouser pocket.

Yes! I have my phone - but I must turn it off, it's my only hope.

She glanced at the men, who were leaning forward over the front seats and talking to the driver. Slowly she reached into her pocket, ran her fingers gently over the phone and pressed the off button, blessing the fact that she always turned the sound nearly right down as soon as she arrived at work and now the buzzing sound it made when she turned it off was hardly audible.

She called out, "Why have you taken me – where are we going?"

The man called Fish looked over his shoulder. "Just shut up or you'll get another slap to remind you!"

"What are you going to do with me? I haven't done anything to you."

She could hear that her voice was higher pitched than normal, and her whole body felt disorganized in some way, though her mind was clear.

So, this is what physical fear does to you, she thought, destroys your coordination and makes you unable to control your voice. I must pull myself together.

But even as the thought passed through her mind, she realized that the best thing would be to let them think that she was incapacitated by fear. If she showed no signs of opposition or fight, they would not expect her to try to escape.

Fish replied without turning his head. "No questions till we're ready to have a talk. We're going to have a chat about a few things and you're going to help us, and then we'll let you go - if you behave yourself. Now just shut up!"

He clambered over to sit beside the driver, and Sam braced himself against the front seats, leaning forward to look ahead. Frantic thoughts about what they might do to her flew through Mia's mind and she tried to think of ways to attract attention, and how she might escape when they took her out of the van. She had no idea which direction they were going, and from her low angle on the floor she could only see the tops of buildings through the windscreen. The metal bars across the floor were biting into her back, and she was just about to sit up when she thought of the phone again. If they searched her, they would find it and it was the only useful thing she had. But how could she conceal it? Her top was too close fitting to conceal anything, so pushing it under the edge of her bra wouldn't work, but there was one option left.

Staying on her back on the hard metal bars and without taking her eyes off the men, she undid the front button of her trousers and started pulling the zip down very, very slowly. Sam turned around and for a scary moment she thought he had heard the zip being pulled. He stared at her for a moment, while she lay terrified on her back with her knees pulled up and her hands folded on her stomach to hide the half-open zip, then he turned to face forwards again.

Mia got the zip fully open, and agonizingly slowly she eased the phone out of her pocket and pushed it down inside her panties. She paused and tried to imagine what it would feel and look like when she stood up. Where would the bulge be, and would the phone move and maybe slip, when she had to duck through the cage door and climb out? Or maybe they would carry or manhandle her – if they did, they might feel it.

She pushed the phone further down, as far as it would go and turned halfway on her side, still with her knees bent. She was facing the front of the van so she would see the men, but that meant they would see what she was doing if they turned around. Tense and trembling, she lifted her left knee slightly to create a small space between her legs and slowly manoeuvred the phone down between her thighs, until it became a solid floor inside her panties. She pulled her hand out and wriggled gently; her panties held the phone in place, and she hoped it wouldn't slide around when she stood up. If she sat with a slight sideways tilt, it might keep the phone from breaking. She rolled onto her back again and quietly did up the zip and button.

Having accomplished something constructive gave her confidence and a feeling of having gained a measure of control. In her mind she planned the move she would try when they stopped, she would kick her high heels of and make a break for it, but she would have to get them off fast. She was beginning to feel sick now and pushed herself up to sit against the side of the cage.

"How much further is it? I feel sick."

Sam turned round and looked at her with an expression of disgust. "Don't you bloody dare spew in the van!"

Mia stared at him, hoping she gave an impression of someone desperately nauseated. "I feel terrible – I can't help it."

The man called Fish turned his head slightly and shouted, "Shut up you silly bitch! No talking till we get there." And in an aside to Sam, he added, "And if she spews, you'll be the one hosing out the back of the van."

Sam turned away and Mia concentrated on combating her nausea and checking for what she could see through the windscreen. There were no buildings now, just the tops of big trucks and over-bridges, so they were somewhere on the motorway. She caught sight of an overhead sign indicating that the off-ramp to Otahuhu was coming up, and a minute later they drove up a slope before doing a steep right-hand turn. Now she was feeling really sick and started counting backwards from one hundred by threes, an old trick from childhood road trips. She no longer watched for land-marks and knew that she would never remember how many turns they had made or in which direction.

49

———

The van stopped briefly, Fish got out and they moved forward, bumped over a ridge and stopped, and Sam slid the side door open. They were inside a vast space, a huge expanse of concrete floor stretched away into the dim reaches of the building. Sam opened the door to the cage and yanked her arm. "Come on! Time to get out."

Mia crawled through the cage door, but when she put her weight on her right foot to stand up a stab of pain shot up her ankle. She cried out and sank back on all fours, grabbed the bars of the cage and used her left leg to rise. Putting her right foot to the floor sent another jab of pain up her leg and she groaned.

"Something's happened to my ankle. I don't know if I can walk."

Sam took hold of her right arm and helped her quite gently out of the van. Once they were out of the van he reached over and pulled her trouser leg up, and they both looked down at her swollen ankle.

"Hey, guys!" said Sam gleefully. 'Have a look at this. Lucky break, eh? She's not going to be running away, is she?" He grinned and let go of her trouser leg.

Fish came over and stood right in front of her, intimidatingly close; she could smell cigarettes on his breath. He had a Star of David tattooed under his right eye and looked like someone, who was used to getting his way, an aggressive bully.

"Now you listen to me, lady," he said, and his voice was full of quiet menace. "We're going to sit down and have a chat - and then

267

you'll spend the night in the Black Plastic Hotel over there." He gestured towards a huge tank a few meters away.

"A classy place – you get a bucket to pee in and a bottle of water and a floor to lie on. You stay there for the night, and we come back in the morning and have another little chat. The sooner you tell us what we need to know, the sooner you can go home."

Mia nodded and made no comment and thought that her best bet was to keep up the helpless image, and not argue. The weaker she seemed, the better were her chances of taking them by surprise.

Sam helped her hobble towards a thick pipe, which ran on raised supports across the floor from the tank, made a right angle turn and disappeared into the gloom of the building. She looked around; the place was big enough to house a jumbo jet, and she couldn't imagine what kind of factory it might have been. And that tank! She had never seen one so big, much bigger than regular water tanks. It had a round hatch door with a large metal handle shaped like a steering wheel - it reminded her of submarines she had seen in films.

Sam motioned to her to sit down where the pipe turned the corner. She used her ankle as an excuse to lower herself slowly and sat well forward, leaning slightly to the left at an angle to avoid sitting directly on the phone. She hoped it looked natural, slid her backside to the left and made an obvious play of moving her right foot into a comfortable position. Sam and the driver stood one on each side, of her and Fish resumed his position close in front of her, forcing her to bend her head back to look up at him.

Ideas and options had been running through Mia's head nearly constantly since the initial surprise of the attack and now she added another touch to her new persona.

"Oh, no - I dropped my keys beside my car, what if someone steals it? It's not insured."

That must be the most idiotic statement anyone could make in a desperate situation, she thought, now they'll know for sure that I'm a totally harmless dill-brain.

Fish made no response to this opener. "We know you're the girl who predicted that the Crocodile Hunter was going to be killed by that stingray. *And* you said that some famous church in Russia was going to burn down – which it did. And now we've heard that you're working with the cops. Apparently, you're going to help them make sure certain things don't happen. Or maybe it is more in the line of identifying people involved in certain things?"

He looked straight into her eyes and waited for a reaction. His stance was menacing, and Mia tried to avoid thinking of those big fists so close to her head and so quick to strike. Trying to inject an incredulous tone to her voice, she made an attempt to talk the tension down.

"I don't know what you're talking about – it sounds insane."

But to no avail; she noticed Fish glancing at Sam as if scoring a point.

"Yeah, right! We were told you'd say that. But we know what we know, so let's cut the crap and be sensible. We have a big job on the go - very soon, and we need to know if you've warned the cops about it."

Mia had no idea what he was talking about and could recall no particularly noteworthy crime in the spring in That Time. She had to use part of the truth now to convince them that she was being frank, and to make them believe her when she said she knew nothing about their job.

"OK, you're right. I *have* been able to predict some events, just a couple. And I'm trying to keep it quiet because I don't want people to think I know every single thing that's going to happen. I don't even know how it works or why it was those things."

She stared seriously into the watchful eyes of Fish, hoping she gave the impression of someone telling the truth. "I just get odd flashes of details, like pictures in my mind. Right now, I only know one more thing that I think will happen and that's my sister having a baby in April. And she doesn't even know she's pregnant yet."

Fish never took his eyes off her face. "That's better! At least you've admitted you can predict stuff - but I think you probably know a whole lot more than you say."

Sam broke in impatiently. "So have you told the cops about something happening at the Casino?"

The look on Fish's face spoke volumes. He glared at Sam, furious that he had been careless with information. "Shut up you bloody fool!" he roared and turned back to Mia. "Well, what's the answer?"

"I haven't told the police anything! I happen to have a personal friend who's in the police and I told him about the Crocodile Hunter thing and the church fire."

She was thinking quickly of how to pitch her response. "But that was only so he would help me try to prevent those things happening. And it didn't work out anyway. I haven't had a single premonition about crimes – only disaster type things. Oh, and my sister's baby."

"So why did you go through that whole business of having people witnessing your predictions at a police station? Don't tell me the cops aren't interested – I wasn't born yesterday!"

"We only did it at the police station because my friend works there - it's nothing to do with the police. All I was after was getting people to believe that those two events would happen. I thought the fire would happen first and if I had witnesses to that prediction, I thought they *would* believe me, when I said the Steve Irwin was going to be killed. And then we would be able to stop that happening."

Fish was still pushing for more. "So why did Irwin die? Didn't you tell him what you knew?"

Her only option was to lie, he would never believe that the parcel had been stolen in transit; it sounded too much like an excuse.

"They didn't believe me, even with the evidence of that church fire. They thought I was some kind of weirdo. And I told everyone, who was there when we recorded that prediction, that I only know a couple of things."

"So, this gift or whatever it's called, that you have – does it only give you a bit of a peek at some things that are happening fairly soon? Is that what you're saying?"

Her tension was mounting; she had never been under such intense scrutiny. Fish seemed to suspect that she was only telling him half the truth and she didn't know what she could say to convince him. She tried to sound indignant and upset that he was doubting her.

"But I *don't* know how it works! I told you already! I've no idea why I can predict some things and not others. It's not a very comfortable thing to have - it isn't a gift, it's a horrible thing!"

She had let her voice rise to a shrill tone to sound as if she meant it, but she was so scared now that real fear was helping to change her voice.

"I've only ever known a few disaster type things. Maybe the bit about my sister is the last thing I will predict? I've no way of knowing, do I?"

She hoped she sounded realistically aggrieved and slightly whiney. She was desperate to make them believe that she was a reluctant prophet and had no idea why she could predict only some things. In the back of her mind sat the terrifying thought that after Sam's revelation about the Casino, they would never let her go.

Fish was frustrated now and getting angrier by the minute. He ordered the driver to keep an eye on Mia, motioned Sam to follow him and the two of them retreated into the van and closed the doors. Though she couldn't hear what they said, it was obvious that Fish was furious – he was banging the flat of his hand on the steering wheel and speaking forcefully. Sam seemed to be protesting, but spoke less than Fish, and after a few minutes they got out and came back to where Mia was sitting on the pipe.

"We're going to leave you in the tank and come back tomorrow and have another chat. That will give you some more time to think about what you can tell us. Nobody comes near this place, and we'll lock the doors. It hasn't been used in years and there's nobody nearby, so it's no use making a ruckus - nobody will hear you."

Fish was speaking less harshly now, sounding nearly friendly, as if he was giving her advice for her own good, and suddenly she was more scared than she had been at any time since they snatched her from the street. Because Fish was not a kind man, and she did not for a moment believe that he felt any concern for her.

She caught a fleeting look of something on Sam's face while Fish was speaking – was it guilt or perhaps embarrassment? He stepped closer, reached out to help her up from the pipe and they made their way closer to the tank. The driver swung the round hatch inwards and Mia instinctively took a step backwards – the tank was totally dark inside and she could see nothing of the inside.

Sam pushed Mia up closer. The lower edge of the opening was just above her knees, so she would have to bend down to climb inside, which meant that the last thing they would see was her backside with her pants pulled tight. There was a strong possibility that they would spot the outline of the phone.

"What's been in there? Will I be able to breathe?"

She tried to step backwards, and her voice trembled. She was terrified now and could see no way out. They would never let her go whether she told them anything useful or not and keeping the phone was vital, it was her only lifeline.

Fish was getting irritated. "Oh, for fuck's sake, it's just as safe as your own bedroom, probably safer. Don't make such a bloody fuss! Sam, get that water bottle and the torch from the van, so she has a light."

He took a hard grip on her arm just above the elbow and shook her roughly. "Now, get in before I lose my patience!"

Mia kicked her shoes off and took a hobbling step right up close to the tank and stood side-on, bent and put her left leg in first, so she straddled the rim of the hatch. She could feel the bottom of the tank with her foot; at least it was dry. She bent further, held on to the upper edge of the opening with one hand and moved inside sideways, avoiding giving the men any more of a view of her backside than she had to. Inside she straightened up, and Sam bent and passed her a plastic bottle of water and a small torch. She took both, tucked the bottle under her arm and turned the torch on.

Fish bent and looked in at her, pretending concern, but his smirk told a different story. "Don't waste the batteries, we don't have any spares to give you."

She turned the torch off, and the driver reached in and grabbed the hatch, she stumbled backwards, and he pulled it shut. Instantly it became completely dark, darker than the darkest night. She heard the wheel being turned to lock the hatch shut and instant fear flooded her mind. She quenched the scream about to erupt from her mouth and her heartbeat accelerated. Terror threatened to overwhelm her. In the midst of near panic, her mind insisted that her only hope was to stay in control of fear.

She could hear muffled voices and leaned forwards with her free hand outstretched, touched the wall and tried to hear what they were saying. Only the odd word here and there was audible, then doors slammed, and the van drove out, the big doors graunched shut, and all that remained was silence and darkness.

. . .

There was a stale smell in the tank, a mixture of plastic and something vaguely acidic like vinegar, but the air was cool and dry. She lit the torch and looked around, but the light only showed curving sides of matt black and a floor with slightly raised partitions like spokes from the centre of the floor out to the sides.

There was no bucket and no more water. She shone the torch upwards. She knew the dimensions of the tank from looking at it from outside and thought it must be about four meters tall and perhaps five meters across. Looking at it from the inside by torchlight created a strange illusion, no light reflected back from the matte walls and there was nothing to give it perspective. It could have been two meters across or ten. At the top were a couple of pipes or vents, but they were too high and too small to get out through.

A cold feeling settled in her chest. She turned the torch off and put it and the water bottle on the floor beside her feet; this wedge-shaped segment of floor would be home base, right in front of the hatch. There were five segments, and she wanted to be able to find her things were in the dark.

The phone seemed perfectly all right when she got it out and turned it on. She had one voice message and several texts but decided to ignore them for now. The battery indicator was quite low, and she knew she must preserve what power she had left. She would send a message for help, but to save the battery she would turn the phone off, work out exactly what she would text, then turn the phone back on and send the message.

Composing the message took several minutes and while she concentrated on it, the intense feat receded, and she felt better. In her mind she lined up all the facts she could muster and repeated them all under her breath each time she thought of an additional thing. Keeping the message short would save power; she would abbreviate as much as possible to reduce the time the phone was turned on. When she had the message clear in her mind, she turned the phone back on, keyed her message in and addressed it jointly to John, Thomas, Lorraine and Paul.

Tkn by fake mech in white van. In empty fctry, lckd in big plstc tank. Left mway Otahuhu exit then appr 15 min. No way out. Big job @ casino v soon. Names r fish and sam. Fish boss star tattoo R cheek. Dont call or txt. Ph off low pwr.

She was just about to press Send when she thought that the vinegar smell might be a useful clue if they tried to find out which old factory she was in. She added it, sent the message and turned the phone off. When the friendly little glow from the screen went out, the darkness was like a physical black mass. Having no visual references made her feel unbalanced, and she lay down on the floor. She was very frightened and very lonely.

50

An hour earlier Thomas had called Mia's cell phone but only got the voice mail message. Now he tried once again, but still no answer. He left another message for her to call him and waited half an hour. He looked out his office window, feeling vaguely uneasy, and told himself that there was no need to panic. She could be busy or in a meeting, but just to make sure he called her office. His brief conversation with Alice, after she had spent several minutes trying to locate Mia, sent a surge of adrenalin though him, something was very wrong. He asked Alice to put him through to Alan and after what seemed like an eternity Alan answered.

"Sorry that you had to wait - Alice was filling me in on Mia going missing and who you are. I'm afraid I didn't even know she was out. Alice says she was only going out for a minute to show the mechanic where the car was parked, but she never came back – Alice went upstairs for lunch just then and she thought Mia was back, but now she thinks that she never returned at all. Nobody in our section has seen her."

"But what on earth can have happened? She's not answering her phone or replying to texts, and I've no idea where she has her car serviced. The garage had a recall of the tyres she had put on a couple of weeks ago - they called her last night."

"I know which garage it is," said Alan. "She and I use the same one – I recommended it to her when she started here, because it's so handy to the office. I'll call them right away. What's your number, so I can call you back?"

While he waited, Thomas sat rigid at his desk, unable to do anything or even move, until Alan called back.

"They had no idea what I was talking about. They put the new tyres on her car, but they didn't call her about a recall - they know nothing about it. What would you like to do? Should we report her missing?"

"I'm coming over right away. I want to see if her car is still there, and I'll call a friend of ours, who's in the police. I'll be there soon."

He left a message for John, whose phone was busy, told the administrator that he might not be back for a few hours and left the office.

Accompanied by Alan, Thomas walked along the street until they found the Honda where Mia had parked it, now with a parking ticket under the windscreen wiper. The car was unlocked, and the keys lay on the street just below the driver's door, the ignition key detached from the key ring. Alan bent to pick them up, but Thomas stopped him.

"I think we'd better leave them for the police. Just in case they need to fingerprint them - we don't know what happened yet. Someone must have taken her, or why would the keys be here, and the car unlocked? That mechanic Alice told us about must have been involved."

"Of course - I wasn't thinking, but you're right. It's a matter for the police."

Standing on the pavement next to the car Thomas called John again, told him what had happened and promised to wait by the car. He turned to Alan. "I suggest you go back to the office – I'll stay here until the police come and then I'll come and tell you what's happening."

Alan nodded and started walking away, but halfway down the block he stopped and looked back, as if he was reluctant to leave Thomas alone. Thomas lifted his hand and Alan walked on.

Standing guard over the Honda with frantic thoughts racing through his mind, Thomas waited for what seemed like an eternity, until John turned up in an unmarked car with a uniformed driver and pulled into a parking slot two bays further along.

"Have you touched it?"

Thomas shook his head. "I haven't even picked the keys up from the ground – I wanted you to see it exactly as we found it."

John told his driver to arrange for the car to be towed and taken to be fingerprinted and walked around it looking in through the windows while Thomas told him all he knew.

"OK, we'll go back to see that girl at Mia's office and talk to her boss - just hang on a minute."

Having told his driver to guard the car until the tow-truck arrived, he made a call to get a couple of detective constables to come and make enquiries in the shops in the vicinity and took a photo of the keys lying on the street. Thomas watched in frustrated silence while John went back to his car and got a plastic zip-lock bag and gloves out of the boot, picked up the keys and handed the bag to the constable.

"Write the place and date on it and give it to the crew when they arrive and tell them where they were found."

He peeled off the gloves and put them in his pocket and turned to Thomas.

"OK, let's go. I need a description of the man who picked her up and I want to know what Mia was wearing."

They received Mia's text messages simultaneously as they walked through the foyer towards Alice's desk and stopped side by side to read it. Thomas held out his phone and raised his eyebrows at John, who nodded; they had the same message.

"What should we do? Do we dare send her a reply?"

"No, not if she thinks it's risky. Maybe she's worried they've left someone to guard the place. We can't risk her losing the phone, it's our only link to where she is. I need to make a call."

Thomas waited while where he was, nearly unable to contain his impatience.

"Hi Lorraine," said John. "Did you get a text from Mia just now? Yeah, that's right. She's been taken by someone. From work, yes – they tricked her out of the building. We've just started working on it now. Yes, of course I'll let you know! No, Thomas is here with me. Can you warn Paul not to call Mia or talk about this until we know more? We don't want any calls going to her phone."

He ended the call and turned to Thomas. "God knows how she managed to keep that phone. Either they're a bit stupid and didn't search her, or else she's very clever and managed to hide it somehow."

He introduced himself to Alice, who had been watching and listening from the reception desk, looking increasingly worried.

"Are you comfortable answering a couple of questions here, or should we go and sit somewhere more private? It won't take long."

"I'm OK here," said Alice. "I'll just divert the calls to another phone." She did something to the phone console on her desk. "What do you need to know?"

"I want to know what Mia was wearing, with as much detail as you can remember. And I want you to tell me everything you possibly can about the man who came to fetch her car. Start with Mia's clothes."

He got a pad and a pen from his inside pocket.

"All right." Alice narrowed her eyes, as if she pictured Mia walking across the foyer with the man from the garage.

"She was wearing dark grey tailored pinstripe trousers, high heeled black shoes and a lime green fitted top with a fairly deep scoop neck. I think she had something in her hand, but not anything big like a bag. It might have been her car keys, but I'm not sure."

"We know she has her phone," said John. "And don't call her! It's important that she gets to keep the phone, so we don't want anyone to call her in case they take it off her. And that's a good description – you are very observant. What can you remember about the man?"

"He was about this much taller than Mia – but remember, she has heels on." She held her hands out and John said,

"About 15 centimetres taller. How tall is Mia, do you think, Thomas?"

Thomas put his hand horizontally just above the level of his collarbone.

"Exactly to here without high heels. About 160 centimetres, I guess."

John turned back to Alice. "What did this chap look like, how did he talk and what was he wearing?"

She replied instantly, without any hesitation. "He had dark brown hair, slightly wavy, and a very sharp haircut. He was slim, and he wore a navy blue overall, very clean, still with the creases from where it had been folded - you know, the kind they wear in workshops."

"Was there a logo or any writing on the overall?"

"No, nothing that I noticed. But I did think it was funny that a mechanic was wearing a fancy gold bracelet at work."

"I'd like you to work with the police artist to get a likeness sketch of him. Do you think you can remember his face well enough?"

"Yes, of course, but you don't need to send an artist. Just find a picture on the internet of Adam Sandler – he was the spitting image, but much younger and with shorter hair."

John looked at Thomas and then they both turned to Alice. "Remind us!" said John. "I know he's an actor. What does he look like?"

"Longish face, very masculine - pretty definite nose. Good looking in an interesting kind of way, looks intelligent – doesn't matter that he mostly plays total losers. Truly – this guy was the spitting image, could have been a very look-alike younger brother, probably only twenty-four or twenty-five, I think."

John was making notes and nodding as he wrote. "Well done, very useful. You have a good eye for detail."

Alice responded with her usual dead-pan honesty. "Well, it does help if they are nice looking, doesn't it? I mean you always have another look and check them out. Not that I'm interested - call it a spectator sport."

She stopped abruptly and looked past them towards the street, and her worried frown returned. "She's been kidnapped, hasn't she? But why?"

"It looks like it," said Thomas, trying to sound calm. "I'll let you know as soon as we know anything, and please keep this to yourself for now. Where is Alan's office?"

"Second door on the right," said Alice and pointed at the corridor, suddenly struggling to hold back tears. "And the mechanic is called Sam – I heard him tell Mia."

Five minutes later they had compared notes with Alan, who had nothing to contribute and kept repeating that he was baffled. "What on earth can it mean? It's dreadful - I don't understand why someone would snatch her. And how could it happen on a street full of people in broad daylight?"

John tried to calm him. "I'm going to try to get the location that message was sent from and we'll proceed from there. We have a very good description of the man and what Mia was wearing – Alice is an excellent witness. Thomas, can you come with me in my car? Reinforcements will have arrived now. We'll go back to the station, and we can talk in the car. If you get a ticket, we'll fix it later."

In the doorway, Thomas turned. "I'll keep you informed, but don't call me unless something new comes up – I want to be available in case Mia calls me."

Mia's car now had crime scene tape and road cones forming a cordon around it and a uniformed police officer standing guard.

"You stay here," said John to man beside the car. "Tell the guys when they get here that I have a photo of the keys on the ground on my phone. Did my driver give you the bag? OK, then, we'll be off."

As they drove John called his team and issued a stream of orders and requests. Thomas sat silent and tense, listening to instructions to track Mia's cell phone location, asking for the crime register to be searched for local armed robbers not in jail, a search for criminals with history and the names Fish and Sam, with or without star tattoos. Eventually the call was finished, and he turned to Thomas.

"As soon as we know where that text came from, we'll get someone down to the Council's planning department. Somewhere in that cell there is a disused factory or warehouse. And whatever used to go on there, involved storing something acidic in a large tank. Very useful that Mia has her phone."

With no idea of what would happen next, Thomas knew he must call his office; he had left abruptly and not told anyone where he was going or why.

"It's a family emergency, and I haven't got time to go into details," he told the administrator. "Just tell Regan I don't know when I'll be back, but I'll be in tough later." The receptionist was ready to commiserate, but he cut her short and said he had to rush and would call back later.

He put the phone back in his pocket and smiled ruefully at John. "I keep promising to call people to tell them things – I hope I remember them all. How do you think they knew about the tyres and how to trick her? Do you think someone at the garage is involved?"

"Could be anything, but of course we'll check if there's a link at the garage. But people talk, you know - about this and that, to all and sundry. Often, it's coincidental - one person hears two facts from two sources, realizes they relate to the same story and that the facts mesh - they put two and two together." He glanced down at his phone as a message flashed across the screen. "I know it sounds unlikely, but you'd be surprised how often luck or chance comes into these things. Mind you, I'm prepared to bet that our journalist friend has been gossiping all over town about who Mia is and perhaps even where she works."

His phone buzzed again, and his face registered satisfaction as he listened. He ended the call and smiled at Thomas. "Good news, they'll have the cell location for us very shortly. Meanwhile we'll organize a rescue party and get the armed offenders' squad on stand-by."

Thomas's imagination instantly produced a stream of horror images – a shootout in a concrete building, bullet ricocheting off steel beams and bullets penetrating the plastic tank, and his hackles rose.

"You're not serious! You can't go in shooting before you know where Mia is - what if she gets hit?"

"No, we'll make sure everyone knows about the tank," said John calmly, "and we won't have any shots fired into the building before we know where the tank is, but we have to be prepared. Don't worry, these guys know what they're doing, but criminals who plan to rob the casino are definitely going to be armed, so we have to be able to meet threat with equal threat."

Thomas understood the logic, but he was unable to share John's confident view that everyone would do the right thing in a situation that might turn messy.

"Let's hope you are right!" was all he said, but inside his head he was shouting "No!"

51

Mia lay on the floor with her eyes shut. It felt more natural that way, looking at total darkness with open eyes was depressing and disorientating. She had spent some time trying to remember if she had ever heard what the minimum amount of water was that you could survive on. She knew that she could survive for a long time without food, but water was more urgent, so she turned the torch on for a moment and checked the water bottle, and it was a small bottle, only half full. As soon as she had discovered how little water she had, her thirst increased a hundredfold and her mouth felt dry. With a major effort of will, she stopped herself from having a drink straight away. She felt panic standing behind her breathing down her neck, waiting to jump if her grip on her composure slipped.

What would be calming, she thought, maybe yoga, though she didn't know the first thing about it. It might calm her down and relax her. She arranged her arms down the length of her body with the outer edges of her hands resting on the floor. Probably the trick would be to see that no part of her body supported any other part, so she would try to let everything just rest on the floor. She started with her shoulders, making sure they were flat on the floor and worked down her body, trying to consciously relax her muscles and become a dead weight. She could feel that she was not exhaling properly, too keen to snatch the next lungful of air and

282

breathing in a shallow way, so she forced herself to slowly and deliberately push the used air out of her lungs and slowly inhale each new, deep breath.

After a few minutes she was no longer aware of her body – she could think of her arm but not feel it, as if her mind was disassociated from her body. Well done, she told herself, that's much better. Being able to do something positive and constructive gave her a feeling of being in control. After what seemed like an hour of lying motionless, she opened her eyes and to her surprise she could see two dark grey circles above her.

That must be those holes through the roof of the tank, she thought, and now that my eyes have adjusted to the dark, I can see that they aren't attached to pipes or anything, just holes – not that they're any use to me. I can't climb up there, and they are quite small, but at least I know I have lots of air, and maybe if I shout the sound will carry.

She sat up and did some stretches before she carefully got to her feet and wriggled her ankle. It was swollen and sore, no more than it had been earlier, but she could only hobble. She lay down again and closed her eyes and wondered what else she could tell Thomas and John to help them find her, but gradually the urge to go to the toilet increased until it could no longer be ignored. She sat up, turned the torch on and looked round, but as expected there were no holes in the floor.

The pie segments that had been moulded into the floor created five completely separate depressions; she would have to decide which one was to be the toilet. She poured a few drops of precious water from her bottle in the segment opposite the hatch to see which way the floor sloped and watched it run towards the outer wall.

That's it then, this is where I pee, she whispered to herself, and it will collect as far away from me as possible, and maybe there's enough air coming in to make it bearable. Hearing her own whispered words was a comfort, nearly like a conversation. I'll take my trousers and panties right off and just stand with my feet wide apart, because I can't bear to think of crouching on this ankle – I'd probably fall over. Let's hope I can avoid having to do anything apart from peeing – that would be really nasty.

She felt a lot better once she was back at home base and dressed again. Every little practical thing she did, even deciding that one segment was home base, contributed to a feeling of having some control over her existence.

Maybe that's what happens to some hostages, she whispered into the dark, and the sound of her whisper was like a ghost of company. Maybe they lose the ability to resist or have hope when they feel they have no control over their fate. Perhaps it makes them unable to try things. I must keep myself going and be strong. Everything I do, every silly little thing, even checking which way my pee would run, has made me feel stronger, so it must be a good thing.

She drank one sip of water to celebrate the idea that she could empower herself by small actions. The tank was cool, and she was not perspiring - the water would last for a while. She forced her mind to drop the subject, because in the back of her mind she knew that it would not take a lot for fear to overwhelm her resolve to stay calm. It was frustrating to have nothing to tell the outside world. If only she had seen a little more from the van, she might have got some specific points of reference. Even when she got out of the van inside the factory, she saw nothing useful before the driver shut the big doors.

With no warning her mind started down the sloping path to fear and despondency. They would never let her go, not now that she knew about the Casino, and what bad luck that her phone had just been put on the charger when the garage man came, though of course, he wasn't a garage man, he was a criminal. Should she turn the phone on and check for messages? What if the phone must be on for the police to be able to track where she was? Best to wait and check in a couple of hours seeing she had told them to not call or message her.

She lay down on the floor again. There was little she could do apart from try to relax or think, but she had run out of thoughts, apart from very frightening ones, which were better pushed to the back of her mind. She knew that if she loosened her grip, she would see mental images of herself screaming and sobbing, starving to death or more likely thirsting to death, hallucinating, and losing control, clawing at the hatch. And once she had let that demon out of the bottle, she might never be able to push it back in. Better to invent silly games to keep her mind safely busy.

She lay in the dark with her eyes shut and tried to compose a mental crossword on a grid of 8 x 8 squares but failed after five words. She reduced the grid to 5 x 5 and thought she got it finished, but it was hard to check. Next, she tried to list as many states in the USA as she could remember and thought she got to thirty-two before she lost track.

And then suddenly acute panic swamped her mind. There was no warning, the calm she had achieved with her relaxation session evaporated instantly. She knew that if she could not take some sort of constructive action right away, she would either start to scream or cry. She clutched at a thin strand of reason, held on for dear life, breathing fast and feeling it slip between her fingers. She scrambled to her feet, turned the torch on and looked round.

Two segments to her right there was a hole in the wall; the start of the big pipe she had sat on before she got into the tank. Shining the torch into it, she saw only discolouration and grit, and the torchlight bouncing off the inside of the pipe at the right-angle turn. She knelt, groaning at the pain in her ankle, and checked to make absolutely sure that she would not be able to wriggle through, but she could only fit her head and one shoulder inside, and that bend would be impossible to negotiate. She could visualize the squat metal supports it rested on as it traversed the floor of the factory; there was no way it could be dislodged by one person from inside the tank.

She straightened and supported herself against the side of the tank before she limped back to home base, and then a sudden thought made her shine the torch directly at the hatch. Curved metal rods shaped like the letter 'c' fitted into channels around the opening and locked the hatch into place when the wheel on the outside was turned. She went hot with excitement. How did it work? Could she open it from the inside? The hatch would never have been designed to prevent anyone getting out, so maybe it could be undone from inside. She looked closely at the mechanism and traced it with her fingers.

There was a circular metal plate in the centre that the wheel on the outside was attached to. She imagined that she was standing outside and about to open the hatch; she would turn it anti-clockwise, so from the inside things would turn clockwise. If the central disc moved clockwise the curved rods would be pulled along and retract from the channels, and the hatch would open. That was how it worked, and to lock it again you would turn the wheel and the curved rods would be pushed into the channels and hold the hatch shut. She should be able to open it by rotating the central disk.

She put the torch on the floor and took a firm grip on the rods and tried to force them clockwise, but they didn't budge, there was not the slightest movement. She let go and considered things again. Where would she be able to exert the most effective force? As close to the central plate as possible or out by the rim? If it worked like a lever, then the end seemed the best bet, but this was not a straightforward lever action, so perhaps taking hold closer to the centre would be more effective.

She tried to imagine what it would look like under that central plate. There must be something that happened when the wheel was turned that allowed the curved pieces to come out of the channel.

Oh, I think I know, she said quietly to herself. The rods have another joint somehow under that round disc, so you only need to turn the wheel perhaps a quarter turn or so, and then they fold underneath the central plate and pull back and that makes them a bit shorter, and they pull out of the channel.

She stuck her fingers under the edge of the round plate and tried to feel what was there. The plate was quite thick and had raised areas on the back – it felt like the raised partitions on the floor of the tank. Perhaps it made things stronger? She felt the rods and their connections and thought, I'm right, that's how it works; they are designed to fold. Elated and with renewed energy she took hold of the rods again and strained as hard as she could, but nothing happened. Her hands ached, but there was no indication that anything was loosening.

She straightened, pushed her hair back from her sweaty forehead and took another small sip of water, before she picked up the torch and tried to look sideways behind the plate, but she saw nothing that gave her any clues. Sitting on the floor she played a film clip in her mind of someone standing outside turning the wheel, with herself standing inside watching it happen, and suddenly she knew what to try next.

She turned the torch on and jumped to her feet with no thought for her injured ankle, and nearly fell over when the pain hit her. She put the torch on the floor and propped it up with the water bottle, so the beam of light was aimed straight at the hatch. Gripping the disk itself with both hands, she tried to rotate it clockwise as hard as she could. Her hands slipped and something under the plate ripped her right forefinger. She pulled her hand out and wiped the blood on her pants and tried again. She had never exerted such pressure on anything in her life; she was holding her breath and her heart was pounding, she grunted with effort. And then she felt it move, a tiny move, but definitely movement.

She let go, lowered herself to the floor and rested. She was panting, her hands ached, and her forefinger was bleeding steadily, she felt the blood dripping on her leg. Again, she wiped the blood off on her trouser leg, used her left hand to put pressure on the ripped flap of skin, and held on tight for several minutes. Her breathing slowed and the sweat dried on her face and neck. She took another sip of water and went back to work, got a grip on the plate and put her entire strength into trying to turn it.

The plate rotated, and a metallic click told her it had gone as far as it was meant to. The curved pieces had come out of the circular channel. She pulled on the hatch, and it swung silently inwards.

She poked her head out and peered cautiously around. The big space was empty, the light through the high windows was fading, and the big doors were shut. Fish had said they were locked, but she must check if she could get out that way. The urge to get out of the building was the driving force now. She must check the doors first and get out, if not through those big doors, then some other way. The men could return at any time and the thought of them finding her outside the tank in the locked building made her shudder with fear. If they knew she could get out of the tank, they would tie her up before locking her in again, or simply kill her.

52

Mia pushed the phone into her pocket and picked up the torch, sat astride the opening and clambered out.

First things first, don't rush it, she whispered to herself, and reached in, swung the hatch closed and spun the wheel to lock it in place. The shoes would stay where they were, it must look as if she was still inside.

She limped across the dirty floor to the doors, but they were securely locked and no shaking or pushing would move them. She knew there must be other doors, normal sized doors for people to get in and out, and windows that she could reach. Exploring the giant building was her top priority now, but she must have something to use as a walking stick or she would never make it. Further along the wall were piles of debris, left when the factory closed, and the machinery was moved out and sold.

As she limped along towards the mess, she got her phone out and turned it on, but nothing happened. She tried again, still nothing. The phone was dead! Mia stood staring at it with tears pooling in her eyes. The battery must be completely empty, but how had it happened? She had turned it off again after that short text message and now it wouldn't turn on again. Perhaps turning it off didn't save power, perhaps it used up more power than just leaving it on?

She wiped her wet cheeks with her fingers and turned her attention to the piles of rubbish. There were bent and broken

289

lengths of pipe, metal brackets, a square metal container that had contained engine oil, but nothing of the right length. Of the various pieces of pipe, the best one was a thin copper pipe about a meter and a half long, everything else was too short or too heavy.

I'll look like one of those shepherds in picture books, she thought, the ones with long staffs, but it works, and I can move a bit faster. Too much noise, though – I need to muffle it. Every time it hits the concrete floor it sounds like a nail gun going off. If the men return, they will hear it and know that I am out of the tank, perhaps before I'm even aware of them.

She thought for a moment, then she tore her top off, removed her bra and put the top back on. With some effort she clamped the pipe between her knees and managed to fold the bra and fashion a pad, which she tied on tight by winding and knotting the shoulder straps. With only a muffled thumping sound she set out down the length of the building.

The light was going fast and soon it would be dark inside. The only windows were high up and the space was a vast darkening expanse stretching into the distance behind the tank. Steel pillars stood like tree trunks, supporting the structure of the roof. There were man-high partitions here and there, and a lot of debris. She could make out the footprints of long-gone pieces of machinery, and in places the floor was studded with treacherous bolts embedded in the concrete. It was a difficult floor to negotiate in the near dark, but as long as she could see anything at all, she would not turn the torch on. Fish had said that the factory was far from habitation, and she might need the torch to navigate outside in the dark.

Mia progressed slowly down the length of the building, carefully watching the floor and trying not to stub her toes, stopping every few steps to listen for sounds of vehicles or movement outside. The gloom was deepening, and she peered at the walls on both sides as she walked, checking for doors. She found two normal sized doors, but both were locked. Using the staff to try to force them didn't work and going back to find other things to use in the rubbish piles was out of the question. The most urgent thing was to investigate what was at the end of the building; she hoped for a toilet block with windows she might be able to reach or a locker room.

When she reached what had looked like the end of the building, it turned out to be a concrete block wall and behind it were offices and toilets, and a lunchroom with a water boiler on the wall. The windows were at normal height, but they were barred. She tried to open one, hoping to attract attention by shouting, but the clasp was corroded and didn't budge. She smashed the glass with her staff and stood for a few minutes shouting for help as loudly as she could. There were not lights to be seen and she could only hear distant traffic noise.

It was nearly dark now and all she could see was a concreted yard with some sheds and piles of debris, surrounded by a tall wire mesh fence and a bit further away a tall, corrugated iron fence. On the far side of the fence some distance away, she saw the roofs of other buildings; factories or warehouses by the look of them, and at this time of the day probably empty. She shouted and banged with her metal staff on the bars across the window, stopping now and then to listen, but there was no response and the bars held firm.

There was nothing she could use to barricade herself in the offices, nothing to push against a door or prop under a door handle to prevent someone turning it from the other side, and her heart sank.

She would have to cross the open factory floor again, return to the end where the doors were and get back in the tank. The thought of it made her feel sick, but at least she could take her walking stick in with her and try to attack them when they came back tomorrow and opened the hatch. But what if they didn't come back? Perhaps they never intended to come back and interrogate her further, perhaps they were just going to leave her there, in which case she might be able to work out a way to attract attention or force one of the smaller doors.

She limped down the length of the now dark factory space with the torch shining at the floor, thirsty and thinking of the water bottle she had left in the tank. And then a sound, a rough sound, something scraping against a hard surface. The big doors! She stopped and turned the torch off, stood still, held her breath and listened intently. The tank blocked her direct line of sight to the doors, but now she could make out indirect light from the far side of the tank. Someone had entered and left a vehicle outside with the lights on.

A man's voice called out, but she was too far away to hear the words. Oh, thank God, it might be someone coming to rescue her, she thought excitedly, and opened her mouth to call out, but common sense cut her shout off even as she was drawing breath to yell. How would anyone know where to find her? And wouldn't it be more likely that police would come, not just a single person? Had she recognized the voice? The echo in the vast space made it hard to be certain but thinking back she wondered if it might be Sam's voice, a light voice for a man.

And then suddenly the sound of another vehicle and a stronger light. A shouted exchange erupted, between a deep, angry voice and the lighter one. Furious voices ricocheted off the hard surfaces and it was impossible to hear what was said, but she took advantage of the racket and advanced slowly towards the tank. Shuffling cautiously forward across the treacherous floor in the dark with no light, she felt her way with her toes. It would only take one stumble and she might drop her metal staff, and then they would find her, but she must get closer to hear what they were saying. If they were about to discover that she was not in the tank, she wanted to know before they started searching for her. Cold sweat broke out on her face as she inched forward at a snail's pace, not letting her staff touch the floor and clenching her teeth against the pain in her ankle. After a few meters of slow progress, she stopped to listen again.

She could identify Fish's voice now and the other was probably Sam. They were arguing in raised voices, but no longer shouting.

"How many times do I have to say it - there's no fucking way you're doing this. What the fuck were you thinking? You stupid bastard - get your hands off that hatch. You weren't just giving her water, you were going to let her out, weren't you, you soft bugger!"

Fish was furious and she shivered at the thought of him taking it out on her; she could imagine those big fists slamming into her face and hearing bones breaking.

Sam was flustered and his voice rose to a higher pitch. "No, I bloody wasn't! I'm not that stupid. I was just gonna give her another bottle of water and something to eat."

"You're a fucking idiot, mate! There's no *point* giving her anything - she's going to stay in that tank, I told you already. Get this into your thick skull - we *can't* let her out. She knows our faces and you mentioned the Casino – we can't ever let her out. Even if the others pull off the perfect job tomorrow and get away without trouble, she's still dangerous to the lot of us. She's dead."

Sam was getting stroppy; he was shouting again. "I don't care what you say - I'm *not* leaving her in there to die. We agreed right at the start that there wouldn't be any killing, and this is just the same as shooting her."

"Listen, you bloody wimp – you'd better get this, real fast! If there's got to be killing, there will be killing - that's just how it is. What do you think I have this for - to start the fucking running races? The only point of having a gun is so you can use it when you need it."

There was a scuffle and some grunts and then Sam said clearly, on a high note of fear, "Don't! Don't you point that gun at me!"

Fish was furious, his mind was made up. "You're going to keep your mouth shut, you dumb bastard. If you make things too hard, I'll shoot you right now."

Mia was holding her breath and her heart was pounding. Perhaps she should try to get behind one of those steel columns, because there was nothing much to hide behind apart from those flimsy, low partitions and she was nowhere near them. If she could make it back to the offices she would, that concrete block wall would stop a bullet, but the risk of tripping made her hesitate.

Then came sounds of a scuffle, and Fish swearing and grunting, a furious shout of protest from Sam, followed by a dull thud, then a long moment of silence. Had Fish knocked Sam out cold? Or had he been felled by Sam?

But then Fish roared a final message to Sam, his voice reverberated through the dark space. "There you are, you bloody idiot - now you can keep each other company in there and I don't have to shoot either of you."

Footsteps moved away and she expected him to shut the door and drive off, but instead there were more creaking and scraping sounds. He had opened the big doors wider, an engine started up and headlights swept across the opposite wall before the engine noise died and the lights were turned off. More footsteps, the big doors scraped shut again, and the muffled sound of a vehicle faded to silence.

Good grief, she whispered to herself, I think he's thrown Sam into the tank and locked it again. They both thought I was in there. And poor Sam probably has no torch, so he'll be feeling his way around and he won't understand what's happened to me, he'll find nothing - what a mad thing!

A hysterical urge to giggle came and went when she imaged Sam crawling arounds inside the tank and realizing that she had been spirited out somehow. She couldn't remember if she had heard the big doors being locked, perhaps Fish had left them unlocked in his furious hurry to get away. She must get down to that end fast and check, and if she could open the doors, get as far away as she could. Urgency flooded her senses, her heart hammered in her chest. Now speed was vital.

What if Fish returns to lock the doors, she thought, and I'm still inside? I must get to those doors!

53

There was no need to be quiet now, and with the help of the staff, she limped as fast as she could towards the doors with the torch aimed at the floor. The dark shape of the tank loomed to one side and muffled sounds came from it. She was close enough now to shine the torch past the tank and saw a car parked in the open area inside the double doors, and her blood ran cold; was someone still there? But no, of course, Fish would have driven Sam's car inside to conceal it before he left, which might mean he didn't intend to come back.

Her staff made a muffled thump on the floor with each step she took, but her only thought was to get to the doors. She shone the light at the car as she approached and wondered if the keys were still in the ignition. Sam was hammering his fists on the inside of the tank and yelling for help.

He must have heard the thumps from my staff, she thought, but I'm not letting him out. I *have* to get out of here - now!

And them, from outside came the sound of a car approaching fast and she saw light in the crack between the double doors. He was coming back! Ducking down in front of Sam's car, she turned the torch off and peeped over the bonnet and through the windscreen. A vehicle had stopped outside and one of the big doors was groaning open again. Against the background of the headlights, she saw the outline of a man approaching. She knelt on one knee and bent her head right down. Adrenaline took over and urged her body to flee, to run for her life – the one thing she couldn't do.

She stayed hunched, her mind nearly paralyzed with terror, held her breath and waited to be discovered. It must be Fish; he had come back for some reason. Now he was rummaging around inside Sam's car and her skin prickled with fear at the thought that he was only a metre or two from her hiding place. Then his footsteps moved around the back of the car towards the tank again, and she lifted her head a tiny bit so she could peek around the corner of the front wing.

Fish was standing in front of the tank, only a few metres from her. His silhouette was crisp in the light shining in through the door, and his shadow fell in a long dark column across the floor, past her hiding place. He had a gun in his hand, and he was aiming it at the tank. His voice was triumphant.

"I came back for your phone, you silly bastard. Lucky for you it was in your car, so I don't have to open the tank and shoot the two of you. I might just put a few bullets into that tank anyway and make you dance, just for the fun of it!"

His voice was still echoing through the building when another voice called through a loudhailer from outside, and Fish swung towards the door, gun in hand.

"Put your gun down and raise your hands above your head. The building is surrounded by armed police. Your best chance is to come out quietly."

Fish didn't hesitate, his voice was a raw scream of fury. "No fucking way! If you come any closer, I start shooting into that tank and they'll both die."

As he spoke, he moved slightly to his right. He was edging closer to Mia, and also closer to the shadow cast by the tank. If he got in behind the tank, it could turn into a gun battle, and nobody knew she was there. She processed options at lightning speed.

He'll get behind the tank and then it will be too late to do anything, and I can't shout to alert the police, because then Fish might shoot me, he will turn his head and see me. If he manages to get behind that tank the police won't be able to see him, and I can't make a run for it either.

She made no conscious decision to act, she simply rose to a semi-crouched position, and with her staff in her hand she launched herself forward, oblivious of her protesting ankle. She swung the staff horizontally with both hands, from her right to her left, and caught Fish hard behind the knees. He crashed down like a felled tree, and several things happened seemingly simultaneously. Fish's gun flew through the air in an arc when his hand hit the floor, there were several shots, something struck her hard, and she too crashed to the floor.

Mia lay half stunned while around her chaos broke out; rapid footsteps, the sound of boots on the concrete floor, shouted instructions, strong lights. Her mind seemed detached from her physical body, and she looked up into the dark space high above her and wondered what would happen now. She felt quite calm and peaceful, and her ankle no longer hurt. Unaware of a lump forming on the side of her head where she had hit the floor, she thought vaguely of sitting up and moved her hand across the floor and felt a wet patch, wondered what it was, but lost interest. Now someone was kneeling beside her, and she looked up at the dark shape that seemed to have no face, and her voice came out as a croak: "please let poor Sam out of the tank", and then darkness claimed her.

When she opened her eyes, she looked straight up at a low white ceiling. There was something hard on her face, around her mouth, and she tried to raise a hand to remove it, but her arm wouldn't move, and a face appeared directly above hers.

"Just stay still, everything's OK. You're in an ambulance and you have an oxygen mask over your face to help you breathe. We'll be at the hospital in a few minutes."

Mia blinked. Her voice seemed to have disappeared or she had forgotten how to use it. Dispassionately she studied the face above her – a middle-aged man with glasses and a luminous jacket.

OK, I can figure that out, she thought, he's an ambulance man. Wonder where I'm hurt? I feel weird, my ankle feels heavy - I'm exhausted, but I'm not in pain.

The face disappeared and now Thomas looked down. She felt his warm hand on the top of her head. "Take it easy Mia, we'll be there soon."

She tried to smile, but she was too tired. She blinked her eyes to try and keep them open, then darkness swamped her again.

54

Mia opened her eyes and saw blue sky through a large window. It was daylight and very quiet. Every part of her body ached and when she tried to move the effort made her groan. She heard a chair move and then Thomas's face came into view. He smiled and put his hand on her cheek.

"Welcome back."

Her voice came out like someone else's, from far away, hoarse and faint. "Everything hurts."

"I'll ring the bell and get them to give you some pain relief. They took your drip out an hour ago. They said you'd start waking up soon."

He held her hand and looked carefully at her. "You seem surprisingly wide awake, I must say. They had you sedated to stop you moving around too much."

Now there was a nurse on the other side of the bed. "Hi there, nice to see you with your eyes open. I'll just check a few things and let the doctor know you're awake."

Mia turned her head and saw that she was hooked up to some sort of monitor. The nurse pressed a couple of buttons and smiled. "All good! I'll be back soon."

Thomas put his hand over hers. "Do you remember what happened?"

"I remember the factory. And being in the tank. And Fish. I hurt my ankle in the van." She tried to move her legs, but decided it wasn't worth the effort.

The nurse returned and gave her an injection while Thomas

was on the phone telling someone that Mia was awake now, and they could come and visit.

He turned back and smiled. "I've told Lorraine to let John know you're awake now, so they'll be here soon."

Mia fell asleep again.

When she woke up the second time, Lorraine, John and Thomas were sitting by the window drinking coffee out of paper cups and talking quietly. There were flowers and cards everywhere.

"Thomas, my throat hurts." Her voice was still gravelly and talking was an effort. They all got up and came over and stood around the bed, looking concerned and pleased at the same time.

"You poor little wrecked thing - let's give you a drink." Lorraine patted her cheek and motioned to Thomas. "I'll raise the bed a bit with this remote gizmo, if you hold that mug with the bendy straw."

Mia sucked water through the straw and Lorraine lowered the bed again. "Your throat is sore from the tubes you had down your throat – you've had two operations, but you'll feel better soon."

Mia tried to smile. "I feel totally wiped out. Why can't I move?"

Lorraine held her wrist in a gentle grasp. "Well, you nearly did get wiped out. I'll let John tell you what happened because he was right there when you were shot."

"Shot? Someone shot me?" She tried to think, but only vague impressions surfaced.

They all moved their chairs closer to the bed and sat down, and Thomas reached for her hand again.

John cleared his throat. "I'm very sorry, Mia – one of the guys in the armed offenders' squad shot you, but not on purpose. We didn't even know you were there - we thought you were still in the tank. And then you erupted out from behind that car like a cartoon warrior and whacked Fish behind the knees with a length of pipe. The guy who shot you saw Fish turning to shoot at us, but suddenly he went down in a heap and his gun flew in the air and hit the deck. Our chap fired at Fish, not realizing that Fish wasn't still holding the gun – it all happened simultaneously, you understand – and you got hit you in the side, you were right there behind Fish."

He reached out to pat her leg, drew his hand back and said,

"God, I don't know which part of you I can touch, you seem to have so many injuries."

"Oh, all right. That's why I feel so tired then."

She was gradually recalling more detail. the loud and chaotic scene in the factory was taking shape in her mind.

"It's coming back to me now. I remember hitting Fish, but that's the last thing I know."

Lorraine took over and provided the details. "The bullet hit you in the side, from a front angle, just under the ribs. It went right through you on a diagonal track and exited close to your spine. The surgeon said it's the most miraculous escape she's ever seen – it missed your liver, no vital organs destroyed, but your spine is untouched, thank God."

"But", said Thomas, "that means that your flawless body is slightly the worse for wear. You've got stitches front and back, a twisted ankle with a couple of ligaments torn, a lump the size of an egg on one side of your head and a badly ripped finger with *more* stitches - and some bruises."

Lorraine laughed. "Sorry, I'm not being callous, but when you list her injuries like that it makes *my* body hurt and I'm just a spectator."

Thomas smiled at Mia and gave her hand a squeeze. "But on the other hand, you are the nation's heroine, and the media are clamouring to interview you. TV and newspapers have promoted you to Girl Hero, Fearless Girl Fighter and Resourceful and Dangerous. I hope you can hear the capital letters."

John smiled. "Lorraine has bought every newspaper she could lay her hands on and collected all the cuttings, so you can read them when you feel better. You're the most famous person she's ever known. And Thomas has been welded to your bedside for two days - and I've been busy arresting and interviewing people."

"Two days? What day is it now?" Mia's voice was barely louder than a whisper.

"It's Thursday afternoon – you were snatched on Tuesday at lunchtime, and we got to you, hot on the heels of Fish, at half past seven that evening. We have him and Sam and another chap on kidnapping and assault charges – no bail - and some of their mates on a conspiracy charge for now. Plenty of search warrants being acted on, and the more we dig the more we find."

He chuckled, delighted with the outcome, but he still had more to tell. "I haven't told you yet, Thomas - I managed to get our mate

Miles and Grace Wright to come in for a chat this morning. They didn't want to come, Miles was particularly reluctant, so I said we had grounds to suspect that they had links to Fish and his gang and were involved in the kidnap conspiracy. That got them in there really fast." He laughed. "Even faster than I had hoped for – I barely had time to work out what I was going to charge them with if negotiations didn't work."

"And I bet they brought the big legal guns along," said Thomas. "This could ruin both their careers."

"No, they didn't - and I must admit I was surprised. We were expecting the whole thing to be hampered by legal eagles querying every question, but they came alone."

"But why?" Thomas was intrigued. "They must have known they could be in serious trouble."

Mia shut her eyes and listened. "Of course, they did," said John. "But I think they had decided that if they could convince us they weren't linked to Fish and his gang, then nobody else need ever find out - or something along those lines. Miles said he represented both of them, and they were going to cooperate completely with the inquiry."

"Really? And did they tell all? Or did you bring out the thumb screws?" asked Thomas and sounded as if he wished he'd been there and in charge of the equipment.

Lorraine looked proudly at John. "You wait till you hear it - it's a master stroke of deviousness and manipulation."

"Well, I should be modest, but it was pretty damned clever. I had a list of things that I said I could use to back up a charge of conspiracy - most of it impossible to prove, but they didn't know how much or how little I had - I wasn't specific. They were too keen to save their hides and get off without any formal charges being laid to delve into the details. So, everything just fell into place. I said we would have half an hour of unofficial chat and then we would start a formal interview, and everything would be on record. And believe it or not, after twenty-five minutes we made a deal."

"Is that legal?" Their heads swivelled in surprise towards Mia's hoarse whisper, and John smiled at her and patted her hand.

"I thought you were asleep - I'd nearly forgotten you were there. No, it's not really legal, but then it's not totally illegal either - call it a creative grey space. Up to that stage they were 'helping with the inquiry' and we did a private deal. Nothing official, they weren't under arrest."

Thomas was avid for details. "How water-tight do you think this agreement is?"

"Oh, I think it will hold water. They know that I can resurrect the conspiracy theory at any time. I could claim to have come across new evidence or something like it – not that I would. They're trying to make sure they will never be officially inter-viewed or charged – that would be a stain neither of them can afford. I would never do it of course, because that sort of exposure is exactly what we don't want for Mia, but they don't know that."

Lorraine touched Mia's arm gently and she opened her eyes again and smiled.

"I *am* listening, I'm just resting my eyes. Can I have some more water please?"

Lorraine and Thomas gave Mia a drink, and Lorraine said, "Well, I want to ask John a question – because I want us all to hear the answer. Do you think Fish and the others will drag Mia's prophesies into it, when they appear in court?"

"Yeah, they probably will, but it won't matter. It will sound so bloody silly that nobody will believe it. If they refer to that stupid newspaper column, then Grace Wright will promptly write about it in her next article and make fun of them for falling for such a ludicrous idea. And at the same time, she will apologize for having started the rumour, which she suspected was a hoax right from the start. That's part of the deal." He laughed.

"Some deal!" Thomas was impressed. "And it saves me risking my reputation by threatening physical violence. Thank you, John."

"You're welcome - but back to the story, Mia, and this is the best bit. I never in my life saw anyone as furious as Fish, when he real-ized who had felled him. The guys thought they would have to user the Taser on him. He fought and shouted and swore for several minutes. If we hadn't been holding him back, I think he would have tried to kick you to death where you lay in a pool of blood. He just couldn't believe that you had managed to get out of the tank and then attacked him like that. I thoroughly enjoyed it, and everyone loved the way you took him down." He grinned. "We have it on video, so you can see it if you want to - like something out of an action movie."

He laughed at the memory but then he got serious. "Though I must say that when you fell and we saw you lying there, out cold and blood spreading rapidly around you – well, that's the first time I've understood what it means when people say their heart stopped. I literally felt my heart stop for a moment." He leaned over and patted her arm. "It's just so good to see you awake and not permanently damaged."

Thomas smiled. "I don't know if you remember telling us to get 'poor Sam' out of the tank, Mia? Well, they did, and I must say he seemed truly pleased that you weren't dead – quite touching really, because he was getting arrested at the same time. But he kept asking how you'd managed to get out and if you were going to be all right, and what with Fish shouting and raving and the ambulance crew doing their thing – it was like a madhouse for a while."

Lorraine was itching to ask Mia questions now that she was awake.

"Well, come on, tell us! How did you get out? I made John take me down there to see the place, and I went into that tank – and my God, it's awful! When you close the hatch it's the worst place ever."

But Mia's eyes are closing; their voices fade into the distance, and she doesn't hear Lorraine and John leaving a few minutes later. Thomas leans back in his chair and sits with her hand in his and watches her sleep.

MANY THANKS

We hope you've enjoyed reading this story and would consider leaving a review on your favourite review site, or with the retailer you purchased from.

These are not only much appreciated, they also help other readers discover new authors.

For more about other titles in this series, please read on.

LETTERS FROM THE PAST

Letters from the Past is a series of stand-alone novels where a letter from or about the past reveals something that changes a woman's perceptions of herself or of her family, and that affects her outlook on life.

These books are such fun to write, and I am always working on the next title in this series. I hope you will enjoy reading them as much as I enjoy writing them!

Tina

Having had nobody in her life since her husband died, Lara unexpectedly finds herself involved with three men. One is planning to use her, one she plans to use for her own ends, and one becomes a "friend-with-benefits" with surprising results. Sometimes a quiet schoolteacher is not all she seems at first glance.

Callista experiences an event of apparent ESP at the Okehampton Castle ruins and becomes a media sensation, but the effect it has on her life is dramatic. How do two people, one calm. one seriously claustrophobic, who feel they are poles apart, cope for an hour and a half in total darkness in a stalled lift? And can they handle the consequences?

Sofia's life is in turmoil: a difficult diva mother, a letter with a confession about a family killing and having to accept help from a man she loathes when she is injured. Can reluctant attraction turn into love?

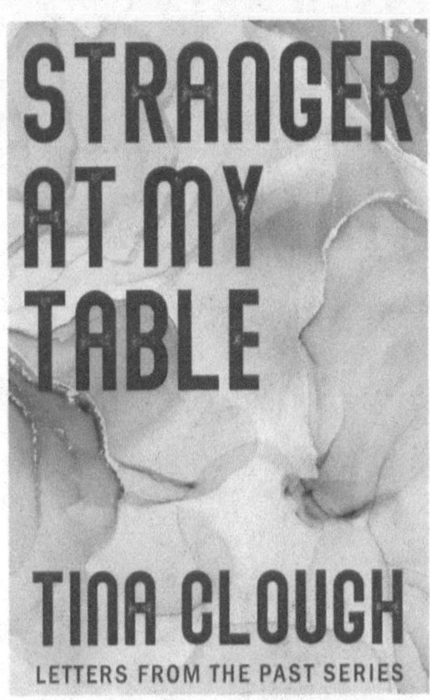

Who is the stranger living in the empty house Miranda inherited from her grandmother? Why is he living like a secretive recluse in someone else's house? Reckless Miranda decides to confront him, and what she discovers prompts her to set out on a fearless quest to bring justice to a man who has given up hope. But is the gamble too great or a risk worth taking?

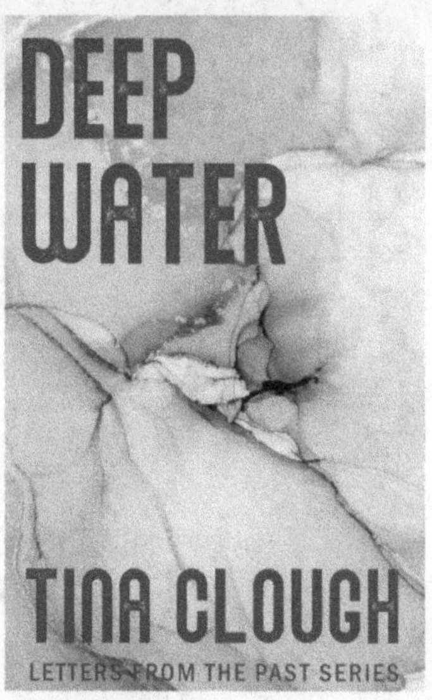

When Emma finds an old letter in a library book she is instantly intrigued, but by researching the origin of the letter she unwittingly opens the door to danger and becomes the target for threats and harassment. Nearly desperate, she takes a leap of blind faith into the unknown and accepts an offer of help from a stranger - but can she trust him?

Jamie, an ardent protester against the gigantic Vista Resort development and Leo Masters, the high-powered developer, seem unlikely to ever agree on anything. But unexpected coincidences and chance brings them together in a fragile state of mutual respect. Will courage and kindness resolve the situation, or do they need help?

After a bizarre accident with ESP overtones, the media haunt Arapera. But can she trust an offer of help from a man she has only met once? Or will she regret it for the rest of her life if she doesn't take the chance? Sometimes life is a knife-edge balance between staying safe and taking risks, and there is no way of predicting if the gamble is worth it.

When crime-writer Saskia finds an unconscious stranger, she has a strange and strong emotional connection. Pretending to be his cousin and with no thought for the consequences, she spends weeks at his hospital bedside. But what will happen when he wakes and discovers she has invaded his life, breached his privacy and made crucial decisions on his behalf?

ALSO BY TINA CLOUGH

THE GIRL WHO LIVED TWICE

What would you do if you woke up one morning and found that time had rewound exactly a year? Would you revisit your past mistakes and try to do better? Would you try to get revenge on those who had wronged you? Or would you use what you knew to get rich? When Mia finds herself in her own past, she must decide how best to use her pre-knowledge of one year's worth of events and personal issues.

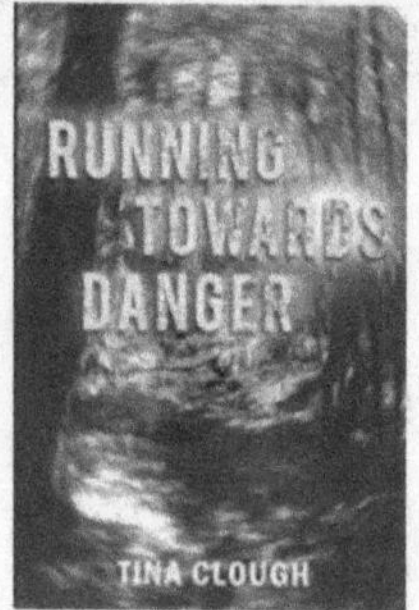

When Karen's flat-mate Nick is gunned down in front of her in the street her life is turned upside-down. Everything she thought she knew about him turns out to be a lie. She becomes a suspect in the police investigation and drug bosses think she knows where Nick has hidden a large sum of money. When her life is threatened, she decides to leave town and disappear.

Karen becomes Cara and creates an anonymous existence, severs all links to her past and adopts a cash-based way of life that leaves no electronic traces. But despite her careful planning danger still stalks her and she is forced to make dramatic choices in the face of threats and brutal violence.

Can she trust the man she is attracted to, or has he been sent by the killers to gain her confidence and find the money they believe she has?

THE CHINESE PROVERB

Book 1 - Hunter Grant Series

Army veteran Hunter Grant thought he had left war behind in Afghanistan – a conflict that left him with physical and psychological scars.

But finding an unconscious girl in the Northland bush and gradually untangling her story involves him in warfare of a different kind in his own country.

Hunter sets out to find and punish the man Dao calls Master, but he soon finds there is more to this story than enslavement. Before long he himself is being hunted by the overlord of a drug empire whose sole objective is to kill Dao because she knows too much.

Protecting her and waging war while trying to keep the police from stifling his enterprise takes all Hunter's ingenuity and determination and puts him in deadly jeopardy.

ONE SINGLE THING

Book 2 - Hunter Grant Series

Journalist Hope Barber disappears two weeks after returning to New Zealand from an assignment in Pakistan, leaving her front door open and her bag and phone inside. The police are tight-lipped about their reluctance to act, and Hunter Grant and Dao agree to help Hope's brother Noah find her. Details about Hope's time in Pakistan gradually emerge but only raise more questions.

Was Hope under surveillance?

Was she linked to terrorists?

And who is the man Hope called 'my stalker'?

FOLDED

Book 3 - Hunter Grant Series

First notes asking for help and folded into tiny origami shapes are found outside a city apartment building, then a physics textbook with tiny writing between the lines and then the woman who found them abruptly resigns and disappears. Are the notes asking for help real or is it a game? Hunter Grant, ex-army and with a pragmatic view of justice, reluctantly agrees to help find the missing woman.

Things get complicated when a high-powered lawyer arrives form the US, and shortly after his meeting with Hunter and Dao, a "cease and desist" letter arrives from the Cayman Islands. Inspector Bakker - a woman, who in Hunter's words "looks as if she would be useful in a brawl, provided she was on your side" - takes instant exception to his involvement and threatens to arrest him for interfering in an investigation.

Dao sets out alone on a dangerous mission, driven by a compulsive need to find out what has happened to the girl who wrote the notes, and Hunter looks death in the face when he decides to risk everything to put an end to the Darknet forces that threaten their lives.

THE SHADOW BROKER

It is 2026 and individual freedoms are severely curtailed, with state surveillance everywhere. State Security has a Watch List, and being on it means that nothing you do or say escapes the authorities, but does the Kill List really exist? And if it does, how would you know if you were on it?

Coded messages on a found burner phone, top-level government corruption and a shadowy mastermind who calls himself The Broker. In this climate of state control, three unlikely friends start quietly looking for connections and set in motion a deadly game of hide and seek that will change their lives forever.

Trying to uncover the truth means risking your life, and nothing is more dangerous than searching for evidence of government corruption.

ABOUT THE AUTHOR

Tina Clough grew up in Sweden and now lives in New Zealand; dividing her time between writing fiction and translating and editing medical research papers.

Between working and writing she looks after an acre of fruit trees, vegetable gardens and roaming hens.

Apart from reading her interests include photography, wine, growing organic vegetables, making jam and kayaking.

https://lightpoolpublishing.com